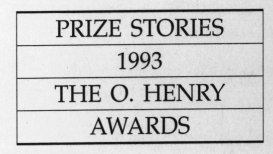

PRIZE STORIES
1993
THE O. HENRY
AWARDS

PRIZE STORIES
1·9·9·3
·THE·
O. HENRY
AWARDS

*Edited and with
an Introduction by*

William Abrahams

Anchor Books
DOUBLEDAY

NEW YORK LONDON TORONTO SYDNEY AUCKLAND

AN ANCHOR BOOK
PUBLISHED BY DOUBLEDAY
a division of Bantam Doubleday Dell Publishing Group, Inc.
666 Fifth Avenue, New York, New York 10103

ANCHOR BOOKS, DOUBLEDAY and the portrayal of an anchor
are trademarks of Doubleday,
a division of Bantam Doubleday Dell Publishing Group, Inc.

Book Design by Patrice Fodero

Library of Congress Cataloging-in-Publication Data
Prize stories. 1947–
New York, N.Y., Doubleday.
v. 22 cm.
Annual.
The O. Henry awards.
None published 1952–53.
Continues: O. Henry memorial award prize stories.
1. Short stories, American—Collected works.
PZ1.011   813'.01'08—dc19   21-9372
MARC-S

ISBN 0-385-42531-7
ISBN 0-385-42532-5 (pbk.)

April 1993

1 3 5 7 9 10 8 6 4 2

First Edition

CONTENTS

PUBLISHER'S NOTE

This volume is the seventy-third in the O. Henry Memorial Award series, and the twenty-seventh to be edited by William Abrahams.

* * *

In 1918, the Society of Arts and Sciences met to vote upon a monument to the master of the short story: O. Henry. They decided that this memorial should be in the form of two prizes for the best short stories published by American authors in American magazines during the year 1919. From this beginning, the memorial developed into an annual anthology of outstanding short stories by American authors, published, with the exception of the years 1952 and 1953, by Doubleday.

Blanche Colton Williams, one of the founders of the awards, was editor from 1919 to 1932; Harry Hansen from 1933 to 1940; Herschel Brickell from 1941 to 1951. The annual collection did not appear in 1952 and 1953, when the continuity of the series was interrupted by the death of Herschel Brickell. Paul Engle was editor from 1954 to 1959, with Hanson Martin coeditor in the years 1954 to 1960; Mary Stegner in 1960; Richard Poirier from 1961 to 1966, with assistance from and coeditorship with William Abrahams from 1964 to 1966. William Abrahams became editor of the series in 1967.

In 1970, Doubleday published under Mr. Abraham's editorship *Fifty years of the American Short Story,* and in 1981, *Prize Stories of the Seventies.* Both are collections of stories selected from this series.

The stories chosen for this volume were published in the period from the summer of 1991 to the summer of 1992. A list of the magazines consulted appears at the back of the book. The choice of stories and selection of prizewinners are exclusively the responsibility of the editor. Biographical material is based on information provided by the contributors and obtained from standard works of reference.

INTRODUCTION

Specifics first; then the observations, generalizations and speculations they give rise to.

This is the twenty-seventh O. Henry collection for which I have had the sole editorial responsibility; the first was *Prize Stories 1967.* I began my introduction to that volume with specifics: "Here are sixteen short stories chosen from among the thousand or more published in American magazines this year. Six of the sixteen appeared in magazines of large circulation; ten in the so-called 'little magazines.' The disproportion, which I hasten to point out is not the result of prejudice or preconceptions on the part of the editor, is significant enough to deserve comment. At the least it reminds us of the debt that dedicated readers and writers continue to owe the 'little magazines.'"

Adjusting the specifics for this year, I find that that debt continues. Here are twenty-three stories, sixteen from the little magazines, seven from magazines of large circulation. The disproportion is even more indicative than the latter figure may suggest for only three magazines account for the seven stories—four in *The New Yorker,* two in *The Atlantic,* and one in *Playboy.* In 1967 I raised the question, What if the little magazines did not exist? "Suppose that in one year they were all together to cease publication, having run afoul of creditors, having lost the good will of a foundation or a patron or a board of regents, or for whatever reason—the effect upon the American short story would be immediate and lamentable."

That gloomy prospect has been averted. In the 1990s the little magazines, more important than ever, thrive, burgeon, bringing forward the work of newcomers and established writers, while the number of large circulation magazines that regularly publish stories each year decreases. *The Atlantic* is an exception that comes promptly to mind, and a handful of others. Most rewarding of all has been *The New Yorker*, where year after year, week after week, stories of outstanding merit have appeared on a scale (more than a hundred a year) unrivaled by any other magazine intended, as it is, for a large readership. Now—late summer 1992—its future is something of an enigma, entrusted to a new editor famous thus far for her achievements in a magazine devoted exclusively to nonfiction. One hopes that in her new post she will prove to be equally welcoming to fiction. Meanwhile the stories from *The New Yorker* I have included in this year's collection represent standards established at the magazine more than fifty years ago, maintained up to the present moment, and likely—if allowed—to continue there in the future.

Late summer 1992—when political rhetoric clamors for our attention and simultaneously contrives to elude our close inspection—is perhaps not the ideal time to discuss standards, literary or otherwise. Even at its best, the rhetoric of politics, attempting to describe the reality of American life in the 1990s, blurs, muffles, and waffles, as though simple truth is too threatening to be communicated truthfully. At its worst, it distorts and falsifies, stupidly or slyly, so that the reality it purports to describe, ours and others' as we know it and live it, is palpably unreal.

At such a moment it seems permissible to say that fictions reveal what politics conceal. The twenty-three stories in this collection, for all their differences in style and content, are alike in this: they are the work of American writers in the early 1990s, seeking out the truth in the stories they choose to tell (or are chosen by). As they communicate to us a sense of the here-and-now or the past, we feel and respond in a vibration of recognition. The time of the story may be long ago, as in Rilla Askew's "retelling" in "The Killing Blanket" of an episode in Native American history, "Back when our word *okla humma* that called us the red people had not yet turned over to mean white man's land." Or it may be the more recent past that we have lived and lied through, the war in Vietnam and its still wounding aftermath, as in Thom Jones's "The Pugilist at Rest."

Mostly, though, these are contemporary and private stories. As such, they move among the complexities, contradictions, and tangles of the present—comic, ironic, tragic, and all the registers between—each with its own truth brought into our view, in a kind of window or mirror, reassuring, sometimes painful to discern, but ultimately rewarding. In the transaction between the reader and the story the reward is to acknowledge, "I am the Other."

Once again, warm thanks to Arabella Meyer and Jon Furay at Anchor/Doubleday for their invaluable cooperation and assistance.

—William Abrahams

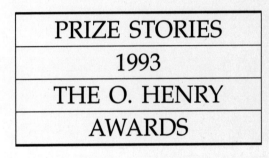

PRIZE STORIES

1993

THE O. HENRY

AWARDS

Thom Jones

THE PUGILIST AT REST

Hey Baby got caught writing a letter to his girl when he was supposed to be taking notes on the specs of the M-14 rifle. We were sitting in a stifling hot Quonset hut during the first weeks of boot camp, August, 1966, at the Marine Corps Recruit Depot in San Diego. Sergeant Wright snatched the letter out of Hey Baby's hand, and later that night in the squad bay he read the letter to the Marine recruits of Platoon 263, his voice laden with sarcasm. *"Hey, Baby!"* he began, and then as he went into the body of the letter he worked himself into a state of outrage and disgust. It was a letter to *Rosie Rottencrotch*, he said at the end, and what really mattered, what was really at issue and what was of utter importance was not *Rosie Rottencrotch* and her steaming-hot panties but rather the muzzle velocity of the M-14 rifle.

Hey Baby paid for the letter by doing a hundred squat thrusts on the concrete floor of the squad bay, but the main prize he won that night was that he became forever known as Hey Baby to the recruits of Platoon 263—in addition to being a shitbird, a faggot, a turd, a maggot, and other such standard appellations. To top it all off, shortly after the incident, Hey Baby got a Dear John from this girl back in Chicago, of whom Sergeant Wright, myself, and seventy-eight other Marine recruits had come to know just a little.

Hey Baby was not in the Marine Corps for very long. The reason for this was that he started in on my buddy, Jorgeson. Jorgeson was my main man, and Hey Baby started calling him Jorgepussy and began harassing him and pushing him around. He was down on Jorgeson because whenever we were taught some sort of combat maneuver or tactic, Jorgeson would say, under his breath, "You could get *killed* if you try that." Or, "Your ass is *had*, if you do that." You got the feeling that Jorgeson didn't think loving the American flag and defending democratic ideals in Southeast Asia were all that important. He told me that what he really wanted to do was have an artist's loft in the SoHo district of New York City, wear a beret, eat liver-sausage sandwiches made with stale baguettes, drink Tokay wine, smoke dope, paint pictures, and listen to the wailing, sorrowful songs of that French singer Edith Piaf, otherwise known as "The Little Sparrow."

After the first half hour of boot camp most of the other recruits wanted to get out, too, but they nourished dreams of surfboards, Corvettes, and blond babes. Jorgeson wanted to be a beatnik and hang out with Jack Kerouac and Neal Cassady, slam down burning shots of amber whiskey, and hear Charles Mingus play real cool jazz on the bass fiddle. He wanted to practice Zen Buddhism, throw the I Ching, eat couscous, and study astrology charts. All of this was foreign territory to me. I had grown up in Aurora, Illinois, and had never heard of such things. Jorgeson had a sharp tongue and was so supercilious in his remarks that I didn't know quite how seriously I should take this talk, but I enjoyed his humor and I did believe he had the sensibilities of an artist. It was not some vague yearning. I believed very much that he could become a painter of pictures. At that point he wasn't putting his heart and soul into becoming a Marine. He wasn't a true believer like me.

Some weeks after Hey Baby began hassling Jorgeson, Sergeant Wright gave us his best speech: "You men are going off to war, and it's not a pretty thing," etc. & etc., "and if Luke the Gook knocks down one of your buddies, a fellow-Marine, you are going to risk your life and go in and get that Marine and you are going to bring him out. Not because I said so. No! You are going after that Marine because *you* are a Marine, a member of the most élite fighting force in the world, and that man out there who's gone down is a Marine, and he's your *buddy*. He is your brother! Once you are a Marine, you are *always* a Marine and you will never let another Marine down." Etc. & etc. "You can take a Marine out of the Corps but you can't take the Corps out of a Marine." Etc. & etc. At the time it seemed to me a very good speech, and it stirred me deeply. Sergeant Wright was no candy ass. He was one squared-away dude, and he could call cadence. Man, it puts a lump in my throat when I remember how that man could sing cadence. Apart from Jorgeson, I think all of the recruits in Platoon 263 were proud of Sergeant Wright. He was the real thing, the genuine article. He was a crackerjack Marine.

In the course of training, lots of the recruits dropped out of the original platoon. Some couldn't pass the physical-fitness tests and had to go to a special camp for pussies. This was a particularly shameful shortcoming, the most humiliating apart from bed-wetting. Other recruits would get pneumonia, strep throat, infected foot blisters, or whatever, and lose time that way. Some didn't qualify at the rifle range. One would break a leg. Another would have a nervous breakdown (and this was also deplorable). People dropped out right and left. When the recruit corrected whatever deficiency he had, or when he got better, he would be picked up by another platoon that was in the stage of basic training that he had been in when his training was interrupted. Platoon 263 picked up dozens of recruits in this fashion. If everything went well, however, you got through with the whole business in twelve weeks. That's not a long time, but it seemed like a long time. You did not see a female in all that time. You did not see a newspaper or a television set. You did not eat a candy bar. Another thing was the fact that you had someone on top of you, watching every move you made. When it was time to "shit, shower, and shave," you were given just ten minutes, and had to confront lines and so on to complete the entire affair. Head calls were so infrequent that I spent a lot of time that might otherwise have been neutral or painless in the eye-watering anxiety that I was going to piss my pants. We *ran* to chow, where we were faced with enormous steam vents that spewed out a sickening smell of rancid, super-heated grease. Still, we entered the mess hall with ravenous appetites, ate a huge tray of food in just a few minutes, and then *ran* back to our company area in formation, choking back the burning bile of a meal too big to be eaten so fast. God forbid that you would lose control and vomit.

If all had gone well in the preceding hours, Sergeant Wright would permit us to smoke one cigarette after each meal. Jorgeson had shown me the wisdom of switching from Camels to Pall Malls—they were much longer, packed a pretty good jolt, and when we snapped open our brushed-chrome Zippos, torched up, and inhaled the first few drags, we shared the over-mastering pleasure that tobacco can bring if you use it seldom and judiciously. These were always the best moments of the day —brief respites from the tyrannical repression of recruit training. As we got close to the end of it all Jorgeson liked to play a little game. He used to say to me (with fragrant blue smoke curling out of his nostrils), "If someone said, 'I'll give you ten thousand dollars to do all of this again,' what would you say?" "No way, Jack!" He would keep on upping it until he had John Beresford Tipton, the guy from "The Millionaire," offering me a check for a million bucks. "Not for any money," I'd say.

While they were all smoldering under various pressures, the recruits were also getting pretty "salty"—they were beginning to believe. They were beginning to think of themselves as Marines. If you could make it through this, the reasoning went, you wouldn't crack in combat. So I remember that I had tears in my eyes when Sergeant Wright gave us the spiel about how a Marine would charge a machine-gun nest to save his buddies, dive on a hand grenade, do whatever it takes—and yet I was ashamed when Jorgeson caught me wiping them away. All of the recruits were teary except Jorgeson. He had these very clear cobalt-blue eyes. They were so remarkable that they caused you to notice Jorgeson in a crowd. There was unusual beauty in these eyes, and there was an extraordinary power in them.

Apart from having a pleasant enough face, Jorgeson was small and unassuming except for these eyes. Anyhow, when he caught me getting sentimental he gave me this look that penetrated to the core of my being. It was the icy look of absolute contempt, and it caused me to doubt myself. I said, "Man! Can't you get into it? For Christ's sake!"

"I'm not like you," he said. "But I am into it, more than you could ever know. I never told you this before, but I am Kal-El, born on the planet Krypton and rocketed to Earth as an infant, moments before my world exploded. Disguised as a mild-mannered Marine, I have resolved to use my powers for the good of mankind. Whenever danger appears on the scene, truth and justice will be served as I slip into the green U.S.M.C. utility uniform and become Earth's greatest hero."

I got highly pissed and didn't talk to him for a couple of days after this. Then, about two weeks before boot camp was over, when we were running out to the parade field for drill with our rifles at port arms, all assholes and elbows, I saw Hey Baby give Jorgeson a nasty shove with his M-14. Hey Baby was a large and fairly tough young man who liked to displace his aggressive impulses on Jorgeson, but he wasn't as big or as tough as I.

Jorgeson nearly fell down as the other recruits scrambled out to the parade field, and Hey Baby gave a short, malicious laugh. I ran past Jorgeson and caught up to Hey Baby; he picked me up in his peripheral vision, but by then it was too late. I set my body so that I could put everything into it, and with one deft stroke I hammered him in the temple with the sharp edge of the steel butt plate of my M-14. It was not exactly a premeditated crime, although I had been laying to get him. My idea before this had simply been to lay my hands on him, but now I had blood in my eye. I was a skilled boxer, and I knew the temple was a vulnerable spot; the human skull is otherwise hard and durable, except at its base. There was a sickening crunch, and Hey Baby dropped into the ice plants along the side of the company street.

The entire platoon was out on the parade field when the house mouse screamed at the assistant D.I., who rushed back to the scene of the crime to find Hey Baby crumpled in a fetal position in the ice plants with blood all over the place. There was blood from the scalp wound as well as a froth of blood emitting from his nostrils and his mouth. Blood was leaking from his right ear. Did I see skull fragments and brain tissue? It seemed that I did. To tell you the truth, I wouldn't have cared in the least if I had killed him, but like most criminals I was very much afraid of getting caught. It suddenly occurred to me that I could be headed for the brig for a long time. My heart was pounding out of my chest. Yet the larger part of me didn't care. Jorgeson was my buddy, and I wasn't going to stand still and let someone fuck him over.

The platoon waited at parade rest while Sergeant Wright came out of the duty hut and took command of the situation. An ambulance was called, and it came almost immediately. A number of corpsmen squatted down alongside the fallen man for what seemed an eternity. Eventually they took Hey Baby off with a fractured skull. It would be the last we ever saw of him. Three evenings later, in the squad bay, the assistant D.I. told us rather ominously that Hey Baby had recovered consciousness. That's all he said. What did *that* mean? I was worried, because Hey Baby had seen me make my move, but, as it turned out, when he came to he had forgotten the incident and all events of the preceding two weeks. Retrograde amnesia. Lucky for me. I also knew that at least three other recruits had seen what I did, but none of them reported me. Every member of the platoon was called in and grilled by a team of hard-ass captains and a light colonel from the Criminal Investigation Detachment. It took a certain amount of balls to lie to them, yet none of my fellow-jarheads reported me. I was well liked and Hey Baby was not. Indeed, many felt that he got exactly what was coming to him.

The other day—Memorial Day, as it happened—I was cleaning some stuff out of the attic when I came upon my old dress-blue uniform. It's a beautiful uniform, easily the most handsome worn by any of the U.S. armed forces. The rich color recalled Jorgeson's eyes for me—not that the color matched, but in the sense that the color of each was so startling. The tunic does not have lapels, of course, but a high collar with red piping and the traditional golden eagle, globe, and anchor insignia on either side of the neck clasp. The tunic buttons are not brassy—although they are in fact made of brass—but are a delicate gold in color, like Florentine gold. On the sleeves of the tunic my staff-sergeant's chevrons are gold on red. High on the left breast is a rainbow display of fruit salad representing my various combat citations. Just below these are my marksmanship badges; I shot Expert in rifle as well as pistol.

I opened a sandalwood box and took my various medals out of the large plastic bag I had packed them in to prevent them from tarnishing. The Navy Cross and the two Silver Stars are the best; they are such pretty things they dazzle you. I found a couple of Thai sticks in the sandalwood box as well. I took a whiff of the box and smelled the smells of Saigon—the whores, the dope, the saffron, cloves, jasmine, and patchouli oil. I put the Thai sticks back, recalling the three-day hangover that particular batch of dope had given me more than twenty-three years before. Again I looked at my dress-blue tunic. My most distinctive badge, the crowning glory, and the one of which I am most proud, is the set of Airborne wings. I remember how it was, walking around Oceanside, California—the Airborne wings and the high-and-tight haircut were recognized by all the Marines; they meant you were the crème de la crème, you were a recon Marine.

Recon was all Jorgeson's idea. We had lost touch with each other after boot camp. I was sent to com school in San Diego, where I had to sit in a hot Class A wool uniform all day and learn the Morse code. I deliberately flunked out, and when I was given the perfunctory option for a second shot, I told the colonel, "Hell no, sir. I want to go 003—infantry. I want to be a ground-pounder. I didn't join the service to sit at a desk all day."

I was on a bus to Camp Pendleton three days later, and when I got there I ran into Jorgeson. I had been thinking of him a lot. He was a clerk in headquarters company. Much to my astonishment, he was fifteen pounds heavier, and had grown two inches, and he told me he was hitting the weight pile every night after running seven miles up and down the foothills of

Pendleton in combat boots, carrying a rifle and a full field pack. After the usual what's-been-happening? b.s., he got down to business and said, "They need people in Force Recon, what do you think? Headquarters is one boring motherfucker."

I said, "Recon? Paratrooper? You got to be shittin' me! When did you get so gung-ho, man?"

He said, "Hey, you were the one who *bought* the program. Don't fade on me now, God damn it! Look, we pass the physical fitness test and then they send us to jump school at Benning. If we pass that, we're in. And we'll pass. Those doggies ain't got jack. Semper fi, motherfucker! Let's do it."

There was no more talk of Neal Cassady, Edith Piaf, or the artist's loft in SoHo. I said, "If Sergeant Wright could only see you now!"

We were just three days in country when we got dropped in somewhere in the western highlands of the Quang Tri province. It was a routine reconnaissance patrol. It was not supposed to be any kind of big deal at all—just acclimation. The morning after our drop we approached a clear field. I recall that it gave me a funny feeling, but I was too new to fully trust my instincts. *Everything* was spooky; I was fresh meat, F.N.G.—a Fucking New Guy.

Before moving into the field, our team leader sent Hanes—a lance corporal, a short-timer, with only twelve days left before his rotation was over—across the field as a point man. This was a bad omen and everyone knew it. Hanes had two Purple Hearts. He followed the order with no hesitation and crossed the field without drawing fire. The team leader signalled for us to fan out and told me to circumvent the field and hump through the jungle to investigate a small mound of loose red dirt that I had missed completely but that he had picked up with his trained eye. I remember I kept saying, "Where?" He pointed to a heap of earth about thirty yards along the tree line and about ten feet back in the bushes. Most likely it was an anthill, but you never knew—it could have been an N.V.A. tunnel. "Over there," he hissed. "God damn it, do I have to draw pictures for you?"

I moved smartly in the direction of the mound while the rest of the team reconverged to discuss something. As I approached the mound I saw that it was in fact an anthill, and I looked back at the team and saw they were already halfway across the field, moving very fast.

Suddenly there were several loud hollow pops and the cry "Incoming!" Seconds later the first of a half-dozen mortar rounds landed in the loose earth surrounding the anthill. For a millisecond, everything went black. I was blown back and lifted up on a cushion of warm air. At first it was like the thrill of a carnival ride, but it was quickly followed by that stunned, jangly, electric feeling you get when you hit your crazy bone. Like that, but not confined to a small area like the elbow. I felt it shoot through my spine and into all four limbs. A thick plaster of sand and red clay plugged up my nostrils and ears. Grit was blown in between my teeth. If I hadn't been wearing a pair of Ray-Ban aviator shades, I would certainly have been blinded permanently—as it was, my eyes were loaded with grit. (I later discovered that fine red earth was somehow blown in behind the crystal of my pressure-tested Rolex Submariner, underneath my fingernails and toenails, and deep into the pores of my skin.) When I was able to, I pulled out a canteen filled with lemon-lime Kool-Aid and tried to flood my eyes clean. This helped a little, but my eyes still felt like they were on fire. I rinsed them again and blinked furiously.

I rolled over on my stomach in the prone position and levelled my field-issue M-16. A company of screaming N.V.A. soldiers ran into the field, firing as they came—I saw their green tracer rounds blanket the position where the team had quickly congregated to lay out a perimeter, but none of our own red tracers were going out. Several of the Marines had been killed outright by the mortar rounds. Jorgeson was all right, and I saw him cast a nervous glance in my direction. Then he turned to the enemy and began to fire his M-16. I clicked my rifle on to automatic and pulled the trigger, but the gun was loaded with dirt and it wouldn't fire.

Apart from Jorgeson, the only other American putting out any fire was Second Lieutenant Milton, also a fairly new guy, a "cherry," who was down on one knee firing his .45, an exercise in almost complete futility. I assumed that Milton's 16 had jammed, like mine, and watched as AK-47 rounds, having penetrated his flak jacket and then his chest, ripped through the back of his field pack and buzzed into the jungle beyond like a deadly swarm of bees. A few seconds later, I heard the swoosh of an R.P.G. rocket, a dud round that dinged the lieutenant's left shoulder before it flew off in the bush behind him. It took off his whole arm, and for an instant I could see the white bone and ligaments of his shoulder, and the red flesh of muscle tissue, looking very much like fresh prime beef, well marbled and encased in a thin layer of yellowish-white adipose tissue that quickly became saturated with dark-red blood. What a lot of blood there was. Still, Milton continued to fire his .45. When he emptied his clip, I watched him remove a fresh one from his web gear and attempt to load the pistol with one hand. He seemed to fumble with the fresh clip for a long time, until at last he dropped it, along with his .45. The Lieutenant's head slowly sagged forward, but he stayed up on one knee with his remaining arm extended out to the enemy, palm upward in the soulful, heartrending gesture of Al Jolson doing a rendition of "Mammy."

A hail of green tracer rounds buzzed past Jorgeson, but he coolly returned fire in short, controlled bursts. The light, tinny pops from his M-16 did not sound very reassuring, but I saw several N.V.A. go down. AK-47 fire kicked up red dust all around Jorgeson's feet. He was basically out in the open, and if ever a man was totally alone it was Jorgeson. He was dead meat and he had to know it. It was very strange that he wasn't hit immediately.

Jorgeson zigged his way over to the body of a large black Marine who carried an M-60 machine gun. Most of the recon Marines carried grease guns or Swedish Ks; an M-60 was too heavy for travelling light and fast, but this Marine had been big and he had been paranoid. I had known him least of anyone in the squad. In three days he had said nothing to me, I suppose because I was F.N.G., and had spooked him. Indeed, now he was dead. That august seeker of truth, Schopenhauer, was correct: *We are like lambs in a field, disporting themselves under the eye of the butcher, who chooses out first one and then another for his prey. So it is that in our good days we are all unconscious of the evil Fate may have presently in store for us—sickness, poverty, mutilation, loss of sight or reason.*

It was difficult to judge how quickly time was moving. Although my senses had been stunned by the concussion of the mortar rounds, they were, however paradoxical this may seem, more acute than ever before. I watched Jorgeson pick up the machine gun and begin to spread an impressive field of fire back at the enemy. Thuk thuk thuk, thuk thuk thuk, thuk thuk thuk! I saw several more bodies fall, and began to think that things might turn out all right after all. The N.V.A. dropped for cover, and many of them turned back and headed for the tree line. Jorgeson fired off a couple of bandoliers, and after he stopped to load another, he turned back and looked at me with those blue eyes and a smile like "How am I doing?" Then I heard the steel-cork pop of an M-79 launcher and saw a rocket grenade explode through Jorgeson's upper abdomen, causing him to do something like a back flip. His M-60 machine gun flew straight up into the air. The barrel was glowing red like a hot poker, and continued to fire in a "cook off" until the entire bandolier had run through.

In the meantime I had pulled a cleaning rod out of my pack and worked it through the barrel of my M-16. When I next tried to shoot, the Tonka-toy son of a bitch remained jammed, and at last I frantically broke it down to find the source of the problem. I had a dirty bolt. Fucking dirt everywhere. With numbed fingers I removed the firing pin and worked it over with a toothbrush, dropping it in the red dirt, picking it up, cleaning it, and dropping it again. My fingers felt like Novocain, and while I could see far away, I was unable to see up close. I poured some more Kool-Aid over my eyes. It was impossible for me to get my weapon clean. Lucky for me, ultimately.

Suddenly N.V.A. soldiers were running through the field shoving bayonets into the bodies of the downed Marines. It was not until an N.V.A. trooper kicked Lieutenant Milton out of his tripod position that he finally fell to the ground. Then the soldiers started going through the dead Marines' gear. I was still frantically struggling with my weapon when it began to dawn on me that the enemy had forgotten me in the excitement of the firefight. I wondered what had happened to Hanes and if he had gotten clear. I doubted it, and hopped on my survival radio to call in an air strike when finally a canny N.V.A. trooper did remember me and headed in my direction most ricky-tick.

With a tight grip on the spoon, I pulled the pin on a fragmentation grenade and then unsheathed my K-bar. About this time Jorgeson let off a horrendous shriek—a gut shot is worse than anything. Or did Jorgeson scream to save my life? The N.V.A. moving in my direction turned back to him, studied him for a moment, and then thrust a bayonet into his heart. As badly as my own eyes hurt, I was able to see Jorgeson's eyes—a final flash of glorious azure before they faded into the unfocussed and glazed gray of death. I repinned the grenade, got up on my knees, and scrambled away until finally I was on my feet with a useless and incomplete handful of M-16 parts, and I was running as fast and as hard as I have ever run in my life. A pair of Phantom F-4s came in very low with delayed-action high-explosive rounds and napalm. I could feel the almost unbearable heat waves of the latter, volley after volley. I can still feel it and smell it to this day.

Concerning Lance Corporal Hanes: they found him later, fried to a crisp by the napalm, but it was nonetheless ascertained that he had been mutilated while alive. He was like the rest of us— eighteen, nineteen, twenty years old. What did we know of life? Before Vietnam, Hanes didn't think he would ever die. I mean, yes, he knew that in theory he would die, but he *felt* like he was going to live forever. I know that I felt that way. Hanes was down to twelve days and a wake-up. When other Marines saw a short-timer get greased, it devastated their morale. However, when I saw them zip up the body bag on Hanes I became incensed. Why hadn't Milton sent him back to the rear to burn shit or something when he got so short? Twelve days to go and then mutilated. Fucking Milton! Fucking Second Lieutenant!

. . .

Theogenes was the greatest of gladiators. He was a boxer who served under the patronage of a cruel nobleman, a prince who took great delight in bloody spectacles. Although this was several hundred years before the times of those most enlightened of men Socrates, Plato, and Aristotle, and well after the Minoans of Crete, it still remains a high point in the history of Western civilization and culture. It was the approximate time of Homer, the greatest poet who ever lived. Then, as now, violence, suffering, and the cheapness of life were the rule.

The sort of boxing Theogenes practiced was not like modern-day boxing with those kindergarten Queensberry Rules. The two contestants were not permitted the freedom of a ring. Instead, they were strapped to flat stones, facing each other nose-to-nose. When the signal was given they would begin hammering each other with fists encased in heavy leather thongs. It was a fight to the death. Fourteen hundred and twenty-five times Theogenes was strapped to the stone and fourteen hundred and twenty-five times he emerged a victor.

Perhaps it is Theogenes who is depicted in the famous Roman statue (based on the earlier Greek original) of "The Pugilist at Rest." I keep a grainy black-and-white photograph of it in my room. The statue depicts a muscular athlete approaching his middle age. He has a thick beard and a full head of curly hair. In addition to the telltale broken nose and cauliflower ears of a boxer, the pugilist has the slanted, drooping brows that bespeak torn nerves. Also, the forehead is piled with scar tissue. As may be expected, the pugilist has the musculature of a fighter. His neck and trapezius muscles are well developed. His shoulders are enormous; his chest is thick and flat, without the bulging pectorals of the bodybuilder. His back, oblique, and abdominal muscles are highly pronounced, and he has that greatest asset of the modern boxer—sturdy legs. The arms are large, particularly the forearms, which are reinforced with the leather wrappings of the cestus. It is the body of a small heavyweight—lithe rather than bulky, but by no means lacking in power: a Jack Johnson or a Dempsey, say. If you see the authentic statue at the Terme Museum, in Rome, you will see that the seated boxer is really not much more than a light heavyweight. People were small in

those days. The important thing was that he was perfectly proportioned.

The pugilist is sitting on a rock with his forearms balanced on
his thighs. That he is seated and not pacing implies that he has
been through all this many times before. It appears that he is
conserving his strength. His head is turned as if he were looking
over his shoulder—as if someone had just whispered something
to him. It is in this that the "art" of the sculpture is conveyed to
the viewer. Could it be that someone has just summoned him to
the arena? There is a slight look of befuddlement on his face, but
there is no trace of fear. There is an air about him that suggests
that he is eager to proceed and does not wish to cause anyone
any trouble or to create a delay, even though his life will soon
be on the line. Besides the deformities on his noble face, there is
also the suggestion of weariness and philosophical resignation.
All the world's a stage, and all the men and women merely players.
Exactly! He knew this more than two thousand years before
Shakespeare penned the line. How did he come to be at this
place in space and time? Would he rather be safely removed to
the countryside—an obscure, stinking peasant shoving a plow
behind a mule? Would that be better? Or does he revel in his
role? Perhaps he once did, but surely not now. Is this the great
Theogenes or merely a journeyman fighter, a former slave or
criminal bought by one of the many contractors who for months
trained the condemned for their brief moment in the arena? I
wonder if Marcus Aurelius loved the "Pugilist" as I do, and
came to study it and to meditate before it?

I cut and ran from that field in Southeast Asia. I've read that
Davy Crockett, hero of the American frontier, was cowering under a bed when Santa Anna and his soldiers stormed into the
Alamo. What is the truth? Jack Dempsey used to get so scared
before his fights that he sometimes wet his pants. But look what
he did to Willard and to Luis Firpo, the Wild Bull of the Pam-
pas! It was something close to homicide. What is courage? What
is cowardice? The magnificent Roberto Duran gave us *"No
más,"* but who had a greater fighting heart than Duran?

I got over that first scare and saw that I was something quite
other than that which I had known myself to be. Hey Baby

proved only my warm-up act. There was a reservoir of malice, poison, and vicious sadism in my soul, and it poured forth freely in the jungles and rice paddies of Vietnam. I pulled three tours. I wanted some payback for Jorgeson. I grieved for Lance Corporal Hanes. I grieved for myself and what I had lost. I committed unspeakable crimes and got medals for it.

It was only fair that I got a head injury myself. I never got a scratch in Vietnam, but I got tagged in a boxing smoker at Pendleton. Fought a bad-ass light heavyweight from artillery. Nobody would fight this guy. He could box. He had all the moves. But mainly he was a puncher—it was said that he could punch with either hand. It was said that his hand speed was superb. I had finished off at least a half rack of Hamm's before I went in with him and started getting hit with head shots I didn't even see coming. They were right. His hand speed *was* superb.

I was twenty-seven years old, smoked two packs a day, was a borderline alcoholic. I shouldn't have fought him—I knew that —but he had been making noise. A very long time before, I had been the middleweight champion of the 1st Marine Division. I had been a so-called war hero. I had been a recon Marine. But now I was a garrison Marine and in no kind of shape.

He put me down almost immediately, and when I got up I was terribly afraid. I was tight and I could not breathe. It felt like he was hitting me in the face with a ball-peen hammer. It felt like he was busting light bulbs in my face. Rather than one opponent, I saw three. I was convinced his gloves were loaded, and a wave of self-pity ran through me.

I began to move. He made a mistake by expending a lot of energy trying to put me away quickly. I had no intention of going down again, and I knew I wouldn't. My buddies were watching, and I had to give them a good show. While I was afraid, I was also exhilarated; I had not felt this alive since Vietnam. I began to score with my left jab, and because of this I was able to withstand his bull charges and divert them. I thought he would throw his bolt, but in the beginning he was tireless. I must have hit him with four hundred left jabs. It got so that I could score at will, with either hand, but he would counter, trap me on the ropes, and pound. He was the better puncher and was truly hurting me, but I was scoring, and as the fight went on the momentum shifted and I took over. I staggered him again and again. The Marines at ringside were screaming for me to put him away, but however much I tried, I could not. Although I could barely stand by the end, I was sorry that the fight was over. Who had won? The referee raised my arm in victory, but I think it was pretty much a draw. Judging a prizefight is a very subjective thing.

About an hour after the bout, when the adrenaline had subsided, I realized I had a terrible headache. It kept getting worse, and I rushed out of the N.C.O. Club, where I had gone with my buddies to get loaded.

I stumbled outside, struggling to breathe, and I headed away from the company area toward Sheepshit Hill, one of the many low brown foothills in the vicinity. Like a dog who wants to die alone, so it was with me. Everything got swirly, and I dropped in the bushes.

I was unconscious for nearly an hour, and for the next two weeks I walked around like I was drunk, with double vision. I had constant headaches and seemed to have grown old overnight. My health was gone.

I became a very timid individual. I became introspective. I wondered what had made me act the way I had acted. Why had I killed my fellow-men in war, without any feeling, remorse, or regret? And when the war was over, why did I continue to drink and swagger around and get into fistfights? Why did I like to dish out pain, and why did I take positive delight in the suffering of others? Was I insane? Was it too much testosterone? Women don't do things like that. The rapacious Will to Power lost its hold on me. Suddenly I began to feel sympathetic to the cares and sufferings of all living creatures. You lose your health and you start thinking this way.

Has man become any better since the times of Theogenes? The world is replete with badness. I'm not talking about that old routine where you drag out the Spanish Inquisition, the Holocaust, Joseph Stalin, the Khmer Rouge, etc. It happens in our own back yard. Twentieth-century America is one of the most materially prosperous nations in history. But take a walk through an American prison, a nursing home, the slums where the homeless live in cardboard boxes, a cancer ward. Go to a Vietnam vets' meeting, or an A.A. meeting, or an Overeaters Anonymous meeting. *How hollow and unreal a thing is life, how deceitful are its pleasures, what horrible aspects it possesses.* Is the world not rather like a hell, as Schopenhauer, that clearheaded seer—who has helped me transform my suffering into an object of understanding—was so quick to point out? They called him a pessimist and dismissed him with a word, but it is peace and self-renewal that I have found in his pages.

About a year after my fight with the guy from artillery I started having seizures. I suffered from a form of left-temporal-lobe seizure which is sometimes called Dostoyevski's epilepsy. It's so rare as to be almost unknown. Freud, himself a neurologist, speculated that Dostoyevski was a hysterical epileptic, and that his fits were unrelated to brain damage—psychogenic in origin. Dostoyevski did not have his first attack until the age of twenty-five, when he was imprisoned in Siberia and received fifty lashes after complaining about the food. Freud figured that after Dostoyevski's mock execution, the four years' imprisonment in Siberia, the tormented childhood, the murder of his tyrannical father, etc. & etc.—he had all the earmarks of hysteria, of grave psychological trauma. And Dostoyevski had displayed the trademark features of the psychomotor epileptic long before his first attack. These days physicians insist there is no such thing as the "epileptic personality." I think they say this because they do not want to add to the burden of the epileptic's suffering with an extra stigma. Privately they do believe in these traits. Dostoyevski was nervous and depressed, a tormented hypochondriac, a compulsive writer obsessed with religious and philosophic themes. He was hyperloquacious, raving, etc. & etc. His gambling addiction is well known. By most accounts he was a sick soul.

The peculiar and most distinctive thing about his epilepsy was that in the split second before his fit—in the aura, which is in fact officially a part of the attack—Dostoyevski experienced a sense of felicity, of ecstatic well-being unlike anything an ordinary mortal could hope to imagine. It was the experience of satori. Not the nickel-and-dime satori of Abraham Maslow, but the Supreme. He said that he wouldn't trade ten years of life for this feeling, and I, who have had it, too, would have to agree. I can't explain it, I don't understand it—it becomes slippery and elusive when it gets any distance on you—but I have felt this down to the core of my being. Yes, God exists! But then it slides away and I lose it. I become a doubter. Even Dostoyevski, the fervent Christian, makes an almost airtight case against the possibility of the existence of God in the Grand Inquisitor digression in "The Brothers Karamazov." It is probably the greatest passage in all of world literature, and it tilts you to the court of the atheist. This is what happens when you approach Him with the intellect.

It is thought that St. Paul had a temporal-lobe fit on the road to Damascus. Paul warns us in First Corinthians that God will confound the intellectuals. It is known that Muhammad composed the Koran after attacks of epilepsy. Black Elk experienced fits before his grand "buffalo" vision. Joan of Arc is thought to have been a left-temporal-lobe epileptic. Each of these in a terrible flash of brain lightning was able to pierce the murky veil of illusion which is spread over all things. Just so did the scales fall from my eyes. It is called the "sacred disease."

But what a price. I rarely leave the house anymore. To avoid falling injuries, I always wear my old boxer's headgear, and I always carry my mouthpiece. Rather more often than the aura where "every common bush is afire with God," I have the typical epileptic aura, which is that of terror and impending doom. If I can keep my head and think of it, and if there is time, I slip the mouthpiece in and thus avoid biting my tongue. I bit it in half once, and when they sewed it back together it swelled enormously, like a huge red-and-black sausage. I was unable to close my mouth for more than two weeks.

The fits are coming more and more. I'm loaded on Depakene, phenobarbital, Tegretol, Dilantin—the whole shitload. A nurse from the V.A. bought a pair of Staffordshire terriers for me and trained them to watch me as I sleep, in case I have a fit and smother face down in my bedding. What delightful companions these dogs are! One of them, Gloria, is especially intrepid and clever. Inevitably, when I come to I find that the dogs have dragged me into the kitchen, away from blankets and pillows, rugs, and objects that might suffocate me, and that they have turned me on my back. There's Gloria, barking in my face. Isn't this incredible?

My sister brought a neurosurgeon over to my place around Christmas—not some V.A. butcher but a guy from the university hospital. He was a slick dude in a nine-hundred-dollar suit. He came down on me hard, like a used-car salesman. He wants to cauterize a small spot in a nerve bundle in my brain. "It's not a lobotomy, it's a *cingulotomy*," he said.

Reckless, desperate, last-ditch psychosurgery is still pretty much unthinkable in the conservative medical establishment. That's why he made a personal visit to my place. A house call. Drumming up some action to make himself a name. "See that bottle of Thorazine?" he said. "You can throw that poison away," he said. "All that amitriptyline. That's garbage, you can toss that, too." He said, "Tell me something. How can you take all of that shit and still walk?" He said, "You take enough drugs to drop an elephant."

He wants to cut me. He said that the feelings of guilt and worthlessness, and the heaviness of a heart blackened by sin, will go away. "It is *not* a lobotomy," he said.

I don't like the guy. I don't trust him. I'm not convinced, but I can't go on like this. If I am not having a panic attack I am engulfed in tedious, unrelenting depression. I am overcome with a deadening sense of languor; I can't *do* anything. I wanted to give my buddies a good show! What a goddam fool. I am a goddam fool!

It has taken me six months to put my thoughts in order, but I wanted to do it in case I am a vegetable after the operation. I know that my buddy Jorgeson was a real American hero. I wish that he had lived to be something else, if not a painter of pictures then even some kind of fuckup with a factory job and four divorces, bankruptcy petitions, in and out of jail. I wish he had been that. I wish he had been *anything* rather than a real American hero. So, then, if I am to feel somewhat *indifferent* to life after the operation, all the better. If not, not.

If I had a more conventional sense of morality I would shitcan those dress blues, and I'd send that Navy Cross to Jorgeson's brother. Jorgeson was the one who won it, who pulled the John Wayne number up there near Khe Sanh and saved my life, although I lied and took the credit for all of those dead N.V.A. He had created a stunning body count—nothing like Theogenes, but Jorgeson only had something like twelve minutes total in the theatre of war.

The high command almost awarded me the Medal of Honor, but of course there were no witnesses to what I claimed I had done, and I had saved no one's life. When I think back on it, my tale probably did not sound as credible as I thought it had at the time. I was only nineteen years old and not all that practiced a liar. I figure if they *had* given me the Medal of Honor, I would have stood in the ring up at Camp Las Pulgas in Pendleton and let that light heavyweight from artillery fucking kill me.

Now I'm thinking I might call Hey Baby and ask how he's doing. No shit, a couple of neuro/psyches—we probably have a lot in common. I could apologize to him. But I learned from my fits that you don't have to do that. Good and evil are only illusions. Still, I cannot help but wonder sometimes if my vision of the Supreme Reality was any more real than the demons visited upon schizophrenics and madmen. Has it all been just a stupid neurochemical event? Is there no God at all? The human heart rebels against this.

If they fuck up the operation, I hope I get to keep my dogs somehow—maybe stay at my sister's place. If they send me to the nuthouse I lose the dogs for sure.

Andrea Lee

WINTER BARLEY

1. THE STORM

Night; a house in northern Scotland. When October gales blow in off the Atlantic, one thinks of sodden sheep huddled downwind and of oil cowboys on bucking North Sea rigs. Even a large, solid house like this one feels temporary tonight, like a hand cupped around a match. Flourishes of hail, like bird shot against the windows; a wuthering in the chimneys, the sound of an army of giants charging over the hilltops in the dark.

In the kitchen a man and a woman sit eating a pig's foot. Edo and Elizabeth. Together their years add up to ninety, of which his make up two-thirds. Edo slightly astonished Elizabeth by working out this schoolboy arithmetic when they first met, six months ago. He loves acrostics and brain teasers, which he solves with the fanatical absorption common to sportsmen and soldiers—men used to long, mute waits between bursts of violence. Edo has been both mercenary and white hunter in the course of an unquiet life passed mainly between Italy and Africa, between privilege and catastrophe. He is a prince, one of a swarm exiled from an Eastern European kingdom now extinct, and this house, his last, is a repository of fragments from ceremonial lives and the web of cousinships that link him to most of the history of Europe.

The house is full of things that seem to need as much care as children: pieces of Boulle and Caffiéri scattered among the Scottish furniture bought at auction, a big I.B.M. computer programmed to trace wildfowl migrations worldwide, gold flatware knobby with crests, an array of retrievers with pernickety stomachs in the dog run outside, red Venetian goblets that for washing require the same intense concentration one might use in restoring a Caravaggio. In the afternoons Edo likes to sit down with a glass—a supermarket glass—of vermouth and watch reruns of "Fame" magically sucked from the wild Scottish air by the satellite dish down the hill. With typical thoroughness he has memorized the names and dispositions of the characters from Manhattan's High School of Performing Arts and has his favorites: the curly-haired musical genius, the beautiful dance instructor he calls "la mulâtresse." The television stands in a thicket of silver frames that hold photographs of men who all resemble Edward VII, and women with the oddly anonymous look of royalty. Often they pose with guns and bearers on swards blanketed with dead animals, and their expressions, like Edo's, are invariably mild.

To Elizabeth, Edo's kitchen looks unfairly like a men's club: brown, cavernous, furnished with tattered armchairs, steel restaurant appliances, charts of herbs, dogs in corners, Brobdingnagian pots for feeding hungry grouse shooters, and green baize curtains, which, as they eat tonight, swell and collapse slowly with the breath of the storm. The pig's foot is glutinous and spicy, cooked with lentils, the way Romans do it at Christmastime. Edo cooked it, as he cooks everything. When Elizabeth visits, he doesn't let her touch things in the kitchen—even the washing up is done in a ritual fashion by the housekeeper, a thin Scottish vestal.

"These lentils are seven years old," he announces, taking another helping.

"Aren't you embarrassed to be so stingy?"

Dried legumes never go bad, he tells her, and it's a vulgar trait to disdain stinginess. His mother fed her children on rice and coffee during the war, even though they crossed some borders wearing vests so weighted with hidden gold pieces that he and his sisters walked with bent knees. Edo grew up with bad teeth and an incurable hunger, like the man in the fairy tale who could eat a mountain of bread. He has a weakness for trimmings and innards, the food of the poor.

Elizabeth knows she adopts an expression of intense comprehension whenever Edo reminisces; it pinches her features, as if they were strung on tightening wires. Still, she doesn't want to be one of those young women befuddled by lives lived before their own. She grew up in Dover, Massachusetts, went to Yale, and hopes that one day she'll believe in more than she does now. At the same time she has a curiously Latin temperament—not the tempestuous but the fatalistic kind—for someone with solid layers of Dana and Hallowell ancestors behind her. This trait helps her at work; she is a vice-president at an American bank in Rome. Tonight under a long pleated skirt she is wearing, instead of the racy Italian underwear she puts on at home, a pair of conventual white underpants and white cotton stockings held up with the kind of elastic garters her grandmother's Irish housemaid might have worn. Edo has been direct, and as impersonal as someone ticking off a laundry list, about what excites him. She is excited by the attitude in itself: an austere erotic vocabulary far removed from the reckless sentiment splashed around by the men she knows in Rome, Boston, and Manhattan.

Elizabeth discovered early on that the world of finance, far from moving like clockwork, is full of impulse and self-indulgence, which extend into private life. When she met Edo she had just come out of a bad two years with a married former client from Milan, full of scenes and abrupt cascades of roses, and a cellular phone trilling at all hours. In contrast, this romance is orderly. She supposes it is an idyll when she thinks about it, which, strangely, is almost never; it flourishes within precise limits of ambition, like a minor work of art. The past he sets before her in anecdotes—for he is a habitual raconteur, though rarely a tedious one—keeps the boundaries clear.

Africa; dust-colored Tanzania. Edo is telling her how his mother once got angry on safari, blasted a rifle at one of the bearers, missed, and hit a small rhinoceros. Under a thatch of eyebrows

Edo's hooded blue eyes glow with a gentle indifference, as if to him the story means nothing; the fact is that he couldn't live without invoking these memories, which instead of fading or requiring interpretation have grown more vivid and have come to provide a kind of textual commentary on the present. His hair is white, and he has a totemic Edwardian mustache. His cheeks are eroded from years of shooting in all weathers on all continents. It's the face of a crusty old earl in a children's book, of Lear, and he is appropriately autocratic, crafty, capricious, sentimental.

He watches Elizabeth and thinks that her enthusiasm for the gluey pig's foot and the rhino story both grow out of a snobbish American need to scrabble about for tradition. Americans are romantics, he thinks—"romantic" for him is the equivalent of "middle-class"—and she is no exception, even if she does come from a good family. Accustomed to judging livestock and listening to harebrained genetic theories at gatherings of his relatives, he looks at her bone structure with the eye of an expert. She is beautiful. Her posture has the uncomplicated air of repose which in Europe indicates a well-born young girl. But there is an unexpected quality in her—something active, resentful, uncertain, desirous. He likes that. He likes her in white stockings.

She says something in a low voice. "Speak up!" he says, cupping his ear like a deaf old man. He is in fact a bit deaf, from years of gunpowder exploding beside his ear. He often claims it turned his hair prematurely white and permanently wilted his penis, but only the first is true. "You're a gerontophile," he tells her.

She'd said something about storms on Penobscot Bay. The rattling windows here remind her of the late August gales that passed over Vinalhaven, making her grandmother's summer house as isolated from the world outside as a package wrapped in gray fabric. She recalls the crystalline days that came after a storm, when from the end of the dock she and her cousins, tanned Berber color and feverish with crushes, did therapeutic cannonballs into the frigid water. She sees her grandmother in long sleeves and straw hat, for her lupus, dashing down a green path to the boathouse with a hammer in her hand: storm dam-

age. In the island house, as in Edo's, is a tall clock whose au-
thoritative tick seems to suspend time.

Elizabeth and Edo finish the pig's foot and stack the dishes in
the sink. Then they go upstairs and on his anchorite's bed make
love with a mutual rapacity that surprises both of them, as it
always does. Each one has the feeling that he is stealing something from the other, snatching pleasure with the innocent sense
of triumph a child has in grabbing a plaything. Each feels that
this is a secret which must be kept from the other, and this
double reserve gives them a rare harmony.

Later Edo lies alone, under the heavy linen sheets, his lean
body bent in a frugal half crouch evolved from years of sleeping
on cots and on bare, cold ground. He sent out the dogs for a last
pee beside the kitchen door, and now they sleep, twitching, in
front of the embers in his fireplace. He has washed down the
sleeping pill with a glass of Calvados that Elizabeth left for him
and lies listening to a pop station from Aberdeen and feeling the
storm shuddering through the house, through his bones. He
imagines Elizabeth already asleep in the bedroom with the Russian engravings, or—hideous American custom—having a bedtime shower. He has never been able to share a bed with a
woman, not during his brief marriage, not during love affairs
with important and exigent beauties. It gives him a peculiar
sense of squalor to think of all the women who protested or
grew silent when he asked them to leave or got up and left
them. Alone among them, Elizabeth seems to break away with
genuine pleasure; her going is a blur of white legs flashing under his dressing gown. Attractive.

After immersion in that smooth body, he feels not tired but
oddly tough, preserved. An old salt cod, he says to himself, but
for some reason what he envisions instead is a burl on a tree. At
Santa Radegonda, a vast country house in Gorizia that nowadays exists only in the heads of a few old people, there was in
the children's garden an arbor composed of burled nut trees
trained together for centuries. The grotesque, knobby wood,
garish with green leaves, inspired hundreds of nursemaids' tales
of hobgoblins. Inside were a rustic table and chairs made of the

same arthritic wood. The quick and the dead. A miracle of craft
in the garden of a house where such miracles were common—
and all of them grist for Allied and German bombs. He seems to
see that arbor with something inside flashing white, like Elizabeth's legs, but then the Tavor takes hold and he sleeps.

2. REMEMBERING EASTER

The storm has blown itself out into a brilliant blue morning, and
Elizabeth lies in bed below an engraving of a cow-eyed Circas-
sian bride and reads the diary of Virginia Woolf. Volume II,
1920–1924. She imagines Bloomsbury denizens with long faces
and droopy, artistic clothes making love with the lighthearted
anarchy of Trobriand islanders. Through the window she can
hear Edo talking in his surprisingly awful English to the gardener about damage to *Cruciferae* in the kitchen plot. Rows of
broccoli, brussels sprouts, and a rare black Tuscan cabbage have
been flattened. The gardener replies in unintelligible Scots, and
Elizabeth laughs aloud. She finds it shocking that she can feel so
happy when she is not in love.

They met when she was depressed over the terrible, common-
place way things had ended with her married lover from Milan,
with all her friends' warnings coming true one by one like
points lighting up on a pinball machine. She had sworn off men
—Italians in particular—when a gay friend of hers, Nestor, who
spoke Roman dialect but was really some kind of aristocratic
mongrel, invited her to Scotland to spend Easter with him and
some other friends at the house of a mad old uncle of his. Nestor and the others didn't show up for their meeting at Gatwick,
so Elizabeth bought a pair of Argyle socks at the airport shop
and took the flight up to Aberdeen on her own. It didn't feel
like an adventure, more like stepping into a void. After the
tawny opulence of Rome, the obstinate cloud cover through
which she caught glimpses of tweed-colored parcels of land far
below suggested a mournful Protestant thrift even in scenery.
She listened to the Northern British accents around her and re-

called her mother's tales of a legendary sadistic Nanny MacKenzie. In her head ran a rhyme from childhood:

> There was a naughty boy,
> And a naughty boy was he
> He ran away to Scotland,
> Scotland for to see.

Nestor was not in Aberdeen, had left no word, and the mad uncle was disconcerting: white-haired, thin-legged, with the pitiless eyes of an old falcon. He was exquisitely unsurprised about her coming alone, as if it were entirely usual for him to have unknown young women appear for Easter weekend. Jouncing along with her in a green Land Rover, he smoked one violent, unfiltered cigarette after another as she talked to him about Rome, trying to conceal her embarrassment and her anger at Nestor. Air of a near-polar purity and chilliness blew in through the window and calmed her, and she saw in the dusk that the landscape wasn't bundles of tweed but long, rolling waves of woodland, field, and pasture under a sky bigger than a Colorado sky, a glassy star-pricked dome that didn't dwarf the two of them but rather conferred on them an almost ceremonial sense of isolation. No other cars appeared on the road. They passed small granite villages and plowed fields full of clods the size of a child's head, and Elizabeth felt the man beside her studying her without haste, without real curiosity, his cold gaze occasionally leaving the road and passing over her like a beam from a lighthouse.

Edo was wondering whether his young jackass of a nephew had for once done him a favor. But he himself had offered no kindness that merited return, and Nestor was ungenerous, like the rest of Edo's mother's family. Perhaps the girl's arriving like this was a practical joke: he remembered the time in Rome when a half-clothed Cinecittà starlet had appeared on his terrace at dawn, sent by his friends but claiming to have been transported there by group telekinesis during a séance. But Elizabeth's irritation, barely lacquered with politeness, was genuine, and lent a

most profound resonance to her odd entrance. In the half-light
he admired the gallant disposition of her features below her
short, fair hair, the way she talked in very good Italian, looking
severely out of the window, from time to time throwing her
neck to one side in her camel-hair collar, like a young officer
impatient with uniforms.

"We're on my land now," he said after forty minutes, and she
observed ridges of pleated dark forest and a jumble of blond
hills. Down a slope behind a wall of elms was the house—a
former grange, two hundred years old, long and low, with
wings built on around a courtyard. With windows set deeply
below an overhanging slate roof, it looked defensive and determined to endure; on each wing, black support beams of crudely
lapped pine gave it the air of an archaic fortification. When Edo
opened the Land Rover's door for her and she stepped out onto
the gravel, the air struck her lungs with a raw freshness that
was almost painful.

"Why do you live here?" Elizabeth had changed from jeans into
a soft, rust-colored wool dress that she wore to the bank on days
when she felt accommodating and merciful. She stood in front
of the fire with one of the red Venetian goblets in her hand,
feeling the airiness of the crystal, balancing it like a dandelion
globe she was about to blow, watching the firelight reflecting on
all the small polished objects in the long, low-ceilinged room so
that they sparkled like the lights of a distant city. She knew the
answer: gossipy Nestor had gone on at length about Byzantine
inheritance disputes, vengeful ex-wives, and drawn-out tan-
trums in climacteric princes. However, with Edo standing before her so literally small and slight but at the same time vibrant
with authority, so that one noticed his slightness almost apologetically—with him playing host with immaculate discretion,
yet offering, subtly, an insistent homage—she felt strangely de-
fenseless. She felt, in fact, that she had to buy time. Already she
was deliberately displaying herself, as the fire heated the backs
of her legs. Before she let everything go she wanted to understand why suddenly she felt so excited and so lost and so un-
concerned about both.

"Why do I live here? To get clear of petty thieves," he said with a smile. "The daily sort, the most sordid kind—family and lovers. When I got fed up with all of them a few years ago, it occurred to me that I didn't have to go off to live in Geneva like some dismal old fool of an exile. Africa was out, because after a certain age one ends up strapped to a gin bottle there. So I came up here among the fog and the gorse. I like the birds in Scotland, and the people are tightfisted and have healthy bowels, like me." He paused, regarding her with the truculent air of a man accustomed to being indulged as an eccentric, and Elizabeth looked back at him calmly. "Are you hungry?" he asked suddenly.

"I'm very hungry. Since breakfast I've only had a horrible scone."

"Horrible scones are only served in this house for tea. I have something ready which I'll heat up for you. No, I don't want any help; I'll bring it to you as you sit here. It will be the most exquisite pleasure for me to wait on you. There is some snipe that a nephew of mine, not Nestor, shot in Sicily last fall."

"What do you think happened to Nestor?" asked Elizabeth. "Could you call him?"

"I'd never call that bad-mannered young pederast. He was offensive enough as an adolescent flirting with soldiers. Now he's turned whimsical."

When Edo went off to the kitchen Elizabeth walked back and forth, glancing at photographs and bonbonnières, touching a key on the computer, looking over the books on cookery and game birds, the race-car magazines, the worn, pinkish volumes of the *Almanach de Gotha;* and she smiled wryly at how her heart was beating. In the kitchen Edo coated the small bodies of the snipe in a syrupy, dark sauce while from her corner the Labrador bitch looked at him beseechingly. His thought was: How sudden desire makes solitude—not oppressive but unwieldy, and slightly ludicrous. It was a thought that had not come to him in the last few years—not since his last mistress had begun the inevitable transformation into a sardonic and too knowledgeable friend. Randy old billy goat, he said genially to himself, employing the words of that outspoken lady; and with the alertness he used to follow trails or sense changes in weather he noted that his hand was unsteady as he spooned the sauce.

The next day, Good Friday, they drove a hundred miles to Loch Ness and stood in the rain on a scallop of rocky shore. Edo broke off a rain-battered narcissus and handed it to Elizabeth in silence. He was wearing a khaki jacket with the collar turned up, and suddenly she saw him as he must have been forty years earlier: a thin, big-nosed young man with a grandee's posture— an image now closed within the man in front of her, like something in a reliquary.

On the drive back, he asked her abruptly whether she knew who he was, told her that his curious first name (Edo was the third in a procession) had set a prewar fashion for hundreds of babies whose mothers wanted to copy the choice of a princess. It was a rather pathetic thing to say, thought Elizabeth, who from Nestor knew all about him and the family, even down to alliances with various unsavory political regimes. Long beams of sunlight broke through over pastures where lambs jumped and ewes showed patches of red or blue dye on their backs, depending on which ram had covered them; shadows of clouds slid over the highlands in the distance. Edo drove her across a grouse moor and talked about drainage and pesticides and burning off old growth, about geese and partridge and snipe.

Then he said: "I want the two of us to have some kind of love story. Am I too old and deaf?"

"I don't know," said Elizabeth.

"I've quarrelled with nearly everyone, I'm solitary and selfish, and I understand dogs better than women. I have been extremely promiscuous, but I have no known disease. That's just to prevent any misunderstanding."

"It doesn't sound very appealing."

"No, but I have a foolish, optimistic feeling that it might appeal to you. The thing I like most is a girl from a good family who dresses vulgarly once in a while. Nothing flashy—just the cook's night out. And schoolgirl underclothes, the kind the nuns made my sisters wear. Do you think you'd be willing to do that for me?"

"I might." Elizabeth felt as if she were about to burst with laughter. Everything seemed overly simple—as it did, she knew, at the beginning of the most harrowing romances. Yet, laughing inside, she felt curiously tender and indulgent toward him and toward herself. Why not? she thought. During the rest of the trip home they traded stories about former lovers with a bumptious ease startling under the circumstances, as if they were already old friends who themselves had gotten over the stage of going to bed. His were all bawdy and funny: making love to a fat Egyptian princess on a bathroom sink, which broke; an actress who cultivated three long, golden hairs on a mole in an intimate place.

The telephone rang before dinner that night, and it was Nestor. He was in France, in some place where there were a lot of people and the line kept dropping; he wanted to know whether Elizabeth had arrived. His uncle swore at him and said that no one—male, female, fish, or fowl—had arrived and that he was spending Easter alone. Then Edo slammed the phone down and looked at Elizabeth. "Now you're out of the world," he told her. "You're invisible and free."

They stood looking out of the sitting-room windows toward the northwest, where a veil of daylight still hung over the Atlantic, and he told her that when seals came ashore on the town beaches people went after them with rifles. He came closer to her, felt desire strike his body like a blow, called himself an old fool, and began to kiss her face. Her hair had a bland fragrance like grain, which called up a buried recollection of a story told him by his first, adored nurse (a Croat with a cast in one eye), about a magic sheaf of wheat that used to turn into a girl, he couldn't remember why or how. Elizabeth remained motionless and experienced for the first time the extraordinary sensation she was to have ever after with Edo: of snatching pleasure and concealing it. "We won't make love tonight," he said to her. "I've already had you in a hundred ways in my mind; I want to know if I can desire you even more. Prolonging anticipation—

it's a very selfish taste I have. But without these little devices, I'll be honest with you, things get monotonous too quickly."

Later he told her not to worry, and she said happily, "But I'm not at all worried. In a few months we'll be sick to death of each other."

This arrival at Easter has become currency in Elizabeth's sentimental imagination, but unlike other episodes with other men it doesn't pop up to distract her during work or even very often when she's not working. She has never been anxious about Edo, but she wants to see him often. Though he is never calm, he calms her. When he sends for her and she takes the now familiar flight up to Aberdeen, she feels her life simplified with every moment in the air. It's a feeling like clothes slipping off her body.

She thinks of it this morning as she sits in the sunlight with her knees up under the covers, and she takes possession, a habit of hers, of a phrase from the book she is reading. "So the days pass," she reads, half aloud, "and I ask myself whether one is not hypnotized, as a child by a silver globe, by life, and whether this is living."

3. SPORTSMEN

For the last ten minutes Elizabeth, the old prince, and three young men have been sitting around the table talking about farts. The young men are Nestor and two cousins of his, whom Elizabeth knows slightly from parties in Rome. All three are tall and thin, with German faces and resonant Italian double last names; they wear threadbare American jeans and faded long-sleeved knit shirts. They are here for a few days' shooting, and in the front hall stand their boots—magnificent boots the color of chestnuts, handmade, lace-up, polished and repolished into the wavering lustre of old furniture. The front hall itself is worth a description: wide, bare, pine boards, a worn, brocade armchair, antique decoys, a pair of antlers twenty thousand years old dug from a Hungarian bog, ten green jackets on wall pegs, exhaling scents of rubberized canvas and dog.

The three young men worship Edo—since their nursery days he has been a storybook rakehell uncle, wreathed in a cloud of anecdote unusually thick even for their family. They are also very interested in Elizabeth—two of them because she's so good-looking, and Nestor from a piqued curiosity mixed with sincere affection. She has stopped confiding in him since he mischievously threw her together with his uncle at Easter. He owns the condominium next to the one she rents in Via dei Coronari and knows that she has been using a lot of vacation time going up to Scotland; he assumes that the old skinflint is laying out money for the tickets and that they're sleeping together, but he can't understand what they do for each other, what they do with each other. She is not an adventuress (in his world they still talk about adventuresses), and she is clearly not even infatuated. Elizabeth's non-whim, as he is starting to call it, only serves to confirm in Nestor's frivolous mind the impenetrable mystery that is America.

Elizabeth sits among them like a sphinx—something she learned from watching fashionable Italian women. But she feels conflicted, torn between generations. Edo feels a growing annoyance at seeing how her fresh face fits in among the fresh faces of the young men. Her presence makes the gathering effervescent and unstable, and all the men have perversely formed an alliance and are trying with almost touching transparency to shock her.

"It's a sixteenth-century gadget in copper called 'la péteuse,' " continues Edo in a gleeful, didactic tone. "It consists of a long, flexible metal tube that was used to convey nocturnal flatus out from between the buttocks, under the covers of the seigneurial bed, into a pot of perfumed water where rose petals floated. I own three of them—one in Paris and the other two in Turin. I keep them with the chastity belts."

Everyone is crunching and sucking the tiny bones of larks grilled on skewers, larks that the guests brought in a neat, foil-wrapped parcel straight from Italy, it being illegal to shoot songbirds in Great Britain. They eat them with toasted strips of polenta, also imported. Elizabeth hates small birds but is determined this evening to hold up the female side; she draws the line at the tiny, contorted heads, which make her think of holocausts and Dantean hells. Game, she thinks, is high in the kind of amino acids that foster gout and aggressive behavior.

"The worst case of flatulence I know of," Edo says, "was the Countess Pentz, a lady-in-waiting to my mother. She was a charming woman with nice big breasts, but she was short and ugly, and farted continuously. It was funny at receptions to see everyone pretending not to notice. I believe she used to wear a huge pair of padded bloomers that muffled the noise to a rumble like distant thunder."

They go on to discuss Hitler and meteorism. One of Nestor's cousins, Giangaleazzo, sends Elizabeth a swift glance of inquiry, perhaps of apology. There is something sweet about that look. Edo sees it and glowers. Elizabeth seizes the opportunity to contribute, mentioning—she realizes it's a mistake the minute she does—Chaucer. Blank looks from the men, although only Edo is truly uneducated. Edo says: "The middle classes always quote literature. It makes them feel secure."

Elizabeth has lived in Rome long enough to be able to throw back a cold-blooded barb of a retort, the kind they don't expect from an American woman. She knows that the young men aren't even surprised by Edo's remark, since it seems to be a family tradition to savage one another like a pack of wolf cubs. But she is looking at the row of restaurant knives and cleavers stuck in back of the long, oiled kitchen counter, and she is imagining the birds heaped in the freezer—small, gnarled bodies the color of cypress bark. She decides that she would like not simply to kill Edo but to gut him swiftly and surgically, the way she has watched him so many times draw a grouse.

When they have finished the larks and the young men are eating Kit Kat bars and drinking whiskey, they complete the fraternal atmosphere by launching into a *canzone goliarda*, a bawdy student song. This one has nearly twenty verses and is about a monk who confesses women on a stormy night and the various obscene penances he has them perform:

> Con questa pioggia, questo vento,
> Chi è chi bussa a mio convento?

Between verses Edo looks at her without remorse. He's thinking, She's tough, she holds up—which is one of his highest compliments. "You look like a wild animal when you get angry," he tells her, and she hates herself for the way her heart leaps. Just before midnight she lies in bed wondering whether he will come down to her. She will not go to him; she wants him to come to her room so she can treat him badly. She lies there feeling vengeful and willfully passive, imagining herself a Victorian servant girl waiting for the master to descend like Jove; at any minute she expects the doorknob to turn. But he doesn't come, and she falls asleep with the light on. At breakfast the next morning he greets her with great tenderness and tells her that he sat up till dawn with Nestor, discussing fishing rights on a family property in Spain.

4. HALLOWEEN

Bent double, Edo and Elizabeth creep through a stand of spindly larch and bilberry toward the pond where the wild geese are settling for the night. It is after four on a cold, clear afternoon, with the sun already behind the hills and a concentrated essence of leaf meal and wet earth rising headily at their footsteps—an elixir of autumn. Edo moves silently ahead of Elizabeth, never breaking a twig. His white head is drawn down into the collar of his green jacket, and his body is relaxed and intent, the way he has held it stalking game over the last fifty years in Yugoslavia, Tanzania, Persia.

Even before they could see the pond, when they were still in the Land Rover, chivying stolid Hertfordshire cows, and then on foot working open a gate that the tenant farmer had secured sloppily with a clothesline and a piece of iron bedstead—even then the air reverberated with the voices and wingbeats of the geese. The sound created a live force around the two of them, as if invisible spirits were bustling by in the wind. Now, from the corner of the grove, Edo and Elizabeth spy on two or three hundred geese in a crowd as thick and raucous as bathers on a city beach: preening, socializing, some pulling at sedges in the water of the murky little pond, others arriving from the sky in un-ravelling skeins, calling, wheeling, landing. Sometimes during the great fall and spring migrations, over two thousand at a time stop at Edo's pond.

He brought them here himself, using his encyclopedic knowl-edge of waterfowl to create a landscape he knew would attract them. He selected the unprepossessing, scrubby countryside af-ter observation of topography and migratory patterns, and en-larged the weedy pond to fit an exact mental image of the shape and disposition needed to work together in a kind of sorcery to pull the lovely winged transients, pair by pair, out of the sky. After three years, the visiting geese have become a county curi-osity. Local crofters have lodged repeated complaints. Edo doesn't shoot the geese; he watches them. This passion for the nobler game birds is the purest, most durable emotion he has known in his life; it was the same when he used to lie in wait for hours in order to kill them. Now he's had enough shooting, but the passion remains.

He grips Elizabeth's arm as he points out a pair of greylags in the garrulous crowd on the water. His hand on her arm is like stone, and Elizabeth, who loves going to watch the geese, never-theless finds something brittle and old-maidish in the fixity of his interest. Crouching beside him, she experiences an arid sense of hopelessness, of jealousy—she isn't sure of what. Casting about, she thinks of his ex-lovers who sometimes call or visit—European women near his own age who seem to have absorbed some terrible erotic truth that they express in throaty laughter and an inhuman poise in the smoking of cigarettes and in the crossing of their still beautiful legs. They are possessive of Edo, and they make her feel raw as a nursery child brought out on display. But she knows they aren't the real reason that she feels cold around the heart.

"You're not interested in getting married, are you?" He says it abruptly, once they have returned to the Land Rover. He says it in French, his language for problems, reasoning, and resolution. He hears his own terror and looks irritably away from her. It is six months since they met.

"No, I'm not," replies Elizabeth. She is embarrassed by the

fatuous promptness with which the words bound out, like a
grade-school recitation. Yet she hadn't prepared them. She
hadn't prepared anything. They are bouncing across stubble,
and to the west, where the evening light is stronger, a few green
patches shine with weird intensity among the autumn browns:
barley fields planted this month to be harvested in January or
February. On the horizon, below a small, spiky gray cloud, a
bright planet regards them equably. Without another word, Edo
stops the motor and reaches over to unzip her jacket and unbut-
ton her shirt. With the same rapt, careful movements he used in
approaching the geese, he bends his head and kisses her breasts.
Then he straightens up and looks at her and a strange thing
happens: each understands that they've both been stealing pleasure. For a second they are standing face-to-face in a glass corridor; they see everything. It's a minor miracle that is over before
they can realize that it is the most they will have together. Instantly afterward, there is only the sense of a bright presence
already departed, and the two of them faltering near the edge of
an indefinable danger. As Elizabeth buttons her shirt and Edo
turns the ignition key, they are already engaged in small, expert
movements of denial and retreat. The jeep pulls out onto the
darkening road, and neither finds a further word to say.

A tumult of wind and dogs greets them as they pull up ten
minutes later to the house. Dervishes of leaves spin on the
gravel beside the rented Suzuki that Nestor and his cousins
used to get to that day's shoot, near Guthrie. Both Elizabeth and
Edo stare in surprise at the kitchen windows, where there is an
unusual glow. It looks like something on fire, and for an instant
Edo has the sensation of disaster—a conflagration not of his
house, nothing so real, but a mirage of a burning city, a sign
transplanted from a dream.

"What have they gotten up to, the young jackasses?" he says,
climbing hurriedly out of the jeep. But Elizabeth sees quite
clearly what Nestor and his cousins have done and, with an odd
sense of relief, starts to giggle. They've carved four pumpkins
with horrible faces, put candles inside, and lined them up on the
windowsills. She interprets it as a message to her, since yester-

day she and Giangaleazzo, who went to Brown, had been talking about Halloween in New England. "It's Halloween," she
says, in a voice pitched a shade too high. She feels a sudden
defensive solidarity with the jumble of young men in the
kitchen, who are drinking Guinness and snuffing like hungry
retrievers under the lids of the saucepans.

"Jackasses," repeats Edo, who at the best of times defines as
gross presumption any practical joke he hasn't thought up himself. In this mood, his superstitious mind is shaken, and he can't
cast off that disastrous first vision. He hurries inside, telling her
to follow him.

Instead, Elizabeth lets the door close and lingers outside,
looking at the glowing vegetable faces and feeling the cold wind
shove her hair back from her forehead. She wills herself not to
think of Edo. Instead she thinks of a Halloween in Dover when
she was eight or nine and stood for a long time on the doorstep
of her own house after her brothers and everyone else had gone
inside. The two big elms leaned over the moon, and the jack-o'-
lantern in the front window had a thick dribble of wax depending from its grin, and she had had to pee badly, but she had
kept standing there, feeling the urine pressing down in her blad-
der, clutching a cold hand between her legs where the black
cheesecloth of her witch costume bunched together. She'd stood
there feeling excitement and terror at the small, dark world she
had created around herself simply by holding back. It's an erotic
memory that she has always felt vaguely ashamed of, but at the
moment it seems curiously appropriate, a pleasure she'd enjoyed without guessing its nature.

Edo opens the kitchen door and calls her, and she comes toward him across the gravel. For a moment before he can see her
clearly, he has the idea that there is a difference in the way she
is moving, that her face may hold an expression that will change
everything. Once, thirty years ago, in Persia, he and his brother
Prospero saw a ball of dust coming toward them over the desert, a ball of dust that pulled up in front of them and turned into
a Rolls-Royce, with a body made, impossibly, of wicker, and,
inside, two young Persian noblemen, their friends, laughing,
with falcons on their wrists. He and his brother and the

gunbearers had stood there as if in front of something conjured up by djinns. He watches Elizabeth come with the same stilling of the senses as he had that afternoon in the desert. When she gets closer, though, the dust, as it were, settles, and his wavering perspective returns to normal, there on the doorstep of his last, his favorite house, in the cold October night. He thinks of the unspoken bargain she has kept so magnificently for a woman of her age, for any woman, and he says to himself, Very well. He has studied nature too long to denigrate necessity. Then why the word thudding inside him, first like an appeal, then a pronouncement: "Never, never, never"? Never, then.

Laughter comes from behind him. His nephews to summon him have launched into the ribald student song from the other night. When Elizabeth reaches him he doesn't look anymore but takes her arm firmly, draws her inside, and shuts the door.

William F. Van Wert

SHAKING

Hard to remember the beginning with people. The end, no. The end is different. The end gets written in indelible ink. But beginnings are so alive. They require the force of memory to be recaptured, and even then they're never as alive as they once were. The aliveness is missing.

This was the case with Jenny Winslow, the Shaker woman. The Free Clinic in Canterbury. Fall colors. The annual blood drive. The bonnet on her brittle head. Shawl across her lap like a tablecloth. Nubby fingers that never stopped twitching. Cobbler's shoes that clacked, like in the fairy tales. All remembered in great detail, like pieces of a patchwork quilt. But the aliveness is missing.

It was fall at the Free Clinic in Canterbury. The trees outside were on fire with colors: raw sienna, robin's breast, roan and burnt henna. The perfect time for a blood drive, except that the wind was blowing bone-cold outside and the whole country was afraid of AIDS, so nobody was giving blood.

I was in the office working on the books when Alice Perry, one of the volunteer nurses, came in.

"Doctor Lazarus? Sorry to bother you . . ."

"What is it?"

"I think you better come out and see for yourself."

I started to follow her to the intake station. I stopped in the doorway to put on my white coat and stethoscope, and I saw the woman. Nurse Perry had gotten her as far as the chair next to the table with the curtain partially pulled around, although there was no one in the outer room to see her.

I knew she was a Shaker woman from the flat mesh bonnet, which looked like a snarl of cobwebs on the white mat of hair. She had little hair left, and the bonnet gave the appearance of even less. Like rain after snow, I thought. Anything added to white makes white look gray.

She wore horn-rimmed glasses with thick curved lenses that made her eyes look big and smeared. Everything else on her face looked pre-shrunk, from the small nose to the pursed lips to the bags of chin. She had spread a white shawl like a table-cloth across her black dress, upon which her fingers shook and rubbed against each other, the only visible sign of any nervousness.

"This is Jenny Winslow, Dr. Lazarus, and she wants to give blood," Alice Perry said, then added, "She insists upon giving blood."

"Does she now," I said, trying to be cheerful. "I'm Dr. Lazarus, Miss Winslow. Or is it Mrs.?"

I held out my hand to shake her hand as I asked. But, instead of giving me her hand, she held it up, palm towards me, as though to stop me from coming any closer.

"I'm legally blind, you know," she said in a scratchy voice, "but I can tell you've got your hand out there. I'm a Shaker and the Shakers have always been celibate, so of course there's no Misses to me. You can call me Sister Jenny if you have to call me anything, and I don't mean to hurt your feelings, because the Shakers love everybody, and we *are* permitted hand-shaking with a man, no harm in that if it goes no further, but you're a young man and I never made your acquaintance before and I'm already nervous enough about giving the blood, so if you don't mind . . ."

I knew there was a Shaker settlement in Canterbury, but I never expected to meet one of them at the clinic. She was very old and dignified in her demeanor, and I suppose I was amused by her presence there, but when she spoke she seemed to be talking about fourteen things at once, the way old people do, and I think I felt a little put off that she had to give me the Shaker belief system in order to avoid my handshake.

"That's fine, Sister," I said, wanting to be done with her.

"I told her I didn't know if I could find a vein," Alice said.

I nodded to Alice Perry that I understood her predicament. She had done right to come get me. We didn't want to poke into this woman's flabby arms, trying to find a vein and possibly triggering something that might lead to a malpractice suit.

"How old are you, Sister, if I may ask?"

"I'm eighty-nine. How old are you?"

"I'm twenty-six, but that's not the point. You see, we don't usually take blood from someone who's over . . ."

"Pardon me," she interrupted, "but it's you who doesn't understand. I have to give the blood this time."

"This time?"

"Yes. I came the other time, but I was too young to keep my wits. I got sick to my stomach just thinking about the needle and I got out of line and ran away."

"When was that?"

"Nineteen-what? Seventeen, it was. For the war."

I could believe it somehow. The more outlandish a thing she said, the more I believed it. She had come to repay a debt, an obligation, a chance missed of seventy years. She had to be nineteen at the time. All those years: the blood not given, the needle avoided, the wars that followed. There was a strength in that kind of obsession. As a rule, we didn't take blood from people over sixty.

"The thought is beautiful, Sister, but maybe it's better left as a thought than as a deed. You don't actually have to . . ."

"I know you must think I have no manners at all, interrupting you all the time and such, but I won't be talked out of it. I know it's old blood, but it has to be worth something to somebody. It's kept me going all these years."

"Well, okay then," I said finally. "Let's do it."

"If I must be penetrated, it would be my wish that this good woman do it."

"We'll just have to respect your wish then, won't we? Would you excuse us for a moment, Sister? We'll be right back."

Alice Perry followed me into the lab. The way the Shaker woman had said "penetrated" sounded too sexual to me. Something as neutral as drawing blood shouldn't have carried such connotations. But then the way she said it gave me an idea.

"I really don't think I can find a vein in either arm," Alice Perry said.

"You don't have to," I said. "You just have to pretend to find one."

I got some blood we had on hand in the refrigerator and extracted some into the syringe. We went back to the patient, I distracted her with questions about the Shaker way of life and Alice Perry pretended to draw blood.

"I thought it would be darker," Jenny Winslow said when she finally looked at the blood up close to her face.

I wasn't sure that she was convinced.

"Alice has a patch to give you," I said, distracting her once again. "It says you gave."

"That's nice," Jenny said. "That's exactly how I'd want to be remembered."

"Can I call a cab for you?" I said.

"No, my legs are good," she said. "I like to walk. It's what I do best."

I felt relieved to see her go, but I also felt a slight twinge of guilt for having tricked an old woman. I had no idea that she would be coming back every day after that.

I came to do my internship at the Free Clinic in Canterbury with a chip on my shoulder. My wife had left me, I was still heavily in debt, and I didn't want to deal with the humiliation of hierarchies and political intrigues at a big hospital, so I opted out.

I came to Canterbury to clean out my lungs on country air and put my damaged manhood on hold. I thought I would find some lost ideals in healing the poor, but I soon found out I hated the poor: their basic ignorance of the body, their fierce pride at not paying, their repetitive diseases. New Englanders are supposed to be hardy and harsh, like the weather, and silent as proverbial sticks. They doctor themselves and pretend away coughs and colds until they're bed-ridden, and then they like to mistake the doctor for the disease. A deep distrust of doctors, a blind belief in God and self-sufficiency, they seem to go hand-in-hand, one nurturing the other. What keeps them here, rooted for generations? Fall colors, winter quilts and family farms all conspire to keep them, but these have become as much a reason for other people coming as for them going, as much a tourist attraction as their beloved tombstones. Why do they live in places that do not protect them?

I say "they," but I am one of them.

Jenny Winslow kept coming to the clinic, day after day, at first a few hours at a time and then gradually half a day, usually in the mornings. She came with knitting or crochet-work and she sat in a corner, speaking to no one. At first, I ignored her, because I thought she had come to give blood again. Then I thought she might be there to proselytize, and I didn't want to encourage that, so I ignored her. And then all sorts of possibilities occurred to me, and I wanted to ignore all of them. She may have experienced some sort of bonding, because of the blood donation. She may have become senile, with no place to go but places of habit or unusual experience. She may have been waiting for the right moment, after wearing us down with her presence, to ask for a drug, some sort of "twilight sleep" to end it all. I was ashamed of all these thoughts, and finally I felt ashamed of having ignored her, but a doctor, even an intern, learns to let trouble come to him. He doesn't go looking.

I heard her tell Ruth Halliburton, one of the nurses, that the Shakers stopped shaking in chapel a long time ago. That kind of dancing took place in the old days, when Mother Ann Lee was founding the Shaker settlements and there was a need to communicate physically with God by dancing. She told Ruth there were only eight of them left now at Canterbury and at Sabbathday Lake in Maine, all women in their nineties, who kept to the simple ways, still did some farming, canned jams, wrote cookbooks and watched Jerry Falwell and Johnny Carson on TV.

"I can't remember the last time I shook," she told Ruth.

I don't think Ruth or any of the other nurses believed her. An old woman, celibate all her life and living apart from other human beings in a sect like that, has to have a secret, and the secret had to be some sort of shaking. The name still held. Why not the practice?

I waited until she had dozed off, as she often did, and I left my office to go stare at her. Bonnet on a brittle head. Shawl across her lap like a tablecloth. Stubs of fingers that never stopped pointing and twitching and rubbing, even while she slept. And those quaint cobbler's shoes, like in the fairy tales. I found myself staring at her shoes. The shoes of old people are never in style. They reflect the feet inside, not the times around them. Shoes that age with them, gnarled and irregular, encompassing ingrown toenails, corns, bunions, broken arches, swollen ankles. Her shoes were black and bulbous. Mannish shoes. I remembered my grandmother in shoes like that, shoes that had to be resoled a dozen times, because there was no buying new ones to fit. Old women in men's shoes, clacking on linoleum floors, and clapping time for an old Disney tune from the seven dwarfs: "Shoes, to set my feet a dancing, dancing, dancing all my cares away." Or maybe it was Gepetto, before he made the real boy.

I came out of my office one afternoon and there was nobody there except the Shaker woman. I didn't expect to see her in the afternoon like that and I certainly didn't expect to find myself alone with her.

"The school called," she said. "Her little boy was throwing up, so Ruth had to go. You were in the bathroom, so she asked me to tell you."

"Did she say she was coming back?"

"She didn't say. She said she would call."

"Thanks."

I started to walk back to my office, then stopped. I felt that I was being rude somehow, turning my back on her like that.

"You want a cup of tea or something?"

"Thanks, no. I'm just fine."

"We don't seem to have many patients these days."

"An apple a day," she said, smiling.

"Do you mind if I sit with you for a minute?"

"It's your clinic," she said.

"I wanted to ask you that first time you came in. Why did you think it was so important to give blood in 1917?"

"Oh, that. I don't know. We still had a lot of brothers with the Shakers then. I have to say I didn't much like any of them, even though Shakers are supposed to love everybody. I don't think they cottoned much to me either, but they sure enough took off to war. Soon as we'd declare a war, they'd be off in a bunch. We lost our last brother that way in 1938. I knew it was the end of the Shakers then, and sure enough. We couldn't take in new men, because we didn't have any brothers left to serve as their counselors. We stopped taking in children because the town wanted them to go to public schools. Then in 1957 the leaders agreed we wouldn't take in any new members. That was what? Thirty years ago?"

I wasn't sure she had answered my question, and I think she could feel that. She turned her body toward me and put her knees together, dropping the shawl to cover her legs.

"You wonder about men, don't you? Everybody does. You're a man and you wonder about the men. And you wonder how come a bunch of men and women choose to live together communally and then be celibate. It wasn't hard, I can tell you that much. 'Hands to work and hearts to God,' Mother Ann said. And so it was."

"You never missed having children?"

"There are women who have had children who had less children than I did. I had them in the kitchen for cooking. I had them in the schools. All gone to God before me, though. That's what hurts."

"If you didn't like the brothers that much, why did you come to give blood in 1917?"

"That was a long time ago. You ask an old woman like me the

reasons for what she did or didn't do that long ago and you're like to get a pack of lies."

"Are you evading my question, Sister?" I teased.

"Maybe so," she said, squirming a little. "If I tell you, do you promise not to tell another living soul?"

"Cross my heart and hope . . ."

"Don't hope for that. Okay, then. There was a fellow went off to the Great War. That's what we called it then. His name was Archie Bishop. He wasn't exactly a Shaker. He wasn't with us long enough. His folks died of flu right after they came to us. His little sister stayed on with us, but Arch, he joined up. I didn't know him very long, but I never seen a boy that could dance as good as he could. He had sweet feet. And he kinda took a shine to me and me to him. Of course, we never touched or anything like that. But we did converse, and there was the dancing. So, when he enlisted, I decided to give blood. But then I got scared, and well, you know the rest."

"So, you were sorry when he left?"

"Guess I was. I was all of nineteen then. I had visions of making him a wife and we'd go off and have a pack of kids in Pennsylvania or somewhere. I still had urges then. But, after he left I didn't have them anymore. Probably a good thing he left too."

"Why's that?"

"Boy named Arch Bishop in this town? Land sakes."

"And you never heard from him again?"

"I took him for dead all these years. Then I got a letter from France with a picture. It was of him in his doughboy costume. Nothing more recent than that. He was leaning on his carabine, all smiles, and you could tell the war was over when the picture got took. He said he married a French woman and they had six kids. Near the end of his letter he said his wife had just died and he was left to wondering, not what it all meant with her, but what it might have been with me. And he said he never told his wife in all those years that he was still thinking of me and couldn't put the dancing out of his head. Very old men have the same cheek sometimes as very young boys. I found the whole thing a bit disrespectful. That was ten years ago."

"You never wrote back?"

"My lord, no. I said a hominy straight away."

Hominy for homily. Jenny Winslow sometimes mixed words. Like Louise Erdrich, saying, "I'm in a laundry" instead of I'm in a quandary. Both could be excused, I decided.

"And you," she said. "You're not from here, are you?"

"How can you tell?"

"You're not solid, that's how. You feel to me like Arch Bishop. You haven't found the place you're bound to be."

"Maybe I ought to go to France," I said.

"Wars aren't good for much else," she said. "You don't have any children."

"No."

"But you'd like to?"

"Are you a mind-reader too? Yes, when the time is right."

"But there is a wife . . ."

"She left me last year."

"Why would she do that?"

"She said she couldn't wait any longer. Said she wanted to 'try on' new things. Like clothing."

"She wasn't right for you."

"Obviously," I said, scornful of such a trite conclusion. "So, who is?"

"There may not be many people right for you. But, when you find one that is, you will be happy a long long time. You have the right last name for that."

"I didn't have much to do with it. It was my father's last name."

"And what's your prefix?"

"My what? You mean my Christian name? It's James."

"Nothing remarkable about that."

"Well, once again, I didn't have much to do with it. My mother chose it."

"Look, then, to your father, not your mother."

Just then, the phone rang. It was Ruth, explaining why she had to leave the clinic. When I hung up, Sister Jenny was gone.

I took to spying on Jenny Winslow after that. Actually, what I took to was staring at the Shaker woman from my office, especially when I caught her napping. Espionage seemed more palatable than voyeurism.

It's hard to imagine that old people were ever young once. When Jenny Winslow fell asleep and her jaw went slack, her whole face caved in at the center, the two long lines compressing her nose and mouth, looking more like puppetry than human flesh. Old people have to strain to look kind and loving. When their features are at rest, they look burrowed and surly, like forgotten apples.

There was not even a hint of a woman's body underneath the black baggy dress that made her look like a penitent in Pilgrim times. And yet her legs were still strong. They weren't muscled, but they weren't flabby either. They were barreled. No varicose veins, no extreme cellulose, no fluid build-up. And those shoes, those black deformed hunchback's shoes. There was an aliveness to them I cannot describe.

I realized finally that there was a conspiracy going on around me. Sister Jenny had somehow made fast friends with all the nurses, who, while they never mentioned her by name at weekly staff meetings, were extremely protective of her. She was, I assumed, some sort of fairy godmother to them: some kind of avuncular good-luck charm, mascot and matriarch rolled into one. What I didn't realize was that her stature among them went way beyond that.

After a series of missed appointments and sudden "cures" among my patients, I discovered that Sister Jenny was doing more than her kitchen samplers in the outer room. I confronted Alice Perry with my suspicions. Although she was only a volunteer nurse, Alice was the oldest person who worked in the clinic and the only one who sometimes called me by my first name.

"Mrs. Neary is supposed to be seeing me for her arthritis. When I don't see her, I call her and she thanks me for the Shaker woman who massaged her feet and hands. Mrs. Chandler is a different story. You know, the one with diabetes? She tells me Sister's recipes have stopped her seizures altogether. And there's more. What's going on here, Alice?"

"We knew you were overworked, Jim. Patients, prescriptions,

house calls, doing the books, scheduling our shifts. It's more than one person ought to be doing. Sister Jenny seems to have a knack. I watched her myself. I can promise you she's never been without supervision. We're all amazed at what she can do."

"It has to stop right now, Alice. We could be in serious trouble if anyone complained."

"Far from it. People are singing her praises."

"No more. Tell the good Sister I'd like to see her in my office, would you?"

Jenny Winslow made her way into my office as though sleepwalking through a thick fog, her hand outstretched, palm toward me. I started to help her to a chair, but she found it first.

"I have a nose for chairs," she said, smiling. "It's like they got my name on them."

"Sister Jenny, I wanted to talk to you about helping the patients here."

"You don't need to thank me, Brother James. The Shakers love everybody."

"That's not the point, Sister. I have to ask you to stop."

"Oh? A matter of professional jealousy, is it?"

"No, a matter of licensing. You aren't licensed to practice medicine in this state. I am."

"Oh, bother," she said, clearing her throat. "What I'm doing isn't any practicing medicine. It's commonsensical. Starve a cold, feed a fever. The Shakers have a good recipe for everything that ails a body."

She wasn't contrite at all. I had to try another approach.

"Let me put it to you this way. If I catch you touching another patient or giving another patient advice, I'll have to bar you from coming here. Do you understand what I'm saying?"

"You think the Shakers are all air and fairy tales, don't you? Did you know that we Shakers invented the circular saw, the common house broom, a washing machine and the common clothespin? We've been here close to two-hundred years. You've been here one year, not even that, and you're telling me what I can and cannot do?"

"I'm telling you what I have to tell you. If my patients want to go out to your farm to be treated, then who am I to stand in your way or theirs? But, if they come to my clinic to be treated, then I have to be the one who treats them. Can you see what I'm saying?"

"I'm legally blind, you know, but I see better than most. The rose don't come without the thorns. That's what I see."

It was her exit line. The phone rang. It was my ex-wife wanting to know if I had paid the car insurance premium that she had sent me. By the time I explained to her that I had never received the forms and got off the phone, Jenny Winslow was gone.

Right was on my side, of course. Not just anyone can practice medicine. I knew the difference between real medicine and the short-term healings of a Shaker woman. If a smoker gets a bad enough cough, he'll stop smoking. But, as soon as the cough goes away, he'll start smoking again. Mrs. Neary's arthritis would flare again. Mrs. Chandler would have new seizures. And, even if they were only interested in short-term relief, I was there for the whole ballgame, all nine innings, the long-term prognosis, even if there were no cure for either one of them.

Jenny Winslow stopped coming to the clinic after our talk. The nurses took it personally and blamed me. Alice Perry stopped calling me Jim. Everything was done by the book after that, the way it should be. I was glad for the routine that followed, but I sometimes missed the aliveness.

My father trembled, but he never shook. He took to his Parkinson's as though he were married to it after my mother died. His fingers trembled in place, so much so that he banged his coffee cup against his teeth and finally had to stop drinking coffee altogether. He sat in his rocking chair for hours at a time, and I got so used to him sitting there that it didn't shock me when he went from the rocking chair to the wheel chair. His jaws turned to stone, and he drooled sometimes when he tried to talk. I told him I loved him one day when I was cleaning food off his chin and shirt, and he grimaced, a kind of shriek where a smile should have been, and he mumbled: "My son, the doctor."

I didn't know if it was pride or scorn.

I thought about writing Jenny Winslow before I left Canterbury. My year was nearly up and I remembered that she had told me about the letter from Archie Bishop in France, and having that information somehow gave me the right to write her if I wanted to.

Doctors go from one crisis to the next, blown out of all proportion by the patients who only know the quick cure. And doctors prescribe: amoxicillin for the ears, hydrocortisone for rashes and eczema, alophyllin or Alupent for bronchial wheezing, L-Dopa for Parkinson's. They hurry up their hand-scrawl: drug name, proper dosage, possible side-effects or contraindications and whether there's to be a refill or not. Paper in hand, the patients hurry to the pharmacy, already half-healed. So it goes. But the doctor knows, if he looks long and hard enough at the patient, that the wins are only temporary. One day he will lose the patient. The patient dies one day, not from cancer or Alzheimer's or Parkinson's or AIDS, but from something simple, something impromptu and whimsical, like pneumonia.

The trick is to deceive the patient one more time, always one more time, into his or her aliveness. Doctors are paid high salaries for this sleight-of-hand.

I never went to a prom in high school, because I was afraid my friends would find out I couldn't dance. I love music, but I don't know what to do with my hands and feet, so, when I am moved by a piece of music, I sit uneasily on the edge of my chair, a little frantic, a little lonely, unable to move. My mother offered to teach me to dance once, but I refused.

When I left Canterbury, I was more than ready to go. I felt like my time at the clinic was like a stint in the Peace Corps. You don't have to go very far from home to feel deprived. I was ready for the city again, for long hours and shift work at a big hospital, for real paychecks, real restaurants and night life, real women. My ex-wife, my medical school debts, my parents' deaths, they were part of a past from which I felt vaguely disconnected, as though it had been surgically removed.

I have never quite believed in a personal God.

I want to shake just once before I die.

Joyce Carol Oates

GOOSE-GIRL

She wanted very much to know why, yet she dreaded knowing why, her son, newly home after four months away, was avoiding her. And then he reared up suddenly before her, as she was descending the stairs, tall, long-boned, his deep-set eyes shiny with misery, and said, "I'm—so ashamed of something." It was typical of Barry, Lydia's youngest child, twenty years old but as likely to appear, in strangers' eyes, older, as he was likely to behave, at home, as if he were younger, that, though he'd been replying to Lydia's remarks in laconic monosyllables, shrugging nervously, shifting his shoulders like a wild creature unaccountably trapped in clothing, as in this household now depopulated of all save his wanly attractive and resolutely cheery forty-six-year-old divorcée mother, Barry would address Lydia as if, all along, they'd been having a conversation; as if this raw, mildly stammered, wholly unexpected statement was in response to a question of hers. And invited a question, which Lydia asked immediately, with warmth, her hand on his arm, "Oh, Barry— what is it?"

He stood on the step below her, yet nearly of her height. Tense, perspiring, giving off a scent (though he'd showered, at length, that morning: Lydia had heard him, early) of anguish and excitement, that faintly briny smell she recalled, with a pang of nostalgia, from his high school days as an athlete. But now Lydia had asked the question, Barry was naturally on the defensive. He said, "I don't know if, if I can tell you, Mom. I mean," he said, shaking his head, turning away, "right now."

Lydia, trying not to become alarmed, trying not to wonder what this intelligent and well-mannered and altogether admirable young man might mean by saying he was ashamed of something, followed Barry downstairs into the hall, it seemed he was headed for the kitchen, then he veered sharply in another direction and went into the garage, and Lydia was trying to stop herself from wondering, fearfully, Had he been expelled from Amherst?—Was the spring semester not really over, and Barry had come home early, banished, disgraced? Even as she reasoned this could not be so, she'd nearly memorized the salient dates of the school's academic calendar. She was calling, "Barry, honey—wait!" but of course he wasn't going to wait, like an arsonist who has dropped a lighted match on flammable material he wasn't about to wait, nor even to glance over his shoulder to see how the damage he'd caused was progressing. Barry opened the garage door and wheeled his Yamaha out into the May sunshine, and Lydia, ever attentive, even in the exigency of worry, snatched up the grimy black helmet from the concrete floor and followed after him. She said, calmly, "Barry, please. You can't run off. You've upset me by saying—"

Barry murmured, "Yeah, Mom, okay, I know, I'll tell you later, I just can't tell you now. I *can't*."

"Is it about school?"

"No."

"Is it about—Chris?" Chris was Barry's girlfriend, from high school, now at Middlebury; or rather, one of his girlfriends. He had not spoken of her lately, but Lydia knew from her former husband, with whom she spoke frequently on the phone, that they still saw each other.

Quickly, irritably, his back to her, Barry said, "No, it isn't about Chris."

"Is it—"

"I'll tell you later, Mom. I *said*." He paused, wiping the accumulation of cobwebs off the Yamaha, rubbing the chrome with spittle. "Don't bug me, okay?"

There was an old semi-jokey history in the family of Lydia's exaggerated dislike of the motorcycle, perceiving it, as Lydia thought quite reasonably, as the possible instrument of her son's death or disfigurement, but there was an old history of Barry's fanatic attachment to it: he'd worked at exhausting jobs, including emergency snow removal for the State of New York, to pay for it. Lydia, with her anthropological-sociological bent, thought the shiny black vehicle with the flaring handlebars and high-backed seat and the near-deafening roar of which its motor was capable, a sign of Barry's rejection of his own natural introversion and good sense, a proclamation of his distinctly American, thus public, masculinity; Sam, her former husband, graced with a placidity regarding their children's welfare that Lydia sometimes thought maddening, at other times enviable, had merely shrugged and said, "It's cheaper than a car."

Barry straddled the Yamaha and labored to start it, and after several abortive attempts it started, roaring into demonic life, eager to be gone. Lydia handed Barry his helmet, for otherwise he might have forgotten it. A womanly figure in a medieval tapestry, handing over armor to a knight on a steed. A visor to obscure the youthful, and in this case embarrassed and sullen, face.

She asked where he was going, and he told her, naming names she'd heard from junior high school onward, and she asked when he thought he might be back, and he said, fumbling to fasten the helmet strap beneath his chin, lowering the smoked-plastic visor, "Maybe around lunch—I don't know," and he drove noisily off, like an upright insect on the black vehicle, down the sloping asphalt driveway, onto Somers Brook Road, within seconds curving out of sight. Lydia stood alone shading her eyes against the warm sunshine, feeling more than usually diminutive; diminished; a bit foolish, like a spurned woman. Except for the stink of the exhaust, and an agitation of the air, there was no evidence Barry had been there at all.

It was nine thirty-five A.M. He'd fled without eating breakfast. Lydia, who had set this day aside for Barry, canceling appointments, rearranging her schedule, saw that it would be a long day.

Of the three Manning children, Barry had taken his parents' protracted separation and speedy divorce the most seriously—with an almost romantic seriousness, Lydia and Sam thought. Believing that the erotic passion that had generated *him,* of all the world's population, was too extraordinary ever to be extinguished?

The week before, talking with Sam on the phone, Lydia had asked, "Does Barry talk to you?—confide in you?" steeling herself for information that might reawaken an old, demeaning jealousy, but Sam had laughed his explosive laugh, and said cheerfully, "Are you serious, Lydia? The kid hates my guts." Which wasn't true, for no one hated Sam, least of all his youngest and most tender-hearted child.

Lydia was thinking guiltily that she'd neglected Barry, this past year. She was working again, and she had her friends, and the days passed swiftly, and smoothly—as they had not passed smoothly during the years of her marriage. It was easy to comply with Barry's neglect of her, in the heady maelstrom of undergraduate life: a few late-night telephone calls, snatched from the waning day, postcards and not letters, no time, no time. Once, seated at the dining room table with his mother, his brother, and his sister, this would have been Christmas of his freshman year, Barry had solemnly denounced a friend, now at Berkeley, who'd sent out a computer-printed newsletter to Barry and many others, taking no time to make the individual letters individual, thus worthy of being read. Josh, Barry's brother, his elder by three years and so by family tradition his mentor, said, "Yes, but a newsletter is better than no letter, isn't it, assuming you care about your friend at all," and Barry said, incensed, his dark nostrils fairly flaring, "No! No it isn't."

He was fierce and hawklike in profile; he wanted to be an "environmental science writer," or maybe a lawyer, something in the line of environmental protection, yes, but he was being drawn toward the classics too, what a mesmerizing professor he had, making Homer, the Greek lyric, the tragedies, come *alive.* Like many shy people, he could talk excitedly, and at length, as if words were pent up inside him, exerting a sweet painful pressure. Yet listening to Barry, Lydia sometimes felt she didn't know him, at all. For the words he actually spoke somehow did not match the words she imagined pent up inside him; as his purchase of the Yamaha, and the fever of excitement surrounding it, had stunned her, his mother—Yes, she wanted to protest, other boys do such things, but not *you*.

In families, courtships prevail. Someone is forever pursuing someone else; that person, another; and there are those who, so strangely, so perversely, prefer, yes unmistakably prefer, to be alone.

For a long time, Lydia had believed herself to be in pursuit of her children, who, even as they clearly loved her and behaved very decently to her, nonetheless eluded her. For a brief while, Lydia had believed herself in pursuit of her husband—talky, gregarious, clumsy Sam, who of course meant no harm, blundering amid the wreckage of their marriage, perennially meaning well. Then, by degrees, she'd realized, No, no, I am not like this at all, I am the person I always was, from the first, I don't need others to define me, it's in fact others who misdefine me. Armed with such knowledge, Lydia had surprised Sam—so conciliatory, so fair-minded. When, another time, he'd asked if he could come back to her, try again, he loved her of course and she loved him, Lydia had laughed and laid her hands on Sam's arms, in the manner of a coach springing the news to a dazed second-string player. "No, Sam. No. *No.*"

Now Sam was living with a woman friend, in Dobbs Ferry, a half-hour drive from his old house in Hazelton-on-Hudson. Lydia hoped they would marry soon, to restore tidiness, formality, to the situation.

Lydia herself had numerous male friends, amid the large, heterogeneous circle of her Hazelton friends, but no romantic prospects or interests—assuredly not. She was slim, impeccably groomed, beautiful in a fading, dusky-golden way, as if touched with pollen, like a day lily just past its prime; she supposed herself attractive to men but gave no encouragement, made no overtures. Her women friends, those still married, made no secret of envying her what's called, in the simplest language, *peace and quiet.* Everyone loved Sam, but who would have wanted to live with him? And their own husbands? Who would want to live with *them?* So, lunching together at the tennis club, or in town, Lydia and her friends of many years would succumb to fits of girlish, exhilarating laughter, given a special buoyancy by glasses of white wine, cool, dry, tart, low in calories. The wittiest and most brazen among them (this would not be Lydia, however) might even be led to do imitations of certain husbands, and how the women laughed, laughed—for domestic life, seen from the perspective of youthful middle age, is as amusing as a comic opera by Mozart. More hilarious still if the beautiful arias are sung by wavering, amateur voices, as in a summer stock production.

Lydia wondered if, at such giddy times, she might not be betraying not only Sam, but her children—Josh, Roslyn, Barry—so defining herself as a *self* wholly independent of them.

Once, during the time of the divorce, Lydia confessed, of Sam, that while she still loved him she could not, often, *bear* him. "In a way, the thing that upset me most," Lydia said, as her friends leaned forward attentively, like medical students at their first dissection, "was his, I don't know, mendacity?—that's too strong a word. His ranking of people—of friends. For instance, when we'd give a dinner party"—and here Lydia's friends did indeed listen attentively, for they and their husbands had many times been guests at the Mannings', as the Mannings had been guests at their homes—"Sam would deliberate for days over the wine." Sam Manning's wine cellar was much talked of in Hazelton, a good deal of the talk by Sam himself. "Everything he serves is precisely chosen—there are A wines, red wines, from the 1960s; there are B wines; God knows what the C wines are, these days. And Sam would rank the wines to fit the guests, and I was always so worried the guests would *know*."

Lydia's friends erupted in laughter. "Of course we knew, we knew all along, everyone knew," they told her.

Lydia did something she'd promised herself she would never do, again. When Barry didn't return for lunch, she telephoned in pursuit of him—making three calls before she tracked him down, yes, he'd been visiting his friend Trig, just home from Wesleyan, but he was gone now, off on his Yamaha.

"I see. Thanks!" Lydia said cheerfully.

She thought, The next thing will be going through his things. She thought, I will *not*.

Lydia had been trained as an educational psychologist and had more recently taken graduate courses at SUNY-Purchase; she was working as a consultant for a film company that did educational films; she'd been contracted to prepare the script for such a film herself. And she had plans to invest, with a Hazelton friend, a divorcée like herself, in a documentary film series on children and the arts. Through the years of her marriage she had worked sporadically, but only part-time; she'd rarely had the luxury of periods of concentration that professional work requires; when the children and Sam had all been home, her consciousness was as easily broken and scattered as—what? A flock of sparrows pecking in the dirt, when a stone is tossed into their midst. Since Barry had come home she'd been reduced to *that* again—not just the edginess of confrontation, but the apprehension of it. She could not imagine how their conversation would go, only that there would be a conversation.

She recalled his words. The startling gravity of "ashamed." "So ashamed."

She recalled his eyes, evasive, very dark, as if all pupil.

She recalled the awkwardness, and the hurt, of the previous evening, when she had prepared a light supper for the two of them, and Barry had had little appetite, picking at his food, scarcely hearing what she said, answering her questions quickly and abstractly, as if with the most superficial part of his brain.

He'd been nervous, excited about something, yet, so strangely, he'd gone to bed early, at eleven. Lydia herself usually went to bed around midnight.

The thought had occurred to her, He's uncomfortable alone in the house with me. The two of us, now that the others are gone.

It was a thought she pushed from herself.

It was a thought, yes, she'd had herself, without fully articulating. Quite deliberately, she pushed it from herself.

The previous afternoon, Lydia had talked Barry into coming with her to a small impromptu gathering at the home of neighbors on Somers Brook Road. Though he had been home only a few hours, and might have pleaded tiredness, he agreed to accompany her, provided he didn't have to wear a coat or tie (Lydia assured him he didn't) and they wouldn't stay too long (Lydia promised no more than an hour). The Brewers were old family friends, they'd seen Barry grow up, Barry understood that they would be hurt if they knew he'd returned from school but hadn't cared to see them. He understood that, like other young men and women of his age, he represented something binding and reassuring to his parents' friends, particularly those of an older generation than his parents, and that this fact carried with it a curious obligation. *He meant something. He "stood for" something.* So he'd accompanied his mother, and they'd stayed for two hours, and Lydia was covertly proud of her tall, attractive, well-mannered son, who now shook hands with adults as if he were one of them.

He'd even been drawn off, in a mysteriously intense conversation, by a local woman with whom the Mannings were slightly acquainted—the married daughter of friends of the Brewers, in her late twenties, back in Hazelton on a visit.

"How does Barry like Amherst?" Lydia was asked, and "Is he home for the summer?" and "What is he studying?" and "Is he still serious about—what was it, track? swimming? diving?" The Brewers, now well into their seventies, never tired of exclaiming, "How he's grown!" out of Barry's earshot, to Lydia, as if his height were an accomplishment of Lydia's. She smiled, and blushed, as if, indeed, it were.

The day had been balmy, fragrant with the sweet catkins of pussy willows and Lombardy poplars. The party was held on the Brewers' terrace overlooking their lawn and cattail-choked pond, and Lydia watched absently as Barry and the young married woman strolled down to the pond, the woman leading the way, talking animatedly, gesturing, conspicuous in her tight-fitting glove of a dress and spike-heeled shoes, her hair, clay-colored, with a look of being glazed, springing in shoulder-length curls around her thin face. The woman's name was Phoebe Stone, and Lydia could not recall her husband's name, though she knew he was a prominent Manhattan financier, and much had been made, in Hazelton, when the wedding had taken place—surely no more than two years ago? Phoebe Stone was painfully and defiantly thin; she wore black silk, no doubt to emphasize her thinness; she was not beautiful, nor even pretty, with close-set wary eyes and a large dissatisfied mouth, yet she had an air of reckless glamour, inappropriate to the setting, comically out of place amid the Brewers and their guests, several of whom were white-haired. Of the gathering, only Barry was near Phoebe Stone's age, if twenty is near twenty-nine. Only Barry, lanky and self-conscious in jeans, pullover shirt, canvas shoes, with that maddening habit of continually brushing his hair out of his eyes, provided any interest for her.

Sam had had an apt name for the haughty Ms. Stone, whose parents were very wealthy. Now what was it?

It was after such Hazelton gatherings that Lydia most missed her husband. Her old pal, her confidant. Blunt, funny, unsparing and outrageous in his judgments, Sam had allowed Lydia, all those years, to remain *nice;* yet, with a delicious sense of abandon, to *laugh.*

So Barry had accompanied his mother to the Brewers' party, and had seemed to be enjoying himself. At least, saying good-bye, he'd shaken his host's hand vigorously, and leaned to accept a kiss and a cheek from his hostess, and thanked them both with his sweetly shy dimpled smile. On the way home in the car, however, he lapsed quickly into one of his moods; staring out the window, fidgeting, replying in monosyllables to Lydia's remarks, as if he were, so suddenly, twelve years old again. Lydia was surprised, and Lydia was hurt. How like sunshine on a day of high scudding clouds these adolescent beings are—patchy, unpredictable, unreliable. She foresaw that the evening, the supper she'd so looked forward to, just Barry and her, would be an ordeal; and she was not mistaken.

He wasn't very hungry, Barry mumbled, picking at Lydia's food. He'd had a lot to eat, he guessed, at the Brewers'.

"I guess you know her. You and Dad. The woman at the Brewers'. Yesterday."

Barry was speaking haltingly, his face visibly warm, eyes lowered. There was a faintly sour smell of beer on his breath.

Lydia said, more perplexed than startled, "Phoebe Stone?"

"She— I— Oh Christ, I'm so *ashamed*."

"What happened, Barry?"

Barry was sitting directly in front of Lydia; hunched a bit, flexing his big-knuckled hands. It was nearly six o'clock. He'd stayed away all day, and when Lydia heard the motorcycle approaching the house, heard the damned thing sputter to a stop in front of the garage, she'd felt almost faint with anger and apprehension. She was in the sunporch at the rear of the house —the glassed-in room that was also her study—and she'd been working, though of course she'd been waiting, all day.

Lydia said, rather sharply, "What happened, Barry?"

Barry squirmed. Ran his fingers through his hair. Spoke in so soft a voice Lydia could barely hear. Now plunging headfirst, with that air of calculated desperation he'd brought to high school swim meets . . . where, as a diver, he'd climbed the ladder to the high diving board as everyone watched, a skinny, scared-looking boy, near to naked, streaming water like rippling nerves. It had seemed to Lydia and Sam that their son ran the length of the board to fling himself into—what? Space, oblivion, destiny.

Barry told Lydia shamefaced that, at the party, Phoebe Stone had "come on pretty strong" to him; he'd been surprised and, he guessed, flattered; he wasn't used to that sort of attention from older women—"Heck, from anyone." She was such a— beautiful woman. Such a glamorous woman. And married. And in her thirties.

Lydia, who was profoundly shocked, nonetheless corrected her son. "Oh, I don't think so. Phoebe Stone is no more than twenty-nine."

Barry shifted his shoulders miserably and ran his fingers through his hair. His hair, though washed that morning, looked dirty—oily. It stood up in frantic tufts about his head like the damp-feathered tufts of a newly fledged bird.

Lydia had time too to register bemusement—of course, Phoebe Stone's exact age could hardly matter. She was *older*.

Gently, Lydia asked Barry again what had happened; and Barry hesitated and said, still in a low, mumbly voice, "Mom, she wants me to come over to her place, tonight. She gave me the address and all. She's staying with her parents but there's a separate house she's in—nobody would see, she said, if I came after dark. Her telephone number too." Barry removed from his jeans pocket a much-crumpled little piece of paper and laid it on Lydia's desk, awkwardly smoothing it; this little task required several seconds. Lydia caught a glimpse of a harshly slanted handwriting, words and numerals in red felt-tip pen. "She said," Barry continued, suppressing a nervous belch, "she wanted me to—make love to her." Again he paused; swallowed; his face so darkly mottled with blood it looked like a recrudescence of his old acne. "She, uh—didn't use that word, exactly. She used other words."

There was another pause; a pang of mutual misery; and now Lydia looked down at her own hands, whitely clenched in her lap. What were they talking about? How was this possible? Her Barry, her son? Recruited for a sexual adventure? Under her very eyes? At the Brewers' home on Somers Brook Road, of all unlikely places? Barry continued, rapidly, "She said she didn't think she really knew *how*, the kind of man her husband is, something wrong with him I guess, or maybe with other men she'd been—involved with. She said I looked like I would know *how*. So I"—Barry broke off, giggling suddenly—"I said yes."

"You said *yes*—?" Lydia's voice was faint.

"I was flattered, I guess. She's so beautiful and so—glamorous. So strange. Like nobody I know my own age, or any age. I didn't have time to think, it was like something in a movie—but the kind of movie that never would happen to *me*. She said she 'felt a rapport' with me—'felt desire' for me—as soon as she saw me arrive at the Brewers'. She didn't know who I was, or who you are, Mom—or anyway she pretended not to. Jesus, it was weird! I knew at the time it was weird, but I—couldn't say no. We were walking down by the pond and she looked at me, her eyes are so big, and her skin's so white, like she was getting over being sick, she's got a sort of feverish look, it just went through me. 'Promise me you'll come to me, and promise you'll never tell anyone,' she said, she squeezed my arm, dug in her nails so they hurt, 'promise, promise, promise.' I said yes, sure, I'd come, and I wouldn't ever tell anyone, I guess I'd have told her anything, she had me so—" Barry's face contorted as he searched for a word that eluded him, and that Lydia, listening with a painfully beating heart, did not want to supply. "Anyway, I said those things. And now I'm telling you, Mom, so that makes me a liar, I guess, and I'm not going to her place tonight, so I'm backing out on that too—oh God, I'm so fucking *ashamed*."

He was too agitated apparently to notice the profanity that had slipped from him, which Lydia had never heard from his lips before. Not that she was surprised—much.

So he talked, confessed. Doubled back and repeated what he'd said, with amplification. It was clear that the situation greatly distressed him; that, apart from the sexual embarrassment, he simply did not know what to do. Where another young man would have torn up the note, or gone to the tryst and afterward boasted to his friends, Barry was too sensitive, and too inexperienced. In Lydia's place, Sam would have dropped a heavy hand on the boy's shoulder and told him the incident was funny, why not just laugh? For Sam, that would about sum it up—*funny*. And maybe that was so.

Lydia said, suddenly, "The Goose-Girl!"

Barry squinted at her, perplexed.

Lydia explained, "That was what your father used to call Phoebe Stone—not to her face, of course. It was one of his comical names. She reminded him—and me too—of the drawing of the poor Goose-Girl, in our copy of *Grimms' Fairy Tales:* that sort of gangly, frazzled look, the enormous staring eyes, stork legs— do you remember the Goose-Girl? No?" Barry's eyes had gone opaque. Any attempt on Lydia's part to remind her children of their common childhood, especially their remote babyhood, was usually met with such blank resistance. "Phoebe used to always dress conspicuously, as she did yesterday. For a while it was tie-dyed things, like rags. Once she wore what looked like a PLO uniform, khaki fatigues, leather boots to the knee. Now it's black. And always skintight. She's so terribly thin—anorexic, I suppose. And the extreme high heels, with her height—she must be five feet ten. And the bizarre makeup." Lydia paused, breathless. She was unable to recall whether in fact Phoebe had been excessively made-up the day before, or whether she'd worn no makeup at all. The young woman's pale, pinched face floated before her, indistinct as a ghost's. "We'd heard that she was having 'emotional problems,' a breakdown in college. Then she got involved in demonstrating against—I think it was nuclear power plants. She was always what you'd call eye-catching. Always seeming to cry, 'Look! Look at *me!*"

Barry was too caught up in his own emotion to notice his mother's. He said, face contorted as a small boy's, "If only she hadn't made me promise. If only I hadn't been such an asshole. I had a quick glass of wine, and it's sort of, you know, disorienting, to be back home, and—everything went to my head. And now—"

Lydia smiled, encouragingly. "And now—"

"—I'm not going."

The words were a vow, vehemently uttered.

Lydia said, "Well, I wouldn't think, under the circumstances, you would."

Still he stared at her, imploring her. To what? Saying, tears glistening in his eyes, "I'm not going and I—I can't call her." There was a pause. Lydia, now knowing what was coming, began to shake her head. Barry pleaded, "Mom, please, would *you?* Just call her, and tell her—some excuse? Anything? Like, I'm gone out of town, had to go back to school, I'm not—*here?*"

Lydia said sharply, "Barry. *No.*"

"You could make up any excuse, you could simply—"

"Lie? For you? And you're twenty years old, and you got yourself into this predicament?" Lydia laughed, though without much mirth. She could scarcely force herself to look at Barry:

such adolescent misery quivered in his face, he seemed about to cry.

She got abruptly to her feet, anger coursing quicksilver along her veins. Why she was so radiantly angry she didn't know, and didn't want to know. She seized Barry's forearms, each in a tight grip, and said, firmly, "No. No. *No.*"

Lydia hid herself away upstairs, she was so upset.

Was she furious with the Goose-Girl for daring to proposition her son, her young, beautiful, innocent son, or was she furious with her son for being so propositioned—and so flattered? So, it was clear, sexually mesmerized? Wryly Lydia thought, I'm angry because it's the one thing, for her son, a mother can't do.

And then, of course, she relented.

For Barry *was* miserable, as only the young can be miserable, perceiving their betrayal of another person as self-betrayal; too humiliating, at the core, to be remedied. "And please don't tell Sam," Barry pleaded. (Lydia's former husband was one of those fathers who request that their children call them by their given names, as if, apprehended as equals, they might then be expected to bear less parental responsibility.) Lydia sighed, and Lydia laughed, and Lydia said, in disgust, "Oh, all right. *But never again.*"

Barry stared at her as if she'd uttered an obscenity.

So Lydia relented, and at ten-fifteen P.M., with Barry out for the evening, she poured herself a glass of dry white wine, and smoothed out the wrinkled scrap of paper bearing Phoebe Stone's telephone number, and, her hands slightly trembling, dialed the number. By Barry's account, Phoebe had asked him to come to her house, a former carriage house on the Stones' property, "anytime after nine-thirty." So she would have been waiting for him, expecting him, for forty-five minutes.

As the phone rang, and rang, Lydia's face burned. She felt—what? Vindictive, elated?—gloating? Why should *she* have him, even for a night, Lydia's son?—the gawky-gangly Goose-Girl, who deserved only rejection, repudiation?

The phone was answered at the other end, a faint, guarded

voice ventured, "Hello?" and Lydia, swallowing, suddenly very
nervous, said, "Hello? Is this Phoebe Stone?"

There was a pause. Then Phoebe Stone said, Yes, yes this is
she, and Lydia cleared her throat, and said, in a voice of warmth
and apology, as evenly as if she'd practiced this little speech for
hours, "Phoebe, this is Lydia Manning—Sam Manning's wife—
we were both at the Brewers' yesterday, but I don't believe we
had a chance to speak?" There was no reply to this cast-out
remark, casual and imprecise as it was, not even the usual murmured assent or encouragement for Lydia to continue, so Lydia
plunged forward, a bit clumsily, her face now burning, "I—I'm
calling for my son Barry. He said you'd invited him and some
of his friends over tonight," a lie, but an inspired lie, one which,
Lydia reasoned, would allow the Goose-Girl to save face, "and
he's asked me to call you and apologize, something came up, a
friend from college—" Lydia's voice trailed off in just the right
tone of exasperation and indulgence.

A pause. No reply.

Lydia added, with a weak laugh, "You know how they are—
at that age."

Then came Phoebe Stone's voice, clear and distinct and small,
like crystal being struck, "I'm afraid I don't, Mrs. Manning." In
that instant Lydia could see the young woman's thin, pinched-
pale face, the eyes brimming with tears. That Goose-Girl tumble
of curly, crinkly hair with its synthetic luster. "But thank you
for calling, you're very kind."

Exhausted, Lydia went to bed early. But though the house was
empty, and silent as a tomb, and the painful ordeal was over,
she couldn't sleep. (No, she wasn't waiting for Barry to come
home: she'd given up such wasted effort, years before.) Toward
two A.M. she got out of bed and wandered downstairs, switching
on lights as she passed. She was drawn as if by instinct to a
swaybacked old Workbench bookshelf in one of the spare bedrooms, located the aged copy of *Grimms' Fairy Tales*, leafed
through it. . . . The book was a children's edition, hardcover,
oversized, with illustrations for most of the tales . . . in very
bad condition (in fact, hadn't it slipped from her or Sam's hands

once and fallen into the tub, where one of the children was being bathed?) . . . untouched for years. Lydia located the
Goose-Girl, and was startled to see that the drawing bore very
little resemblance to Phoebe Stone after all.

The Goose-Girl in the book was pretty in a conventional way,
plump-cheeked, curly-haired, sweet-faced, vacuous. Lydia
scanned the tale and saw, too, that it wasn't the fairy tale she
might have surmised, from the title, but a rather cruel, primitive
tale—yet another variation on the "mistaken princess." The
Goose-Girl *was* a princess, mistaken as a commoner.

So Sam had been wrong after all. But then, Sam had been
wrong about so many things.

Lydia closed up the book, her eyes stinging with tears. Poor
Goose-Girl! She'd deserved better treatment, at the hands of
such good people.

Charles Eastman

YELLOW FLAGS

I remember little of my father from the time we all lived together in Hollywood, and only a few disturbing moments from
that period, including the afternoon when he took out after another car that had in passing splattered ours with muddy water
from the gutter. He was suddenly furious, as though he had
been injured or insulted. What he planned to do when he
caught up with the offender I didn't know, but I saw that he
was all the more determined, fiercer in his pursuit, for my
mother's high-pitched objections from the passenger seat—as
our car, a Ford sedan, hit the hazardous dips of the cross streets
and barreled forward. I think I felt that my mother was over-
reacting, more fearful than need be, and was feeding my father's
rage, but I did not know about alcohol then and so assumed
that she saw the peril more clearly than I, on my feet in the
back seat like a charioteer and more entertained than frightened.

I also remember him at a card table in the middle of the living
room on Western Avenue. The floor lamp is at his right, out of
place, pulled from behind the couch to illuminate the card game
he plays with our guests—childless, unfettered friends my parents knew from high school. My father lifts his arm suddenly to
thwart some attempt to calm him down, make peace, and the
lamp goes over with the gesture. I hear raised voices, concilia-

tory, then pandering, before an abrupt, intimidated silence. The room is tipped upside down in the spilled light.

Here again it is my mother's reactions that stay more acutely with me, her keening moan of desperation, her see-what-you've-done-now despair. She, who would go to any lengths for the sake of appearances, suddenly surrendered and began wildly overstating her embarrassment, goading my father's temper, I think, and feeding his penchant for making scenes, on those card-playing nights of the Depression.

Otherwise, my father seemed to be laughing most of the time, or asleep, in the memory I have of him, in the few, brief years before the divorce. I can recall his teasing sense of well-being, his self-satisfaction, fixed on my mother, and the long, heavy hours of sudden, untimely slumber: eventless Sunday afternoons, when after some aborted pastime I was obliged to honor an uncommon, unreasonable quiet.

Then he was gone, his absence hardly noted in the abrupt change in our circumstances. My mother was at work now, and my grandmother was running the house—or the succession of houses—we shared with her and with my working aunts, sometimes my uncle, and finally, for a while, a stepfather.

And then, after several years, he was back.

He was in uniform, in the Army, a sergeant, and he was leaving town. It was early summer and I was not in school. The kids, my brother and sisters, were somewhere, I don't know where. Perhaps it was not summer vacation but Easter week.

My grandmother let him in and called my mother on the phone. The phone was in the hall, on a small, cluttered desk invariably lacking a pencil, with a chair in front of it, though my grandmother did not sit down. She wore a patterned pinafore apron, blue; it was damp from her interrupted work at the sink or at the tubs on the back porch. I can only think she was torn over how to handle this emergency.

"He's here and he wants to take Conrad to the beach," she said to my mother at her office across town. It was gloomy in the hall, as it always was when the bedroom doors were closed. My father stood in the door to the den, taller than anyone I knew, blocking light from that source, too. My grandmother did not turn the light on.

"No, he doesn't seem like it," she said.

"Could I speak to her?" my father said.

My grandmother gave him the phone. With her apron she wiped her wrists where suds had climbed when she'd dried her hands.

"I had one beer at lunch," my father said, as though my mother were being unreasonable. "A beer."

I sat down on the third step from the bottom of the narrow staircase that led to the rooms above. I knew that some higher order of things regulated my fate now, some jurisdiction where I didn't belong exclusively to my mother and my grandmother anymore, and where their preferences could be overruled. He was my father, after all, if currently underprivileged and in disgrace, and was thereby entitled to the sympathy and the subordination of my protectors, female. Still, I had the dim hope that my mother might prevail, would say a firm no, from the obstinate streak I knew she possessed.

"But I'm sober and I'll stay sober while he's with me," my father said. My grandmother swatted him with her dish towel, good-naturedly, warningly, and got back on the phone, her job to lighten things up.

"Tell her I'll behave," my father said, recognizing an ally. And then, turning to me, addressed the jury: "But I'm leaving for a while and I just thought I might like to go to the beach for once with one of my kids, for Christ's sake."

I could not hear my mother on the other end of the line, and yet I have no doubt about what she said: "I'm pretty busy just now, Mama," as though she recognized my grandmother's divided loyalty and was feeling outnumbered, overruled. This was not indifference or callous disregard but simply the truth. Our welfare depended on my mother's salary now. Which we knew, my brother, my sisters, and I. Our mother's attention during the day, in our larger behalf, was owed elsewhere, even if we did not always temper our emergencies to that priority.

As she listened to my mother, my grandmother looked between my father and me. She said she was sure Edward was a good man and would take good care of me. If she looked as though she doubted her own argument, it was because she understood our conflicting feelings fully, and her heart went out to all three of us.

"But I want him to give Conrad five dollars, in case something happens—right now, in front of you, Mama, so he'll have money to get home at least, or to phone."

When my grandmother hung up and repeated this codicil to my father, he said, "For crying out loud."

At the beach it was not warm or crowded enough to be summer, and the briny smell, like laundry soap and sulfur, was caustic; the wind was blowing.

We stayed for a while in my father's borrowed car and stared at the wind-combed sand. The car belonged to a woman, I suspected. Someone who kept it clean, anyway, who had left a half-peeled roll of Life Savers on the seat. Wint-O-Green.

My father said that maybe we wouldn't go swimming after all, maybe we'd just walk along the Strand. He asked whether I wanted to see the apartment building where he and my mother honeymooned when they got married. It was called the Ocean Arms. It was right across the street; we didn't even have to leave the car. He pointed out the very room where he and my mother had stayed.

"She took the afternoon off," he said. "And I wasn't working." He was speaking of their wedding day.

They had liked the Ocean Arms for its Spanish arch over the entrance, for a living-room tapestry of dancing gypsies deep in the woods, held up by iron rings at the top, and for a wrought-iron grille over the front window, which was leaded, with sections of colored glass. (I'd heard about all this before, from my mother, from my grandmother.)

"We lived here two whole months," my father said, as though it were a lifetime and all anyone could expect of paradise. Then he reached to the heart of his nostalgia: "I had a straw hat that was really quite the thing."

My mother always spoke of him as "a dresser," as though looking for something to explain it all, to make some sense of it. Four kids.

I liked the past and didn't mind this information, but I was not as interested as I was at home in our dining room, when my mother opened her hope chest (the heavy relic of her life with my father and the one off-limits in the house which I respected) and a world before my own emerged in the form of folded scarves and strange lapel pins, beads and thick letters and flaking snapshots, and posed, tinted portrait pictures of remote and unrecollected people, people in their youth looking older than they would today, serious, formal, preliminary people, fixed in receding time and smelling of cedar. In my view the circle had closed, and my father was not entitled to his side of our history anymore; he was dealing in stolen goods when he presumed to speak of our past.

"But the sound of the sea made her nervous," he said. "She wanted things set—I understand that. I wanted things special. She'd get embarrassed by things, little things. For instance, everyone came down on Sundays because we had the beach. But only tenants could use the showers, which made your mother feel ashamed."

The building was now painted turquoise. A cardboard sign in the ground-floor front-room window read ROOMS. The wrought-iron grillwork remained, but the leaded patterns and the colored glass were gone.

"You thirsty? Want a Coca-Cola or something?"

A block from the Ocean Arms was a flat-faced market, and before it a dented red refrigerator box with cold drinks. My father opened a Hires for me on the rusty lip of the cap receptacle and went into the market counting his change; he came out with a bottle of Lucky Lager.

He tucked his sergeant's cap under his belt and put his foot up on a crate half filled with empties. He leaned his elbow on his elevated knee.

"Your mother should have come down with us today," he said. He held his beer before him thoughtfully, as though his right to it were without question, as if broken promises were inevitable.

"She doesn't like the beach," I said, feeling at once that my tone might sound too in-the-know and challenging. My mother was beautiful; she was easygoing, and could, in my experience, be persuaded in almost any direction. But she had positions, out of nowhere and seemingly on small points, and she held to them stubbornly. For example, she hated the beach. It was sandy, too far to go, too much trouble. She burned.

My father took a long swallow of beer. "I guess not," he said. "She never did."

He looked up and down the Strand. He nodded then, as though he felt some gesture were required, some conclusion. "Funny," he said. "It doesn't seem to have changed all that much."

I looked up and down the street as well, in case my opinion of the neighborhood was pertinent.

"You get good grades in school?" my father asked.

"Pretty good," I said, embarrassed for him, his remark so parental, obligatory.

"Just pretty good?"

"I guess."

My father cleared his throat, looking for the right voice, as if he hadn't intended to get businesslike but the issue was too important to ignore. "Well, work on your grades and keep them up there," he said.

In another swallow he had almost finished his beer. "What do you play? Do you play—what? Basketball?"

"They play kickball at my school," I said, feeling immediately some deep prevarication in my soul, an effort to cover up, slide by the abyss.

"You play, don't you?"

We were addressing the mystery of the ball, and I was at a terrible, threatening loss. I shook my head.

"How's that?" my father asked, baffled but concerned, squinting at me.

"I'm not very good," I said, recognizing in this admission a glaring want of character.

"Well, that's the way you get good," my father said. "By playing." He seemed relieved to have found what to say to me. "Ball."

"I don't like it," I said. I was down to the foam of my root beer.

"You should play, Conrad," my father said.

"I put out the yellow flags," I said.

"The what?"

"They tell when recess is just about over," I said. "Lunch period. And your time is running out."

My father said nothing. He might have been wondering what to say next, he might have been through with the conversation, but I felt the interrogation continuing, more pressing for his silence.

"At a quarter to one someone has to put out the yellow flags," I said. "That tells everyone if they have to go to the bathroom or clean up their area, they have fifteen minutes left."

"You do that instead of play?" my father said.

I said nothing. I might plead the importance of my charge, but I had my mother's integrity and would claim no distinction that another failed to grant me freely.

"I was a quarterback when I went to school," my father said. "That's how your mother met me."

"I've seen the picture of you," I said, envisioning the cedar-smelling staged photo of a high school celebrity that my mother had shown me from the chest in the dining room—shown me too often, too pointedly, I thought, trying to do my father justice and make sure I got the image of him that she herself had fallen for. This she did as faithfully as she sent me to Sunday school and to violin lessons, and in the same spirit—for my greater good, else she be charged with bias or neglect.

"She ever talk about me?" my father asked, and I knew that the subject had traveled beyond me, a duty stop, to the destination it was headed for all along.

I was relieved, of course, that my rank on the playground was no longer being investigated and that I'd slipped past the theosophy of ball without being further disgraced. But I felt awkward, as you do when you have mistaken someone's waving at you across a distance—when you've quickened, perhaps even brightened a little, and lifted your hand to respond—only to see that happy look spear past you to someone behind your back. You feel the fool then, and cheated, as you witness the reunion made in heaven you almost interrupted.

"She said she doesn't want me to dislike you or anything," I said. "Or hold anything against you."

He had bought a quart of whiskey, which he left in the paper bag, the bag held tightly around the neck of the bottle, and he drank as we walked along the Strand, his bathing suit wrapped up under his arm. I carried our towels, my grandmother's reminder at the last minute. I wore my bathing suit under my pants.

Then he said he was tired of walking.

We crossed the sand and sat down by the water.

He saw that the cuffs of his Army pants were filled with sand and he cursed, lightly, to himself, as though I weren't there. He opened his belt, because the buckle cut into his stomach now, doubled up as we were. He threw his cap aside. He warned me that he might fall asleep, and then he lay back and fell asleep.

A gathering of gulls had settled into the sand upwind, and occasional feathers blew against my father and stuck to his khaki, as though he had been punctured and his stuffing were coming out. Sometimes I reached to pull them off, these soft, curly innards, and sometimes I didn't.

Every few minutes the surf cracked at my back with the sound of a whip, and when I looked around, I could see a whooping spray thrash backward, like a mane over the breakers. After a while I took the bottle of whiskey by its brown neck; the bag lifted with it. It was heavy enough to be not empty yet, and smelled of khaki and cigarette smoke and moustache and neck. It was, as I knew it would be, warm when I drank, like something that should not be consumed. I put the bottle back where I found it, having tasted my father and my own stale origins.

· · ·

My father ran into the water, his legs stabbing a fountain of clear fire up over his body. He had awakened with the desire to swim after all, and now he vanished beneath the surf.

I went in only as far as the water wrapped my waist.

The sun had fallen to the horizon, and the surface of the water was blinding. The tide had gone out while my father slept, and the breakers were louder than ever and sudden and shallow, if not fierce. The wind had stopped, though, and the cool evening air on our shoulders made the water seem warm enough.

He came back toward me. "What's the matter?" he said. "Can't you swim?"

"I can but I don't want to," I said. I stood with one hand held up to my eyes to protect them from the glare of the sun. I could see my father only when a wave broke the reflection and cast a shadow, and then I had to stagger back as the wave hit me. I thought I might return to our towels, but a pair of dark surf fishermen had appeared on the beach, and for some reason I was reluctant to pass them.

My father, riding a wave, surfaced beside me. He lifted me up and carried me farther out, without asking, marching through the crackling edges of incoming water.

"I don't like it," I said tightly.

He held me up as a wave pulled under us; we continued out.

"Please."

"Come on."

"I don't want to."

"Just jump when they—just hold your breath and squat down."

"I—"

"Don't be a baby."

His body was slippery, and I could not hold on. I felt also some other prohibition against my clinging, some manners or taboo.

"Hold your nose!" I heard his wet laughter against my ear. "I said open your eyes for crying out loud!" His whiskey breath was like a muzzle clamped over my nostrils.

"I can't!"

"I got hold of you!"

"No!"

"This one we'll jump, and see—"

We did.

"—how easy it is?"

I felt the buoyant lift, the possibility of pleasure, trust.

"See?"

"I want to go back."

"What fun it is."

"Yeah, but."

"You'll get used to it."

My teeth were so tightly locked together that I took in no water when the wave hit and I was pushed down and torn from my father's hands. I bounced against the bottom and hit the top again almost immediately, surprised at my survival and a bit exhilarated, to find the surf suddenly still, covered with a hissing froth that moved in every direction at once. I felt myself riding it, a spinning marble racing away from the disinterested figures on the shore, the surf fishers.

But my father was gone and I had no foothold.

My neck tightened to keep my head above water, and twisted as another sudden locomotion struck me from behind, smashing me like a giant paw. I sprawled into the depths again, feet over head in a black cartwheel; my head struck sand. I fell over on my arm, on my back, and again over and upside down.

I came to the surface crying, put my feet down, and stood. I fell and crawled and staggered up the sand yelling *no* to my father, who was pursuing me, calling my name and swearing.

He stood over me, his hand on my shoulder. He was breathing loudly. I was shuddering. I felt him quivering in the cold.

"Rip, huh?" one of the surf fishers said. "I seen you out there."

The other one said, "This time of year."

We walked, dressed now, but damp and sandy underneath our clothes, through the evening light along the surf's edge, a golden dust rising from the breakers. The sun, which was out of sight, sank in the sand at our feet, the last of the moist dye of

day. My father's strides were long and enthusiastic, and promised *You're going to like this place.*

"If it's still there, that is," he said. "I don't know if it's still
even there."

He was thinking about my mother again.

"Even after we had moved away, we'd come back down for
our dinners sometimes," he said. "To have the best steak and
seafood dinners I ever ate. Do you like steak?"

"No."

"You don't like steak?"

I didn't answer.

The bar was through an arch to the right of the door from the
beach. I could see a dining room in the back, with a stage at the
far end, where tables and chairs were stored under fake palm
fronds, beyond a bare, dusty dance floor reflecting the light of a
jukebox living there in the dark, a glowing troll. The place was
called The Palms and was on the Strand where the pier began; it
had an L-shaped counter under a low roof around a large grill.

We took the one booth in the bar section, and when we sat
down, I could see, out the windows over my father's head, the
purple sky where the sun had gone. The table wiggled when I
put my elbows on it.

"It's the wrong time of year," my father said.

He sighed, a blunt, naked statement of his disappointment.
"Or early, maybe." Other than a man in the dining room, we
were the only customers. "Me and your mother used to come
here all the time."

Beyond the counter, by the grill, I could see a black man
wearing a tall chef's hat, as if it were New Year's Eve or Halloween. He hit a flat bell with the palm of his hand as we sat down,
as though summoning someone from the dining room, where
Hawaiian music was playing.

My father said, "How are the steaks tonight, Cooky?"

The cook said, "Yes, sir, the steaks are real good." He rang the
bell again, smiling vaguely at nothing.

"You wouldn't kid me, would you, Cooky?"

"The waitress will be right with you, sir, yes, sir."

My father reached to the counter for a menu, a typed page under clear plastic, ringed in black leatherette. "Do you like a New York steak?" he asked. "Or a Spenser steak, or a filet mignon, which is four dollars."

Then, "What's this here steak, Cooky, this here house steak, is that any good?"

The cook said, "Yes, sir, that's a real good steak." He rang the bell for the waitress again.

"Why don't we have two of them house steaks then," my father said, folding up the menu.

Then, "How do you like your steak? Rare? Medium?"

The cook hit the bell again, sharply. He had been listening to the radio when we came in, and now he turned it down.

"Medium rare or what?"

I looked around to the bar for the waitress. For some reason my father didn't seem to understand that we needed the waitress before our order was official.

"Or well done? Do you like your steak well done?"

"I guess so," I said.

"Or medium rare? That's the way I like mine."

"I guess," I said.

"Medium rare," my father said to the cook. "And we'll have two shrimp salads—I mean cocktails."

The waitress came in from the dining room. She was flipping pages in her pad as she approached us. "Salad with my prime rib," she said over her shoulder to the cook. My father repeated his order to her, adding french fries. "And I'll have a beer."

He said to me, "Do you like milk, or what do you have with your dinner at home—Hires root beer, or what?"

"Coca-Cola."

"Ginger ale," the waitress said, looking up as two men came in from the Strand.

"They only have ginger ale here," my father said.

"Ginger ale," I said, recognizing the new arrivals as the surf fishers we had seen earlier.

"He'll have milk," my father said to the waitress, who gave the cook a page from her pad and proceeded toward the surf fishers settling in at the counter, putting their tool kits on the floor by their feet, their poles against the wall. They ordered beers.

One of the surf fishers put a large red thermos onto the counter when the waitress had gone. "You want to fill this with more of that chowder there, Henry?" he said, moving the thermos to within reach of the cook. "Before we go."

My father was quiet, even when the waitress came back with everyone's beer. Then, suddenly, loudly, he said to the huddled backs of the fishermen, "Anytime I go out the only thing biting is the goddamn groupers."

The fishermen looked over from the counter. One nodded, the other shook his head. One was drinking his beer from the bottle, the other slowly pouring his into a tipped glass to regulate the foam. They were both hunched over, leaning as though into a fire; they were pulled from that warmth by the necessity of responding to my father, and I could see that they were eager to return to their comfort.

"And I'm not just only some Sunday fisherman either," my father said, as the waitress set two silver urns down before us. "I know fishing." The urns contained chipped ice and clear glass dishes of red sauce, chunks of pale flesh protruding, looking like carnage, something from first-aid class, civil defense.

My father was quiet for some time; then he turned back to me and our meal. He picked up the baby fork sticking out of the ice as though he were already angry at something. He wagged the fork at the backs of the men at the counter, at the cook prodding our steaks on the grill beyond.

"This last time," he said. "This last time—?"

The men looked around, but only briefly.

"This goddamn manta ray, this goddamn manta ray—?" My father's mouth was full. "Comes along and takes my line and snaps it right off."

"You got that chowder, Henry?" one of the surf fishers said, getting to his feet.

Once more my father turned back to me, finishing his shrimp cocktail. "Why aren't you eating?"

"I'm eating."

"I don't see you eating . . ."

I said nothing. I could hear the cook's radio program.

The other surf fisher got to his feet also as the waitress brought them their full thermos and their check. They finished their beers on their feet.

"Hey," my father said to the waitress, extending his empty beer bottle to her. "Buy those two men over there a drink, will ya?"

The surf fishers gave my father a sidelong look. One picked up his tool kit; the other went for their poles.

My father was getting to his feet, reaching for his wallet. "What are you drinking there, boys? Tell this lady here what you're drinking."

"Never mind, thanks," one of the surf fishers said.

"No, come on, I want to buy you one."

"We'll catch you another time, soldier," the other one said.

"If you reach low enough, eh?" my father said, sinking back to the booth again, laughing.

The cook hit the bell on his counter with his heavy fork. I could see that our steaks were ready.

The waitress brought my father another beer.

I watched our plates steaming on the counter.

The waitress lit a cigarette and leaned against a pillar in the back. She did not see our plates. She was taking a rest.

The surf fishers headed for the bar with their check.

"Are those your friends?" I said when they had gone.

It was cold walking down the Strand from The Palms, back to the car, under the streetlamps painted black for the dimout, and to keep warm I took my arms out of my sleeves and folded them across my chest under my sweater. "You're going to stretch your sweater that way," my father said, annoyed at my posture. Or at something, someone—the surf fishers, maybe.

He drove slowly then, very carefully, and said nothing more until we were back in my neighborhood, on my street and parked before our house.

"I don't think I'll come in, though," he said. "Your mother's probably home by this time and—" The burglar alarm in the poultry shop at the corner rang briefly as the place was being shut up for the night.

"Well, it's her home," he said. "She's probably relaxing and everything. After a hard day's work and everything. Not looking forward to company or anything—some other time." As though I had asked him to come in and kept insisting. "You tell her I'll write her, though, soon as I know where I'm at and can make the allotment a little bit bigger."

He was quiet for a minute. "Which I think I ought to be able to do."

Then, "Do you need anything or anything?"

I said no.

"You're probably cold, so I don't want to keep you," he said.

"I'm not so cold," I said. "Now."

I returned my arms to my sweater sleeves, the damp of the beach gone. The light from the streetlamp, not painted over this far inland, filtering through the trees, made a pattern on the car, shadows shuddering in a slight breeze. "Where do you guess you'll go in the war?" I said.

"Well, they don't tell you that." I saw the hand of a drowning sailor sinking in the water, his stricken ship in the background. Somebody Talked! I felt un-American for having asked.

"You take care of your mother, though," my father said.

"I will," I said. But I was chilled at the possibilities inherent in this request, the prospect of such responsibility.

"Can you think of anything you need?" he said.

"A new notebook for school," I said. "That's twenty-nine cents. The good ones." I was grateful to have thought of something.

"Well, here's—fifty cents is all I got right now, I got to get gas."

He opened the glove compartment and studied his fuel gauge in the light it shed, though with the motor off this was pointless, wasn't it? "I really meant for you to keep that five dollars," he said. I had returned it to him, his deposit, when the bill for dinner had come and he was short. "But I don't want to take it back empty." He shut the glove compartment. "That wouldn't be nice." I wondered who she was, where, waiting impatiently, worried, the owner of the car.

We were quiet, my lap heavy with the damp towel wrapped around my bathing suit.

"I sure wish you could think of something I could do for you," my father said. "Besides a school notebook."

Then, "I mean, if there was any problem or anything that you were having."

"I can't think of any problems," I said.

"Well, I'm glad you haven't got any problems." In laughter he reached for my knee. I didn't move, but recoiled just the same. He withdrew his hand.

"Oh, hell, I know I'm going to be all right," he said. "I'm not the least bit concerned about that part of it."

Then, "What I mean is, I know I haven't shown you much in the way of being a father, Conrad." The amateur living of my parents, I thought. I thought of bad actors in the movies. "I mean, if today was the only chance I had and the last chance, well, I wouldn't want you to remember me—well, I'm just thankful, that's all, that I know you're in good hands. I'm grateful for that. And, I mean, I just hope you had a good time today, that's all."

"I had a real good time," I said.

"Well, good," he said. "That's what I wanted to hear."

"But I guess I better go in."

"Because if you ever felt like writing any letters to me sometime—" he said. "I sure would like that."

I was looking down the street, across the dancing light on the car hood. I could see my father in snapshots again, yellowed snapshots, dog-eared and chipped, in woolen trunks and a belt, leaning against the wall of the Ocean Arms with one of his friends from cards and high school, his moustache tilting with his grin. I could see what my mother saw in him, but I could smell the cedar of her hope chest, too, and I knew it was all in the past.

"And tell me about your grades in school and everything, and all your friends."

"I will," I said.

"You know, Conrad, what I wish you would do?"

"What?"

"I would take more interest in ball if I were you."

"In ball?"

"Sports."

I was silent.

"I'd let someone else take out the yellow flags."

"I can't," I said.

"Yes, you can," he said. "If you make up your mind."

"There's no one else to take them out."

"There is. That's foolishness, Conrad."

"The person who gets a hundred percent in fractions every day for a week takes out the yellow flags," I said. Then I said, "You get to leave class early and come back late."

"That's fine, but—"

"So you got to have mastery in fractions."

"Mastery?"

"—so only the highest kids."

He made no further attempt to touch me, and I got out of the car without touching him, though I felt some awkward debt in that regard.

I looked back once before I opened the door of our white-pillared house. He was still sitting there in the borrowed car, a black silhouette, a lawn between us. I could not be sure if he was looking at me. I was in shadow too. He didn't wave, I didn't.

I went into the house and closed the door.

Cornelia Nixon

RISK

Margy and Webster needed a vacation, after the year they'd had. After the year they'd had, they couldn't afford one, but that didn't worry them. Nothing further, they decided, was going to worry them. Their house was in Hyde Park, in the middle of the Chicago Southside, and once when they were only out to brunch burglars had drilled through the door, ripped the alarm out of the wall. But this time they didn't find anyone to stay in it while they were gone. They packed the credit cards, turned out the lights, and didn't even bother to close the blinds.

They got onto an aging DC-10 and flew to San Francisco, where an earthquake, possibly major, was predicted to happen within five days. In those five days they slept in a room on the nineteenth floor, drank in revolving bars atop tall buildings floating on landfill, and idled in traffic on the lower decks of freeways and on bridges over the bay. In a new rental car, with no replacement insurance, they took a drive along the San Andreas Fault and parked near a fissure that swallowed a cow in 1906. They hiked the crumbling coastal mountains, on paths made famous by the Trailside Killer, and loitered on the edge of a sandstone cliff that once slid 16 feet in 45 seconds, watching seals cavort in the ocean below.

They ate sushi without inspecting it, though a man in Webster's lab was studying the worm that lives in raw fish and digs

into the human stomach, from which it must be surgically removed. They drove to a deserted headlands parking lot at midnight, left their wallets in the car under a sign saying not to do
that, slid down a narrow path through poison oak and rattle-
snakes by moonlight to a secluded beach, and swam in the icy
waters where a Great White Shark ate a swimmer in 1964. They
drove to Yosemite and carried backpacks up 10,000 feet, though
altitude made Webster sick, could leave him retching on the
trail, unable to walk, and they timed the trip to see the full
moon in eclipse, though Margy was having her period, and
bears in other parks had killed menstruating women. They slept
on the ground in a tent and did not hang their food in a tree.
The moon rose, shimmering white, and tinted bloodstain red.

"We seem to be taking our chances here," they noticed, everywhere they went. They didn't mind, so long as they were holding hands. The winter before, Margy had left him for another
man, and Webster had retaliated with a series of girls, all a great
deal younger than Margy. Several times a day they called each
other up, shouting words they'd hardly ever used before, like
"slut," "fuck you" and "kill myself," howled back and forth
through phone lines, New York to Chicago, Chicago to New
York. One month their phone bills came to six hundred dollars.

But now they were back together, and happier than they'd
ever been. Breaking up had cleared the air, and they could fall
in love again. Nothing else was going to worry them. Was that a
mossy rock on the brink of a high waterfall? A hidden beach,
soon to be cut off by the advancing tide?

"Now there's an inviting spot," they'd say. "Let's just go over
there and check that out."

And they'd clutch hands, and kiss each other, and look for
some new way to risk their lives.

On their last day in California, having exhausted the possibilities for disaster, they called old friends who had lately moved to
Berkeley. David was Webster's friend from graduate school, and
until a few months before he and his wife had lived in Hyde
Park, close enough for Webster to stumble through the streets
and throw himself tragically on their carpet. Margy and Webster

were still apart when David and Isa left, and they had not seen them since getting back together. Webster had sent a postcard, saying they were coming west, but he'd put off calling until now.

"We've rebuilt our marriage from the ground up," he said on the phone, trying to sound relaxed. He remembered other calls he'd made to them, like the night he took the hedge clippers to Margy's wardrobe. She'd called to say she wasn't coming home, the symphony tour was over but she was staying in New York, with a man she'd met. When he had it all in pieces, the Belle France dress he'd hacked up first, weeping and tearing the silky fabric with his teeth, he put his head in the oven, took it out, and called David and Isa.

"The main thing is," he told them now, "The main thing is, we're all right. I mean, we're better than all right. Things are better than they've ever been. Of course there might have been a better way to do it, something less confusing for our friends. But that was the way we did it, and therefore, in the Zen sense or something, the way it had to be done."

David and Isa sounded wary, but they agreed to meet them for a peripatetic dinner, progressing course by course through Berkeley restaurants. Margy felt a little wary too, crossing the Bay Bridge. How much did David and Isa know, about the year they'd had? How much had Webster told them?

He would've emphasized the part that hurt, how she'd left him, and not the reasons why. She'd met a man who wanted children, which Webster did not—but to Webster that was no excuse for leaving him. In fact, there could be no excuse for leaving him. It didn't matter that he'd once agreed to have children (in the early, besotted phase of their love) and changed his mind after the wedding, or that he kept track of every cent she spent—once he forbade her to go to a free car wash, because even for free it pampered the car. It didn't matter that he refused to buy products packaged in plastic or let Margy kill a bug. He studied animals too small to see, charting their destruction in lakes and oceans, and because of that she had to find shampoo and lotion and meat in paper or glass, while in their house the kitchen counters were patrolled by ants, and spiders fattened overhead, sending offspring through the air on tiny fil-aments. Once he kept a housefly as a pet, closing it in the guest room, where it lived in safety for several weeks, since it was winter and the spiders were asleep. Flies are losing ground, he said. The human race is already redundant. Once he said he'd leave her if she got pregnant.

"Sweetheart," she said, glancing back and forth expertly from him to the road. She did most of the driving, since she was better at it, and cared more. Webster didn't care what lane they were in, or how to get where they were going. He had no sense of direction, and his eyes were bad at night, when the thickness of his contacts warped oncoming lights. Fingers lightly but alertly on the wheel, as if it were her violin, she glanced at him. "Sweetheart, how much do David and Isa know?"

Webster was looking down, examining his tie, which Margy had just bought for him—it was sage-green silk with a 1920's print, and a little on the lavish side. Only lately had he started wearing ties. The winter before, after Margy broke his heart, he'd made a remarkable discovery, that women noticed him more often when he had one on. All he had to do was walk down the street in a tie, and every young woman he passed would give him a searching look. Here was a man of substance, a tie must say to them, like the courtship displays of certain birds, puffing up the orange air sacs in their necks, doing back-flips over branches, turning feathers inside out. Here was a man who could build a fine nest. Had other men noticed that ties had that effect? He should bring it up to David if he got the chance.

"How much do they know?" he said, absently smoothing his tie.

"You know," she said and tried to catch his eye.

He blinked to resettle his contacts, get them into position so he could focus on her. She was a minnow of a woman, no taller than his chest, and tonight she had her hair in springy ringlets, a way he liked—it made her look about eight, playacting in a grownup dress. She could pretend to be a full-size human, but he knew the truth. He folded her clothes out of the dryer, tiny shirts and socks, and underpants the size of his hand. Lying on her back in bed, she didn't make a bump in the comforter.

He batted some ringlets around. "I know what, Mouse?"

She ducked. "Hey." She'd spent an hour in rollers with the dryer, getting the frizz out of her hair. "You know. About this year. I suppose they heard all about my glorious behavior?"

"Oh, well."

Grimly he looked out the window. Of course he'd talked to David, after what she did. "You are the victim of a terrorist attack," David had said, and he was right. Margy believed she could have what she wanted, no matter how impossible or who got hurt, and that she'd always have a second chance. She arrived at airports when her plane was due to leave and ran gaily through the terminal, waving her ticket over her head. She planted peonies in October and felt betrayed when they were under snow. Her credit cards were a disaster. Living with Margy, he had learned to make certain allowances. He could get off a plane and wait for her to meet him, an hour late. He could try to understand, when she left him for another man. He could let her drive. That was the secret of marriage, he'd come to realize: you had to stop yourself from clutching the wheel when your wife turned her back to the traffic trying to look you in the eye.

"Don't worry," he said and focused on the road ahead, hoping she would do the same. He patted her thigh. "When they see how happy we are, they'll forget the whole thing."

David and Isa met them at Christopher's, where they started with rock shrimp, hearts of palm and several bottles of Pinot Blanc—though Isa, who was usually fond of wine, drank mineral water. She was also wearing a sari, which was odd. She'd been in the States since high school, and usually she wore loafers and pleated skirts, or jeans and hospital scrubs. She didn't explain when Margy admired it.

"Feel," Isa said, holding out the piece that looped over her shoulder. It was apricot silk, bordered in cream, and it glowed against her olive skin. "Isn't it delicious?"

They talked about David's new lab, and the progress of Webster's book (*Lake Death: Canary in the Mine*). Isa described the grueling regime of her fellowship in cardiology, widening her big black eyes. Margy listened, smiling and nodding. After the first few awkward moments, seeing David and Isa again, everything seemed to be fine. She didn't mind it that they seldom spoke directly to her. She was used to Webster's friends. They were scientists, who dealt in facts, and she hardly knew any facts. She found it restful to be with them. She didn't have to air her opinion of a certain performance of the *B-minor Mass*, or tell witty stories on the Kronos Quartet. She didn't even have to listen, all the time. And sooner or later someone would ask about her wrists. Decades of daily violin had toughened the fingertips of her left hand, made a sore spot under her chin and inflamed the tendons in her wrists, and these were facts to interest Webster's friends.

She surfaced for a moment. David was telling Webster about a new machine for the analysis of protein chains. Isa pinched the sleeve of Margy's new Italian sweater. "What's this? Pretty!" she said in mime. Everything was definitely fine.

They moved on to the Fourth Street Grill, for mesquite-seared salmon and shoestrings and white Zinfandel. Isa still drank mineral water. Finally Webster leaned forward smiling.

"So, Isa. California appears to have gotten to you. Or is it cardiology?" He held up his glass. "Do you know something about this stuff that we don't know?"

Isa smiled, appeared to blush, and told a story about a bypass patient who'd demanded wine with his hospital food, on grounds that any meal could be his last. "He'll probably live to be a hundred. I don't think there's very much wrong with wine." She straightened the fork in the middle of her plate. "Except at certain times." She lifted her big eyes at David.

David nodded. He faced Webster and Margy.

"We have something to tell you," he said. "Which is maybe a little surprising. We're with child."

On the wall above him, safety-orange chipotle peppers and puce eggplants danced in space.

Margy was surging across the table. "You are? But that's *wonderful*. That's really *wonderful*."

The blood withdrew from Webster's skin, down his spine and into the chair. He couldn't look at Margy. She seemed to be shining, with a moist radiance, like a lightning bug. The happiest moment of her life, she'd told him once, would be on the delivery table, when they held up her child.

David smiled apologetically. "It took us years to decide to do it. In fact, the first time we thought she was pregnant, we almost jumped out the window. But now that it's for real, it's strange. We're completely glad."

"But we had no idea," Margy cried. "Is that why you're wearing a sari? For maternity clothes?"

Grinning, Isa tugged the sari a little this way, a little that. "I think that may be what they're for, you know. Infinite adjustability, no matter how big you get. You don't create a country of a billion people with a taste for tight clothes on women."

Briskly, cheerful as Mozart, Margy asked questions. She wanted Isa to know that it was fine to talk about it, that she personally would not be depressed or upset that Isa was having a baby while she, Margy, was not. How did she feel, when was she due, what were her plans?

Webster looked mournfully at David. They'd never talked much, not about their lives. But they could take long runs on Sunday mornings, and sit together sweating on the porch when they got back, eating M&M's by the two-pound bag. And David knew what to say at important times. When Webster'd first met Margy, he kept showing up at David's too tired to run, and he apologized for letting him down. "What do you think we're working out for, man?" David had said and smiled.

Webster tried to move his lips. Did David and Isa lie in bed in the mornings, reading and making love? Did they realize they'd never do that again?

"Do you realize," he said, "that the highest quality of life the human race will ever achieve is right now, in our lifetime? In places like this, where you can still breathe the air, and this class, which can still afford to buy a house? After us, it will be all decline."

David's eyes went slightly crossed. "Geez, is that true? That's a hell of a thing. So why can't you get a decent yo-yo now?"

Isa leaned forward with merry eyes, touched Webster's arm. Isa was from New Delhi, and she'd once said she thought America could use a little more population. "What about you two? eh? Shall we expect an announcement?"

Webster smiled, a fissure in rock. Margy's face went hot. So Webster hadn't told them, as she thought. She shot him a look—did he like the way this felt? Did he realize it was his own fault?

Isa touched her arm, wheedling. "I know that coy look. Hmmmm? You're already trying, aren't you? Temperature in the morning, dots on a chart?"

Beside her, Webster shuddered, like a glass about to shatter from a high-pitched sound. Margy lifted her chin. "We've decided not to."

Isa's hands drifted down to the table. "You've what? But that's impossible. How could you decide a thing like that?"

Her eyes protruded at Margy, bright examining lights coming on inside.

Margy uncrossed her arms from in front of her chest and made her hands relax at her sides—you never knew what Isa was noticing. She'd noticed some odd things herself. Since going back to Webster, she'd noticed that she did not like to sit or walk or even lie in bed without an arm crossed over her chest, gripping the elbow on the other side. When she tried to do without it, the front of her body felt amorphous, as if it were ballooning out, swelling and swirling like a soggy cloud, and only a steady arm could keep it in.

Isa waved her hand. "You'll change your mind. What are you worried about, your career?"

Margy smiled rather distantly—she couldn't have explained it to Isa. It wasn't her career. She had a low chair in one of the world's best orchestras, and if she never got any farther, that would be fine. It wasn't even exactly Webster anymore. Lately Webster'd said he didn't want to do it, no, and it would ruin what they had together now, which was awfully good, and since the earth was already buried in plastic diapers it would be selfish to produce another child, but she could do it if she really

wanted, and now she wasn't sure she really did. Leaving Webster she had learned an awful fact, that he was the one she
wanted, and now she needed to lie with her head on his chest,
while he soothed her like a baby. If they had a baby, Webster
would hold the real baby like that instead, and when she
wanted to put her head there he might say, "Pardon me, but
you see I've got this real baby here. And would you mind cleaning the bathroom?"

Webster felt for Margy's hand, and it was hot and dry, as if
she had a fever. He gave her a glance that meant she didn't
have to answer, but she didn't look at him. She tossed back her
hair.

"Webster doesn't want to," she said. "And the choice doesn't
mean much, does it, if the answer always has to be yes?"

Isa pressed her lips together, black eyes bulging wide. David
tipped his head back, gazing at Webster as if he were a little too
far off to see. He was not, Webster noticed, wearing a tie.

They drove up the hill toward Walnut Square, planning to end
with coffee-chocolate mousse and Meyer-lemon tart at the Chez
Panisse Café. The evening had grown chill, as cold white fog
slid in, falling over the last mauve light like a lid. In Walnut
Square, they had to park several blocks from Chez Panisse.
Walking, they continued to talk, sometimes a little self-con-
sciously, a little artificially, as they broke down to single file or
stepped out into the street to avoid a homeless person, while
pretending not to notice they were being asked for money.

"Of course," Margy said, stepping off the curb in her high
heels, avoiding a suntanned man in a dirty quilt. "You won't
even have to have amnio, will you? You're so young." Margy
was thirty-five, and Isa at most was thirty-one.

"Spare change?" said the man.

Isa strode along with a relaxed expression, one end of the sari
floating behind her like a wing. "Oh, no—I'm going to have it.
It's always a good idea with geriatric pregnancy."

Webster stepped around the suntanned man, avoiding his
eyes, and David followed him. Ever since Margy'd told them,
David had stayed near him, shoulder almost touching his, not

saying anything but letting Webster know he understood. Webster walked beside him in grateful silence.

"Geriatric?" Margy said. The edge of the sari almost brushed a car, but Margy caught it as she stepped back on the sidewalk. "Who're you trying to kid?"

Isa laughed and looked at her. "I'm old enough to be a grandmother in some parts of the world."

A big black man with red eyes blocked their path. "I'm homeless and I'm hungry and it's my own fault. If you could lay a five on me—no, okay, then God bless."

They parted to stream around him and reformed. A few steps further on, a blond man in a button-down shirt held up a sign, "Disabled Vet." When they didn't stop, he shook it frantically, grimacing and weeping. In a doorway, on a pile of bedding, a gray-haired Chinese couple sat with their backs to the sidewalk, the man exhaling acrid smoke, the woman cradling an ornate platter on her lap. Margy fell back slightly, depressed. She couldn't even give them any money without making a scene—Webster carried the cash when they went out. He liked to know how much they'd spent, and she didn't like to lug a purse. He was yards ahead of her now with David and Isa, and if she wanted even a quarter she'd have to run after him and interrupt.

Isa turned, called gaily back. "Besides, I want to know everything. I want a laparoscope, full time, so I can watch the whole thing. But all I have so far is the sonogram. All I know is that it looks like a salamander."

David hooked his arm around her neck and raised his eyebrows over her head. "Oh, yes, exactly like a salamander. There was this gray blob, see, and this black blob, and the gray blob wiggled a couple of times. Sounds like a salamander to you, doesn't it?"

Isa slugged him on the shoulder with her fist.

Webster waited for Margy, but she didn't seem to see him as she passed. Her face had an expression he'd seen before, a damaged look—I have been denied, it said. Clenching his teeth, he followed behind her. What did he care if she ignored him? Why in hell should he mind?

He should never have let it happen to him, marriage. It was like all those other awful relations, brothers and sisters, parents and children, the way it wired your tender parts to someone else's whim. He had enough electrodes on his balls before he met her, thank you very much. Why would anyone volunteer for any more?

A young man stood on the curb ahead, with a rip in the seat of his pants exposing a buttock to the air, the skin chapped raw and red. The four of them passed him in silence. Margy stopped, touched Webster's arm, let David and Isa get ahead.

He stared at her coldly. "What?"

She held her palm out, whispering. "Give me some money."

He touched his pocket—the wallet was in front, where the pockets were deeper, and he could feel it riding on his thigh. "What for?"

"Just give it to me," she said impatiently.

He'd heard that tone before: you are acting like a child, she used to say in fights. Grown men do not act like you. She'd left him for a man of fifty, grizzled, soft in the middle—but mature.

He started walking toward David and Isa, who had turned to watch. Hooking his elbow like an anchor, Margy tried to slide her hand into his pocket. He caught her wrist, kept his voice down.

"Not now, Margy." Releasing her, he walked ahead.

Margy was aware of many things: that she should let it go, that she'd be sorry if she didn't stop, and that she would stop if she hadn't been drinking wine. But she seemed to be propelled by something large and fierce, reaching through her arms like a puppeteer. Catching up to Webster, she restrained his wrist, and plunged her hand in his front pocket.

He did not resist. Lifting his arms away from his body, he made clear who was causing the trouble. She skipped a few steps up the block, worked the money out of the billfold, and tossed the wallet back. She walked away, head down.

He scooped the wallet off the sidewalk—she'd taken all the cash. The pores of his face felt cold—he'd broken sweat. On his toes like a prairie dog, he watched her go. Last time, he hadn't realized what was happening. He'd stood on the porch and waved, while she smiled through the window of the cab. Six weeks later, she called to say she wasn't coming back.

David's big hand fell on his shoulder, gripped his trapezius. "Hey, pal. Everything all right? What's going on?"

Their rickety metal chairs were on the sidewalk, in front of a cavernous café across the street from Chez Panisse. David and Isa had steered him there, so they could watch for Margy. At the other tables, street people hunched in tattered sweaters, stocking caps and gloves with missing fingers, trying to warm their hands around styrofoam cups.

Isa shivered, rewinding the top layer of her sari. David took off his tweed jacket and held it for her while she slid in her arms. She flattened the lapels over her neck and did not thank him. Sighing, she looked up and down the street.

"I thought you two were through with things like this?"

David gave her a warning look. She smoothed down the jacket's cuffs.

"You'd think it would be enough for her, the way you took her back, after what she did."

"Isa," David said. He picked up his cup, held it in front of his mouth.

"That was more than most men would have done." She gave David a sideways stare. "I'd hate to see what would happen if I tried something like that."

David's elbows barely touched the table top.

She tugged at the sari under the jacket. "I really would. What would happen if I tried something like that?"

David's face settled like slag. "Are you sure you want to talk about that?"

Webster looked away, trying not to listen. On the curb across the street, the man with the hole in his pants stood waiting for a light to change, though he was in the middle of the block. Up the sidewalk behind him, Margy came striding. Swinging her arms, she looked fresh and relaxed and innocent, as if she'd just gone off to milk the cows.

Snapping his fingers, the man whirled. He charged toward

Margy, averting his eyes. His hair was matted like a bird's nest, and a shining stream flowed from his nose, clotting in his beard. Snapping his fingers again, he spun back to his spot on the curb.

Margy passed him slowly. She didn't have much money left. She'd given a five to the red-eyed man who asked for it, and a ten to the disabled vet. She'd tried to give a twenty to the Chinese couple, but the woman waved her hands, shaking her head —Margy left a wad of ones on the bedroll, hoping the man would pick it up. Her last two ones she gave to the suntanned man, and a ten to an old black woman she hadn't seen before. All she had left now was the twenty.

The man on the curb continued to remember errands he'd forgotten in the opposite direction. Margy fingered the sleeve of her sweater. It was rose-gray silk, shot with shimmering threads, and all she had to tie around his waist.

She held out the twenty. He looked at Margy serenely and did not take the bill. Gingerly she reached for his wrist, turned up the palm, curled his fingers over it. He had a musty smell, like a wild animal.

Pointing at his bottom half, she waved her fingers up and down. "That's twenty dollars, for new pants. Don't lose it. Okay?"

He did not look at the money. When she walked away, he was still standing with his hand raised to the level where she let it go.

On her way to Chez Panisse, she spotted Webster and the others across the street. They didn't wave, but she knew they could see her as she crossed. David and Webster sat close together, while Isa slumped, staring down into her cup.

Margy got a chair from one of the other tables. No one spoke for several moments.

"Well," said Isa, putting down her cup. "So, Margy. How're your wrists?"

Webster was driving, and too fast. "Get in," he said, yanking open the passenger door, after David and Isa dropped them at their car. Margy leaned back, trying not to watch the road. The fog had vanished, and ahead the bridge was a necklace of cold white stars against black sky. Across the water, San Francisco shimmered, yellow lights molding over rolling hills, like a lolling female body in gold lamé. Bright streaks dangled away from it, undulating with the waves.

Webster leaned across her, jerked open the glove compartment and threw maps out on the floor. Margy clutched the handle on the door. "What do you want? I'll look, you drive!"

"What do you think I want? The bridge is a buck!"

In the gritty felt of the glove compartment, she found a paper clip and a plastic pen. When she glanced up, they were flying past the turnoff for the bridge.

"Turn here!" she shrieked and grabbed the dash.

Swerving across three lanes, they raced into the toll plaza. "Carpool Free," said a sign on the far right. Webster aimed for it. "Carpool is Three Persons," it also said, but the gate was up. He did not slow down.

"Webster! Stop!"

The attendant put his head out, pulled it back in fast. Whoosh, they were past the booth. A dozen lanes merged down to four, drivers jockeying for spots. Webster claimed a lane and blazed right through them.

Her voice was high and thin. "Are you trying to get us arrested? Have you lost your mind?"

His voice was calm. "Let's not talk about losing one's mind. Let's not talk about throwing away eighty bucks on the street."

"Oh, it was not eighty."

"You don't have a clue about money, do you? You don't even know how much you gave away."

"Of course I do. It was . . . less than we spent on dinner. If you're going to be stingy, why don't we talk about that?"

She glanced at the road. He was about to hit an enormous Cadillac, banked with lights.

"Look out!" she screamed.

Webster weaved around it with a grace he'd never noticed at lower speeds. What a relief it was to be driving. How had she ever cowed him into riding on the passenger side?

"You walk by homeless people every day," he said. "And I've hardly ever seen you give a dime."

"That's because you don't pay much attention to what I do. I do it all the time, when I've got money with me. When I'm *allowed* to have money with me. You're the one who walks right by them."

"So now you're going to get self-righteous. Do you really think you did that to help those people? Or was the point to make a scene in front of David and Isa? There I was, trying to convince them I wasn't crazy for taking you back—"

"Oh, I see. You had to convince them of that. Thanks for telling me."

His eyes were on the road, hands on the wheel. He wasn't angry, only Margy was angry.

"Look, I realize you were in some kind of state tonight, from talking to Isa. Some kind of breeding frenzy. But I don't see why that had to make you—"

Leaping out of her seatbelt, she faced his profile, familiar as the blade of an axe. "What an attractive phrase that is. Why don't you give a course in elegant speech for the home? Call it 'Thug Talk Made Easy.'"

They roared through the tunnel and out onto the second bridge, the lights of the city suddenly fat and bright. Webster kept his foot on the floor.

"Have you ever noticed how often you attack me, in how many different ways? I'm a thug, and childish, and stingy, and I've ruined your life. You seem to want to keep me feeling guilty, all the time."

"Oh, I do not. I never said—"

"Why is that? Is it to distract me, so I won't notice what you're doing? So the next time you call me up and say that you've been—"

"I do not!" She put her hands over her ears, knowing what was coming next. "I do not!"

"Opening your legs for a stranger—"

"You know it's your own fault that happened! You know it's your own fault I left!"

"My fault?" he said in wonder. "My fault?"

His brain felt suddenly clear and bright, starlike. He knew what she meant: "Webster doesn't want to," she could say any time she liked, and walk out with another man. Webster didn't want to, and she did—that was her alibi. A thought shot through him in a blaze of light. Margy knew how to get what she wanted. Why hadn't she made it happen, if she wanted it so much?

He imagined a baby, a very small one, his. Of course he'd love the little salamander. He'd probably love it too much—he wouldn't let it out of his sight. The first time he'd found a real one in the wild, a California slender, tiny and black, he'd picked it up, stunned by its minute fingers and thread-size legs. How could anything so vulnerable stay alive? Leaving his hand, it climbed his arm, parting the hairs, and when it came to the bend of his elbow it paused, lifting its small curved face to gaze at him as if it were looking up into the face of God. How could he let it go, in a world full of shoes, and rakes, and tires?

"The truth is, Margy, aren't you the one who doesn't really want kids? If you did, wouldn't you have made it happen by this time?"

She stared at him as if balanced on the head of a pin. Lifting her arm from the shoulder, she slapped his face, his shoulder, his arm, the side of his head. He caught one hand, but she hit him with the other. Striking his eye, she knocked out a contact lens.

The road ahead was now bright fuzz, sliced by the speeding blackness of her arms. Closing the eye that had lost the lens, he could make out the road ahead, flattened into bleeding planes of light and shade. Reaching an exit, he spiralled down to a wharf and stopped.

She was no longer hitting him. Taking hold of her neck, he bent her back against the seat. Her face was a white blur, staring up an inch away. This was not real, it was a play, he could throw her out the window, drive the car into a post, put his fist through the windshield and grind glass into his wrists, but nothing in the real world would be changed. He jerked her throat to emphasize each word.

"If you ever hit me again, I will kill you. I will kill you."

. . .

Lying on the front seat, he searched his face. Only the tips of his fingers tapped spider steps. He checked his eyebrows, his hair, his neck, his clothes, the plush upholstery of the seat, the steering wheel, the sandy floor. He did not find the contact lens.

One hand over the vacant eye, he faced the way she'd gone, toward the rear of the car. To get the depth, he opened both eyes. On his left a row of round-topped warehouses humped along, running together and reforming like nightmare elephants. On his right an elevated freeway sliced out of the dark, a giant wing aimed for his head.

"Margy?" She couldn't have gone far at this time of night. She didn't have a quarter to make a call. All she had was the Italian sweater on her back. "Margy?"

He walked for several blocks, calling her name. The water was close by, exhaling tide rot and diesel oil. Rotating his face like radar, he kept the smell on his left.

Suddenly he was in the dark, without a streetlight. He flipped around—the light had gotten behind him. She wouldn't be out there in the dark. The street along the wharf was wide, and cannily he crossed it to check the other side.

Ahead was an empty lot, a field with grass. Out in the middle, a figure crouched. He could see her hair, springing out around her head. He ran out into the field.

"Sweetheart?" She wasn't going to make him search till he got lost.

At the last second, she turned into a black plastic sack, stuffed with rags. He touched it with his foot—how could he have thought that was his wife?—and darted back across the field the way he'd come.

He stopped. Brick buildings had sprung up around him. He turned in a circle, holding out his arms. Where was the wharf? What had happened to the water?

The pier lay in a slot between warehouse walls, with a view straight up to the bridge. Out on the end, where the breeze licked frigid water, Margy crouched against a piling, knees to chest, sweater stretched down to her stocking feet. Running onto the pier, one heel had caught in a crack, and she'd kicked the other shoe off. She couldn't see them in the dark. She could see streaks of greasy swells, in flitting greenish light, cigarette butts awash, one styrofoam cup riding up and down on its side.

She pictured his face, yelling an inch away. Touching her throat, she tried to distinguish sore spots the size of fingertips. Once, making love on a summer night, he'd left the prints of all four fingers and his thumb in a blue bruise on her upper arm. She had to wear long sleeves for a week, and he kept taking off her blouse to see the marks. "Tiny delicate creature," he'd murmured, kissing them.

Distant sirens cried, broken by wind. The roar of traffic from the bridge subsided. The dark was now as perfect as the bottom of a burrow, even the green light gone. With the piling at her back, the cocoon of sweater warmed. A wave of sleep passed over her.

How did people learn to sleep in public places? Resting her forehead on her knees, she closed her eyes, but she couldn't sleep like that. She stretched out flat, arms crossed over her chest.

Yards below her, water was rising and falling with a rhythmic sigh. Her hands and feet began to swell, until they felt as big as the claws on industrial cranes, and filled with pleasure. She wanted them to keep on growing. Her fingers bulged the size of Florida. Uncrossing her arms from in front of her chest, she let her belly go. Up it sprang, huge and round, grazed the bottom of the bridge, ballooned into space. She was not a tiny delicate creature now. She was a house, a city, a planet, home to rivers and oceans, forests and mountains, a food-delivery system, a sewer, a bed, all that was needed for sustaining life. If she got up and walked, she could dent the ground.

She imagined Webster where he must be now. In their hotel room, he'd wash his face, slide between clean sheets, stare at the dark. She'd open the door, trudge in, enormous belly first. Crossing to the bed, she'd shake the floor.

"Here it is. How do you like it?"

Webster's eyes would open wide, his face become polite.
"Don't hit me," he'd whisper.

And she would say, "All right."

Out of the darkness thrummed a huge white boat, searching the
blank face of water with its lights. Stark glare deflated Margy,
pinned her to the planks, flat on her back. The pier had corners,
cleats, a coil of thigh-sized rope and a heap of rusty rags, etched
with shadows in the light. It wasn't close, dark, safe, but airy
space, part of the street.

The dark was blinding when the boat had gone. Springing to
her feet, she felt her way along the rail. One shoe stuck quivering by its heel, the other near it on its side. She ran to the
lighted street before she shoved them on. The heels slowed her
run, but a woman alone on a wharf near dawn had better not
walk.

Ahead she could see city streets, past an elevated freeway.
The wharf was empty now of cars, except for one, a new American compact half in the street on the wrong side. Swerving
wide, she ran beyond it, before she realized she'd seen that car
before.

"Kill you," he'd said. "I will kill you." She ran another block,
cast back a glance. The car didn't only look empty. It looked
derelict, left to drift.

Warily she circled back. Doors unlocked, the keys dangled in
the ignition, glinting in the artificial light. In the tray between
the bucket seats lay the square gold key to their hotel, the only
one they had. Turning away, she took a few steps and stopped.
Where exactly had he gone?

She was alone now, in a way she had not been before, when
she could aim what she was doing in his direction. The vacant
breath of the street passed over her. Nothing was moving, but
everything looked like it might the second she turned her head.
She ran back to the car, leaped in, locked all the doors.

She felt watched as she started the engine, and she left the
wharf like a hand off hot metal. Racing to the hotel, she did not
stop for lights. Webster wasn't in their room. He'd left no message.

She called the police, and they filled out a report. Had her husband been feeling despondent? the officer asked. She called David and Isa, woke them up. No, they hadn't heard from him, why should they? Was something wrong?

"Yes, no, I'll let you know. Sorry I woke you."

"Margy?" David was saying as she hung up.

She changed into jeans and sneakers, got back into the car. The dark was beginning to fray as gray light leached in, giving the empty streets an illusion of safety, like a person sitting beside her, doing what she did. Doors locked, windows up, she rolled along the wharf and the streets around it. He was not in an all-night restaurant on Market. He was not sleeping on the sidewalk or in a doorway.

Passing the ferry building for the third time, she noticed a pedestrian tunnel to the landing. Through the tunnel, she could see a body lying on the ground. Parking the car, she checked the street and ran for it.

The tunnel stank of wine and urine. On the other side, a plaza opened over the water, with huge cement planters circled by redwood benches. On the benches, and under them, and mashing down the tall blue lilies in the planters, people were sleeping. The preferred position was on one side, knees drawn slightly up, arms crossed over the chest. Most were prepared for cold, with a jacket or a blanket, a hat or a scarf around the head, but one had only a linen jacket, and a silk tie. Lying on his side, hands between his knees, he'd flipped the sage-green tie up over the side of his head, like a dog with one ear inside out.

She took a step closer. His lids snapped open. A spark lit his eyes and died, as iron came down behind them. Neither of them moved a millimeter.

Finally Margy took a chance. She raised her eyebrows, faintly pulling up the corners of her mouth. Bravely she held onto it.

He glanced away from her, closing one eye—she was mistaken if she thought they were all the way to smiling yet. It might be days or weeks before they got to that, if they ever did. But slowly, inch by inch, his frozen body started rising from the bench.

Rilla Askew

THE KILLING BLANKET

This is an old story.

White man does a good job turning the people against themselves. Here's how he done it one time.

My daddy told me this story.

There was a lot of fighting back then. It was like that all over. Some of the people wanted to cut up the land, make allotments to the different families, do like the whites and act like they owned it. Said it would be good for the people. Said it was no choice anyhow. This was back yonder. 1892, I think it was. Back when the Nation was all in one piece.

So some of the Choctaws wanted allotments, but there were plenty others thought it was a bad thing. Tribal election was coming, and the people were divided. Anger and bitterness cut hard between them. Some said it was on account of outsiders living in the Nation that the people were divided. Three whites for every Choctaw lived here by then. Carried their United States dollars in with them. Married our women. Paid money to build their houses then wanted papers to say they owned it. Paid money to trade here. Snuck around against our laws and sold the people Choctaw beer. These whites wanted allotments, wanted to see the Nation cut into pieces. They wanted to see the people stirred up.

Other Choctaws, a bunch of them mixed bloods, they said the people had to see what was coming, take advantage, get profit from the land before the white man took it anyhow. They said the Choctaw had to adapt.

Now in that time two men lived near this place here called Cedar, and these two men were friends. One of thems name was Silan Lewis, and the other was Moshulatubbee District Sheriff Tecumseh Moore. These men grew up together, played stick ball together at Skullyville. Their folks come over the trail together in the first year of the removals when so many died in the blizzards and floods. They'd known each other a long time. Tecumseh Moore didn't practice any politics but just kept the peace in the District. Silan Lewis was a farmer, a pureblood, married to a white woman, and he was one of the Choctaws who believed allotments was bad.

Silan Lewis and some others made it up that they'd just have to kill a bunch of these Choctaw Progressives who favored allotments, worry the rest of them, stop all this talk about cutting up the homeland. They were going to do these executions at night. Some of them were going to strike in Cedar County, some in Nashoba, Sans Bois, Jack's Fork, Kiamitia. All over the Choctaw Nation. All on the same night. It'd be done and over with then. The people would go back to living and taking care of themselves then. That's what Silan Lewis and these others thought.

So they made it up, and come time on that night, nine men rode west through the long valleys south of the Sans Bois. This was the time of the high corn before harvest, and it was hot.

My daddy told it to me this way.

The land was different then. The earth had not turned over and grown up clawed and scrabby. The rocks were buried deeper. The water wasn't brown then. This is how they say. Them that went with Silan Lewis had to go over by Hartshorne and kill Joe Hokolutubbee and then get on over to McAlester and kill some others, that was their job, so they had to ride fast. It was a long way to Hartshorne in that time. They crossed over the Little Fourche Maline—it wasn't called that then but I don't know now what it was called—and a yellow panther jumped down off a tree limb onto Eli Holbird's back. They were slowed there to cross the water and they passed under some sycamores and this cat fell down silent from fifty feet up that tree maybe, because the trees were all that tall and taller then, and it landed on Eli Holbird's back. Holbird fell off sideways and the cat sprung off quiet into the night, never let out a sound. They all thought Holbird was dead, but he was just stunned and come to afterwhile and they rode on west again.

But they all knew that to be a bad sign. No panther jumps on a man riding with eight other men and horses.

When they got to Joe Hokolutubbee's they found him sleeping on the porch. Silan Lewis went in first. He went in close enough to see the outline of Joe's body on a bed there in the corner. Joe must've heard him. Who is it? he called out in the dark. Joe sat up, said it again. Who is it? Who's there? Silan Lewis never answered. He fired one shot. That signaled the others and everybody went in firing. They shot Joseph Hokolutubbee all to pieces there on the dark porch. He never even got up from the bed.

Then they rode on again.

Rode fast.

Rode west towards McAlester.

They were set to kill three or four others. They believed that all over the Three Districts other Choctaws were carrying out their executions in the night, same way they'd all made it up together. But it didn't happen like that.

Somebody must've told. Time they got to McAlester, the men they were set to execute were all hiding out. They couldn't find nobody to kill. A fella rode in from Tuskahoma and told how all over the Nation the Progressives were either lined up to fight or else hiding out like rabbits.

So they knew there was some serious trouble.

They had a stand-off there at McAlester for a time. Both sides come together and faced off at McAlester, men from both parties camped out west of town. They sat looking at each other, hundreds of armed Choctaws ready to fight and kill one other. They sat that way for four days.

They never did fight. That's one part of this story.

They started in talking. Afterwhile they finally settled that they'd break up and go home to their families, and Silan Lewis and his bunch would go to trial for the death of Deputy Sheriff Joseph Hokolutubbee.

So them that rode with Silan Lewis surrendered.

Silan Lewis was getting his horse shod one cold morning in South McAlester, and Tecumseh Moore come along and nodded his head at him. Silan paid off the blacksmith and saddled up his red mare, mounted her, followed Moore back to Hartshorne where the other riders were under guard. The two were quiet on the way from McAlester to Hartshorne. They neither one said a word. Tecumseh Moore kept his back to Silan Lewis, walked his horse slow in the dirt of the road.

In this way it come about there was a trial, a lot of talk, a lot of words in the newspapers. The United States government come in on it. The papers took sides and stirred up the people. Each side called the other Buzzards and Skunks.

Choctaw court said the men who killed Joe Hokolutubbee had to be shot. Some of the people said that was right. Others said no, they ought to only receive one hundred lashes. But the court said they had to be shot.

The United States government come in on it again.

There was more trials and papers and lawyering.

Come down to only Silan Lewis and one other was set to be executed.

Come down to it finally, Silan Lewis was the only one they said had to be shot.

So Silan Lewis went back home to wait for the day of his execution. He stayed home for one season and a little more, and then after harvest and just before winter and more than two years after the death of Joe Hokolutubbee, Silan Lewis hitched up his team and set out from the house with his wife sitting silent and staring in the wagon beside him.

There were some in the Nation had already forgot the old ways. They tried to talk Silan Lewis into running. Said he ought to keep going in that wagon and head on down into Texas. Said it was no sense anymore in a man traveling headlong to his own death. But Silan Lewis kept to the old ways. The shame was going to kill him if he went down to Texas, so there he'd be dead anyhow but with shame and not honor. It wasn't any kind of choice for a man. Him and his wife drove twenty miles in one day and set up camp near the courthouse alongside the creek.

Now Tecumseh Moore let it be known about that if anybody wanted to rescue Silan Lewis, why, him and his men would give him up without a fight. That would happen sometimes back in those days, a man who was set to get executed might get took off on horseback by his friends just before he got shot. Most of the people thought that would happen with Silan Lewis. Choctaw government thought it would happen and that's how come them to send in the lighthorsemen. They were swarming around all over the place. Tecumseh Moore thought it would happen. He believed it would happen. He didn't want to shoot his old friend.

He waited past the time when the sun reached its high point. That was the time set for the execution. The day was a color like the breast of a mourning dove, grayish-like brown shaded nearly to pink. Tecumseh Moore acted like he couldn't see when the sun reached its high point, but the sun was one light spot trying to burn through the skymist and anybody could see it. He had them read the death sentence two or three times. The lighthorsemen pranced their horses in and out amongst the people. The people talked in low voices, and then their voices started rising like the slow rise of wind.

Tecumseh Moore could see there wasn't any help for it. He said, I'm not going to shoot this man, we've been friends all my life. He appointed Deputy Sheriff Lyman Pusley to do the shooting, and sent for the blanket.

They spread the blanket according to law on the ground at the side of the courthouse. The people gathered in a great circle all around. Silan Lewis took off his jacket and sat on the blanket. He didn't look at his wife. Didn't look at anybody, just stared between the legs of the people at the courthouse wall straight ahead. His wife stood inside the circle of people. She didn't act like anything but looked across to the other side of the circle with eyes like a blind woman. Eli Holbird took Silan's boots off him. He was the only one of the eight men who helped him kill Joe Hokolutubbee to show up for his execution. Least he was the only one anybody saw. Holbird held Silan's boots inside his hands and went over and stood in the circle next to Silan's wife.

One Choctaw man stretched Silan Lewis's legs out in front of him on the blanket. Silan sat up straight. Two others held Silan's arms stretched out on either side of him. Another walked up behind him and bent over his shoulder and opened his shirt. The shirt was white. This man dipped his fingers in a tin of white powder and put his fingers on Silan Lewis's chest and drew a white circle over the place he figured Silan's heart to be. Silan kept his eyes open and steady on the wall of the courthouse. He sat stiff, his shirt and the powdered circle glaring white, answering each other against the brown of his skin.

Tecumseh Moore looked up the road and down the road. His eyes searched the hills cradling the courthouse on all sides. The people were silent like wind that drops and goes still in the last minute before a twister. There was no sound of horses running. No movement on the road or among the oaks and cedars on the hills. Sheriff Moore waited for some sign of rescue. The pale disc of sun slid long past the high point, and there was no sound. Lyman Pusley held his Winchester ready. Sheriff Moore raised his arm finally, and still there was no movement.

Then a high keening cry came, first light and faraway-sounding so that the sheriff didn't know where it came from, and then close by, high-pitched, tortured, with no stops for breath in between. It came from the closed lips and dead eyes of Silan Lewis's white wife.

Tecumseh Moore swooped his arm down.

Lyman Pusley fired his rifle.

Smoke puffed from the mouth of the rifle, and the white circle on Silan Lewis's chest exploded into red. He jerked back and sprawled face up, arms open, on the blanket. Those two Choctaws still had hold of his hands.

But Silan Lewis wasn't dead yet.

His wife's high cry dropped low and snarling in her belly like the growl of a hurt dog. Silan Lewis jerked and twitched on the blanket, and the two men held him down by the arms. The people watched, silent, and one or two of them walked away.

Still Silan Lewis wouldn't die.

Tecumseh Moore looked at him twitching on the blanket, not living and not dying. Silan Lewis made no sound.

After too much time passed Sheriff Moore knew again that there wasn't any help for it. He went over and knelt on the blanket. He put the palm of his left hand over the mouth of his friend, and felt the warm breath pushing against it. Silan's eyes were glazed over, but he turned them from the sky to look up at Tecumseh Moore's eyes.

Sheriff Tecumseh Moore saw it then.

He saw it like a memory he'd nearly forgotten.

How there was no reason for the people to be all turned against themselves and killing each other. How Silan Lewis had no call to shoot Joe Hokolutubbee in his bed on his dark porch. How Lyman Pusley had no call to shoot Silan Lewis. How in the old time in the old Nation, in the homeland where the bones of the ancestors were buried, in *okla falaya* by the Tombigbee waters, in the long ago time the Choctaw knew how to fight and kill enemies. How enemies were always, in the old time, only others and not the Choctaw people themselves.

And how it was when the white man wanted the land of the old Nation that the people first came to be divided. How the white man said to some of them, here, you give us this land and we'll give you this other, and it will belong to the Choctaw as long as the waters run. How the white man had a good trick then to give whiskey to some and money to others, how he'd name some of them chiefs who had no right or honor to be named so, for the one purpose of getting those Choctaws to sign papers of lies giving away the people's land. How it was the people divided that was the first sign of the loss of the old Nation, before so many died on the long trail of tears when the people left the bones of the old ones and came up the great river, removed by the white soldiers to the new land.

Tecumseh Moore felt the warm living breath of Silan Lewis, felt him jerking and shaking.

He closed the fingers of his right hand over the nose of Silan Lewis and squeezed shut the air holes and twisted his palm into Silan Lewis's mouth. Silan's eyes stayed open, looking up at the eyes of my grandfather, and his twitches and spasms grew slower and softer. My grandfather knew then that he knelt on the death blanket with his killing hand on his friend's mouth because the Choctaw had not known how to turn back that good trick of the white man. They hadn't known how to keep him from turning the people against themselves.

So not long after the death of Silan Lewis the United States government passed the law allowing allotments and carved up the Nation. Not too long after that the land was all gone out of the people's hands. Like some of 'em said, it wasn't any choice anyhow.

Well, this story's an old one.

It happened a long time ago.

Back when our words *okla humma* that called us the red people had not yet turned over to mean white man's land.

Antonya Nelson

DIRTY WORDS

FRUIT

It was a nine-month incarceration. It was solitary confinement. It was dry and stupefying, full of sweets and regression—a hormonal trip to childhood, to cheap candy and bad music and copious tears. It was pregnancy, and Bette saw that she might not be reformed by the end of it; she might not turn out to be a good mother.

Already she'd gone slack with gravity, sad and self-indulgent. Her pets, a cat and a dog, sexual neuters themselves, were as fat as she. "Here," she told them again and again, presenting the open refrigerator for their perusal, "help yourselves." There was no kick to be had anywhere but in the kitchen.

She'd called her own mother after six months. "I'm pregnant," she said into the hissing reception. From far away, two time zones and a chasmal continental divide, her mother answered, "Who is this?" Between them was the white noise of futile hope, misunderstanding, and exhaustion. Bette's mother used to claim she hated pregnancy but in the end felt it worthwhile. Now she left off the last part. She gave thirty-year-old conventional wisdom as advice, which Bette, newly fluent in the rules of the game, would eagerly, incoherently defy. She would gain forty pounds instead of twenty, quit her brown-stain habits of coffee and cigarettes, possibly take up jogging. She would not drink. In La Jolla her mother sniffed. "I drank like a fish the whole time, and you and your sister turned out just fine." Bette wasn't sure.

In her family children drank early on, in the civilized tradition of Europeans yet with the exuberance of Americans, glib and intemperate. They drank early on and, when they grew up, later on—after dinner, post-dessert, into the A.M. hours. Where she came from you sampled every flavor of fun and found it good. She took the "Could *You* Be an Addict?" kind of test whenever she came across it, always failing—or was it passing? —within three humorless questions. She'd attended a single A.A. meeting, staying long enough to feel satisfactorily removed from its ranks. They were hiding vodka in Evian bottles, slipping away to bars far from home, counting hours between drunks, and limiting themselves to one a week—in short, they weren't having a good time. Bette's problem was that she merely missed drinking—it was like a hilarious friend who had moved away, like a party that had ended.

She'd told the A.A. circle—a gritty group of écru-eyed chain-smokers—that she'd grown up next to groves of orange trees. But her stories were nostalgic instead of repentant. It was in the groves that Bette learned to drink—fresh orange juice with vodka. Or with rum. Tequila from across the border. In Chicago, where citrus arrived green and hard and undersized, shiny with wax, she longed for the orange trees, driving alongside them, the rhythmic pattern with which they fractured rays of the sun.

At night she might dream of parking in the groves. A boy was beside her, the heat of the desert and the car bringing out from his freshly laundered shirt his own heat and the scent of soap flakes. They drank in the groves and played with the headlights —switched them off, then on, the trees suddenly surrounding them as in a holdup, then fleeing in the sudden dark like spirits. Sometimes irrigation fog came and settled in the groves, rank moisture that did not evaporate, a dense, pesticidal haze among the orange trees.

Her puberty came back to her. Or she went to it, eating citrus, dreaming of old friends, of the groves. Her dream landscape always had as its backdrop the branches of trees with oranges like bright baubles. When she couldn't sleep she lay resentful beside the baby's father, kicking his ankle whenever she was kicked from within. He would rouse himself enough to put a heavy, forgiving arm across her chest. He was older, willing to delay gratification. Bette liked grown-ups. They were generous. They had patience. In their eyes she was, and always would be, young.

It would have been sweet to have a teen-age adventure—she dreamed giddy car rides into city lights, laughing with boys she didn't know who handed her cigarettes and beers. Only when she rolled the taste in her mouth, allowed it to unfurl in her limbs, might she remember she was pregnant, and wake stricken, heart banging with worry about the baby.

She cried progesterone-born tears, was wrenched by hysterical hiccups. Inside her grew a brutish boy, a leaper, a diver, an insomniac, his angular knees and his feet and skull stirring restlessly through the night like ice cubes, his image on the ultrasound screen one of a swimmer, in focus this moment, blurred by motion the next, scrotum looking bigger than his brain.

Down on the floor Bette's loyal dog wheezed with asthma but was happy to be loved suddenly so well, so weepily. Bette put her face to his and cried and cried, doomed, hugely and miserably unintoxicated.

HUSBAND

Her husband had been born in 1936 to Polish immigrants who never really learned English. They did not want to be absorbed into America; they had simply wished to leave Poland. He was Sergio Petroski, Serge to his friends. He owned a coffeehouse that had a Marxist slant: for your *latte* you paid only what you could. He was a widower. His first wife had been a political poet named Ferosa Rosario, who had been slain—the word itself was enough to unnerve Bette—for holding opinions. Sergio, by virtue of history (because he had one), intimidated Bette. Would this intimidation pass for love, she sometimes wondered. When compared with his past, her California-orange-grove life looked as naïve and sunny as a sitcom. Until she saw him naked, Sergio had made her feel immorally young and uneducated, which was precisely what she'd come to Chicago to feel. She had not been a victim; she did not grasp oppression. His breadth, his resources, the stacks of books that he could quote from and recommend, the people who called him, late at night, long-distance, from prison or deathbed—Bette, alas, had no way to link herself to this international chain of passionate intelligentsia.

Then they ended up tangled on a couch together one Saturday after closing time, after the setting of the alarms and the locking of the doors. It was your basic apolitical clinch. Sergio was stocky and gray, walrus-featured, sadly drooping in the face like Albert Einstein, fifty-three years old, most often found wearing what he called his Greek-fisherman sweater, a sewage-colored woollen garment that covered his barrel-like paunch. Bette was twenty-five, two inches taller than he, wearing clogs to exaggerate the difference, to feel some advantage. He had held her face in his hands and she could not return the direct gaze he gave her, could only close her eyes and give in to what she knew best, which was the fundamental mechanics of love. She allowed her breathing to deepen, and felt him lick her eyelids. He wore a cologne from France, sent to him by a former girlfriend—a pepperminty scent like a cool candy, like sweet schnapps—and Bette, on her clogs, leaned into it and rubbed her cheek against the crosshatched skin of his neck. Still he stared at her; she could feel his eyes on her arms and elbows, but she imagined herself hiding inside his embrace, trying to believe that this thing between them had nothing, nothing to do with age. The room around them—the display rack of hand-lettered cards, the walls of framed manifestos—floated away.

That night, before they eased awkwardly onto the bristly plaid couch Sergio kept in the back office, he brushed his teeth. It was this, and his grandfatherly nakedness, that finally gave Bette a window of confidence. With him she had only one edge, and it had to do with being born in 1964 in California in a grove of orange trees, and with having taut skin still marked by the three triangles of a long-ago tan, and breath she never bothered to freshen.

They were married in the coffeehouse, attended by employees and neighbors, poets and customers. A woman read a poem after the ceremony, though Bette could discern nothing wedding-like or well-wishing in it. There were dark birds circling carnage in Gdańsk, gutters of blood, scalpels and bombs and bones, and clouds that looked like the severed wings of doves. After the woman ended—paused and then dropped her hand, with which she had been conducting her own vibrating voice—the audience, Bette's co-workers and Sergio's friends, gave an artful and depressed appreciative grunt. Bette looked around at them and then laughed, drunk and tall. Sergio tried to smile in her direction, to be a good sport, his face glossy with nervous bravura—he'd married such a young girl, so spontaneously, on so little evidence of worth—then applauded vigorously for the reader, who was small and unadorned and whose expression was utterly venomous. Only later did Bette learn that the poem was one by Sergio's dead wife.

Ferosa haunted Bette like a guilty conscience. Sergio seemed always involved with a project in Ferosa's memory, the details of which Bette could not keep straight. He raised money and circulated petitions—that was the general gist—but each time the funds went to different people: hostages in prison, booksellers going bankrupt, destitute protesters who picketed the *Tribune* or Oscar Mayer. Now it was Iraq and Kuwait. Pregnant, Bette had thought she might find her way in for good, forever. She thought she might appear mysterious and estimable to him, carrying a secret inside her which he could not comprehend, toward which he would have to pay an outsider's homage.

Instead, Bette found Ferosa's book of poems in Sergio's desk. They were, she understood as she read them one long, unsleeping, and unsettling night, all about the politically correct stance of not having children. *We unmake our country*, Ferosa had written of her skinny shrunk-chili-pepper-shaped homeland, *gene by gene, cell by cell.*

TOURIST

For the first three months of the pregnancy Bette was hot. For the next three cold. In Chicago, the weather was either on or off but never what you might call good. She sat on a radiator and watched the parade of service people who kept her building presentable. They all wore uniforms, brown or white or blue; they all stopped just below her window to consult their lists, then buzzed a tenant. Her clothes hung like skeletons in the closet and, unwilling to commit herself to stretch pants, support hose, or underwires, she wore the same frumpy thing every day, her own sort of uniform, once maroon, now weather-washed pink. Her libido, she was told by the OB, might run rampant, might drive Dad out the door. She maintained a look-out for such a development but remained oddly content reading erotica, never missing the real event. Her husband was a grownup; he would wait nine months, if need be. He'd done it before—been celibate for two years when he'd grown disenchanted with himself and his relationships with women. Bette thought him wise and profound, like a Buddha, like a turtle.

How could he love her? He simply did. He found in her something she could not find herself. He laughed at her when she did not mean to be funny. One day, he caught her by the wrist and held her, nearly crying, when she returned from shopping. She deposited bags of cans and eggs and salty snacks on the table, mystified by his damp eyes, horrified to think she might discover him to be weak, standing above him while he closed her skirt around his face like a handkerchief. Inside her body a boy of their making rolled and punched; outside, the father put his ear to the drama and seemed to despair. Bette tried to chart a course of action while she stroked his silky, thin hair and saw herself en route to California, pregnant behind a steering wheel. But it was an abysmal and unconnected image. Her previous life, filled with forgettable family and forgetful friends, would not secure her. This was her place, yet it depended on Sergio's steady presence. She tilted his face toward

her own and squinted into it. "You're all I have," she repri-
manded him.

It turned out he'd been reading the newspaper; it was world
events that had consumed and grieved him, as they frequently
did. Later the two of them shared a pot of licorice tea and
watched reruns on the tiny black-and-white TV they kept
stashed in a closet, Sergio laughing and laughing at the old-
fashioned jokes, hugging Bette and pounding the table with his
fist.

She did not believe he meant to make her feel inadequate.
"You hide what becomes you," he told her when she insisted on
knowing what made her merit his ample affection. "You are
sweet when you cross your arms over your big breasts to make
them disappear. You are shy with them, as if they might embarrass someone. Don't you see?"

She did—his praise thrilled her; she'd always thought of herself as being a size or so too large—but she made him continue
by pretending otherwise. "You love me for my bosoms?"

Though he was smart about her, he mostly played into her
hands. " 'Bosoms,' " he said, laughing. "I was making a metaphor. You don't know those things about yourself which are
appealing. That's what I like."

Still, it was tiresome to be mistaken for his daughter, to have
people, especially women and especially now, in Bette's seventh
month, stare at the two of them with disgust. Sergio's mother,
who lived in a nursing home three blocks from their apartment,
puffed her mouth when Bette came to visit, as if she might spit
a tooth onto Bette's lap. Before moving to the home, before
Sergio's father's death, before the oxygen machine they'd attached her to, Matska had been vaguely senile. Her apartment
always smelled of gas, though Sergio's parents claimed over
and over to have had the problem checked by their super. Matska would smile and invite Bette into her seedy kitchen, humbly
introducing herself and her husband, never sure who the girl
was. Now, purely oxygenated, she knew.

"Child!" she hissed, and Bette did not know whether it was
she being addressed or the one in her womb. Matska's English,
still a foreign language to her, was full of inconsistencies. She

seemed to use "child" as a term not unlike "whore" or "witch." Sergio was protected from her fury by her evident belief that Bette had tricked him into marriage (via sex or incantation, Bette supposed, which, strictly speaking, might not be so far from the truth) and still held him under a spell.

"Most mothers *want* to be grandparents," Bette whined. "She ought to be *thrilled* with me." Sergio agreed, seeming to think the arrival of the baby, this grandson (a genealogy Bette didn't like to consider for long), would soften things among them all.

However, Matska was also a drinker. It had been a useful common denominator, because it was a role Bette inhabited the way she did that of a lover—with assurance. Before Matska went into the home, she and Bette used to sit for comfortable hours in front of an open window, wearing coats, drinking cooking sherry, Matska relating the story of her son's life, his tender childhood. Bette continued to visit the nursing home, hoping one day to discover Matska returned to her former hospitality, with a deck of cards—she loved honeymoon bridge—or a friendly bottle of cheap sherry resting on her bed table.

Sergio did not drink, and he was the only friend Bette had made in Chicago with whom she didn't immediately associate alcohol. Choosing him, she told herself when she worried, showed her willingness to turn her back on frivolity.

At the coffeehouse she had always gotten high with Benjamin. But now that she was pregnant, Benjamin had little to say to her. He was Sergio's oldest friend, a business partner by default, a former this, that, and the other—tired, cynical, gay. What possible use did gay men have for pregnant women? So seeded, so Kansas, so fat. She went to visit one day, dressed not in the artful black clothing she'd learned to wear in her former life but in something floral and baggy.

"Yikes, a romper!" Benjamin said when he greeted her, squinting his eyes as if against glare, laughing.

Bette knocked over a pyramid of Melitta filter baskets when she rounded a corner. Squatting among the plastic cones, she tried not to cry.

"How's things?" she sniffed, hungry for the outer world, collusion, jokes.

"Swell," Benjamin said, making the word as ripe as she, holding himself away from her, as if her condition were transmittable or he might be embarrassed by association. And then he asked, as everyone always asked, always in a great, solicitous, sorry tone: "How are you feeling?"

She smiled thinly and told some version of the truth. "There's only three states of mind for a pregnant woman: suicidal, homicidal, and placid." You woke up and there you were, propped on one pointy corner of the triangle or another.

Ordinarily they might smoke pot together in the back room. Benjamin kept a stash and pipe in a file drawer for the regulars, for civilized, chummy rainy-day intimacies on the plaid couch. How Bette missed her real life. Now the back room reeked of underarm sweat and rotted orange peels.

Benjamin turned to face her suddenly, inspired by something, his eyes unaccountably eager. "Let me see you," he said. He was staring at what had once been her waist. "I've never seen a naked pregnant woman. What do you say—gimme a look-see?"

Bette felt herself redden, horrified at exposing herself. "Go get knocked up yourself if you want to see a freak show." Spinning to leave, she crashed into an adding machine, sending it only as far as the seat of a roll-away chair. Benjamin sighed in disappointment, still mesmerized by her midsection.

Other people stared, too. A dark and craven man followed her around Dominick's, circling aisles so that he continued to approach her head on, staring intently at her abdomen as if she might be about to burst with prophecy. Something maniacal in his eyes kept her from saying a word. In the presence of all the gaping world, Bette remained mute, ashamed of the large evidence of copulation she carried with her every day. It was worse than a scarlet letter; it forced her to waddle, to buy prunes and healthful cereal that looked and tasted like little haystacks, to require carryout service. In the checkout line she managed to overturn a display of horoscopes, tiny rolled tubes that spilled to the floor like a pack of cigarettes. She was too ungainly to retrieve them from under the magazine stand.

Knocking things over was not confined to public spaces. At home pens jumped from tabletops, papers from shelves. "Could you pick that up?" she would ask the cat. "Oh, never mind. Forget it." From tummy to knee she was a map of bruises, a geography of lumpy flesh and tender veins. Sergio had to kneel at her feet to roll her stockings up her ankles. Counters and the newly tight space of their small bathroom conspired against her. She was a large belly, wobbling through the world like an ugly tourist, cloddish, and with a loud, guffawing laugh.

BABY

Memory of life before maternity leave had dried up and blown away. She stood on a vast desert like a Russian nesting doll, shiny and round, and solitary but for the little clone hidden inside.

Her condition, by now, was inescapable, the baby a conundrum like a ship in a bottle. In the park, small children, infants, the mere sight of strollers were terrifying. Parents tried to converse with her. She scurried to dog territory, where others, childless, knelt with plastic bags and paper towels, screeched the names they might otherwise have bestowed on offspring: Maurice, Chloe, Otis.

"Help," she sometimes said at the grocery store, unable to reach the desired brand of rye crackers on a top shelf. She hoped someone might hear and understand, as if she were short and old like Matska.

Sergio decided Bette was to be spoiled and petted. He fawned, he cooked leafy greens, he brought her grotesque bouquets of blood-red roses. Somewhere he found a bottle of wine containing no alcohol, a promising, deeply colored Merlot. Bette sipped, then gulped, but it tasted precisely like what it was: 12.8 per cent absent. Sergio shrugged sheepishly, then lay behind her and kneaded her spongy skin while she sniffed his sleeve for the adult odors he'd picked up on the El—diesel exhaust and mentholated cigarette smoke.

"Only two more months," he said carelessly at one point. He was preparing his future nostalgia for these despicable days. She had never felt so isolated—like an astronaut floating through space. *Reel me in!* she might gesture in her bloated white suit, in a panic, but on board the ship her co-pilot would wave serenely, thinking she was pointing out the idiotic beauty of Pluto.

Denied wine, she substituted chocolate. She'd lost her talent for discrimination; an Oreo was as good as Godiva. The days wore on, not in their usual parade of ups and downs, clowns and cops, but precisely identical to one another. She rolled from bed each morning horrified by how many more times she would have to do it. She walked sluggishly, creating new, deeper-sourced noises in the wood floor, and then sprawled at the kitchen table. She weighed more than Sergio now. Shoes, the one form of clothing that had never betrayed her—had never been outgrown before worn out—no longer fit. She popped from everything—overblown dough, a rhino in her own home.

Sleep was her only recourse, the deeper the better. Each afternoon she prepared a nest. She pulled the phone cord from the wall, shut the blinds, turned the metal radiator up high, stripped naked, and then positioned pillows between her knees and under her neck and over her exposed ear. She drifted as if in the ocean, thinking of weightlessness, of sunshine, of being without a body. She put her hand to her hard belly and felt herself as suspended as her child, dreamy and liquid, without consciousness or conscience.

WAR

Meanwhile the Middle East roiled. Sergio organized one of what were known as Events at the coffeehouse. Antiwar poetry and music. Bette decided against attending. Wasn't it arrogant, after all, to turn up pregnant at a time like this? Besides, she could not interest herself in the war. It was abominable, but she was busy. (She couldn't even think of the word "abominable" without changing it to "abdominal.") She signed petitions but had no idea what they signified. Clever peace slogans went over her head. In the evenings, when Sergio flipped on the news (the television now lived on the kitchen counter), Bette retreated to the bedroom and browsed through baby catalogues. She heard the word "Scud" and still thought of boys who weren't cool enough.

FELLOWSHIP

The first day of their Lamaze birth class, each couple was asked to reveal the length of their marriage, their occupations, and whether this was a first child. In the beginning Bette enjoyed her and Sergio's relative bizarreness. Other Moms and Coaches spent their days at real-estate offices or car dealerships or architectural firms. One Coach, obviously unwillingly associated with the whole project, stubbornly announced himself unemployed. His wife, an enormous red-faced woman who had fallen into her chair as if ready to put down roots there, socked him on the arm. "He does phone solicitation," she explained. "In between jobs."

The group grew to tolerate one another, and Bette found herself looking forward to their meetings. She began wishing Sergio were as clunky as the other husbands, as young and as easily embarrassed by the instructor's frankness. Instead, the lingo rolled right off his tongue: cervix, placenta, lanugo. He read the books, and none of what he read made him squirm. It occurred to Bette that the rest of her life would be abnormal, that Sergio would train their boy to hug dolls and to cry and to wear—without masculine resentment—lumpy Ecuadoran sweaters.

"Remind me why I wanted a baby?" she asked Sergio, over the telephone. Only over the phone could she concentrate on conversation. In person she was too distracted; her body got in her way—the swollen ankles, the popped navel.

"Was it your ticking biological clock?" he teased, squeaking in his chair at the café. "Or maybe mine?" He giggled, and Bette was tempted to join him, but often these days she found herself frighteningly close to turning Sergio's jokes into a tragic version of her life. There was music in the background at the café, loud guitars and drums, manhole covers clashing together. "Benjamin says maybe our marriage was going wrong." Sergio went on playing. "Actually, I can't remember why we got with child. Can't you?"

The truth was—there was truth—she *did* remember. Every now and then a wash of emotion came over Bette so strongly that she had to sit down and cover her eyes for fear of falling. *This* was the reason—the scientific principle governing the teardrop-shaped female body: inertia or vertigo or something not yet discovered and named. It had to do with her tender breasts, with TV commercials about puppies, with the childhood taste of hot oatmeal and raisins, with Sergio's sleeping face under her wakeful, skeptic's scrutiny, with her part in the dreadful, thrilling innocence of new life.

DOG

Three flights of stairs became too many in her eighth month. And the dog had never learned to heel, raised as he had been in lawn-filled, permissive California. Sergio suggested tentatively that he drop the dog each morning at Matska's nursing home, where they encouraged pets and warm, fuzzy feelings, and let the dog make use of the yard the residents themselves hadn't set foot in for the last three months. Sergio spoke out of regard for Bette's precarious physical state, the ice on the back steps, the fact that the dog, which weighed eighty pounds, could be considered dangerous in this weather to someone in her condition.

And it was. Bette recalled a day not more than a week before when she'd slid, clinging with one hand to the frozen pipe that served as bannister, the other hand resting over her baby, the dog, a flight below, sledding comically on his side, legs flailing but catching at nothing.

"O.K.," she said, tearfully. Pregnancy had made her stupid with commitment to the animal, and she choked up over his absence. Sergio dropped off and picked up the dog the way one would a child in day care. "It's great—it's so yuppie," Sergio would say when he got home. Bette squatted—she seemed to do nothing but squat these days—to pull tiny clots of pressed snow from between the dog's toes. The clots were like hailstones, round and solid as pebbles from nestling all day in his paws. Meanwhile, his tongue would work at her hands, reminding her gently though persistently that he did not like his paws touched. It was inconceivable to her that she would love anything more than she did the dog.

The nursing home's director, ambassador to the outside world, called one afternoon, three days before the baby was due, to say that the dog was acting . . . well, funny.

"Funny ha-ha?" Bette asked. "Funny strange?"

After a long pause, the director chuckled uncertainly. "Your dog is digging our fence up. You must come fetch him."

Bette looked down and discovered herself to be sitting in a warm puddle. "Yes!" she cried. "Broken water! Yes!"

She set the receiver in its cradle. A lulling voice was carrying on patiently from far away. "We wouldn't want to be forced to let him escape. We wouldn't want to have to actually give chase. . . ." Before phoning Sergio, Bette stood to survey the damage. Then, while on her feet, she decided to have a drink. It seemed the indubitably correct move, now that her child was about to be washed from her body.

Grownup Chivas in hand—she'd never drunk Scotch before— she dialled the coffeehouse. Her sweatpants were soaked. Inside her, curious movement began, more articulate, less muffled. All lines were busy at the shop, so she waited, sipping distractedly on her drink, wondering if what she felt was contractions. If so, they weren't as bad as everyone made them out to be. When after five or six minutes all lines were still busy, Bette asked an operator to cut in.

"I'm the owner's wife," she told the woman, who had no interest in the nature of the emergency. "And I've gone into labor."

"Uh-huh," the operator said nasally. When she returned to Bette she informed her that no one was on any of the lines; everything was off the hook.

At this, Bette gulped down the remainder of the Scotch and

phoned her doctor, whose nurse told her to take a cab to the hospital.

Before leaving, she brushed her teeth.

MOTHERHOOD

Woozily, she gave birth. On the way to the hospital, she'd had to lecture her cabdriver. He'd made the mistake of expressing his disappointment at his wife's getting a C-section. His accent annoyed Bette, that and the fact that he'd taken a longer route than necessary to Northwestern. Bette swooned on the stiff plastic back seat, feet straddling the floor hump, forehead propped on the back of the front seat. This, she concluded, was it. Hardly breathing, she could smell her cabbie's aftershave, his aging American sedan, the grotesque odors of former fares. "My wife, she did not try hard enough," he said.

"Oh, give me a break!" Bette shouted at the floor, when she could take in enough oxygen to say anything. From rib cage to pelvis she was taut as a basketball.

"Is true!" the driver swore. "She only tried one day for the natural birth."

"As in twenty-four hours?" Bette lifted her head long enough to see him nod vigorously. "I feel sorry for her," she said.

"Yes," he said. "It's very bad she couldn't do it the natural way."

"No," Bette said, struggling to speak now. "I feel sorry she's still your wife." But he couldn't possibly understand her. A barge had come pushing through her, a seizure, a pain like a fired missile.

Sergio made it to the hospital in time to cut the baby's cord. The phones had been off the hook at the coffeehouse because the war had ended. Benjamin and Sergio were toasting the possibility of peace and hadn't wanted to be interrupted.

"My turn to take care of him," Sergio now shouted happily to the room full of green-clothed adoring women. Bette heard one woman say to another, "It's so unusual to have a grandfather in delivery." The obstetrician dashed out the door, due at another birth party down the hall.

From her room she phoned her mother. For a truce-like time they discussed labor while Bette watched Sergio through the nursery glass, walking up and down with little Ed, named for his real grandfathers, both of them, two men long gone from two worlds equally lost. Bette was teary considering it. From La Jolla her mother told her she had begun writing poetry.

"Oh, please," Bette said in exasperation. "I already have one poet too many in my life."

"Listen, here's a line about all these California grandmas. I'm working with Mother Goose here. You ready? Quote, 'There was an old woman who lived in a shoe. She had so many children she *did* know what to do,' unquote. Whaddaya think? I'm taking a class at the branch library."

Bette said, "I better go lactate."

SEX

Toward her pets she held recalled affection, and this is what she now felt toward Sergio as well: habitual love, her response to his caresses like a segment of a routine—this, then that. Not unlike grinding coffee beans in a stupor each morning. For his part, Sergio's affection extended to Eddie via Bette; he still loved her best. But between Bette and Eddie, small red-fisted thing, there was something brand-new. He was a high she knew she didn't deserve: his eager face at her breast every few hours, his confused cross-eyed looks and wrinkled forehead that seemed to pose to her a severe and simple question: Who are you?

Sergio fetched his mother, who came to the apartment bearing a roast to celebrate the baby's birth and the end of the Gulf War offensive. Sitting in the refrigerator, dripping blood onto a milk carton, the clear-wrapped lump of meat looked for all the world like a placenta. Bette gagged down dinner anyway—her mother-in-law was trying to make reparation. At the stove Matska had mistaken one knob for another: a burner on top glowed red all afternoon while, in the cold oven, the meat grew gray, remained raw. They sliced it and fried it before eating it, but still it was unbearably rare.

"He looks like his father," Matska told them, of Eddie. Bette agreed; but, then, all newborns looked like old men to her. Matska held him without supporting his wobbly head, allowing it to loll sideways and back. "You're good, you're good," she cooed into his slow, opaque eyes. Bette drank champagne, one sparkling glass after another, idly subtracting ages until she realized that she was closer in age to her son than she was to her husband, and that her husband was closer in age to his mother than to her.

The baby did many less than pleasant things but they didn't bother Bette. Sergio, however, with his bald head, the hairs in his ears, the saggy paunch of flesh, an odor he couldn't quite disguise—these things began to disgust her, though she spent the day changing diapers full of tar and wiping down the yellow chin of her son. Eddie's skin was remarkably similar to Sergio's, dry as paper and baggy as a pachyderm's. She grew to dread Sergio's touch, to turn her mouth away from his minty kisses. He closed his eyes and groped, like the baby, for the favors of her flesh. She began to wish him dead, to imagine the car accident or heart attack that might take him. In his absence she was ecstatic, autonomous once more, propelling the baby through the neighborhood in his stroller, dragging the dog behind, grinning at strangers, and chatting. But at Sergio's arrival home each evening, Bette might dissolve into tears, complain about her sore breasts and the baby's interminable, choking cry.

Sergio would hold the boy and walk from room to room, listening to Bette without looking at her. She watched him and heard herself as if from a corner of the ceiling. Who was this shrew inside her? She seemed to be set on driving her husband from her life. How much would he take, she wondered. At what point would his adult disposition give way to boyish hurt? Each time, just before she went too far, Bette ran to Sergio and held him tight—she was sorry, so sorry, and he, as ever, forgave.

They could resume relations, her obstetrician informed her. "You really think so?" Bette wanted to ask.

She'd been a prisoner of war; she'd come back metamorphosed, a veteran, politicized. In celebration she drank beer while little Eddie nursed, both of them warm and a little drunk. Now that he was out and fine—above average in all ways, on all scales, ninety-nine out of a hundred—alcohol became Bette's friend again. Everything appeared through the lens of her successful campaign. Ferosa was a beloved but deposed demagogue; Matska a psychological sissy. And Sergio? An anachronism. His son would be blond. And the baby already preferred his mother: Bette. In the back of her mind sat the dirty words "divorce" and "departure," like loot in a secret safe-deposit box. She was healthy, vigorous, young: a pretty American girl with her own car, her body snapped back, pre-pregnant and firm, virgin. The country stretched to either side of her, festooned with yellow ribbons, offering no resistance. She could drive anywhere, and ever after live happily, happily, happily.

John H. Richardson

THE PINK HOUSE

We stood in an empty house looking at a walk-in closet. At least Mom and I did; Dad stood by the window smoking a cigarette and pretending to ignore us. We had been house-hunting for three days, and Dad had been cranky since the middle of the first day, when he realized just how much house he could expect for his money (double what he could get in the States, but there was no telling him that). By now he was impossible. As the real-estate agent ran down the history of the house, he gazed out over the red-tiled rooftops with a look of growing misery. The sun flowing into the dark room etched pits and hollows into his face until he looked as harsh as a monk in a medieval woodcut.

Mom leaned in to inspect the closet. She nodded her head at the shelves, confirming their existence, doing the polite thing, making the agent happy.

"Walk-in closet," Dad muttered. "We don't need a walk-in closet."

My parents had been living in Mexico for almost two years, since shortly after my father retired. They chose Tonala because of its superb climate—second only to Nairobi's, everyone said— and because it housed the largest expatriate community of retired Americans in the world, nearly a hundred thousand of them. There were book clubs, garden clubs, eating clubs, golf courses galore, the American Society and its many functions, and Mom and Dad had quickly gathered a group of friends. Now Mom wanted to buy a house. She promised Dad his own garden, his own library. It would have a high wall, Mexican style. An oasis. They'd pay for it in cash and never have to worry about rent again.

Dad wasn't persuaded. He spoke again, louder: "We don't need a walk-in closet."

Mom avoided the agent's look. She spoke with patient reason, as to a child. "There's nothing unusual about a walk-in closet."

Dad cleared his throat gruffly. "Well, I don't need one and I don't see any point in spending a small fortune to have one."

This was one of his tricks for getting out of something he didn't want to do: simply saying he didn't feel like it would be rude, by his lights, so he worked up a steam of indignation until we gave in to his bad mood. He brought his cigarette to his mouth. The cigarette had a very long ash, nearly half its length. We all looked at it. Despite the slight trembling of Dad's hand, the ash didn't fall.

"Maybe we'd better come back another time," Mom said to the agent, giving her a stretched-across-the-teeth social smile.

In the car she opened her purse in her lap and began adjusting her makeup. We waited. "Really, Richard," she said. "Must you embarrass me like that?"

Dad said nothing.

"That was a perfectly reasonable house. There was nothing extreme about that house."

"It had a swimming pool," Dad said.

Mom made a *tch* sound.

"There'll be bills," Dad said. "Cleaning bills, heating bills, bills for chemicals and whatnot. I don't need a pool. You don't need a pool."

"It might be nice to go swimming," Mom said.

Dad scowled. "I'd say your swimming days are over."

Mom was silent for a moment. Finally she spoke. "Thank you very much," she said, a stop in her voice.

Watching from the back seat, I thought Mom was overdoing it

a bit, enjoying the melodrama of a personal offense. "Looked like a great house to me," I said.

They ignored me. But I knew it would be best to continue to fill the silence, that being one of the primary functions of children. So I babbled. "The acoustics were great, what a place to play guitar, that living room, big kitchen, loved all that tile work, it was just great."

That was for Mom. Now for Dad: "Of course, I don't see what you want to buy a house for down here anyway. I mean, California, that would be cool, near the beach, but that's me, and you guys have your own priorities and needs and stuff, which I guess include living in this God-forsaken, disease-ridden, macho, sexist country."

"I'm not sure I do want to buy a house," Dad said. "Your mother is the one who insists on it."

Dad flipped on the turn signal and glanced at the lane to his right, his face dark with concentration. Mom didn't speak until there was a break in the traffic. "Honestly," she said. "You talked to the accountant. You talked to Dr. Joe. You were the one who said we should do this—and I agreed. Now, when it comes to the point of actually doing something, you make everything impossible. This happens every time we try to make a decision."

Dad just compressed his lips and looked out his side window. Mom could see that continuing the conversation was pointless, and we rode the rest of the way home in silence.

When we got home—home that year being an apartment near midtown—Dad went straight into the kitchen. After a moment we heard the clink of glass and bottle. When Dad emerged, glass in hand, Mom gave him a critical look, which he ignored. "I'm going to read," he said, heading for his bedroom.

Mom shook her head and sighed, moving toward the kitchen. I followed. "Are you hungry?" she asked.

"I thought I'd go out for a while," I said. "Get some tostadas."

I leaned against the counter as she went through the refrigerator. The kitchen was blue—blue fridge, blue counter, blue walls.

"This is the way it's been," she said. "He's been this way ever since he retired. I honestly don't know if I can stand it much longer."

She shifted a few Tupperware containers in search of something.

"Come on, Mom," I said, thinking she was being melodramatic again. "You're not talking . . . divorce?"

"I've thought about it," she said grimly, wiping her mayonnaise knife clean with two definite strokes against the edge of a slice of bread.

I was quiet for a few moments, giving ritual gravity to Mom's statement even though I didn't remotely believe it. Now she was setting up a tray with salt and pepper shakers and a placemat, good china, a Steuben crystal glass, even a miniature vase and one small rosebud. In our house there was always a flower on every tray.

Divorce: the thought annoyed me. The confidence annoyed me. But it had nothing to do with me. I hadn't even seen much of the folks for the past seven years, since I was sixteen and they got hysterical over some minor recreational drug abuse. I got into college early, came home once or twice for vacation—the last time two years ago, the year Dad retired and I graduated from college. That was another disaster. So I was surprised and a little flattered—and secretly pleased—when Mom called me up and said that Dad wasn't doing very well, could I come down?

"This'll blow over," I said. "He's just having trouble adjusting to retired life."

"Some trouble," she said. She looked the tray over, aligned a fork, picked it up, and started for the door.

"Maybe if you didn't wait on him hand and foot," I said.

"He should eat," she said, taking the tray to his bedroom.

When she opened the door, I saw Dad lying sideways on the bed, propped up on his elbow with a cigarette in one hand and a book in the other. He turned a page and looked up, his expression vague. As Mom carried the tray to the bed, he shifted to make room for it and his cigarette ash fell on the bedspread, which was already burned in a half-dozen places. "Oh, Richard," Mom said, quickly brushing the ash away.

Escape! I shot down the stairs of our small apartment building (pillbox balconies, smell of damp cement) and burst out onto the street. The street was narrow here, choked with trees that split the sidewalks, but down a few blocks was a broad divided boulevard with grass and trees and fountains in the middle and a statue on every corner. At one end stood a huge sculpture of the Child Heroes, a few dozen schoolboys who had fought the North American imperialist armies with primitive guns and no grown-up supervision (they were slaughtered, of course, but they showed initiative). At the other end was a huge grocery store, an example of the recent national fad for giant *mercados*. For a while I just strolled around looking at girls. Finally I ducked into my favorite tostada place—wherever I was, I always found a favorite restaurant and always ordered the same thing—and ordered two beers and tostadas, which I wolfed down with sudden hunger. Then I picked up my head and inhaled the balmy, flowered air: jacarandas, bougainvillaea, gardenias. It seemed a terrible injustice that there was no one around to have sex with.

The next morning at nine-thirty mom was already walking around the apartment, picking at things. She fluffed the pillows on the sofa. She ran a finger across the lid of a cigarette box. "I told him we were leaving at ten," she said. "This is just like him." Then she turned to me and confided, "He was up all night." She called out his name.

"I'll get him," I said. I went to Dad's door and knocked once, twice, pushed it open. The room was dark and stank of cigarettes. Dad lay on his back, his mouth open, his fringe of gray hair tufted from his skull. I touched his leg to see if it was warm.

"Dad," I said, shaking him by the shoulder. "Dad." His eyes opened. It took a moment for him to focus. He gave me a weak and pitiful smile. "Oh," he said, clearing his throat.

"Mom's getting antsy," I said, my voice cold. "She wants to get going."

"I'm getting up," Dad said. He folded back the covers. His body seemed smaller than I remembered, his legs and arms brown and wiry, his belly pregnant and white. As he sat up, the fly of his boxer shorts gaped open.

Dad sat on the bed, his feet on the floor, his hands holding the edge of the mattress. His big toes had extremely thick nails that curved sideways, making his feet look almost deformed. The toes were bright red.

"What's wrong with your toes?" I said.

Dad said nothing.

"They look infected," I said.

Dad grunted dismissively. He put his hands on his thighs and moved forward into a half-crouch; then he pushed off the bed, balancing and straightening at the same time. He faced me, gave an absent nod, and then bowed his head and reached for his robe.

An hour later he was dressed in his uniform of double-knit pants and *guayabera*, an open-necked Mexican "dress" shirt, which seemed to me quite a comedown from the expensive suits he used to wear. His face was like a shirt from a suitcase, clean but creased. We rode the elevator down to the garage and got in the car and drove off, Dad maddeningly slow at everything from locking the front door to getting the car out of the garage. As we got to the garage door, Dad said, for the third time in as many days, "This is an electronic door. We have all the latest improvements here."

Despite his hangover, he was trying to be hearty, a proper member of the stoic generation, the Depression generation that never complained, that took pride in bluffing their way through the day no matter how bad they felt (except for those occasional explosions). This annoyed me, and I stayed glumly silent. How could he resolve his problems if he ignored his feelings? When I had a hangover, I babied myself.

An hour later Mom stood in the middle of a kitchen as the real-estate agent threw open cabinets. The agent was talking about how wonderful it was that this house had so much storage space. Mom oohed and aahed. "Is this a microwave?" she asked. "That's the first one I've ever seen."

"Mom," I said, "we owned a microwave. Remember? In Whittier?"

"I meant down here," she said. "You hardly ever see them down here." She turned to Dad, who was standing in the doorway trying to muster an expression of mild bemusement. "Look at that, Richard. A microwave." Dad grunted.

"No walk-in closets this time," the agent said. Mom and Dad forced out social chuckles. "There is a safe, however," she added.

"That would be useful," Mom said. "We could give up the safe-deposit box. Save a few hundred pesos."

Dad put on a mock expression of joyous gratitude—his eyebrows went way up, his smile spread absurdly wide. "Now, that interests me," he said. "Now you have caught my interest. You're appealing to my deepest desires."

The agent laughed. "Would you care to see it?" she said. We trooped off to the bedroom to inspect the safe. It was set into the wall, the paint around it darker where a painting must have hung. It was gray, like gunmetal but stippled, with walls about an inch thick. The inside was just big enough to stack five or six hardback books.

"It looks sturdy enough," Dad said.

"It's fireproof, too," the agent said.

We all stood there for a minute, staring into the gray steel box.

"What was wrong with that house?" Mom asked bitterly an hour later, as we drove home.

"Am I not permitted simply to dislike something?" Dad said. "Did I work my entire life to be forced to buy a house I don't want to buy?"

"It would be nice if you had a reason," Mom said.

"I didn't like it," Dad said. "I just didn't like it. It was too bright, or too dark, or something."

"Too bright or too dark? Honestly."

"Well, damn it," Dad said.

"I agree with Pop," I said. "That house sucked."

"Daniel," Mom said, this time using the same exasperated tone on me.

"It did. It was too close, like a zoo or something, the way all the bedrooms and even the kitchen opened onto the living room. I kept expecting to see bars on the doors and some little cave in the back where the animals go to hide."

"That's exactly it," Dad said. "I couldn't have put it that well myself, son. That's exactly it. A zoo. A Goddamn zoo. At the cost of over one hundred thousand dollars."

Once again Mom sighed, chastising me with her eyes in the rearview mirror.

"And there was no pool," I said, just to be a monster. Dad fell right in with it.

"At that price it should have a pool," he agreed, nodding.

Mom widened her eyes in outrage.

Later that day Mom held out a canapé tray to Frankie Day, her principal ally in the Battle to Buy a House. Frankie was about fifty, with a crewcut and bright red cheeks. He was a retired real-estate mogul, and Mom's confidant.

Even though Dad was sitting right there, Mom spoke in a whisper. "We can't even get through two houses a day, he gets so mad."

Frankie spoke to Dad with his exaggerated, ironic drawl. "Really, Richard, you can't expect to see just the thing you want your first day out. You know Raoul? Who owns that little restaurant in Los Oblatos? He spent two solid months looking, and he found that marvelous place—you were there on Leticia's birthday—with the flowering trees?"

"It is lovely," Mom said.

"What did he pay, though?" my father said. For reasons obscure to all of us, he showed Frankie a lot of respect. "I can't believe these prices."

Frankie nodded. "Everything is going up," he agreed. "It's the market—it's absolutely wild, and I don't think it's going to get better."

Mom gave him a look. "At least not soon," Frankie said quickly. He knew the rules.

But it was too late. Dad went off on a fret about the local stock market. For the past year or two it had been his personal gold mine, and every time he'd mentioned it he had preened like a proud father. But he also seemed to worry about it constantly. What if it were all a delusion, a mirage? What if he lost his *guayabera*? These doubts made him even more fiercely loyal. When I wondered out loud if the Mexican stock market was the best place to put his money, he gave a little chuckle that said he knew better. But when Frankie said he had his doubts too, Dad started asking fearful questions. What have you heard? Which stocks are weakening?

Finally Frankie and Mom managed to steer the subject back to the house. "You know, Richard," Frankie said, "if you want to save money, the best places are outside Chapultapec altogether. Even Providencia is getting expensive."

Mom had suggested this dozens of times, but Dad would have none of it.

"You can get a mansion out at the lake for . . ."

"I will not live at the lake!" Dad blurted.

Mom frowned at him; his sudden vehemence was inappropriate. "Richard," she said.

Dad shook his head and waved his cigarette, refusing to be shushed. "Everyone we know lives here," he said to Frankie. "Margaret wouldn't want to live too far from here."

"Nobody said we had to buy at the lake," Mom said. "We're just talking."

"I don't like the lake," Dad continued. "It's too damn remote from everything. It's isolated. There's no hospital. I just don't like it."

"Okay," Mom said.

"Well, damn it," Dad said.

Frankie and Mom sipped at their drinks while Dad pouted.

"I always liked the lake," I said.

Frankie took over again. "What you want to think about, Richard, is somewhere out on the outskirts, like Chapalita or Oblatos. Quiet, close to town, cheap. Lots of people are moving out there now. Rancho Contento is a lovely place, for instance."

"Which one?"

"The one near Oblatos, away from the *barranca*," Frankie said.

"The one that changed its name?" Mom said. There had been a lawsuit between the two Rancho Contentos, and one was now called Rancho Mirage, but everyone still enjoyed the confusion and refused to use the new name.

Frankie nodded. "Remember, Richard? Where Dette and Bo live? The Breeces, from Texas?"

Dad shrugged.

"And Serena, the actress," Frankie said.

"It's nice, isn't it?" Mom said. "Remember the cobbled streets?"

Dad nodded grudgingly. "I don't think I could live in a place named Rancho Contento."

"It really is a charming place," Frankie said. "I hear you can get a three- or four-bedroom house with a half acre for about sixty thousand American. That won't buy you maid's quarters in Chapultapec."

"Sixty thousand?" Dad asked.

Dad was weakening, and Frankie ran with it. He mentioned the convenient shopping center, and the advantage of access to the back road to the airport, and the popular Aguas Calientes hot springs nearby. The Rancho even had its own little nine-hole golf course, splitting the older, top half of the development from the newer half below, with the lowest green fees of any course in the area. There were lovely places to walk. It was well protected, surrounded completely by a wall, and always had a guard at the gate. Not to mention the convenient Club Deportivo de Tonala, with its tennis courts, indoor pool, and popular bar. And the nearby town of Los Oblatos was so historic. "You know the Arabian Nights, that marvelous little restaurant," Frankie said. "With the patio? We ate there. With the peacocks?"

All this was according to Mom's plan. We weren't surprised when, immediately after Frankie left, Dad solemnly observed that perhaps we should look a bit out in Rancho Contento, despite its awful, unfortunate name.

Mom looked at me and rolled her eyes.

Later Dad confided in me. "Your mother prefers it here," he

said, "but it's just too damned expensive. I can't afford to buy here. I have to think how she's going to manage when I pass on."

The next morning Mom made a few calls, and by lunch we were driving out to Rancho Contento. It was a rustic-looking private development with wide, rough-cobbled streets, completely surrounded by a mossy brick wall. In the lower half most of the houses had open lawns, in the American manner, but above the golf course the streets wandered into the foothills and the houses all had walls. There were even a few crumbling haciendas dating back to just before the Mexican Revolution, huge shady estates as quiet and timeless as monasteries. On the widest of five avenues horses moved slowly along the dusty center divide. It looked exactly like an older Mexican neighborhood, but without any of the dark little corner stores that sell nothing but bread, sodas, cigarettes, gum, and tired-looking fruit.

Dad had never been above the golf course before, and was quite impressed. As we explored, the real-estate agent told us the peculiar history of the Rancho. It was originally settled near the turn of the century by an American who had made a fortune in the Alaska gold rush and came south to found the proverbial gleaming city on a hill. But the American got chased out by the revolution and returned north a broken man; not only was his wife killed in the fighting, but his sister took up with a young Mexican revolutionary and actually carried a rifle into battle by his side. The American left behind only a few scattered haciendas and the rough outline of imagined streets.

Half an hour later we were standing outside a huge house. We were in the highest part of the Rancho, where the streets parted around giant gnarled cottonwoods and all the gates looked like entrances to Aztec tombs. The house before us was at least fifty years old, maybe sixty, one of the first large places built on the hillside after the revolution. The wall around it was massive, ten feet high and at least two feet thick. The agent was saying we could get the house "for a song," because the owner wanted out quickly.

"It's quite impressive," Dad said.

Mom didn't say anything.

The agent pushed open the door. Inside, the house was dark and dusty; Mom's nose wrinkled in immediate distaste. At the back of the foyer a curving staircase rose up to a narrow balcony. On one side was a living room, on the other what seemed to be a library. "Well," Dad said. He was still standing just inside the door. "It's quite baronial."

The agent said the house was selling for just ninety thousand dollars. Dad appeared to be pleasantly surprised—this house was twice the size of the ones we had been looking at.

Mom ran her finger along a table and brought it up for inspection. It was black. She looked at the ceilings dubiously.

"It hasn't been cleaned for months," the agent said quickly. "Not since the owner went back north."

"It is dusty," Mom said.

"Look, Margaret," Dad said. "Built-in shelves!"

Dad led the way into the library, admiring the floor-to-ceiling bookshelves. He then posed himself with his back to the fireplace and actually clasped his hands behind his back. The agent smiled.

"Does it work?" Mom asked, nodding at the fireplace.

"Of course it works," Dad said.

"Yes, it works," the agent said. She led us back through the foyer and across the living room to a set of French doors. They opened onto the back yard. She opened the doors and displayed the yard with an upheld hand. "No pool," she said.

Mom narrowed her eyes and sniffed.

By the time the tour was over, Dad was clearly in love with the crumbling old house. He went on and on about its charm and scale and what a wonderful place it would be to entertain. Mom was pointedly silent. When we got to the foyer, Dad said he thought we should make an offer. Mom paused in the middle of a step, took Dad's arm, and smiled sweetly at the real-estate agent. "Could we have a moment?" she asked.

The agent said she would wait in the car; we could just close the door behind us when we were finished. The minute she got out of sight, Mom exploded.

"I can't believe you, Richard," she said. "Here you are, ready to make an offer. Look at this place! It's huge."

Dad looked confused. "I thought you wanted space," he said.

"Space, not a warehouse," Mom said. "This place is so old, I'll bet anything it has a million things that need repairing, old rotted this and that and rusted pipes and whatnot. You can't just make an offer. This place should be surveyed by a professional. We don't know what we'd be getting into. And why has it been on the market for months if it's such a good deal? Just imagine cleaning it!"

Dad appeared to be dumbfounded. "Well . . . ," he said. "I thought . . ."

"You didn't think," she said, turning and walking out the door.

After a moment Dad looked at me and shrugged. I shrugged back. "Looked okay to me," I said.

That night Dad went on one of his horrible benders. Mom and I sat in the living room talking in hushed voices, and every now and then Dad would come walking through in his boxer shorts with a crystal water glass in his hand. He'd nod his head to acknowledge us. Once he said, "Still up?"

"I don't want him going with us," Mom was saying. "He gets so upset, and then this. I'm afraid he'll have a heart attack."

"He's going to feel awful in the morning," I said.

"I hope he's alive in the morning," Mom said. "I always go in there wondering."

After a moment I suggested that I stay with Dad while Mom went house-hunting alone. "I mean, if it upsets him that much."

"You know your father," Mom said. "There's no way he'll let me go alone."

"Why don't we commit him to a mental institution for a week?" I said. "We'll say it's a case of temporary insanity—ours, if we don't get him out of our hair."

Mom laughed. Then she sighed. "I wish I could," she said.

At that moment I noticed something dark on the floor.

"What's that?" I said. "Look."

It was a bloody footprint. Looking down the room I saw another, and another, and another, a whole series of bloody footprints leading to my father's room.

"He probably dropped a glass and cut himself," Mom said, not getting up. "He's done it before."

I went to the pantry where we kept the liquor, looked around, and came back out. "No sign of any glass," I said. Mom got out of her chair and we headed toward Dad's room. We knocked, heard a grunt, and pushed open the door. Mom gasped. The whole bottom half of Dad's bed was soaked with blood. Dad was lying there reading, completely oblivious.

Twelve hours later we stood at the foot of Dad's hospital bed. Mom was shaking her head. "You really are a strange and stubborn person," she said. Dad looked sheepish.

His feet, it turned out, were horribly infected after being gouged deep and long by two fierce ingrown toenails that had actually imbedded themselves nearly half an inch into the pulp of his big toes. Apparently he'd been trying to dig out the ingrown toenails with a nail file when he drunkenly stabbed himself in the ankle deep enough to require three stitches. Then, it seems, he'd given up his efforts at home surgery, dabbed at the wound with his sheet, and gone to get another drink.

We left Dad in his private room and walked down the hall with Dr. Joe.

"It's really not that serious," he said. "What's surprising is that he let it get that bad—he must have been in pain for months. Anyway, I can have him out of here tomorrow."

Mom's reaction was instantaneous. "Oh, no," she said.

Dr. Joe looked at her curiously. His hair was going prematurely white—he wasn't much more than thirty—and that, combined with his stodgy bedside manner and the medicinal smell he gave off, made him seem almost as old as his patients.

"Can't you keep him for a while?" Mom said.

Dr. Joe laughed. There were people waiting for the bed, sick people, he said. He had no right to mislead an adult patient about his true condition. Besides, Dad would kill him if he ever found out.

"If he keeps drinking the way he has been," Mom said, "he won't live long enough to kill you."

Dr. Joe puffed out his lips and clasped his hands, tapping his thumbs together.

"You know how he is about spending money," Mom continued. "This house thing has got him rattled so; I've never seen him like this. If you could just keep him for a week, we could buy something and it would be over."

Dr. Joe pondered. "He really shouldn't be drinking with his EKG," he said.

"He smokes two packs a day," Mom said.

"More like three," I offered.

Dr. Joe nodded and said that maybe keeping Dad for a week's detox wouldn't be such a bad idea. He was amazed that the old man survived the things he put his body through, he said. Maybe a week in the hospital would put the fear of God into him.

Mom said she thought that was a great idea.

When we got back to his room, Dad was offering his pathetic smile to a nurse, who was shaking her head and saying no, no, no. "¿Por favor?" Dad said, holding up a finger and speaking in a voice full of mock anguish. "Solamente uno, solamente uno."

"Eres un hombre muy malo, Señor Sinclair," the nurse said, shaking her finger back at him. "Tu sabes aquí no se puede fumar."

He was begging for a cigarette.

With Dad in the hospital, house-hunting became much more efficient. Instead of touring every house at length (Dad thought that saying no at first glance would insult the agent), Mom took a quick walk through and said it would never do. In this way we got through three or four houses in a morning. During the afternoons I would visit Dad and tell him about the day. Though he would never admit it, the old man seemed relieved to be out of the picture. Most of the time when I came in, he was flirting with a nurse, playing the pitiful invalid to cadge a cigarette or a smile. The nurses seemed to get a big kick out of him; the lecture Dr. Joe had apparently given him had worked, giving him an apologetic, sheepish quality that made him, I had to admit, pretty damn lovable.

I learned not to dwell on the specifics of a house; some detail was sure to set Dad off. I tried to stay vague and bright. When things got tense, I diverted the subject to my latest scheme for making money: I was thinking of importing fire agates to the States with the help of a Mexican kid I had met at the tennis club. Dad was always pleased when I showed signs of entrepreneurial enthusiasm. But he seemed happiest of all when I told him I didn't like any of the houses we'd seen that day, as if that were a sign of our toughness as buyers. He was very concerned that we were not tough buyers.

Mostly we played chess. Once or twice I beat him, and Dad praised my playing. "You're a natural player," he said. But he added immediately that I was too hasty, too impatient, and the unhappy speculations these criticisms raised about my future turned him dark for the day.

Once, he told me I was growing up "to be a fine young man," which left me in shock.

Four days after Dad entered the hospital, the real-estate agent told us that another house had become available in Rancho Contento. It was an emergency sale, solidly below the market price, and another buyer was already interested. We drove right out. It was the Pink House. Mom loved it at first sight—the gazebo and cactus garden out front, the faded pink paint a perfect pastel against the white wrought-iron bars on the windows, the sun-room that doubled as an entrance, the arched brick ceilings (also white), the red-tile floors, the flagstone back porch with its awning heavy with vines, the narrow staircase to the roof choked with bougainvillaea, the swimming pool with inlaid angelfish winking from the bottom, bubbles of white tile rising from their mouths. It was a lovely place, a true oasis, abstracted by high white walls from the dust and tumult of Mexico.

"It's lovely," Mom said. The agent watched us with a knowing smile.

Without showing any particular enthusiasm (she was canny in that way), Mom asked the agent about price and closing costs and so on. It was selling for around eighty thousand, which was at least ten and probably fifteen thousand dollars below the going price for that much house in that neighborhood.

As we drove away, Mom asked me what I thought.

"It's nice," I said.

"Did you see the kitchen?"

"Lots of space."

"The yard?"

"Dad'll freak about that pool."

Mom gave her head a little impatient shake and actually said *pooh*. She nodded her head several times and gripped the steering wheel. "I'm going to make an offer," she said very firmly.

A few days later we were ready. Back at the hospital, I went in to talk to Dad first—the shock troops in Mom's battle plan. "Build it up," she had told me. And I did. "It's really beautiful, Dad," I said. "It's like the perfect house."

"You say it's pink?" Dad asked, frowning.

"Yeah. You can paint it if you don't like it."

He seemed very skeptical. " 'Yeh,' " he repeated, mocking my diction in a blatant attempt to stall for time.

"You're focusing on the negative," I said. "You can paint a Goddamn house. The point is, Mom's in love with it, and it's really a great house. It's everything you wanted. It's even cheap."

"I wouldn't call eighty thousand dollars cheap."

Patience, I told myself. "You'd pay twice that in Chapultapec," I said.

Dad shook his head, dubious about my statement and the general state of the world.

"But the Rancho," Dad said. "I really don't think your mother will like being so remote."

"Dad! She loves it! She's the one who wants to move there! And you're the one who wants to save money! It's perfect! You're driving me crazy!"

Dad continued to shake his head. "I don't know."

"Dad! You haven't even seen it!"

Calm down, I told myself. This is not productive. Dad lifted his hand to his mouth and laid his fingers against his lips.

"It's hard for me to think," he said, indicating with a slight wave the absent cigarette.

"Blackmailer," I said.

He smiled.

Mom and Dr. Joe were waiting out in the hall. Mom gave me a questioning look. I shrugged. "He wants a cigarette."

"The condemned man," Mom answered wryly, unsnapping her purse and pulling out her pack. Dr. Joe shook his head and said he couldn't approve of this at all, but he seemed amused. We all trooped into the room, me in front holding the cigarette forward like a white flag. Dad snatched it as soon as I got within range. He examined it. "I shouldn't smoke this," he said.

He wasn't talking about health. Mom had given me one of her American cigarettes, which cost twice as much as the local brands. Dad was offended by the lapse in his sterling record of self-denial. But he lit it anyway and leaned back in his pillows, inhaling deeply and gratefully.

"A pink house," he said, shaking his head at the world's infinite peculiarity.

Mom pulled a chair up to the bed and sat down, all business. She'd been hard at work since finding the house, and already the offer had been accepted and the purchase contract had been vetted by our lawyer. It was now in an envelope in the purse on her lap, waiting for Dad's signature.

"A pink house," Dad repeated. "It sounds like something for a chorus girl."

Mom made the *pooh* sound.

"I'll tell you right now," he continued, taking another deep drag on his cigarette. "I will not live in a pink house. I will never live in a pink house."

We returned the next day with Frankie. "Look at the fabulous invalid," Frankie said as he swept into the room. "I hear you're flirting shamelessly with all the nurses."

"Oh, no, not me," Dad said, too heartily. "I'm too damned old."

He didn't look well. His toes, however, poking from the bottom of the sheet so that the infection would get air, had gone back to nearly a normal color.

"You look like hell," Frankie said. Dad chuckled weakly, and Frankie leaned over the bed and pulled something out of his pocket. I saw the flash of glass. "Don't abuse it," Frankie said. It was a half pint of vodka. Dad looked puzzled at first, and then smiled with touching gratitude.

"So, have you heard about your gorgeous new house?"

Dad pushed the bottle under the covers and reached for his bedside glass. "Can you empty this for me?" he said. As I headed for the bathroom, Dad turned to Frankie and answered, "I don't know about that."

"I saw it this morning," Frankie said. "It is really, truly a beautiful place—you will absolutely love it. The yard! The garden! And I'm telling you, as an investment you couldn't do better. You know they're expanding the shopping center and building a whole new development between Oblatos and the turnoff —that whole part of town is coming up faster than downtown Dallas."

"Margaret didn't tell me about a development," Dad said, taking the empty glass I held out. He clamped it between his legs, unscrewed the vodka top, and poured out a fist of booze.

"Well," Frankie said, his tone forgiving. "She's just in love with that house."

"What about the neighborhood?" Dad asked, taking a grateful first sip.

I slipped out and went to the office, where Mom sat gossiping with Dr. Joe. "How're they doing?" Mom asked.

I shrugged. "He's listening."

Mom shook her head, a gesture at once understanding and a little bitter. She knew exactly what I meant. Dad would give Frankie the respectful attention he could never give a member of his own family.

It took a few more days. Dr. Joe helped too, painting the house as an oasis where Dad could finally find the peace to reform. In the end Dad was ready to sign the papers. Dr. Joe and Frankie were there to give last-minute support. Mom handed Dad a pen.

"I need a cigarette," he said.

"Richard . . . ," Dr. Joe scolded.

"For God's sake," Dad said. "It's a huge amount of money."

"Oh, give the poor man a cigarette," Frankie said. Mom opened her pack and handed Dad a cigarette.

"Two," Dad said.

She gave him two.

The next day I went to pick Dad up. Dr. Joe was finally releasing him. I wondered if Dad knew that the whole hospital stay was just a vicious conspiracy by his family and friends to force him into buying a house he really didn't want to buy. He seemed frail as he walked to the car, bent from the week in bed. He shuffled; maybe his feet still hurt him. His head hung. I could see his gray hair clumped against his neck, which seemed as rough as elephant skin. It made me feel tender and sad. I opened the car door and held back a branch so that the old man could squeeze into the shotgun seat. It took a few long moments.

"Let's go visit the house on the way," I suggested. "Have a look at what you bought."

"Oh, no, son," Dad said. "I don't . . ."

"Come on, Dad," I pleaded. I wanted to be there with him, see the pink house through his eyes. I wanted him to like it and be happy. "Mom gave me the key."

He said okay. We didn't talk much as we drove out to the Rancho. Finally I pulled the car up outside the wall and helped Dad to the gate. I unlocked it and pushed it open and stood back. "Ta da," I said.

For a moment he just stood there, looking through the gate at the faded pink house. His face showed no reaction, but his eyes were hooded and a bit sad. There was a little foreboding in them, a little anxiety. In the flame tree that rose above the gazebo to the left, a bird trilled a long series of notes. The tree was in flower, and Dad, looking up in the direction of the bird, let his eyes linger on the bright orange blooms. Then he looked back at the house where he would live until he died. He sighed once and began walking toward it, moving past me without a word, composed and ready to inspect his fate.

Diane Levenberg

A MODERN LOVE STORY

It is the summer of '75, and I am fed up with loving a married man—brilliant young novelist though he is. Adele decides to offer me her version of the "talking cure"—the story I had longed to hear of her famous sister's renunciation of love.

Adele lived not far from me in Greenwich Village, was married to a struggling writer who divided his time between poems and editing a fledgling literary magazine, and had set up house in what was to be a charming railroad flat on Barrow Street. I thought that narrow winding street, that apartment with its huge windows facing the tree shaded street below was just the place for a passionate bearded poet with his papers and books strewn all over the middle room's bare pine floor. She hoped someday to do something more than serve as editorial secretary at the *Jewish Daily Forward* and sometimes seemed weary of her Bohemian marriage. Never one to complain, she had engaging stories to tell—of eager Yiddish poets and displaced critics rushing up to her office with a courtly air handing her their weekly wares.

Married to a man who loved to recite his latest masterpiece, Adele, friend of all of us trying to publish our poems and our stories, editor and translator, was then helpmeet to the word. To her, listening was an active act, and she paid "passionate atten-

tion"—to our stories of rejected manuscripts, delayed and un-
cashable checks, and unrequited love.

I was flattered when one cool Sunday afternoon, after serving
both of us Turkish coffee (mixed with just a hint of hazelnut) in
her sunny living room, she settled herself in the oak rocking
chair brought from her parents' home in Baltimore. In that
graceful meticulous way she had, she smoothed the green and
blue throw across her lap and began her sister's tale of passionate adoring love which had erupted the summer before.

You know my sister only from occasionally reading her articles.
And once or twice I think you've heard her speak? Yes? So it
would be hard for you, for anyone, to know how intensely self-
conscious she is. How painfully shy. Who knows what brought
that on? She used to be so lively, so vivacious, until she was
about ten and I was twelve, yes, I remember because I was pir-
ouetting before the mirror in my bat mitzvah dress. She
watched me wistfully and assured me she would never look as
pretty in that dress.

My narcissistic dance was halted. I turned away, embarrassed
because the sister I adored was now stepping aside and I wasn't
ready to accept the responsibility of protecting her. Yes, I knew
even then she would need protection because, though I never
understood it, I knew her pride had been broken. And I don't
think it returned until years later when . . . but wait, here I am
getting ahead of myself. Let me tell the story in its correct order.

She came to New York to study at the Jewish Theological
Seminary. At that time, there was no chance that they would
ever ordain women rabbis, but they had read her essays, they
were indebted to her for the work she had done editing the
papers of their founder's wife, and, as they interviewed her, I
believe they saw something special. She has a passion for scholarship, my sister. And an uncanny energy. She sleeps only
about five hours a night and can work long hours. Without hesitation, they accepted her as a special student.

She returned to Baltimore to pack her meager belongings—a
few dresses, some records—she used to say she couldn't live
without the optimism of Mozart—and her books. Not knowing

yet where she would live, she put most of them in storage but I remember how she described what would become the basis of her New York library—the newly translated Bible, a set of Proust, Thomas Mann's *The Magic Mountain*, a volume of Heine, a biography of Herzl, and *The Woman's Room*, a novel she didn't like but to which she felt, "uncommonly drawn." How had she decided to come to New York? Hmmm. Yes, now I remember.

Mama had come to Papa's study to find her asleep at his desk. My sister had tried once again to edit his papers, but like many young women of her generation, though she had studied Bible, Hebrew literature and the Code of Jewish Law she had never formally studied the Talmud. What did "taku" mean? Or "hakhi dami"? My father had written almost an entire book on his understanding of *Ketubot*—a tractate of the Talmud dealing with, among other things, the marriage contract. She had neither the skills nor the required knowledge to translate and organize his chapters. Moreover, whenever she began to open his yellowing notebooks, a wellspring of grief would invariably open in her.

Tired and distracted, she missed Papa. She longed for a man in her life; she was sorry to be alone and unmarried. Mama brushed back a few stray wisps of hair—her unfashionably long hair which each morning, in a hundred strokes, my sister, in her one homage to vanity, brushed to a silky shine. Appreciating this comforting gesture, my sister opened her eyes.

"Have some tea," offered Mama.

"I need more than that," complained my sister.

"I have an idea. Why don't you apply to the Jewish Theological Seminary as a special student? They haven't as yet ordained any women rabbis, but how could they refuse to let you audit some Talmud classes? Then, you will feel more competent working on Papa's book."

I think Mama cared more about a possible husband for my sister than she did about Papa's manuscript. And for once, she was sensitive enough to approach my sister through her brain. It worked. They spent the summer closing down the old house in Baltimore, and by the end of September, she was living on

102 Street—two subway stops, or a quick busride to the Seminary. Mama moved in with us, here in the Village and quickly became the president of her Hadassah chapter which entailed frequent visits uptown to the national office. My sister had her studies, more books to edit—my husband Toby was then working as an editor at Schocken and found my sister work. Things were thus peaceful and purposeful—for a while.

In the Seminary Reading Room, transformed now into a synagogue, with its geometric patterned ceiling and leaded glass windows filtering the light, my sister found true sanctuary. For a moment she imagined pulling down one of the cookie cutter shapes from the ceiling. She would bake her cookies to resemble star shaped coins—in the center of each she outlined the head of a man to whom she had dared not yet speak.

She giggled softly to herself. It had been a long time since she had felt so light and free. It was Rosh Hashonah, and caught as she was by how the light played on the books lining the room, she felt a surge of hope. Yes, finally, after the sweaty heat of her burdensome move, she was feeling sexually alive. What should she ask for in this new year, in a new city, with challenging tasks to fill her days? She looked out the open window to catch sight of the foliage in the courtyard. The branches decked out in their finest golds and ambers seemed, also, as they beckoned and retreated to be praying. For what did she want to pray? When she turned back to her siddur, Mama's comforting hand on her arm reminded her.

She had seen him once in the library preparing for his class. As she approached the reading table, he stared straight at her, but then, bringing his glasses from the top of his head he continued to write. It was all the moment she needed to see that he had the most extraordinary blue eyes. Every time she tried to enter his Talmud class, she saw those eyes again and retreated. In the cafeteria, she heard his students talking. He was brilliant and sarcastic. He was intimidating and humbling. Frequently, his cynical retorts embarrassed them. Yet, they loved him. It was rumored that he had been hired because the Seminary's former chancellor, Rabbi Louis Finkelstein, believed that under his guidance, the young Russian immigrant would grow to become the world's greatest scholar.

"Today," said the young rabbinical student, "he raised his infamous eyebrow, and hooked his thumbs into his vest pockets." The student assumed an exaggerated posture, and imitating a Russian accent, continued. "If you could run the bath water for Rabbi Akiva's most illiterate student you might be more constructive than you are now, yes?"

"Who knows? There may be some truth to that," said his friend.

"You think so? That's why I left the Ashram and came here. I never could quite accept it that washing dishes was as holy as studying sacred texts. But that's what's so appealing about him —he seems to know some secret of the universe that we are still too stupid to grasp. So I forgive his sarcasm and return to his class—almost like, well, like a chastised lover."

His friend blushed. "Yes, I know what you mean. We are all afraid of him and yet when I sit in his class I seem suddenly to become aware of my own soul."

My sister cleared her dishes onto her tray. So, she thought, even the boys are fatally attracted. She would need daily contact with him to become adjusted to his imperious manner. She would want to see him human, and flawed, and to know that despite his brilliance in regard to Talmudic matters, in the ways of the world he was still an innocent. She prayed that second day of Rosh Hashonah that the next time he cast his blue eyes upon her he might really see her.

The rest of the month she suffered from a raging flu which kept her in bed and away from the synagogue on Shabbat. Rabbis Eskolsky and Mintz called at the apartment to ask how she was and to inquire whether the American poetry class she had been informally offering would be held that evening. I was there, with Mama, visiting, reading aloud to her from a new Borges collection, and I was surprised that she consented to teach them. They enjoyed the poetry—a subject new and foreign to them, and were beginning to incorporate lines from Wallace

Stevens and D. H. Lawrence into the sermons they were delivering at the Seminary synagogue and elsewhere.

I stayed on to participate in the discussion. She stiffened beside me when, without warning he too appeared. She had Mama offer them some tea and then fled with me into the bedroom. Her hands were shaking as she tried to brush her hair. "I'm a mess," she wailed. "I didn't dress—just this old robe." This from my sister who never once had I heard mention a word about her wardrobe.

Perhaps I understood sooner than she did but I kept my own counsel. My sister had had suitors—yes, she even had been engaged twice. And, though we never shared such intimacies, I'm sure there were others with whom she had had romances. But I had never heard her speak of them. I had met only two men in her life—each time at my home, for dinner, when it seemed clear to her that she might marry. I cooked my kosher version of chicken kiev for each of them, but knew that nothing would come of it. They were, how shall I say it—inappropriate. One hopelessly pedantic, repeatedly pressing his pencil point down to emphasize his point, the other too naïve, preparing to set up a newspaper commune in Soho. No, these were not men for my sister.

She stumbled through the class, her voice shaking, her hands sweating. Fortunately, these are, in addition to the signs of love, also the symptoms of the flu from which my sister was suffering. They offered their condolences and as though to repay the energy she was expending, offered her their insights to which the poems had opened them. He was silent throughout; then he offered her his gift from which she never quite recovered. In his mellifluous voice, with his unforgettable Russian accent, he leaned back, closed his eyes, and recited from memory one of her favorite poems—*Peter Quince at the Clavier*. We were all silent, and for a second I believe her breathing stopped. She wiped her brow, and then to protect her I insisted they leave and let her retire.

"So now you know," she said. "You saw for yourself."

"Yes," I replied to save her the indignity of further revelation. He had shown no sign of feeling for her and my sister was not one cut out for unrequited love. Later that week, when he met her outside the Seminary cafeteria, he asked whether she would be good enough to edit a paper he was preparing for a scholarly journal. She had no time to think. "By the way," he said, his eyebrow arched to its full height, "I haven't seen you in my Talmud class yet. Aren't you enrolled?"

"Yes," she mumbled. "Good. Then here's the manuscript. My deadline is two weeks from now. I will call you." And he handed her his paper. Just like that. With stains on it from the blintzes and sour cream he had been eating for lunch.

She read his paper and wondered why he had to look for his material among the writings of the church fathers but he hadn't asked her to criticize. Merely to edit. And she pleased him with the result.

"You've worked diligently on this," he said approvingly. "Look, how about some entertainment now. Brodsky is here from Russia. He's reading tonight at New York University. Would you join me?"

She nodded.

"I'll pick you up at seven, all right?"

Is it her imagination or as the subway lurched past 72nd Street, did his arm really brush hers? Did he lean closer than he had to? She wished that first they might have eaten together. Or ridden down in a cab. Anything to be able to talk to him, just as one person to another.

He kept his eyes closed throughout the entire reading. Afterward he left her standing to one side while he went up to shake Brodsky's hand. They seemed to be old friends. "Would you like to come to a party?" he asked her. "Susan Sontag has invited some of Brodsky's friends to her place. Just some crackers and cheese, some wine. And perhaps some good talk. Though I never expect much from these post-reading affairs. But who knows? Maybe Brodsky can be asked to read another poem. Will you come?"

This time they shared a cab with four others. He said little, sitting in the front, too preoccupied to turn around and say more than a few words. Once though, he recited from memory a poem he wished Brodsky might have read.

At the party, held in a large apartment on West End Avenue, Susan Sontag, drink in hand, was holding court discussing Walter Benjamin's suicide.

"Hello," she said, moving away from the circle of listeners, "I'm so glad you could come. I read your last piece on Jewish role models. Very interesting. I quite agreed with you—they have to be rediscovered, if not reinvented."

My sister was stunned. Her article had appeared in a literary magazine with a circle of perhaps 500. "It's true," she said, when she returned home that night, "Susan Sontag reads everything."

Was it also true that he wanted to see my sister as often as possible? His articles increased in frequency and number. He would appear at her door at least once a week to pick something up, to deliver another section of a chapter. Then she would make tea, they would discuss a recent novel, a favorite poem, the morning's headlines, or, if it were a Friday, he might offer her his interpretation of that week's Torah reading. Finally, one afternoon, his hand closed over hers as she offered him his tea. In delirious thanks, she invited him for Shabbat dinner. He accepted.

She actually, crazed woman that my sister had become, counted the minutes until he would arrive. He didn't disappoint her. He brought flowers. A poem to recite. In his soft, lilting voice he recited the kiddush and she pictured him standing there, week after week, in the years to come, her soulmate.

They sat on the couch, after dinner, and suddenly, when she rose to find him a book he wanted to see, he took her hand, stood up, and kissed her softly on the mouth. As though something were settled between them, he sat down again pulling her down next to him. He continued to hold her hand, leaned back, closed his eyes, and said nothing more for the next hour. My sister was afraid to break the spell. Besides, as far as she knew, she had died and gone to heaven.

He rose to leave. "Tomorrow," he said, "I will call for you at nine. We will go together to the synagogue. Yes."

"Yes," said my sister, and yes again, many times in the months that followed. He was an old fashioned suitor. He took her to concerts, plays, good restaurants. He had left the waste-land of Russia for the cornucopia of America and he wanted her to share it. But his heart? Did he also want to share that? She was never quite sure. It was an intellectual courtship. His passion was reserved for his scholarship. They held hands, he kissed her hello, goodbye, but no more. And she, despite her own burgeoning sexuality, was content. They had an understanding.

He didn't fail her. Five months later, on an evening walk along Riverside Drive, he said, "We're compatible, yes. We are, how do my students say it, on the same wave length. It would be nice to live together. To be married, yes?"

Yes, of course yes. She had never learned yet how to say no to him. I, of course, wasn't so sure. What did marriage mean to him? Separate bedrooms? He had never more than kissed her. Unlike my sister, I don't find transcendence in social intercourse.

She, however, thought she had discovered a new world where happiness meant a pair of blue eyes looking tenderly down upon her face, or at a manuscript she had just edited. Her own writing and my father's papers remained in a drawer.

I invited them to dinner, to celebrate their engagement. He came into the kitchen, watching me cook, a pleased smile across his face. "That's what I like to see," he said. "A woman preparing dinner. It is so comforting, yes?"

"Yes. It's nice when men cook too. My husband Toby finds it relaxing, after a day deliberating over someone's scrawled notes, to chop peppers, slice mushrooms. He's become quite an accomplished chef."

"Yes? I cannot understand that. I prefer my study. Or my woman to cook. This new American feminism. I am not sure I understand it. It is a puzzle, yes. We take the risks in the world. A home, children, the exercise of loving kindness—these are the domain of women, yes?"

"No," I said. "They are equally the domain of men. And women have as much right to choose love at home or assume the challenge of the risks in the outside world. As much as it is yours, it is their right to choose."

"To choose? Who asked me to become a scholar? I somehow think that for women their most important choice concerns the appropriate man to marry. They have to think of the children they will bear. Shaw was right. It is in this way, in this exercise of choice, that women really rule the world."

"And what if there is no man to marry?" my sister asked quietly. She had been standing at the kitchen door.

"Come, sit down," bellowed Toby. "Dinner is ready."

So I never heard his answer. Whether or not they discussed it, I never knew. A month later, Toby had a heart attack, and two months later he had to leave Schocken. He needed a rest and a less pressured job. They asked my sister to become the senior editor. The rest, as they say, is history.

"You mean, that her scholar left and married someone else?"

"Yes. But only after she told him that she wanted something more out of life than cooking his meals, three a day because he came home for lunch, and editing his lectures. Suddenly her pride returned. She told him no. She would write her own essays, and be paid for her editing. He stormed out angrily, took a leave from the Seminary, went to Israel, and a few months later married Anne. A friend of mine was once invited to their home for dinner. His new wife lovingly wiped the crumbs from his beard and polished each fleischig tablespoon until her smiling face was mirrored there."

"I know my sister has a brilliant career. Ironically, when he returned and brought his book to Schocken, it was she who had to edit it. But if you ask me, he edited her life. She will never marry anyone else. She lives not far from here, talking to the flowers in her garden, reading poetry for comfort before she goes to sleep, alone."

Two years after our talk, Adele and her husband were suddenly killed in a car crash. Adele never knew that in 1978 her sister became the founder of the Jewish Womens' Organization. She never saw her sister off to Israel to become Israel's first woman minister of Arab Affairs. We read in the American press how she is constantly working to achieve a lasting peace between Israelis and Arabs—those with whom Israel is at war and those who wish to become its citizens.

As my phone rings at the appointed hour (my lover, though faithless, is prompt) I think of her, living alone in Jerusalem, in her small stone house, talking to the flowers in her garden. It is midnight there now and I see her, writing in her journal, composing her poems. I think of what it took for her to push aside her love and find her purpose. Thanks to her, there may be peace one day in Israel. But as Adele predicted, won't her stalwart heart always be at war?

After all these years, I let the receiver rest in its cradle.

John Van Kirk

NEWARK JOB

> "Where are we going, Dad?"
> —Ernest Hemingway, "Indian Camp"

Young Henry Bowman woke instantly at the touch of his father's hand on his shoulder. It was not yet light.

"Still want to go, son?"

"Yeah, Dad, yeah," he answered quietly, careful not to wake his brothers, who slept a few feet away. "What time is it?"

"About six thirty," his father said, "plenty of time."

The boy climbed down silently from his upper bunk, and put on the clothes he had set out the night before. In the bathroom, he washed his face while the man shaved—the washrag and safety razor alternately passing through the stream of steaming water—and he combed his hair in the lower part of the mirror while the man was wiping away the last traces of shaving cream in the upper. Black whiskers swirled down the drain. The boy carried his hiking boots downstairs to the kitchen where the kettle was already whistling, made instant coffee and toast for his father, and fixed himself some tea and a bowl of cereal. He was lacing up his boots when his father came in. "You know you don't have to go if you don't want to, son," the man said. "We're gonna be gone all day."

"No, Dad, I want to go."

After they ate, they went down into the cellar where the tools and fittings were arranged in black buckets. The man quickly selected what he figured he would need, and the boy started

Reprinted by permission from *The Hudson Review*, Vol. XLIV, No. 4 (Winter 1992). Copyright © 1991 by John Van Kirk.

carrying the buckets out to the car. The sun was a low, pale glow in a cold, grey sky. Nobody else was out. Some trucks went by on the street at the top of the hill, but that was all. The man carried out the big bottle of gas, cradling it in his arms like a papoose as he laid it gently on its side in the back of the old Ford station wagon. "Two more buckets and we're on our way," he said. When the loading was finished the boy had to get into the car on the driver's side, because both doors on the other side had been wired up with coat-hanger wire and a broom handle after the locks broke. The man turned on the radio as he started the car. He backed carefully down the steep driveway and headed up the hill.

They got to Sarge's Plumbing Supply at about ten after eight. A black boy about Hank's age was washing the windows of the storefront with a long-handled squeegee. Sarge was sitting on a high stool behind the counter with a stained coffee cup in front of him. He was smoking a fat, soggy cigar; and when he put it into his mouth his lips—normally thin as a British major's— would unfold around it, thick and shiny as the lips of a cartoon Ubangi. Behind him was a color picture of a yellow-haired woman kneeling in the center of an arrangement of chrome plated plumbing fixtures: faucets and taps, showerheads, traps and drains. . . . Her breasts were clearly visible through her sheer yellow nightgown. The white paper calendar that was stapled to the picture said: October 1965.

The hot water heater wasn't there yet.

"If that slumlord you're workin' for would shell out for a quality product I'd of had one waitin' for ya," Sarge said to Henry's father. "Hell, I got two Westinghouses out back now and a General Electric on the floor. But this other company . . . you can't hardly depend on 'em, you know? I don't like to deal with 'em."

"I know. I don't like it any more than you do; but work is where you find it. And when you don't have a license. . . ."

"Yeah, I guess so, but. . . . You know I never figured you for this kind of work anyway, you should a been a doctor or somethin'." Sarge looked over at Hank. "You know your ol' man was the best medic I ever seen, he saved a Jap's life when we were over there after the war. He ever tell you that?"

Hank looked at his father.

His father was silent for a moment, looking at nothing; then he looked back at Sarge. "When you expect it to get here?" he asked flatly.

"They were supposed to have it here first thing this morning," Sarge said, rolling the cigar around in his mouth; "but it's a shine outfit, ain't no tellin' when they'll show up."

They waited. The man had a coffee, and he bought the boy a bottle of Coke from the red machine. The heater arrived about twenty minutes later. The driver and his helper put the long box into the back of the old station wagon. They wedged a hand truck borrowed from Sarge in on top of it. Henry slipped into the car through the right-hand window, which he had left open. The man made a wide U-turn in front of the store and snapped off a farewell salute to Sarge, who was now out on the sidewalk inspecting the windows. A tall, loose-jointed black man wearing a bright pink shirt, brown leather jacket, and wide-brimmed purple hat was crossing the street. "Hey, dark cloud," the man called out to him, gunning the motor and accelerating away.

They stopped to eat in a diner converted from an old railroad car. "I know it's early for lunch," the man said, "but I don't like to knock off once we start, and where we're going there's no place fit to eat nearby." The waitress called the man "Honey," and smiled at him like she knew him. They ordered Taylor Ham and egg sandwiches on hard rolls.

"Did you really save a man's life?" the boy asked while they ate.

"I guess so," his father answered, "but that was a long time ago."

The boy waited for the man to say more, but the man just ate in silence. Finally he spoke: "When we get there I want you to watch where you sit down," he said. "Your mom'll kill us both if you bring home any bugs. If you want anything more, you'd better get it now; we probably won't eat again till dinner." The boy had a piece of apple pie and a coffee light with sugar. He felt like a real working man and swaggered confidently on the way out.

"What are they like?" the boy asked as they drove.

"Who?"

"These people, where we're going."

"They're good people," the man said. "Mrs. Williams is kind of like a real life Aunt Jemima, big colored woman with a pack of kids. And she'd do anything for 'em, her kids I mean, or whosever's kids they are. I think they're her grandchildren mostly; she has a couple of daughters who are there sometimes; the little ones are probably theirs. Billy's her boy though. He's a good boy, good-looking too, real light, almost olive, about as good-looking a colored boy as I've ever seen. And his sisters are black as coal."

Hank tried to fit the color olive to a person, but he couldn't.

They entered a bleak neighborhood of vacant lots and boarded-up storefronts; newspapers blew in the cold wind. From the backs of some of the buildings brightly colored laundry flapped between steeply tilting grey wooden porches. In one of the lots some men stood huddled around a burning oil drum, their faces as black as the huge burnt sheets of paper ash that floated up from the barrel on shimmering waves of heat.

It was almost eleven by the time they pulled up in front of the sad-looking brick building where the job was. A few curled flakes of white lead clung to the dry grey wood of the doorway and window frames. The mortar between the bricks was crumbling away, and some of the corner bricks had already fallen out and lay broken in the grey dirt of the yard.

"This Mr. Hallinan's building?" the boy asked.

"Just about all the buildings on this block are Hallinan's," the man answered.

"But they're all so . . . I mean . . . they look like they're ready to fall down."

"Well, son, Hallinan is what you'd call a little tight, and I guess he doesn't want to put any more money into these places than he has to."

"But how can you work for a guy like that?"

"See those shoes you're wearing? You think they grow on trees?"

The man had keys, and he opened the main door and undid a heavy padlock that hung from a rusty hasp on a door off the entryway. This door led to the basement, and when it was opened a smell of dry mold and wet ashes flooded the landing, and the boy heard a rustling sound, like squirrels scrabbling up a tree. "Go get some of those bricks outside and prop open the doors, son, while I get us some light and clear the path for the heater." The boy did as he was told. Then, while the man rigged up a caged utility light with a long extension cord, the boy carried the buckets of tools down into the cellar. He didn't mind the cellar so much, his father there with him; but going out to the car alone—though it was only a short walk across the narrow yard—frightened him a little. He saw no one, yet he felt exposed out there, like a soldier behind enemy lines. His working man's swagger fled him and he felt small and vulnerable.

The man went out for the big torch, and then the two of them working together loaded the hot water heater onto Sarge's hand truck.

"Atta boy," the man said as they eased the rig down the worn and irregular stairs. "Careful there . . . easy does it . . . oookay, that's got her. . . . Yer gettin' stronger, Henry; I don't think I could'a done that part without you."

The boy swelled a little at this. "No sweat, Dad," he said.

They uncrated the big white heater, jockeyed it into position on a small concrete platform sunk into the dirt floor, and set to work. This was the part that the boy liked most. He set out the valves, the tees, and the elbows on a piece of newspaper; he cleaned up the connecting parts with steel wool until they shined, and he brushed the flux onto them when the man was ready. He had learned this while working with his father in his own house and on other jobs back in the suburbs; he had had to work hard to become good at it and to convince the man to take him on a Saturday job, a Newark job. Now the man even let him measure and cut some of the pieces of copper tubing. He measured them with the folding ruler, marked them with the stroke of a small triangular file, and then cut them with the tubing cutter, tightening it gradually as he rotated it around the tube until the circular blade broke through the pipe and the cut piece broke cleanly off. He then reamed out the newly cut part with the flat steel reamer on the back of the cutting tool until the inside edge was smooth and all the sharp copper slivers were scraped away. While he was doing this, the man lit a cigar and got the torch ready. When everything was neatly laid out, the man lit the torch from the end of the cigar and began to solder the pieces in place. Hank laughed when his father asked him, over the hissing roar of the torch, for a female tee. "The one there with the tits," he had said. Looking around while the man methodically sweated the solder into each joint, the boy could see where his father's work began and left off. Most of the pipes in the ceiling, aside from being old and crusted with rust and flaking paint, went every which way; but amidst all that confusion there were a few that ran straight and level, with square corners. Some had little white tags hanging from them to tell what they led to. That was what the cellar ceiling in Hank's own house looked like. But it was only now that Hank realized that not all plumbers worked this way. It made him feel proud of his father. Then the torch went off with a loud pop and sudden silence.

Now the man turned the faucet to let the heater fill with water while he hooked up the electricity. The boy looked at the wires that hung from the ceiling, their tips covered with red plastic screwcaps, ready to be connected.

"Did you run those wires, Dad?"

"About two weeks ago. We do it all, son." He smiled.

By the time the tank was filled, Hank's father had screwed the wires in, turned on the power at the fuse box on the other end of the basement, and switched on the heater. He then shut the water off that went to the Williamses' apartment.

"Time to go upstairs," he said.

Upstairs was like nowhere the boy had been before. The smell hit him first, not the same musty, pissy smell of the basement, but a new hot and smokey thick smell: the smell of burning lard and unaired crowded rooms. It poured out hot and stifling into the shabby landing when the door opened, and the boy swallowed hard and almost gagged on going in. But he got accustomed to it quickly, or forgot it, as the scene before him caught him up. His eyes roamed the place greedily, fascinated, taking it in from the floor to the ceiling, from the nearly vanished pattern of leaves and branches on the cracked and peeling linoleum spread like a carpet in the middle of the floor, to the visibly rotten boards that buckled beneath the feet of the rust-stained radiator hissing and steaming under the lone half-boarded window; from the stains like maps on the cracked grey walls, to the splintery slats of lath in the crumbling plaster ceiling. Dark laundry hung from a makeshift clothesline in one corner of the room, near the entry to what must have been the kitchen, and two small children slept on a narrow bed in another. In the center of the room was a hide-a-bed, extended, and a sleeping woman lay sprawled across it in a tattered slip. Her skin was as black as loam, and Hank wanted to look more because she was really almost naked and he had never seen a woman naked before except in pictures; but he felt embarrassed to be staring, and he had to look away. That was when he saw the trophies. One of the walls was covered with them; there must have been fifty or more, from small medallions and engraved plaques, to two-foot-high plinths and pedestals with Olympic-looking golden athletes on them.

"Those are mah boy Billy's," a soft voice drawled.

He looked to see who was talking to him. It was Mrs. Williams; it had to be. His father was right, she did look like Aunt Jemima, big and black and round and smiling. But in another way she didn't look like Aunt Jemima at all; that is, she didn't look like a cartoon, or a picture on a syrup bottle. She looked real, and there wasn't anything funny about her; and when he looked into her eyes, so dark they seemed black too, he smiled, liking her right away.

"We sure glad to see you, Mr. Bowman," she was saying to the man, "you know how long since we got hot water? Three weeks now. That Mr. Hallinan, he don't care 'bout us over here."

"I'm sorry, Mrs. Williams, but I work durin' the week at my

regular job, and every night this week I had to work on another job where they got no heat.''

"Oh, ah know you come soon as you could; ah don' mean to complain. You a nice man, Mr. Bowman; tell the truth, ah don't know how that Mr. Hallinan get you to work for him, but ah'm glad he do.'' She turned to Hank and then back to the man. "And this your boy?'' she said.

"Yes ma'am, that's my son Henry.''

"Well, he is a fine boy,'' she said, "so handsome.'' Hank felt himself begin to redden. Then she turned to him: "And your fahtha,'' she said, "he's a fine man; you take aftah him an' you be a fine man too, a gentleman.''

"Got the water turned off for a while,'' the man said. "Anybody needs to use the bathroom is gonna have to go over to a neighbor's.''

"Oh, that reminds me; Miz Walker next door axt me to ax you if you come today could you go by her place run that thing you got down her toilet; it's been stopped up three four days now.''

"Yeah, sure . . . okay. . . . Son, go on down to the car and get the snake and my black rubber gloves; we'll do that first.''

Mrs. Walker's apartment was so different from Mrs. Williams' that it was difficult at first to believe it was in the same building. It didn't seem newer, and there was nothing new in it, but everything was clean and shiny. It smelled of lemons. There were carpets—threadbare and faded, but there—on the floor; and there were a lot of framed photographs on the walls. All the people in the pictures were black, and most of them were dressed in formal clothes. Mrs. Walker looked formal too: she was thin, with grey hair, and she stood straight and stiff like a schoolteacher. "Thank you so much for coming over, Mr. Bowman,'' she said, with what sounded almost like an English accent.

The snaking job was slow work. While his father cranked the steel spring down the toilet, Hank stared out into the living room. Behind all of the neatly hung pictures were the same cracked and peeling walls as next door; under the carpet were the same buckling floorboards; but the furnishings were arranged as if it were a fine house. There were doilies on the chair backs and arms.

When the steel snake was pulled back up, the foul stench that came with it was so strong it burned Hank's eyes and he realized that his father's cigar was good for more than lighting torches.

Mrs. Walker offered them sodas when they were through.

"Thank you, ma'am," the man said, "we'd be glad for the drinks, but if you don't mind we'd like to take them with us to the job next door."

"Of course," she said, opening the bottles, "and thank you again, Mr. Bowman."

Again the nauseating smell and stifling heat struck Hank as he and his father went back into the other apartment, but after the snaking job it didn't seem nearly so bad as before. They quickly set to work. First they had to connect a new line under the kitchen sink; and as the man opened the cabinet a swarm of brown bugs scurried away. The boy jumped when he saw them. "Just cockroaches, son," the man said. "They won't hurt you, but watch where you set your jacket; we don't want to take any home." Hank folded his jacket carefully and set it on the newspaper with the joints and pieces of pipe, he then sat cross-legged on top of it, ready to hand his father the tools and fittings as he needed them.

A short while later one of the little boys who had been asleep on the bed wandered up behind Hank to see what was going on. The boy had blue eyes and was sucking his thumb. He rocked a little as he watched the man work, and he put his free hand on Hank's shoulder to steady himself. Hank turned to him and asked his name, but the little boy ran away without answering, and jumped up onto the fold-out bed, waking the woman in the slip. She looked sleepily over toward Hank and his father, and hurriedly covered herself with a blanket.

Next a new shower had to be installed. This was Hallinan's solution to the problem of old rusted-out bathtub faucets: cut the lines and run a new piece of pipe up to a cheap showerhead. It took longer than expected to hook up because of problems anchoring it, and Hank could see that his father was unhappy with the ugly metal straps he had to use to fix the pipe to the crumbling wall. The man showed the boy how the fittings were designed to go inside the wall. When it was all connected, the man went down into the basement again to turn the water back on. When he came up again, they tested the new work, and Hank listened to the water rattle up the empty pipes. The connections were good, and the hot water was hot.

Then they noticed that a pool of water was forming under the old tub, which stood on four short iron legs, and it turned out that a piece of the drain pipe had rusted away. Luckily the man had a replacement part in one of his buckets, but that took time too. When they were at last ready to repack the station wagon, it was already growing dark.

"Will the men be coming home soon?" Hank asked his father.

"Huh?"

"The men, they'll be coming home from work pretty soon, won't they?"

"I don't know, son, I've never seen any men here."

"But . . . the kids . . . I don't get it."

"These people have their own ways, son. Seems like the men don't stick around long . . . they just . . . I don't know . . . run off after a while."

"And the kids?"

"Don't worry about them, son, you worry about you."

Hank noticed that many of the streetlights were not working, including the one nearest the car. As he and his father were carrying the last buckets of tools and fittings, an old pink Buick with a continental kit came screeching around the corner and skidded to a stop in front of the building. Two black boys a few years older than Hank jumped out of the car, and Hank saw his father tense. The young men opened up the back door of the Buick and helped another one to climb out. They were practically carrying him. Then the car drove off as noisily as it had arrived.

"It's Billy," Hank's father said suddenly when the boys got to the bright area at the entrance to the building. They were just dragging the limp body along now, and Hank saw a puddle of what looked like motor oil form beneath its feet as they struggled with the door.

"Stay close to me, son," the man said. "That's Mrs. Williams' boy." The man ran over to the door and the boy followed. "Henry, you go up and clear the way, and tell Mrs. Williams we're coming. One of you boys watch over my tools out there."

"Sure, mister," one said, "he gonna be all right?"

"I don't know, son. I hope so."

The man moved quickly, and by the time Hank had cleared the way to the small bed in the corner of the main room, he was already coming through the door with the bleeding boy in his arms, the other boy now behind him. "Get the kids out of here," the man said. "Henry, get those clean diapers we saw in the bathroom. Mrs. Williams, you get a scissors and some clean towels. If you have any tape, get it. No, don't wet them, there isn't time. He's weak from loss of blood, but I can't see where it's all coming from. Get me some light over here; the blood don't show up like on us. Hank, you mop him with the diapers, tell me when you find a cut."

The man was working on the face, which had a deep gash that cut through one eye and laid the cheek open to the teeth below it. The lens of the cut eye looked like frosted glass and the split white was red. The boy couldn't believe that this was happening. He was watching his father tape the face closed with Scotch tape, which was all Mrs. Williams could find; the man was having difficulty making the tape stick to the black boy's clammy skin. Then Hank found a pool of blood that he couldn't seem to get mopped up. It was down by the crotch and he didn't want to touch it and he couldn't find anything but blood.

"Dad," he said, "there's something wrong down here."

"Let me see," the father said, with surprising calm. "Ah, okay, give me the scissors."

Hank could hear the mother crying while he watched his father cut away the trousers. The other boy was telling her that they had been just sittin' around against the car by the school when these guys they didn't know showed up and started something.

"And why you ain't cut, George Johnson, and mah boy all sliced to ribbons?"

"We tol' Billy to let it go, but they kep' callin' him Indian and high yellow and he couldn't take it and he went for 'em. I think he cut one of them too."

"Oh, mah lord," said Mrs. Williams.

It was a big hole, Hank could see now, as his father wiped up around it. How did the knife get up there practically to his balls? And his leg was like a piece of carved wood, not olive-colored at all, but chestnut, with muscles like a statue, but like an ax had bitten deep into the upper thigh. The life was pouring out of the boy fast. The man took a diaper and cut it with the scissors, then tore it into a long thin strip. This he twisted and then drew up into the boy's groin; he brought the other end around under the leg and then pulled it tight. He must have caught the pressure point just right because the flow of blood slowed even before he got the thing tied off.

"Mama, get the shower warmed up and bring me some towels or blankets into the bathroom," the man said, as he cut or tore away the remaining clothing. He then picked up the naked youth and carried him to the shower. "I got to wash him up to see where else he's cut; thank god they got hot water now." The black boy groaned and shivered as the man slid him into the tub and directed the shower over him. "You're gonna be all right, son. Don't talk. We're gonna get you all fixed up." The water splattered pink against the wall and swirled in a red whirlpool at the drain as the man, getting soaked himself, mopped the boy roughly with a towel. The dark limp body glistened wetly, the drainswirl fading from rose to runny watercolor red.

"Mama, get them blankets now. Looks like I got all the big cuts closed, but we got to get him to a hospital right away."

The man lifted the black boy, wrapped in blankets, onto his shoulder, fireman style, and carried him downstairs and out into the front seat of the car. He then had to clear some of the buckets out to put the seat up for Mrs. Williams and Hank. "You watch this stuff for me," he said to the other two boys on the sidewalk. Mrs. Williams was struggling helplessly with the back door on the right-hand side. "That door doesn't work, ma'am," Hank told her; and he led her gently around to the other side of the car. The man drove quickly and efficiently to the hospital; he did not squeal his tires, but he did go through two red lights, after stopping first to check for traffic. The hurt boy was silent now; he was not even moaning, and Hank was afraid that he might be dead. The fat old black lady, when she wasn't giving directions, was mumbling something over and over to herself. Hank decided that she was praying. Her face was shiny with tears.

At the hospital things did not go as quickly as the man seemed to think they should. The emergency room was not full, but there were a lot of people in it. The only white people there were Hank and his father and two harried looking attendants, who were busy having everyone fill out the complicated admittance forms.

"Can't you see there's no time for this?" the man said. "This boy is dying."

"Yeah, everybody comes in here is dying," said one of the attendants.

"Is he your boy, sir?" the other one asked.

"Of course he's not my boy, you . . . you can see that, but . . ."

"Then he's not your problem, is he? Now Mrs.? What's your name? You have to fill this . . ."

"Hey," the man shouted, "do you hear me? Just how stupid are you? Do you think I patched this boy up and brought him here and kept him alive this long just so you idiots could let him die? Where's the doctor? I wanna see the doctor. . . ."

"I'm sorry sir, but the doctor. . . ."

"Just what the hell is going on out here?" boomed a deep rounded voice. Everybody in the place was suddenly quiet. At the doors that led into the inner part of the hospital stood a distinguished looking black man with a grey moustache and a white lab coat.

"Are you the doctor?" the man asked.

The black man just looked at him.

"This boy is dying. He's been in a knife fight and I had to put a tourniquet on his leg and I think he's gonna lose an eye, but you got to look at the leg, it's an artery that's cut. . . ." The man pulled back the blankets.

The black boy did not look so chestnutty now as he had in the dim light of the apartment. Or maybe it was the blood that he had lost, because he looked grey now. Hank did not know what dead looked like, but he thought that the boy looked dead. The doctor picked up the boy's arm by the wrist and looked at his watch. Then he dropped the wrist and bent low over the boy's ruined face, laying two fingers aside his neck. "The tourniquet?" the deep voice asked gently. The man uncovered the boy's crotch. The doctor looked closely at the torn strip of towel and at the wound just below it. "How long since you put this on?"

"Twenty minutes, half hour," the man said.

"Get a gurney out here." The doctor's voice filled the room. "I want this boy in surgery immediately, get him typed and get some blood into him." Then he turned to the man and said softly, "They work very hard, sometimes they do not see what is in front of them." A black nurse appeared from within with the cart and with the help of the attendants lifted the wounded boy onto it and wheeled him away through two swinging doors. "You have probably saved this boy's life, friend," the doctor said to the man. "Now I must try to save his leg. As for the eye . . ." he shook his head sadly, "first the leg." The doctor turned and walked away through the swinging doors.

Then they waited. They made a strange trio, Hank thought, sitting there in the waiting room, the white man and the boy, both spattered with blood, and the big black woman, rocking silently. Mrs. Williams suggested that Hank and his father go on home, but the man said that he would not leave her there. He made a telephone call to Hank's mother to say that they'd be late. Almost two hours passed before the doctor came back out. He addressed himself to the woman. "Your boy's gonna live, Mrs. Williams," he said. He looked tired and somehow older than before.

"Praise the lord," Mrs. Williams said. "Can I see him?"

"Soon. He's gonna be out for a few hours, you can look in on him before you go. Right now I'd like to ask you a couple of questions."

"What, Doctor?"

"Are you in touch with the boy's father?"

Mrs. Williams' head dropped. "No sir, ah am not."

"Is there a man around who can talk to him? Someone he looks up to?"

"No, sir, they ain't no man around, an' we don't need one. Mah Billy is a good boy."

"I'm sure he is, ma'am. He was an athlete, I could see that; built like a quarter horse, it's probably what saved him; but it didn't keep this from happening did it? I get lots of boys in here cut up, but not athletes like your boy. He shouldn't be here. But he is. And he's been badly hurt. He's lost an eye, and it's going to be a long time before he walks without a cane. But that's done. I'm worried about what happens now. He's not going to be running any races for a long while, if ever. What's he going to do? Who's going to stop him from going for revenge?"

"But Doctor? You said he was going to be all right."

"I said he was going to live. He's not going to be like he was. His leg is in bad shape, there could be nerve damage, other complications. He'll need therapy. It's going to take time. And he's lost an eye."

"Can ah see him now?"

"Yes, but just for a minute. The nurse will take you in. Good-bye, Mrs. Williams. I probably won't see you again."

"But who's gonna see to mah boy?"

"The regular doctors here are very good. They are more up-to-date than I am. I just help out in the Emergency on weekends since I retired from my practice. He'll be well taken care of. But you remember what I said about when he gets out. Maybe you can get a teacher to talk to him. Or a coach. This can't be allowed to happen again. These kids butchering each other like Cowboys and Indians."

As they went deeper into the hospital, the antiseptic smell grew stronger. Billy was in a pale green room with an old black man. Both of them were asleep. One whole side of Billy's face was covered with bright white bandages; the other side was ash grey; the rest of him was covered by the sheets. He looked smaller than before. Some tubes went from a bottle at the top of a pole into a needle stuck in his left forearm. Mrs. Williams knelt beside the bed, touched her son's arm, and seemed to pray softly to herself. After a few minutes the nurse ushered them out again. "Come and see him in the morning," she said. "You'll be able to talk to him then."

Hank and his father drove Mrs. Williams home. As they pulled up to the building, they could see that the buckets of tools that had been left on the sidewalk were gone. The man said nothing. But going in they saw that all the tools had been brought into the entryway and Billy's two friends were leaning against them. Their flashy clothes were rumpled and bloody, and they looked as if they had been sleeping.

"Is he all right?" they asked, almost in unison.

"He's alive," the man said tiredly.

The black boys didn't say anything more, but after the man took Mrs. Williams up the stairs to her apartment, they helped carry the tools out to the car. The man thanked them and held out two dollar bills.

"Thanks for watching my tools," he said, "they're my . . . thanks."

They wouldn't take the money.

"You helped our friend, mister, you don't owe us nothin'," one said.

"Yeah," said the other, "we owes you."

As his father pulled the car away from the curb, Hank looked back at the building, and for a moment, in the dark, he caught a glimpse of it as something other than what it now was, a glimpse, perhaps, of what it had been years before, when the dirt yard had been a lawn, and the mortar between the bricks was hard and white, and the trim was shiny with fresh paint. He saw men with hats in antique cars coming to call on women in dresses. But then the image fled, and he saw the same grey, crumbling wreck of a tenement. The man tuned the radio to the soft music station. They passed the lot where Hank had seen the burning oil drum in the morning, and it was still there, but now the blaze lit up the night like a bonfire, sending sparks up into the black sky, and casting long dancing shadows of the dark men huddled around it. Not long after that they turned onto a brightly lit avenue, and Hank found himself breathing an almost audible sigh of relief to be out of the darkness. He soon fell asleep.

When he awoke, the car was pulling up the steep driveway. It took him a moment to shake his head clear, and after he slid across the seat and out, he leaned lightly on the side of the car and worked his way around to the back to unload the buckets.

"That's all right, son," the man said. "We'll leave 'em till morning. You go inside and get cleaned up for bed. I'll tell your mother what happened."

Upstairs, Hank stretched out in the tub. A few hours ago he had seen another boy stretched out in a tub. The image burned in his mind. He looked down at himself and thought of the fine athletic frame of the other boy, the legs like carved wood. . . . Would he ever grow into a body like that? And then he thought of the blood, of the cut face, the horrible eye, and the gash . . . they had almost cut his . . . god . . . and he thought of that, which he had seen too—he had never seen a black one before— and he felt small and pink and more like a boy than the young man which he so wanted to be. Then he thought of the wounds again, and the foggy eye, and he scrubbed himself hard to wash off the dried blood and the plumber's dirt and all of it. He opened the drain and stood to dry himself, and as he toweled his body off, he watched the blood and grease and dirt swirl down the drain, and he thought of that other drain with the red blood swirling down it, and he wrapped the towel tight around him.

After the bath he went downstairs to eat. His mother had made him some sandwiches and hot chocolate. He had forgotten that he hadn't eaten since lunch. His mother asked him nothing about the day.

"Daddy saved a boy's life tonight," he offered.

"I know," she said.

He looked at her and she at him.

"It's late," she said, "eat up; you have to be up early tomorrow for church. Your brothers are all asleep."

He realized after a moment that he was grateful to her for not asking him more about it, for now that he thought about it he saw that he didn't want to talk about it after all. He ate the cookies she gave him after the sandwiches and then went up to bed.

His father came to see him in his bedroom. It had been a long time since he had come up to say good night. He went to the other bunk bed first, then to the bed below Hank's, gently adjusting the blankets over each of Hank's brothers. Finally he straightened up and stood with his hand on the headboard of Hank's top bunk. "I'm sorry you had to see that, son," he said.

"But I helped you, didn't I?"

"Yes, son, you sure did. I couldn't have asked for a better helper. Now, get some sleep."

"Okay, Dad. G'night."

"G'night, son."

Hank watched his father back slowly out of the room. He looked tired. The part of the floor brightened by the hall light shrunk and then winked out softly as the bedroom door was eased shut. Hank stretched out straight in his bed, worked the back of his head into the pillow, and waited for his eyes to get used to the dark.

Alice Adams

THE ISLANDS

What does it mean to love an animal, a pet, in my case a cat, in the fierce, entire and unambivalent way that some of us do? I really want to know this. Does the cat (did the cat) represent some person, a parent, or a child? some part of one's self? I don't think so—and none of the words or phrases that one uses for human connections sounds quite right: "crazy about," "really liked," "very fond of"—none of those describes how I felt and still feel about my cat. Many years ago, soon after we got the cat (her name was Pink), I went to Rome with my husband, Andrew, whom I really liked; I was crazy about Andrew, and very fond of him too. And I have a most vivid memory of lying awake in Rome, in the pretty bed in its deep alcove, in the nice small hotel near the Borghese Gardens—lying there, so fortunate to be in Rome, with Andrew, and missing Pink, a small striped cat with no tail—missing Pink unbearably. Even blaming Andrew for having brought me there, although he loved her too, almost as much as I did. And now Pink has died, and I cannot accept or believe in her death, any more than I could believe in Rome. (Andrew also died, three years ago, but this story is not his story.)

A couple of days after Pink died (this has all been recent), I went to Hawaii with a new friend, Slater. It had not been planned that way; I had known for months that Pink was slowly failing (she was nineteen), but I did not expect her to die. She just suddenly did, and then I went off to "the islands," as my old friend Zoe Pinkerton used to call them, in her nasal, moneyed voice. I went to Hawaii as planned, which interfered with my proper mourning for Pink. I feel as though those islands interposed themselves between her death and me. When I needed to be alone, to absorb her death, I was over there with Slater.

Slater is a developer; malls and condominium complexes all over the world. Andrew would not have approved of Slater, and sometimes I don't think that I do either. Slater is tall and lean, red-haired, a little younger than I am, and very attractive, I suppose, although on first meeting Slater I was not at all drawn to him (which I have come to think is one of the reasons he found me so attractive, calling me the next day, insisting on dinner that night; he was probably used to women who found him terrific, right off). But I thought Slater talked too much about money, or just talked too much, period.

Later on, when I began to like him a little better (I was flattered by all that attention, is the truth), I thought that Slater's very differences from Andrew should be a good sign. You're supposed to look for opposites, not reproductions, I read somewhere.

Andrew and I had acquired Pink from Zoe, a very rich alcoholic, at that time a new neighbor of ours in Berkeley. Having met Andrew down in his bookstore, she invited us to what turned out to be a very long Sunday lunch party, in her splendidly decked and viewed new Berkeley hills house. "Getting to know some of the least offensive neighbors," is how she probably thought of it. Her style was harsh, abrasive; anything-for-a-laugh was surely one of her mottoes, but she was pretty funny, fairly often. We saw her around when she first moved to Berkeley (from Ireland: a brief experiment that had not worked out too well). And then she met Andrew in his store, and found that we were neighbors, and she invited us to her party, and Andrew fell in love with a beautiful cat. "The most beautiful cat

I ever saw," he told Zoe, and she was, soft and silver, with great blue eyes. The mother of Pink.

"Well, you're in luck," Zoe told us. "That's Molly Bloom, and she just had five kittens. They're all in a box downstairs, in my bedroom, and you get to choose anyone you want. It's your doorprize for being such a handsome couple."

Andrew went off to look at the kittens, and then came back up to me. "There's one that's really great," he said. "A tailless wonder. Must be part Manx."

As in several Berkeley hills houses, Zoe's great sprawl of a bedroom was downstairs, with its own narrow deck, its view of the bay and the bridge, and of San Francisco. The room was the most appalling mess I had ever seen. Clothes, papers, books, dirty glasses, spilled powder, more clothes dumped everywhere. I was surprised that my tidy, somewhat censorious husband even entered, and that he was able to find the big wicker basket (filled with what looked to be discarded silk underthings, presumably clean) in which five very tiny kittens mewed and tried to rise and stalk about, on thin, uncertain legs.

The one that Andrew had picked was gray striped, a tabby, with a stub of a tail, very large eyes and tall ears. I agreed that she was darling, how great it would be to have a cat again; our last cat, Lily, who was sweet and pretty but undistinguished had died some years ago. And so Andrew and I went back upstairs and told Zoe, who was almost very drunk, that we wanted the one with no tail.

"Oh, Stubs," she rasped. "You don't have to take that one. What are you guys, some kind of Berkeley bleeding hearts? You can have a whole cat." And she laughed, delighted as always with her own wit.

No, we told her. We wanted that particular cat. We liked her best.

Aside from seeing the cats—our first sight of Pink!—the best part of Zoe's lunch was her daughter, Lucy, a shy, pretty and very gentle young woman—as opposed to the other guests, a rowdy, oil-rich group, old friends of Zoe's from Texas.

. . .

"What a curious litter," I remarked to Andrew, walking home, up Marin to our considerably smaller house. "All different. Five different patterns of cat."

"Five fathers." Andrew had read a book about this, I could tell. Andrew read everything. "It's called multiple insemination, and occurs fairly often in cats. It's theoretically possible in humans, but they haven't come across any instances." He laughed, really pleased with this lore.

"It's sure something to think about."

"Just don't."

Andrew. An extremely smart, passionate, selfish and generous man, a medium-successful bookstore owner. A former academic: he left teaching in order to have more time to read, he said. Also (I thought) he much preferred being alone in his store to the company of students or, worse, of other professors—a loner, Andrew. Small and almost handsome, competitive, a gifted tennis player, mediocre pianist. Gray hair and gray-green eyes. As I have said, I was crazy about Andrew (usually). I found him funny and interestingly observant, sexy and smart. His death was more grievous to me than I can (or will) say.

"You guys don't have to take Stubs, you can have a whole cat all your own." Zoe Pinkerton on the phone, a few days later. Like many alcoholics, she tended to repeat herself, although in Zoe's case some vast Texan store of self-confidence may have fueled her repetitions.

And we in our turn repeated: we wanted the little one with no tail.

Zoe told us that she would bring "Stubs" over in a week or so; then the kittens would be old enough to leave Molly Bloom.

Andrew: "Molly Bloom indeed."

I: "No wonder she got multiply inseminated."

Andrew: "Exactly."

We both, though somewhat warily, liked Zoe. Or, we were both somewhat charmed by her. For one thing, she made it clear that she thought we were great. For another, she was smart, she had read even more than Andrew had.

A very small woman, she walked with a swagger; her laugh was loud, and liberal. I sometimes felt that Pink was a little like Zoe—a tiny cat with a high, proud walk; a cat with a lot to say.

In a couple of weeks, then, Zoe called, and she came over with this tiny tailless kitten under her arm. A Saturday afternoon. Andrew was at home, puttering in the garden like the good Berkeley husband that he did not intend to be.

Zoe arrived in her purple suede pants and a vivid orange sweater (this picture is a little poignant; fairly soon after that the booze began to get the better of her legs, and she stopped taking walks at all). She held out a tiny kitten, all huge gray eyes and pointed ears. A kitten who took one look at us and began to purr; she purred for several days, it seemed, as she walked all over our house and made it her own. This is absolutely the best place I've ever been, she seemed to say, and you are the greatest people—you are my people.

From the beginning, then, our connection with Pink seemed like a privilege; automatically we accorded her rights that poor Lily would never have aspired to.

She decided to sleep with us. In the middle of the night there came a light soft plop on our bed, which was low and wide, and then a small sound, *mmrrr*, a little announcement of her presence. "Littlest announcer," said Andrew, and we called her that, among her other names. Neither of us ever mentioned locking her out.

Several times in the night she would leave us and then return, each time with the same small sound, the littlest announcement.

In those days, the early days of Pink, I was doing a lot of freelance editing, for local small presses, which is to say that I spent many waking hours at my desk. Pink assessed my habits early on, and decided to make them her own; or perhaps she decided that she too was an editor. In any case she would come up to my lap, where she would sit, often looking up with something to say. She was in fact the only cat I have ever known with whom a sort of conversation was possible; we made sounds back and forth at each other, very politely, and though mine were mostly nonsense syllables, Pink seemed pleased.

Pink was her main name, about which Zoe Pinkerton was very happy. "Lordy, no one's ever named a cat for me before." But Andrew and I used many other names for her. I had an idea that Pink liked a new name occasionally: maybe we all would? In any case we called her a lot of other, mostly P-starting names: Peppercorn, Pipsy Doodler, Poipu Beach. This last was a favorite place of Zoe's, when she went out to "the islands." Pink seemed to like all those names; she regarded us both with her great gray eyes—especially me; she was always mostly my cat.

I find that this is very hard, describing a long relationship with a cat. For one thing, there is not much change of feeling, on either side. The cat gets a little bigger, and you get older. Things happen to both of you, but mostly there is just continuation.

Worried about raccoons and Berkeley free-roaming dogs, we decided early on that Pink was to be a house cat, for good. She was not expendable. But Andrew and I liked to take weekend trips, and after she came to live with us we often took Pink along. She liked car travel right away; settled on the seat between us, she would join right in whenever we broke what had been a silence—not interrupting, just adding her own small voice, a sort of soft clear mew.

This must have been in the early 70s; we talked a lot about Nixon and Watergate. "Mew if you think he's guilty," Andrew would say to Pink, who always responded satisfactorily.

Sometimes, especially on summer trips, we would take Pink out for a semi-walk; our following Pink is what it usually amounted to, as she bounded into some meadow grass, with miniature leaps. Once, before I could stop her, she suddenly raced ahead—to a chipmunk. I was horrified. But then she raced back to me with the chipmunk in her mouth, and after a tiny shake she let him go, and the chipmunk ran off, unscathed. (Pink had what hunters call a soft mouth. Of course she did.)

.   .   .

We went to Rome and I missed her, very much; and we went off to the Piazza Argentina and gave a lot of lire to the very old woman there who was feeding all those mangy, half-blind cats. In honor of Pink.

I hope that I am not describing some idealized "perfect" adorable cat, because Pink was never that. She was entirely herself, sometimes cross and always independent. On the few occasions when I swatted her (very gently), she would hit me right back, a return swat on the hand—though always with sheathed claws.

I like to think that her long life with us, and then just with me, was a very happy one. Her version, though, would undoubtedly state that she was perfectly happy until Black and Brown moved in.

Another Berkeley lunch. A weekday, and all the women present work, and have very little time, and so this getting together seems a rare treat. Our hostess, a diminutive and brilliant art historian, announces that her cat, Parsley, is extremely pregnant. "Honestly, any minute," she laughs, and this is clearly true; the poor burdened cat, a brown Burmese, comes into the room, heavy and uncomfortable and restless. Searching.

A little later, in the midst of serving our many-salad lunch, the hostess says that the cat is actually having her kittens now, in the kitchen closet. We all troop out into the kitchen to watch.

The first tiny sac-enclosed kitten to barrel out is a black one, instantly vigorous, eager to stand up and get on with her life. Then three more come at intervals; it is hard to make out their colors.

"More multiple insemination," I told Andrew that night.

"It must be rife in Berkeley, like everyone says."

"It was fascinating, watching them being born."

"I guess, if you like obstetrics."

A month or so later the art historian friend called with a very sad story: she had just been diagnosed as being very clearly allergic to cats. "I thought I wasn't feeling too well, but I never thought it could be the cats. I know you already have that marvelous Pink, but do you think—until I find someone to take them? Just the two that are left?"

Surprisingly, Andrew, when consulted, said, "Well, why not? Be entertainment for old Pink, she must be getting pretty bored with just us."

We did not consult Pink, who hated those cats on sight. But Andrew was right away crazy about them, especially the black one (maybe he had wanted a cat of his own?): We called them, of course, Black and Brown. They were two Burmese females, or semi-Burmese, soon established in our house and seeming to believe that they lived there.

Black was (she is) the more interesting and aggressive of the two. And from the first she truly took to Pink, exhibiting the sort of clear affection that admits of no rebuff.

We had had Pink spayed as soon as she was old enough, after one quite miserable heat. And now Black and Brown seemed to come into heat consecutively, and to look to Pink for relief. She raged and scratched at them, as they, alternatively, squirmed and rubbed toward her. Especially Brown, who gave all the signs of a major passion for Pink. Furious, Pink seemed to be saying, Even if I were the tom cat that you long for, I would never look at you.

Black and Brown were spayed, and relations among the cats settled down to a much less luridly sexual pattern. Black and Brown both liked Pink and wished to be close to her, which she would almost never permit. She refused to eat with them, haughtily waiting at mealtimes until they were through.

It is easy for me to imagine Black and Brown as people, as women. Black would be a sculptor, I think, very strong, moving freely and widely through the world. Unmarried, no children. Whereas Brown would be a very sweet and pretty, rather silly woman, adored by her husband and sons.

But I do not imagine Pink as a person at all. I only see her as herself. A cat.

Zoe was going to move to Hawaii, she suddenly said. "Somewhere on Kauai, natch, and probably Poipu, if those grubby developers have kept their hands off anything there." Her hatchet laugh. "But I like the idea of living on the islands, away from it all. And so does Gordon. You guys will have to come and visit us there. Bring Pink, but not those other two strays."

"Gordon" was a new beau, just turned up from somewhere in Zoe's complex Dallas childhood. With misgivings, but I think mostly good will, we went over to meet him, to hear about all these new plans.

Gordon was dark and pale and puffy, great black blotches under his narrow, dishonest eyes, a practiced laugh. Meeting him, I right off thought, They're not going to Hawaii, they're not going anywhere together.

Gordon did not drink at all, that day, although I later heard that he was a famous drunk. But occasionally he chided Zoe, who as usual was belting down vodka on ice. "Now Baby," he kept saying. (Strident, striding Zoe—Baby?) "Let's go easy on the sauce. Remember what we promised." (We?)

At which Zoe laughed long and loud, as though her drinking were a good joke that we all shared.

A week or so after that Zoe called and said she was just out of the hospital. "I'm not in the greatest shape in the world," she said—and after that there was no more mention of Gordon, nor of a move to Hawaii.

And not very long after that Zoe moved down to Santa Barbara. She had friends there, she said.

Pink by now was in some cat equivalent to middle age. Still quite small, still playful, at times, she was almost always talkative. She disliked Black and Brown, but sometimes I would find her nestled against one of them, usually Black, in sleep. I had a clear sense that I was not supposed to know about this occasional rapport, or whatever. Pink still came up to my lap as I worked, and she slept on our bed at night, which we had always forbidden Black and Brown to do.

We bought a new, somewhat larger house, further up in the hills. It had stairs, and the cats ran happily up and down, and they seemed to thrive, like elderly people who benefit from a new program of exercise.

Andrew got sick, a terrible swift-moving cancer that killed him within a year, and for a long time I did very little but grieve. I sometimes saw friends, and I tried to work. There was a lot to do about Andrew's bookstore, which I sold, but mostly I stayed at home with my cats, all of whom were now allowed to sleep with me, on that suddenly too-wide bed.

Pink at that time chose to get under the covers with me. In a peremptory way she would tap at my cheek or my forehead, demanding to be taken in. This would happen several times in the course of the night, which was not a great help to my already fragile pattern of sleep, but it never occurred to me to deny her. And I was always too embarrassed to mention this to my doctor, when I complained of lack of sleep.

And then after several years I met Slater, at a well-meaning friend's house. Although as I have said I did not much like him at first, I was struck by his nice dark red hair, and by his extreme directness; Andrew had a tendency to be vague, it was sometimes hard to get at just what he meant. Not so with Slater, who was very clear—immediately clear about the fact that he liked me a lot, and wanted us to spend time together. And so we became somewhat involved, Slater and I, despite certain temperamental obstacles, including the fact that he does not much like cats.

And eventually we began to plan a trip to Hawaii, where Slater had business to see to.

Pink as an old cat slept more and more, and her high-assed strut showed sometimes a slight arthritic creak. Her voice got appreciably louder; no longer a littlest announcer, her statements were loud and clear (I have to admit, it was not the most attractive sound). It seems possible that she was getting a little deaf. When I took her to the vet, a sympathetic, tall and handsome young Japanese woman, she always said, "She sure doesn't look her age—" at which both Pink and I preened.

The vet, Dr. Ino, greatly admired the stripes below Pink's neck, on her breast, which looked like intricate necklaces. I admired them too (and so had Andrew).

Needless to say, the cats were perfectly trained to the sandbox, and very dainty in their habits. But at a certain point I began to notice small accidents around the house, from time to time. Especially when I had been away for a day or two. It seemed a punishment, cat turds in some dark corner. But it was hard to fix responsibility, and I decided to blame all three—and to take various measures like the installation of an upstairs sandbox, which helped. I did think that Pink was getting a little old for all those stairs.

Since she was an old cat I sometimes, though rarely, thought of the fact that Pink would die. Of course she would, eventually —although at times (bad times: the weeks and months around Andrew's illness and death) I melodramatically announced (more or less to myself) that Pink's death would be the one thing I could not bear. "Pink has promised to outlive me," I told several friends, and almost believed.

At times I even felt that we were the same person-cat, that we somehow inhabited each other. In a way I still do feel that—if I did not her loss would be truly unbearable.

I worried about her when I went away on trips. I would always come home, come into my house with some little apprehension that she might not be there. She was usually the last of the three cats to appear in the kitchen, where I stood confused among baggage, mail and phone messages. I would greet Black and Brown, and then begin to call her, "Pink, Pink?"—until, very diffident and proud, she would stroll unhurriedly toward me, and I would sweep her up into my arms with foolish cries of relief, and of love. *Ah, my darling old Pink.*

As I have said, Slater did not particularly like cats; he had nothing against them, really, just a general indifference. He eventually developed a fondness for Brown, believing that she liked him too, but actually Brown is a whore among cats; she will purr and rub up against anyone who might feed her. Whereas Pink was always discriminating, in every way, and fussy. Slater complained that one of the cats deposited small

turds on the bathmat in the room where he sometimes showered, and I am afraid that this was indeed old Pink, both angry
and becoming incontinent.

One night at dinner at my house, when Slater and I, alone, were
admiring my view of the bay and of romantic San Francisco,
all those lights, we were also talking about our trip to
Hawaii. Making plans. He had been there before and was enthusiastic.

Then the phone rang, and it was Lucy, daughter of Zoe, who
told me that her mother had died the day before, in Santa Barbara. "Her doctor said it was amazing she'd lived so long. All
those years of booze."

"I guess. But Lucy, it's so sad, I'm so sorry."

"I know." A pause. "I'd love to see you sometime. How's old
Pink?"

"Oh, Pink's fine," I lied.

Coming back to the table, I explained as best I could about Zoe
Pinkerton, how we got Pink. I played it all down, knowing his
feelings about cats. But I thought he would like the multiple
insemination part, and he did—as had Andrew. (It is startling
when two such dissimilar men, Andrew the somewhat dreamy
book person, and Slater, the practical man, get so turned on by
the same dumb joke.)

"So strange that we're going to Poipu," I told Slater. "Zoe
always talked about Poipu." As I said this I knew it was not the
sort of coincidence that Slater would find remarkable.

"I'm afraid it's changed a lot," he said, quite missing the
point. "The early developers have probably knocked hell out of
it. The greedy competition."

So much for mysterious ways.

Two days before we were to go to Hawaii, in the morning Pink
seemed disoriented, unsure when she was in her sandbox, her
feeding place. Also, she clearly had some bad intestinal disorder. She was very sick, but still in a way it seemed cruel to take

her to the vet, whom I somehow knew could do nothing for her. However, at last I saw no alternative.

She (Dr. Ino, the admirable vet) found a large hard mass in Pink's stomach, almost certainly cancer. Inoperable. "I just can't reverse what's wrong with her," the doctor told me, with great sadness. And succinctness: I saw what she meant. I was so terribly torn, though: should I bring Pink home for a few more days, whatever was left to her—although she was so miserable, so embarrassed at her own condition?

I chose not to do that (although I still wonder, I still am torn). And I still cannot think of the last moments of Pink. Whose death I chose.

I wept on and off for a couple of days. I called some close friends who would have wanted to know about Pink, I thought; they were all most supportively kind (most of my best friends love cats).

And then it was time to leave for Hawaii.

Sometimes, during those days of packing and then flying to Hawaii, I thought it odd that Pink was not more constantly on my mind, even odd that I did not weep more than I did. Now, though, looking back on that trip and its various aftermaths, I see that in fact I was thinking about Pink all that time, that she was totally in charge, as she always had been.

We stayed in a pretty condominium complex, two-story white buildings with porches and decks, and everywhere sweeping green lawns, and flowers. A low wall of rocks, a small coarsely sanded beach, and the vast and billowing sea.

Ours was a second-floor unit, with a nice wide balcony for sunset drinks, or daytime sunning. And, looking down from that balcony one night, our first, I saw the people in the building next door, out on the grass beside what must have been their kitchen, *feeding their cats.* They must have brought along these cats, two supple gray Siamese, and were giving them their supper. I chose not to mention this to Slater, I thought I could imagine his reaction, but in the days after that, every time we walked past that building I slowed my pace and looked carefully for the cats, and a couple of times I saw them. Such pretty cats, and very friendly, for Siamese. Imagine: traveling to Hawaii with your cats—though I was not at all sure that I would have wanted Black and Brown along, nice as they are, and pretty.

Another cat event (there were four in all) came as we drove from Lihue back to Poipu, going very slowly over those very sedate tree- and flower-lined streets, with their decorous, spare houses. Suddenly I felt—we felt—a sort of thump, and Slater, looking startled, slowed down even further and looked back.

"Lord God, that was a cat," he said.

"A cat?"

"He ran right out into the car. And then ran back."

"Are you sure? she's all right?"

"Absolutely. Got a good scare though." Slater chuckled.

But you might have killed that cat, I did not say. And for a moment I wondered if he actually had, and lied, saying the cat was okay. However Slater would never lie to spare my feelings, I am quite sure of that.

The third cat happening took place as we drove down a winding, very steep mountain road (we had been up to see the mammoth gorges cut into the island, near its western edge). On either side of the road there was thick green jungular growth—and suddenly, there among the vines and shrubs I saw a small yellow cat staring out, her ears lowered. Frightened. Eyes begging.

Slater saw her too and even he observed, "Good Lord, people dumping off animals to starve. It's awful."

"You're sure she doesn't live out there? a wilderness cat?"

"I don't think so." Honest Slater.

We did not talk then or later about going back to rescue that cat—not until the next day when he asked me what I would like to do and I said, "I'd like to go back for that cat." He assumed I was joking, and I guess I mostly was. There were too many obvious reasons not to save that particular cat, including the diffi-

culty of finding her again. But I remembered her face, I can see
it still, that expression of much-resented dependence. It was a
way that even Pink looked, very occasionally.

Wherever we drove, through small neat impoverished "native"
settlements (blocks of houses that Slater and his cohorts planned
to buy, and demolish, to replace with fancy condos), with their
lavish flowers all restrained into tidy beds, I kept looking at the
yards, and under the houses. I wanted to see a cat, or some cats
(I wanted to see Pink again). Realizing what I was doing, I continued to do it, to strain for the sight of a cat.

The fourth and final cat event took place as we walked home
from dinner one night, in the flower-scented, corny-romantic
Hawaiian darkness. To our left was the surging black sea; and to
our right large tamed white shrubbery, and a hotel swimming
pool, glistening blackly under feeble yellow floodlights. And
then quite suddenly, from nowhere, a small cat appeared in our
path, shyly and uncertainly arching her back against a bush. A
black cat with some yellow tortoise markings, a long thin curve
of a tail.

"He looks just like your Pink, doesn't he." Slater actually said
this, and I suppose he believed it to be true.

"What—Pink? But her tail—Jesus, didn't you even see my
cat?"

I'm afraid I went on in this vein, sporadically, for several
days. But it did seem so incredible, not remembering Pink, my
elegantly striped, my tailless wonder. (It is also true that I was
purposefully using this lapse, as one will, in a poor connection.)

I dreaded going home with no Pink to call out to, as I came in
the door. And the actuality was nearly as bad as my imaginings
of it: Black and Brown, lazy and affectionate, glad to see me.
And no Pink, with her scolding *hauteur*, her long delayed yield-
ing to my blandishments.

I had no good pictures of Pink, and to explain this odd fact I
have to admit that I am very bad about snapshots; I have never

devised a really good way of storing and keeping them, and tend rather to enclose any interesting ones in letters to people who might like them, to whom they would have some meaning. And to shove the others into drawers, among old letters and other unclassifiable mementoes.

I began then to scour my house for Pink pictures, looking everywhere. In an album (Andrew and I put together a couple of albums, early on) I found a great many pictures of Pink as a tiny, tall-eared brand new kitten, stalking across a padded window seat, hiding behind an oversized Boston fern—among all the other pictures from those days: Zoe Pinkerton, happy and smoking a long cigarette and almost drunk, wearing outrageous colors, on the deck of her house. And Andrew and I, young and very happy, silly, snapped by someone at a party. Andrew in his bookstore, horn-rimmed and quirky. Andrew uncharacteristically working in our garden. Andrew all over the place.

But no middle-year or recent pictures of Pink. I had in fact (I then remembered) sent the most recent shots of Pink to Zoe; it must have been just before she (Zoe) died, with a silly note about old survivors, something like that. It occurred to me to get in touch with Lucy, Zoe's daughter, to see if those pictures had turned up among Zoe's "effects," but knowing the chaos in which Zoe had always lived (and doubtless died) I decided that this would be tactless, unnecessary trouble. And I gave up looking for pictures.

Slater called yesterday to say that he is going back to Hawaii, a sudden trip. Business. I imagine that he is about to finish the ruination of all that was left of Zoe's islands. He certainly did not suggest that I come along, nor did he speak specifically of our getting together again, and I rather think that he, like me, has begun to wonder what we were doing together in the first place. It does seem to me that I was drawn to him for a very suspicious reason, his lack of resemblance to Andrew: why ever should I seek out the opposite of a person I truly loved?

But I do look forward to some time alone now. I will think about Pink—I always feel her presence in my house, everywhere. Pink, stalking and severe, ears high. Pink, in my lap, raising her head with some small soft thing to say.

And maybe, since Black and Brown are getting fairly old now too, I will think about getting another new young cat. Maybe, with luck, a small gray partially Manx, with no tail at all, and beautiful necklaces.

Stephen Dixon

THE RARE MUSCOVITE

I can be such an egotistical self-righteous pompous sonofabitch; unaccepting, nonaccepting, I can't think of the right word but it's what I so often am and all of it's what I was again. Moscow, my wife and I, she to research a book she's anthologizing and introducing, I just to accompany her and see a city and be in a country I've never been to, and it's really just the extra airfare, since restaurants are very cheap and the hotel room's the same for one or two. She—Marguerite—speaks Russian, will be working all day in libraries and with Russian contacts, so through a colleague in America weeks before we left, got an interpreter for me for the five weekdays. Svetlana shows up at our hotel at nine, half hour before she's supposed to. I'm squatting in the little tub, reach over and push the door shut, and Marguerite lets her in. I overhear them: Good mornings in Russian, then "Please, if it's possible, everything in English from now on. I want to sharpen my interpreting facilities even better from your trip, and I'm planning of visiting America in a year. And my earliness—tardiness?—earliness is because the Metro got here faster than I thought and was less crowded than expected. Then our brave police downstairs let me up with a wave when I thought I'd have more difficulties. And I didn't want to walk around in the slippery cold or sit in the dreary lobby with everyone blowing smoke and sturgeon fumes on me and talking in their loud German and English and American voices, present employers—exployees?—excluded of course. I had a stroke, you see, two years ago. Recovered from this side being paralyzed to where I could barely walk. Twelve almonds a day, a healer from Kiev said—the doctors could offer no medicine but time for me. You might think it madness, I know so much how Americans rely on science, but the almonds worked, I'm sure of it, and I don't want to get excited. I can't afford to, you say?—by having to tell them off to their faces, all those bloated businessmen elephants blowing loud smoke and talk on me. I am one of those rare Muscovites who—whom? Let me get it correct now, *who*. Who detests those burning props."

I get dressed in the bathroom, come out, introduce myself, make coffee for us, take out sugar packets and coffee cake and tiny Edam cheeses we got on the plane with our dinner and snack, offer her peanut butter and dried salami and crackers we brought with us. "You don't get anything like this here," she says, "unless you wait on line for hours or buy it in the dollar stores, which I'll take you to," she says to me. "Hams in tins, coffee in cans, the best sardines and cheeses and most over-priced caviar. You won't need those perhaps, for only a week's visit in a hotel. But if you have Russian friends who do or you want to make a gift out of to them, that's also what they have there. And lemon and peppered vodka and Scottish scotch and Ararat, you know what that is?" "Da," I say. "Ah, listen, won-derful—possible he doesn't need an interpreter. But people say it can be as good or as better as the best French cognac. I wouldn't know since I'm also rare in Moscow in that I've never had a taste for alcohol. Maybe for my bad tooth, as a girl, but nothing else. And also at the Beriozka American cigarettes to kill people is what you get there too. One carton of them, none other than Marlboros, would be equivalent to, at black-market rubles for dollars, a month's wages for the average worker here, or fifty rubles less. If you want to, we'll go. For if you return to America and your wife tells Millie you didn't have an opportu-nity to buy the best Russian whiskeys and gifts, because I was taking you to all the more cultural places, I shall be very embar-rassed and dismayed."

"No no," I say. "Any place you take me to is fine, since it'll all be new to me. Though if we want Ararat and vodka, better I hear at the duty-free store at the airport going home."

"But for use in your room? Marguerite tells me she'll be entertaining scholars here. Perhaps you brought the much preferred American whiskey with you. Or you don't drink or once did but went A.A., which is only beginning here. It's not that? If it was, or should it be 'were'?" I throw up my hands, point to Marguerite and say "She knows." "Oh, small difference, since we both know what I meant, and I have the few places and hours the A.A. clubs meet each week. Anyway, it's all up to you. I am simply here to coast you through. And the truth of the matter is that the Beriozkas, though something to see for their glamorous contradictions if not outright falsehoods to the rest of Moscow and present Russian life, have no real appeal to me."

But what am I getting at with all this? I had an idea of saying right at the start "Happens again," and then explaining what does. She gets a stroke our third weekday here, dies, and because I didn't especially care for her almost from the moment I heard her through the bathroom door—actually got irritated, but not visibly, by her almost incessant talking and parading of her knowledge and vast learning. She seemed to know something to a lot about everything we spoke about or saw. She was familiar with the details of Marguerite's project and doctoral dissertation and knew the works of the people Marguerite was going to see, as well as every writer, painter and composer I mentioned and building we visited or I pointed out. Knew the dates, history, influences, inner meanings, could quote lines, cite pages and recite poems and so on—I, what? I forget what I started out saying. But she has this stroke, dies, police have to break down her apartment door to get her two days after her stroke and I feel very bad about it of course and guilty I badmouthed her so much to Marguerite and asked her to phone her to call her off after the second day, at least for a day and then I'd see how I felt. "I want to walk around alone, not meet any schedules, get lost on the Metro if I want with only the few Russian words I know. Find a farmers' market by myself and the Tolstoi Museum and Tolstoi's house again if I like, which I think I would but without her telling me who painted what picture on the wall and who the people are in the portraits and what famous composer played what famous composition on the grand piano there. I just want to feel the place, guess which side of the bed Tolstoi slept, and those desks of his and Sofia's and no electric lights and that sad room behind theirs where their youngest son—I forget his name, though she told me, and I think he was the youngest—died of scarlet fever in that over-sized crib she said was a typical seven-year-old's bed then, or maybe he died in the hospital and she said he only got sick at home. For sure she had it right, whatever she told me. Or just to stay in our room finishing *War and Peace* and maybe going downstairs to the hotel café for a coffee and bun." And I feel if I had let her continue being my interpreter and guide, though we never used that word, instead of giving her a paid day off— paid, it's so absurd, since it was so little money and because she has no survivors we now don't know whom to send it to—she might have somehow survived, or at worst been with me when she had the stroke and I could have got help for her and saved her life. Or been with us, if we again took her to the hotel res-taurant for dinner that night—and why not? Since she knew which foods were freshest, so was an asset of sorts, and she didn't ask for more wages and the dinner was certainly cheap enough. But she died in her room that Wednesday, might not have had anywhere to go except to stand in the cold for hours on different food lines—she was retired but not even sixty—and maybe was incensed at me—knew I didn't like her much for not very good reasons but she stayed because she needed the money—or worried the job wouldn't work out because of what she sensed I felt about her, or grieved or got angry over it or both or something else and that somehow provoked the stroke. But I feel partly responsible for it, also that I wasn't there when I possibly could have been to help her when she got the stroke. And when I say "Happens again" I mean because I've done things like that before—badmouthed people for inadequate rea-sons—there probably aren't any good ones—just to avoid seeing them that night, for example, because they were preventing me from doing something I thought I might want to—just their presence would—or they had achieved some sort of stature or success that let's say I secretly wanted, which I'm not saying she had though I have to admit I admired her intelligence tremendously, and though nothing so bad as a stroke or anything near it happened to any of them I always knew I was wrong in this attitude and regretted it and told myself I wouldn't do it again and sometimes only told myself I should try my hardest not to.

I didn't say what I really wanted to there, only because for whatever it is—my inability to say things clearly and straight and because I really don't have the means to—the language, words, I'm simply unable to do it well, on paper and orally most of the time also, besides not probably having the necessary kind of intelligence and insights. I don't even know if what I just said makes much sense, but let me get on with this. I was where before? Where was I? I'm trying to convey another person and, without being explicit, another person's feelings about her death and the way it changes ordinary life when it suddenly comes and what it can bring out in himself. That and more. Anyway, first place she takes me to the first day—Monday—is Red Square. "*Krasnaya*—red—I'd also like to teach you Russian words connected to the places we go to, which is the easiest way to learn them—through practical identification. Like *ulitsa* —street—which you'll see everywhere after a word like Herzen or Gorki on buildings and streetpost signs, but first I must also teach you the Russian alphabet. And we might as well get *Krasnaya Ploschad* out of the way—see what I mean now? You understand without questioning me. But you can't be allowed to return home without saying you've been there, can you?"

"I think I can. But okay. Even though Marguerite and I went there the Saturday we got here—she insisted I see it at night—I never saw it in the day and nothing was open."

"Shall we walk? It's only two kilometers or and a half, and I can walk that far. It's supposed to be healthy for me besides." I ask how the sidewalks are—"It looks cold and wet out"—and she says icy and I suggest we take the Metro or a cab. I didn't want her falling or holding on to me for so long a walk. "If you have dollars to pay or packs of American cigarettes to show and give away we can get a cab, something most Muscovites can't do here. I doubt you'll want to see inside the Kremlin buildings. They're rather vulgar—glittery jewels and gold and thrones—though you might want to see the domes over the Kremlin. But St. Basil's in *Krasnaya Ploschad* has some of the best of those and later today or tomorrow we'll go to Novodevichy—*novo*, which is one of the forms of 'new'—which I think has the city's most beautiful of them. And I'd like taking you by train to Novgorod, which to me has the world's most beautiful of all."

She goes on like that. Steers me where she wants to go, doesn't think much of my suggestions—Arabat Street, where I'd like to get my gift-buying done with—*matryoska* or *maritroska* dolls—I can never seem to get the word right, and painted wooden boxes and barrettes and decorated potholders and things like that. "Exclusively for tourists," she said, "who want their pockets combed through and gypsy beggar boys to steal their wallets and socks and shoes. Oh, they'll do it, and with baby brothers on their backs to distract you. But if you insist to go there, I won't stop you, but it's walk walk walk through unruly crowds for practically one of your miles." Chekhov Museum—"Ugly, not at all brings to vivid life the personality and living style of the man. But you love him, is that why? He's not Tolstoi, but I like his work very much too. *Toska*—that's 'misery' or 'grief' or really 'long drawn-out sorrow'—not translatable as one word, and you can always remember it by the opera of the same name. A touching story. Very few as good except 'Ivan Ilyich,' which is more than touching—it's terrifying. This man reconciling himself to death after such an empty, trivial—how should I say it?—unenlightened life? I read it once a year. Just as your *War and Peace* there I try to every three years or any time I need some tranquility of spirit and mind. You were right to bring only that book with you—it serves the place of an entire library. Unfortunately there is little left of the Russian soul that's in that novel." The most grandiose Metro stations—"For tour buses to empty themselves out into only, except for regular riders like myself who truly use it. You'll be staring up at the statuary and chandeliers while getting bumped by our rudest inhabitants, too ignorant or impolite or perhaps too eager in a rush to excuse themselves, even to foreigners. But you wish to see these

stations—and the deepest you say, for some unexplained reasons?—then we'll go to these too."

After we all have dinner at the hotel restaurant and Svetlana
leaves I say to Marguerite "Did you see the way she made those
last-minute sandwiches? I mean, she got a free meal—I'm not
begrudging her it, since it was cheap enough and she wasn't too
intrusive at the table and I had enough wine in me to ward her
off when she was. And I know there's a shortage of dairy stuff
in Moscow. But Jesus, have some self-respect and maybe consid-
eration for us, since this is our hotel, and don't stuff the rest of
the table bread into your bag and fill the two slices of bread left
on your plate with a quarter pound of butter and wrap that up
for home too. I shouldn't be saying all this, right? since I probably don't know what I'm talking about."

"It's that you forget. She asked our permission first. She's giving the butter to an old woman in her building who can't get
any and the bread I guess she figures the woman will like also
or else just that the kitchen will throw it away. But suppose she
was drying the bread for herself and hoarding the butter for a
day when she won't have any, like tomorrow perhaps? So
what."

"Okay, fair. But also, when she talks to us I kind of get upset"
—"You get very upset"—"I get a little less than that upset that
she keeps me out entirely, and it's in English. When I do say
something when you're around she often looks at me as if I
were a kid who's barged in when he's been warned not to, as if
this is adult conversation only, so buzz off. You're the big genius and intellectual toiler she's saying—after all, it's your project we've come here for. I'm just a stupid sight-gazer—didn't
know Red Square wasn't inside the Kremlin—but at least I was
honest enough to admit it. Doesn't know the difference between
the Tver—that the way to say it?—and Novgorod Russian icon
schools. Why should I know? Who does but an art expert of that
period or field or someone who has few books to choose from in
libraries and stores but all the time in the world to read. But
credit me with a little intelligence and conversational interest or
skills or whatever you want to call it. Someone who can on occasion talk with some knowledge and depth about the less

poppy and mundane things. For instance, also credit me with—
but nothing, when at the Pushkin, seeing me standing there
staring at the Van Goghs for a few minutes, she asks me do I
like them. 'You bet,' I said, which is what I usually say in front
of Van Goghs, for what am I going to do when I'm still in a state
of enthrallment, go into every crack, dab, dot and corner? But
she gives me the French expression about each to his own taste
or gut and then starts in with this pro-Monet and Cézanne and
anti-Vincent treatiselike argument or lecture I could hardly understand it was so over my head, or else she didn't know how
to deliver it clearly and succinctly in English. But how these
three Van Goghs all on the same wall are critically puffed up by
unscrupulous experts, dealers and museums so people—like
me, I'm sure she's saying—who know little to zero about art
and artistry will pay fifty million bucks apiece for. My point is
she thinks I'm uncultured, or barely cultured—certainly not intelligent. A walking talking absurdity when you think this
shmuck also teaches at a university. Even if it were phys ed or
home ec I taught—still, he represents the academy so should be
much smarter, know several languages backwards, be able to
communicate without hesitation and with full intellectual rigor
and appropriate ornate words what he knows, sees and likes
instead of being someone who probably always needs a thesau-
rus when he writes and talks. The typical example of the stereo-
typed American tourist she's shown around Moscow or just in-
terpreted for before. Except of course you—ah, the intelligentsia.
And those rare nonacademic people like the ones in Boston who
gave you her name—fancy journalists—magazines—but so cultivated she kept telling me: educated, eloquent, polyglot—at
least the guy—worldly and well-read and with even an executed Decembrist count way back in his family. Because I've no
advanced degrees nor easy time with the spoken language and
little political feeling or at least nothing much to say about it for
either of our countries, she thinks I've no mind of my own and
so have to have everything explained to.''

''It can't be all that bad and she has a wonderful itinerary for
you tomorrow. The Tolstoi Museum, a farmers' market or two
where you can get me some cracked walnuts and real Russian

honey and anything that looks unusual there as gifts and will travel well for home. And the Andronikov monastery"—"Great, more icons"—"Don't go if you don't want, but also for its ancient tiny church and onion domes. And the G.U.M. department store to buy records for a quarter and a znachki shop there with the largest selection of them in the city. To impress her, pronounce the store 'goom.' " "Goom, goom." "Then step in with her someplace, get a taste of a workers' restaurant or café—she knows it all, and maybe over food alone you'll get to know and appreciate each other better. Anyway, she'll show you the ropes, how to use the trolley and pay phone and to shop without being cheated and show your dollars without getting mugged. By the time she's through with you you'll be exhausted but have a map of the city in your head. Then you have a day off and she from you. It's for me too you'll be doing this. I'll be too busy to go shopping even one afternoon. And though I've seen most of it before you can tell me what you saw and also take pictures to show me and the kids later on."

Svetlana shows up on the dot next morning. We see things by foot, trolley, Metro, occasional cab for a five-dollar bill Marguerite was told to bring about twenty of to Moscow for just something like this. Svetlana says once "Am I talking too much?" She is but I say "Nah." "I've tendencies towards talk, possibly for being sequestered in my slight space the rest of the days and the one woman I see most to take care of doesn't say three words a time. But I'm an honest person, you're visiting a culture where honest persons with words is almost a belief, so you want to be an honest person too, don't you? Tell me to my face if I'm twisting your ears as the English like to say, and perhaps the Americans too, or showing you too many things too fast to digest." "No no, I mean it, everything couldn't be better, thanks."

I don't want to be with her for lunch so I say I think I'm still suffering from jet lag and would like a nap at my hotel, would she mind eating alone? I give her money for the first-floor café, go upstairs and lie on my bed and drink coffee and read, she rings from the lobby an hour later. More places and constant information and chatter. "Are you sure I'm not talking too much?" "Why, do you think you are?" "Well, I might be." "No, absolutely not, it's all fine." Every monument and theater and famous person's birth or living place and also every building we pass by foot, trolley and cab that looks interesting architecturally or stands out because of its size she has something to say about. "That so? Yes, hmm, so this is where it is, I didn't know that."

We meet Marguerite for dinner at a Georgian restaurant she had to make reservations for two days ago, and in the cab back to our hotel we drop Svetlana off at a Metro station. She hands us each several candies. "Special, hard to get because individually wrapped and the ingredients very select. They're made by an acquaintance of mine in the Kremlin's confectionery kitchen and often given in droves to dignitaries and diplomats. We ought to export them simply for their colorful wrappers. Bears and squirrels—children would love them." "That's very kind, thank you," I say. "I don't eat candy myself but will definitely try one, though not now because I'm too full, and save the rest for my girls." Marguerite's told her tomorrow will be a paid day off and asks if she'd like the first three days' pay now. "All at once, please. I wouldn't want to ride the Metro with it. Too much in dollars and one of our now many clever Moscow thieves might see it on my face." "And on the fifth day?" I say. "Will he see it on my face you mean? No, since that day I'll hire a taxicab or continue with yours, flush like an American tourist or spending as freely as one. But because I'm Russian, all for the sum or extra one of a dollar, and then hide the money in my room for one of your rainy days. That is yours?" "Ours and probably the English too."

Later I say to Marguerite "Know why she wants all her wages at once?" "Something disparaging I suppose." "No, just conjecture born out of insight or something. Because she thinks we'll have to give her a bigger tip for the whole fifty than if we only gave her her last day's pay on Friday. She's a shrewdie all right, and even shrewder how well she disguises it." "Disguises what?" "Everything. Or just things—some. Holding back—being extra gracious to me when we're alone when I know damn well what she thinks of me intellectually, or maybe just culturally—we've spoken of it. And this not wanting her pay day by day because of the increment, the incremental—because with more . . . well, you know—or maybe I'm being farfetched on this. But other things." "That's what I'm asking, what? Did she ever do or say anything in particular to make you question her motives this way?" "As I said, just little things I've picked up but nothing right now, other than what I've mentioned, that comes to mind." "Well I think you're way way off about her. She's a touch sad but decent, and energetic and enthusiastic. And I only wish I had the time to be taken around by such a knowledgeable person who knows the city so well, even if she is so garrulous, and you were the one doing the bookwork all day. Actually, I think you'd like that more." "No, I'm enjoying my rest away from work. And true, I suppose I should feel lucky having her for so little money. But the greater truth is I feel luckier being on my own tomorrow. Anyway, not to change the subject, I was thinking just now: *da, da*—what a nice soft way to say yes."

But to move along. She doesn't call Wednesday morning as she said she would to find out what time she should come Thursday morning. Marguerite calls her and she doesn't answer. She doesn't call Thursday morning. Marguerite calls her every fifteen minutes, thinking maybe she was out all night, slept at a friend's—has a secret life she never gave us a clue about, she says—or got in after midnight last night, when Marguerite stopped calling, and didn't call us after that because she felt it was too late, and was up and out for groceries or something early this morning. We leave the phone off the hook—each room has its own number, so it's all direct—when we go to the hotel restaurant for our complimentary breakfast. Marguerite calls when we get back, then asks me to stick around an hour more before going out on my own if that's what I plan to do. "When she was outside she might have had trouble getting a pay phone or misplaced our number or didn't have the two kopecks on her and nobody could give her change—anything, and she just got hold of a phone. If you want, which you probably won't, call every fifteen minutes or so—she might have just got home. But I'm a little worried about her, aren't you?" and I say "Of course, it doesn't seem like her, but I'm sure it's nothing," and she leaves for her appointment. I wait but don't call, figuring if she just got home first thing she'd do would be to call. I leave after an hour, walk around the old section of the city, try to find some buildings in *War and Peace* Marguerite said are still supposed to be here—the Rostovs' mansion, Pierre's house—but can't find the streets, even though they're on my map, and no one, if they're hearing me right and understanding the few Russian words Marguerite taught me yesterday to make myself understood in something like this, seems to have heard of them; stop in a café for *"odin kofe, mineralenaya voda* and *dva bulka"*—woman shakes her head—*"bulki, bulka,* two," holding up two fingers and then pointing to some rolls on the counter behind her, *"mais*—but not sweet ones, *nyet sakhar, pzhalesta,"* and she gives me mineral water and coffee without the lump of sugar that usually comes with it and takes enough change out of my palm to pay for it while I'm trying to find in it what amount I think she said.

Marguerite calls Svetlana before we go to the hotel restaurant for dinner, calls when we get back to our room. "I'm really worried now," she says, "—I know something's wrong. We know she isn't the type to promise to come—to say she'll call the night before to see precisely what hour we want her—and then just to disappear. And with that stroke she had two years ago—"— "Oh yeah, that's right, the stroke, I forgot. So what do we do?" She calls a scholar she met the other day who said he knows of Svetlana but he only has her phone number, not her address nor knows anyone who does: but he'll make some calls. "Even if we had her address," I say, "what would we do with it? She told me it's about an hour's Metro ride to her stop—lots of changes and at the end of the line. Or a couple of changes, but anyway 'couple' meaning what to her—two, three, four? We'd go out there at this hour when people all over the city are getting bumped on the head and robbed? Even by cab—or of course by cab if we could get one or one would take us that far—we'd be sure he'd wait? If he didn't we'd be screwed." "Not that. But say we found someone who knows her and lives near her? Or someone who doesn't but as a favor to us might want to help her. Maybe that person could phone a friend and go over—two men. Or just you and him. What I'm saying is Russians still do that, put themselves out for strangers, especially one intellectual for another. And if this person didn't want to do it but lived fairly close to her, which would mean you wouldn't go because he couldn't come in for you and then go back there and so on, I'd say we'd pay the fare—cab, anything. And would a carton of Marlboros—a few weeks' salary for some at the regular exchange—encourage a friend of his to go along with him? Meaning, would it encourage *him?* But I've seen the way they've helped me. With leads, contacts, books, unpublished papers and notes and tapes very few American scholars would let me see and hear and copy down. And accompanying me clear across town for something and then waiting there while I worked or saw someone so they could take me back here."

She calls several people she's met, through them friends and colleagues of theirs, but the one person who's heard of Svetlana doesn't even know her phone number. The first scholar she spoke to calls back and says nobody he contacted knows where she lives or how to find out. "I give up for now," she says. "Maybe she's okay and off doing something we haven't thought of yet, but I seriously doubt it." "I hope we're wrong," I say. "You mean you think it's no good too?" "Looks it. But as you said, we've only just met her so there's lots we don't know."

Little past midnight, we just got into our beds and shut the night-table lights, the phone rings. A woman says "Abel, yes? Hello, I'm Katya Sergeyeva, very good friend of Svetlana. Pardon me for upsetting you if this is nothing, but I'm extremely worried for her. Was she with you all of today?" "Let me put my wife on please. This is very important so if there's any language problem, she can speak Russian." She tells Marguerite she and Svetlana have spoken every day with each other since Svetlana's stroke. Yesterday she thought Svetlana went with us someplace outside of Moscow and got back late or stayed overnight at a hotel with us there. Now that she knows we haven't seen her for two days she's sure something's wrong. She's going to go over to her apartment now with a friend. If Svetlana doesn't answer she'll get the police to break down the door.

Marguerite tells her we'll do whatever we can to help so please count on us and call anytime tonight, no matter how late. We read for a few minutes, then she yawns and hearing it I yawn right after and we agree we should try to nap. I wake up once thinking maybe Katya called but we didn't hear it in our sleep, though the phone only rings loudly, and cover Marguerite up and turn off the lights.

Katya calls just when Marguerite's about to dial her. She didn't get back to us last night because it was very late and things were still so unresolved. They got to the apartment, knocked, nobody answered and they didn't hear anything behind the door so they called the police who said they couldn't get there till ten this morning. "They couldn't get there?" I say when Marguerite translates it for me while still on the phone. "What if she still has some breath this minute but dies a few seconds before they get there?" "Shh," she says, signaling she can't hear what Katya's saying. Katya says she and several friends are going to meet the police now at Svetlana's and she'll call soon as she has some news, but she's convinced now Svetlana's dead. She also told Marguerite that after they knocked and called through the door last night they went to about twenty apartments in the building and nobody had seen Svetlana for two days. "They went around asking at one and two in the morning?" "I told you, people here do that. Not the police, as you heard, but you can call on your friends and most of your neighbors any time." "So why didn't they all get together last night and knock down the door? Police wouldn't come, hell with them, or is it it's really maybe some highly penalizable crime?" "Possibly. Probably."

Phone rings two hours later. Marguerite stayed around long as she could but then had to leave for an important appointment that couldn't be rescheduled. "Abel, yes? Katya here, most unexpected news," and then her voice cracks and she speaks excitably in Russian. "Speak English, please, I understand very little Russian. *Nye govoryu po russki, nye govoryu po russki,*" and she says *"Nyet, nyet,* not okay, can't. Wait." A woman gets on and says "Hello, I am Bella, good friend of Katya and Svetlana. It is terrible to speak to you, sir, only this once with only this terrible news for you I speak English not good but try. Svetlana is dead. She has stroke Wednesday, your day, she must have, we and police today believe, that made her that way, killed her. Great pity. Much sorrow. Wonderful woman. Intelligent and kind and so nice to this building and people and everywhere she goes. It is very very sad." "Very. I'm terribly sorry. Please tell Katya that. And what is her phone—telephone number, please, even though I think my wife took it. But what is it if she didn't take it so she can phone Katya later," and she gives me it.

For a couple of days after I think how I would have liked it to turn out. I wouldn't show any signs I disliked her, was annoyed or irritated by her. If I did and it was evident to her I'd quickly apologize, saying it was something in me, personal, being away from my work maybe, maybe worried about my kids, too much of that good lemon vodka last night or bad sturgeon, other excuses, but nothing she'd done. If she apologized for being such a chatterbox, as she said of herself once, covering her mouth with her hand, I'd say "Great, chatter away, don't hold back for my sake, because most of what you're saying is interesting and new to me, and better someone who talks and makes sense than keeps sullen and still." We'd go here, there, lunch, dinner with Marguerite, stop for coffee, tea for her, *bulki, torte* or whatever the plural for them which I'd ask her for, I'd suggest she take me inside the Kremlin, the Tolstoi and Chekhov museums, whatever church and monastery she wants me to see in the city and outside it. At lunch I'd give her some of the plastic sandwich bags I brought from New York and would say "Butter all the bread you want and stick them in the bags and the bags into your pocketbook. Less messy, and the food's only going to go to waste or be taken home by the kitchen staff. I'd take some myself but we do all that kind of buttering and cheese-taking and other secret hoarding at the hotel's breakfast buffet every day." Children's toy store, Pushkin Museum again where I might say maybe she has a point about the Van Goghs and I've been duped as much as the next guy about his work, since I'm no art expert, exhibition hall of contemporary Russian painting she spoke about and I'd wanted to see but begged off because I didn't want her lecturing me. I'd take her up on teaching me ten

Russian words and a couple of phrases and one complete sentence a day and testing me occasionally on the Russian alphabet till I could read or at least sound out all the stores' names and street signs. We'd talk about books and stories we've read, plays we've seen, she here, I in the States. Farewell dinner at a Czech restaurant Marguerite and I had talked weeks ago about ending our trip with. We'd toast to one another, to good literature, to Tolstoi and Chekhov and Babel, Ahkmatova and Tsvetaieva and the endurance of all great art, to the success of Marguerite's project, to my work at home, to Svetlana and everything she does and for being such a fine interpreter and companion and friend and showing and teaching me things I never would have seen or known, to our two girls and all our families and friends, to returning to Moscow soon, to her visiting America and our being her sponsors and me her guide for a day or two, to continuing good relations between our countries, democracy in hers, to eternal peace between them, peace and disarmament everywhere and good health and happiness and cooperation everywhere too and more dinners for the three of us like this one, future toasts. Then we'd ask the restaurant to order a taxi and we'd drop her off at a Metro station, kiss each other's cheeks, give her her five days' salary and a twenty-dollar tip and some kind of present—one of the scarves Marguerite brought as presents from America, cologne from America or probably both if she hasn't given them away yet. Or I'd get out of the cab and help her out and then kiss her, or we'd drive her home no matter how far out of the way and wait in the cab till she got in her building. Or I'd walk her to her first-floor hallway and stay there till she was upstairs and in her apartment or had enough time to get inside. Or we'd cab straight to our hotel and give our presents and enough extra fare in dollars for the cab to take her home.

Back in New York Marguerite says "It's so strange to think the last day you see some person, very active and energetic and seemingly healthy, is the last day of that person's life, or the last night." "Very odd," I say, "very." "And I forgot to tell you. That Katya—you remember her, Svetlana's friend who went over there with the police? Well she said Svetlana was planning to give us a little party at her place after her last workday, or really not so little. After dinner, that she would invite some of her friends—interpreters and people in teaching and editing— and ask me for names of people I'd seen who might want to come, or anyone I wanted. I doubt many of them would have come, unless they lived close by. And I would have done what I could, without hurting her in any way, to dissuade her. But that's something for her to want to do, since she was short of money and you'd think she'd be too tired that day to give it. I'm thinking now though. I'm having this very bad thought, without wanting to sound as if I don't appreciate what she wanted to do, but that her stroke saved us from it. It would have been the last thing I wanted, at her place or any place, but to be honest, less at her place. Her friends were probably bright and nice but a bit dull. Or maybe not, but you know, I just wouldn't see the reason for the party. I don't know how we could have refused it though, do you?" "Too tired and busy. We were leaving in a day and a half and you needed to see some more people or do research or go over your notes or something. And we also had to pack and were almost too tired for even that."

Lorrie Moore

CHARADES

It's fitting that Christmas should devolve to this, its barest bones. The family has begun to seem to Therese like a pack of thespians, anyway; everyone arrives, performs for one another, catches early flights out, to Logan or O'Hare. Probably it's appropriate that a party game should actually appear and insert itself in the guise of a holiday tradition (which it isn't). Usually no one in Therese's family expresses much genuine feeling anyway; everyone aims instead—though gamely!—for enactments.

Each year, now, the stage is a new one—their parents, in their restless old age, buying and selling town houses, moving steadily southward from Maine. The real estate is Therese's mother's idea. Since retiring, Therese's father has focused more on bird feeders; he is learning how to build them. "Who knows what he'll do next?" Her mother sighs. "He'll probably start carving designs into the side of the house."

This year they are in Bethesda, Maryland, near where Andrew, Therese's brother, lives. Andrew works as an electrical engineer and is married to a sweet, pretty, inscrutable cop named Pam. Pam is pixie-haired and smiley. She freezes hams. She makes Jell-O salads days in advance. She and Andrew are the parents of a one-and-a-half-year-old named Winnie, who already reads.

Reads the reading videos on TV, but reads.

Everyone has divided into teams, four and four, and written the names of famous people, songs, films, plays, books on scraps of wrapping paper torn off the gifts hours earlier. There are another few hours until Therese and her husband Ray's flight, at four-thirty, from National Airport. "Yes," says Therese, "I guess we'll have to forgo the 'Averell Harriman: Statesman for All Seasons' exhibit."

"I don't know why you couldn't catch a later flight," says Therese's sister, Ann. She is scowling. Ann is the youngest, and ten years younger than Therese, who is the oldest, but lately Ann's voice has taken up a prissy and matronly scolding that startles Therese. "Four-thirty," says Ann, pursing her lips and propping her feet up on the chair next to her. "That's a little ridiculous." Her shoes are pointy and Victorian-looking. They are green suède—a cross between a courtesan's and Peter Pan's.

The teams are divided in such a way that Therese and Ray and her parents are on one team, Andrew and Pam, Ann and Tad, Ann's fiancé, on the other. Tad is slender and red-haired, a marketing specialist for Neutrogena. He and Ann have just become engaged. After nearly a decade of casting about in love and work, Ann is going to law school and planning her summer wedding. Since Therese worked for years as a public defender and is now, through a fluky political appointment, a county circuit-court judge, she has assumed that Ann's decision to be a lawyer is a kind of sororal affirmation, that it will somehow mean the two of them will have new things in common, that Ann will have questions for her, observations, forensic things to say. But this seems not to be so. Ann seems not to like law school. She has been preoccupied with trying to hire bands and caterers and to rent a large room in a restaurant. "Ugh," said Therese sympathetically. "Doesn't it make you want to elope?"

Ann shrugged. "I'm trying to figure out how to get everybody from the church to the restaurant in a way that won't wrinkle their outfits and spoil the pictures."

"Really?" asked Therese. "You are?"

The names and titles are put in two big salad bowls, each team receiving the other's bowl. Therese's father goes first. "All right! Everyone ready!" He has always been witty, competitive, tense; games have usually brought out the best and worst in him. These days, however, he seems anxious and elderly. There is pain in his eyes, something sad and unfocussed that sometimes stabs at them—the fear of a misspent life or a flash of uncertainty as to where he's left the keys. He signals that his assigned name is a famous person. No one could remember how to signal that, and so the family has invented one: a quick, pompous posture, hands on hips, chin in air. Mustering up a sense of drama, Therese's father does this well.

"Famous person!" Everyone shouts it, though of course there is someone who shouts "idiot," to be witty. This time it is Therese's mother.

"Idiot!" she shouts. "Village idiot!"

But her husband has continued signalling the syllables, ignoring her, slapping the fingers of his right hand hard on his left sleeve. The famous person has three names. He is doing the first name, first syllable. He takes out a dollar bill and points to it.

"George Washington," shouts Ray.

"George Washington Carver!" shouts Therese. Therese's father shakes his head angrily, turning the dollar around and pointing at it violently. It bothers him not to be able to control the discourse.

"Dollar bill," says Therese's mother.

"Bill!" says Therese. At this her father begins nodding and pointing at her psychotically. Yes, yes, yes. Now he makes stretching motions with his hands. "Bill, Billy, William," says Therese, and her father points wildly at her again. "William," she says. "William Kennedy Smith."

"Yes!" shouts her father, clapping his hands and throwing his head back as if to praise the ceiling.

"William Kennedy Smith?" Ann is scowling again. "How did you get that from just William?"

"He's been in the news," shrugs Therese. She does not know how to explain Ann's sourness. Perhaps it has something to do with her struggles in law school, or with Therese's being a circuit-court judge, or with the diamond on Ann's finger that is so huge that, to Therese, it seems unkind to wear it in the presence of their mother's, which is, when one gets right down to it, a chip. Earlier, this morning, Ann told Therese that she is going to take Tad's name. "You're going to call yourself Tad?" Therese asked, but Ann was not amused. Ann's sense of humor has never been that flexible, though she always used to like a good sight gag.

Ann explained officiously, "I believe a family is like a team, and everyone on the team should have the same name, like a color. I believe a spouse should be a team player."

Therese no longer has any idea who Ann is. Therese had liked Ann better when she was eight, with her blue pencil case and a strange, loping run that came from having one leg an inch and a half longer than the other. Ann was attractive as a child. She was awkward and inquiring. She was cute. Or so she had seemed to Therese, who was mostly in high school and college then, slightly depressed and studying too much, destroying her already bad eyes, so that now she wears glasses so thick her eyes swim in a cloudy way behind them. As she stood listening to Ann talk about team players, Therese smiled and nodded, but she felt preached at, as if she were a messy, wayward hippie. She wanted to grab her sister, throw herself upon her, embrace her, shut her up. She tried to understand Ann's dark and worried nuptial words but, instead, found herself recalling the pratfalls she used to perform for Ann—Therese could take a fall straight on the face—in order to make her laugh.

Ann's voice was going on. "When you sit too long, the bodices bunch up . . ."

Therese mentally measured the length of her body and the space in front of her and wondered if she could do it. Of course she could. Of course. But *would* she? And then suddenly she knew she would. She let her hip twist and fell straight forward, her arm at an angle, her mouth in a whoop. She had learned to do this in drama club when she was fifteen. She hadn't been pretty, and it was a means of getting the boys' attention. She landed with a thud.

"You still do that?" asked Ann with incredulity and disgust. "You're a judge and you still *do* that?"

"Sort of," said Therese from the floor, feeling around for her glasses.

Now it is the team player herself standing up to give clues to her team. Ann looks at the name on her scrap of paper and makes a slight face. "I need a consultation," she says in a vaguely repelled way that perhaps she imagines is sophisticated. She brings the scrap of wrapping paper over to Therese's team. "What is this?" Ann asks. There in Ray's handwriting is a misspelled "Arachnophobia."

"It's a movie," says Ray, apologetically. "Did I spell it wrong?"

"I think you did, honey," says Therese, leaning in to look at it. "You got some of the 'o's and 'a's mixed up." Ray is dyslexic. When the roofing business slows in the winter months, instead of staying in with a book, or going to therapy, he drives to cheap matinées of bad movies. "Flicks," he calls them. Or "cliffs" when he's making fun of himself. Ray misspells everything. Is it "input" or "imput"? Is it "averse," "adverse," or "adversed"? His roofing business has a reputation for being reasonable, but a little slipshod and second rate. Nonetheless, Therese thinks he is great. He is never condescending. He cooks an infinite variety of dishes with chicken. He is ardent and capable, and claims almost every night, in his husbandly way, to find Therese the sexiest woman he's ever known. Therese likes that. She is also having an affair with a young assistant D.A. in the prosecutor's office, but it is a limited thing—like taking her gloves off, clapping her hands, and putting the gloves back on again. It is quiet and, she believes, undiscoverable. It is nothing, except that it is sex with a man who is not dyslexic, and once in a while, by God, she needs that.

Ann is acting out "Arachnophobia," the whole concept, rather than working syllable by syllable. She stares into her fiancé's eyes, wiggling her fingers about and then jumping away in a fright, but he doesn't get it. She waves her Christmas-manicured nails at him more furiously. One of the nails has a little Santa

Claus painted on it. Ann's black hair is cut severely in sharp, expensive lines, and her long, drapey clothes hang from her thin shoulders as if still on a hanger. She looks starved and rich and enraged. Everything seems struggled toward and forced, a little cartoonish, like the green shoes, which may be why her fiancé suddenly shouts out, "Little Miss Muffet!" Ann turns now to Andrew, motioning at him encouragingly, as if to punish Tad. The awkward lope of her childhood has taken on a chiropracticed slink. Therese turns back toward her own team, toward her father, who is still muttering something about William Kennedy Smith. "A woman shouldn't be in a bar at three o'clock in the morning. That's all there is to it."

"Dad, that's ludicrous," whispers Therese, not wanting to interrupt the game. "Bars are open to everyone. Public Accommodations Law."

"I'm not talking about the cold legalities," he says chastisingly. He has never liked lawyers, and is baffled by his daughters. "I'm talking about a long-understood moral code." Her father is of that Victorian sensibility that, deep down, respects prostitutes more than it does women in general.

"Whose long-understood moral code?" Therese frowns at him gently. "Dad, you're seventy-five years old."

"Arachnophobia!" Andrew shouts, and he and Ann rush together and do high fives.

Therese's father makes a quick, little spitting sound, then crosses his legs and looks the other way. Therese glances over at her mother, and her mother is smiling at her conspiratorially, behind Therese's father's back, making little donkey ears with her fingers, her sign when she thinks he's being a jackass.

"All right, forget William Kennedy Smith. Your turn, doll," says Therese's father to her mother. Therese's mother gets up slowly but bends gleefully to pick up the scrap of paper. She looks at it, walks to the center of the room, and shoves the paper scrap into her pocket. She faces the other team and makes the sign for a famous person.

"Wrong team, Mom," says Therese, and her mother says "Whoops," and turns around. She repeats the famous-person stance.

"Famous person," says Ray encouragingly. Therese's mother nods. She pauses for a bit, to think. Then she spins around, throws her arms up into the air, collapses forward onto the floor, then backward, hitting her head on the stereo.

"Marjorie, what are you doing?" asks Therese's father. Her mother is lying there on the floor, laughing.

"Are you O.K.?" Therese asks. Her mother nods, still laughing quietly.

"Fall," says Ray. "Dizziness. Dizzy Gillespie."

Therese's mother shakes her head.

"Epilepsy," says Therese.

"Explode," says her father, and her mother nods. "Explosion. Bomb. Robert Oppenheimer!"

"That's it." Her mother sighs. She has a little trouble getting back up. She is seventy, and her knees are jammed with arthritis.

"You need help, Mom?" Therese asks.

"Yeah, Mom, you need help?" asks Ann, who has risen and walked toward the center of the room, to take charge, in her way.

"I'm O.K.," Therese's mother sighs, with a quiet, slightly faked giggle, and walks stiffly back to her seat.

"That was great, Ma," says Therese.

Her mother smiles proudly. "Well, thank you!"

After that there are many rounds, and every time Therese's mother gets anything like Dom DeLuise, or Tom Jones, she does her bomb imitation again, whipping herself into a spastic frenzy and falling, then rising stiffly to great applause. Pam brings Winnie in from her nap, and everyone oohs and ahs at the child's sweet, sleep-streaked face. "There she is," coos Aunt Therese. "You want to come see Grandma be a bomb?"

"It's your turn," says Andrew impatiently.

"Mine?" asks Therese.

"I think that's right," says her father. She gets up, digs in the bowl, unfolds a scrap of wrapping paper. It says "Eckels Street." "I need a consultation here. Andrew, I think this is your writing."

"O.K.," he says, rising, and together they step into the foyer.

"Is this a TV show?" whispers Therese. "I don't watch much TV."

"No," says Andrew with a vague smile.

"What is it?"

He shifts his weight, reluctant to tell her. Perhaps it is because he works with Top Secret documents from the Defense Department; he was recently promoted from the just plain Secret ones. As an engineer, he consults, reviews, approves. His gaze is suppressed, annoyed. "It's the name of a street two blocks from here." There's a surly and defensive curve to his mouth.

"But that's not the title of anything famous."

"It's a place. I thought we could do names of places."

"It's not a famous place."

"So?"

"I mean, we all could write down the names of streets in our neighborhoods, near where we work, a road we walked down once on the way to a store."

"You're the one who said we could do places."

"I did? Well, all right, then, what did I say was the sign for a place? We don't have a sign for places."

"I don't know. You figure it out," he says. A saucy rage is all over him now. Is this from childhood? Is this from hair loss? Once, Therese and Andrew had been close. But she has no idea who he is anymore. She has only a theory: a nice guy victimized by high-school guidance counsellors working in conjunction with the Pentagon to recruit, train, and militarize all the boys with high math S.A.T. scores. "From M.I.T. to M.I.A.," as Andrew once put it himself. "A military-industrial asshole." But she can no longer find that satirical place in him. Last year, at least, they had joked about their growing up. "I scarcely remember Dad reading to us," she'd said.

"Sure he read to us," said Andrew. "You don't remember him reading to us? You don't remember him reading to us silently from the Boston *Globe?*"

Now Therese scans his hardening face for a joke, a glimmer, a bit of love. Andrew and Ann have seemed close, and Therese feels wistful, wondering when and how that happened. She is a little jealous. The only expression she can get from Andrew is a derisive one. He is a traffic cop. She is the speeding flower child.

Don't you know I'm a judge? Therese wants to ask. A judge via a fluke political appointment, sure. A judge with a reputation around the courthouse for light sentencing, true. A judge who is having an affair that mildly tarnishes her character— O.K. A softie, an easy touch, but a judge nonetheless.

Instead she says, "Do you mind if I just pick another one?"

"Fine by me," Andrew says, and strides brusquely back into the living room.

Oh, well, Therese thinks. It is her new mantra. It usually calms her better than om, which she also tries. Om is where the heart is. Om is not here. Oh, well. Oh, well. When she was first practicing law, to combat her courtroom stage fright she would chant to herself, *Everybody loves me, everybody loves me,* and, when that didn't work especially well, she'd switch to *Kill! Kill! Kill!*

"We're doing another one," announces Andrew, and Therese picks another one.

A book and a movie. She opens her palms, prayerlike, for a book. She cranks one hand in the air for a movie. She pulls on her ear and points at a lamp. "Sounds like 'light,' " Ray says. His expression is open and helpful. "Bite, kite, fight, night—"

Therese signals yes, that's it.

"Night," repeats Ray.

"Tender Is the Night," says her mother.

"Yes!" says Therese and bends to kiss her mother on the cheek. Her mother smiles exuberantly, her face in a kind of burst; she loves affection, is hungry and grateful for it. When she was younger she was a frustrated, mean mother, so she is pleased when her children act as if they didn't remember.

It is Andrew's turn. He stands before his own team, staring at the red scrap in his hand. He ponders it, shakes his head, then looks back toward Therese. "This must be yours," he says with a smirk that may be a good-natured smirk. Is there such a thing? Therese hopes so.

"You need a consultation?" Therese gets up to look at the writing; it reads "Surrey with the Fringe on Top."

"Yup, that's mine," she says.

"Come here," Andrew says, and the two of them go back down the corridor toward the foyer again. This time Therese notices the photographs her parents have hung there. Photographs of their children, of weddings and Winnie, though all the ones of Therese seem to her to be aggressively unflattering, advertising an asymmetry in her expression, or the magnified haziness of her eyes, or her hair in a dry, peppery frizz. Surely there must have been better pictures. The ones of Andrew, of Ann, of Tad, of Pam and Winnie are sunlit, posed, wholesome, pretty. The ones of Therese seem slightly disturbed, as if her parents were convinced she is insane.

"We'll stand here by the psychotic-looking pictures of me," says Therese.

"Ann sent her those."

"Oh," says Therese.

"She included the frames and the little hangers. Look," Andrew says, getting back to the game, "I've never heard of this." He waves the scrap of paper, as if it were a gum wrapper.

"You haven't? It's a song. 'Chicks and ducks and geese better scurry, When I take you out in the surrey . . .'?"

"No."

"No?" She keeps going. She looks up at him romantically. " 'When I take you out in the surrey, When I take you out in the surrey with the fringe on—' "

"No," Andrew interrupts emphatically.

"Hmm. Well, don't worry. Everyone on your team will know it."

The righteous indignation is returning to his face. "If *I* don't know it, what makes you think *they'll* know it?" Perhaps this is because of his work, the techno-secrecy of it. *He* knows: *they* don't.

"They'll know it," Therese says. "I guarantee." She starts to turn to leave.

"Whoa, whoa, whoa," says Andrew. The gray-pink of rage is back in his skin. What has he become? She hasn't a clue. He is successfully Top Secret. He is classified information. "I'm not doing this. I refuse."

Therese stares at him. Perhaps this is the assertiveness he can't exercise on the job. Perhaps here, where he is no longer a cog-though-a-prized-cog, he can insist on certain things. The Cold War is over, she wants to say. But what has replaced it is this: children who have turned against one another, now that the gods—or were they only guards?—have fled. "O.K., fine," she says. "I'll make up another."

"We're doing another one," announces Andrew triumphantly as they come back into the living room. He waves the paper scrap. "Have any of you ever even heard of a song called 'Surrey with the Fringe on Top'?"

"Sure," says Pam, looking at him in a puzzled way. No doubt he seems different to her around the holidays.

"You have?" He seems a bit flummoxed. He looks at Ann. "Have you?" Ann is reluctant to break ranks with him, but says quietly, "Yeah."

"Tad, how about you?" he asks.

Tad has been napping off and on, his head thrown back against the sofa, but now he jerks awake. "Uh, yeah," he says.

"Tad's not feeling that well," says Ann.

In desperation, Andrew turns toward the other team. "And you all know it, too?"

"I don't know it," says Ray. He is the only one. He doesn't know a show tune from a chauffeur. In a way, that's what Therese likes about him.

Andrew sits back down, refusing to admit defeat. "Ray didn't know it," he says.

Therese can't think of a song, so she writes "Clarence Thomas," and hands the slip back to Andrew. As he ponders his options, Therese's mother gets up and comes back holding Dixie cups and a bottle of cranberry drink. "Who would like some cranberry juice?" she says, and starts pouring. She hands the cups out carefully to everyone. "We don't have the wineglasses unpacked, so we'll have to make do."

"We'll have to make do" is one of their mother's favorite expressions, acquired during the Depression and made indelible during the war. When they were little, Therese and Andrew used to look at each other and say, "We'll have to make doo-

doo," but when Therese glances over at him now, nothing registers. He has forgotten. He is thinking only of the charade.

Ray sips his drink a little sloppily, and a drop spills on the chair. Therese hands him a napkin, and he dabs at the upholstery with it, but it is Ann who is swiftly up, out to the kitchen, and back with a cold, wet cloth, wiping at Ray's chair in a kind of rebuke.

"Oh, don't worry," her mother is saying.

"I think I've got it," says Ann solemnly.

"I'm doing my clues now," says Andrew impatiently. Therese looks over at Winnie who—calm and observant in her mother's arms, a plump, incontinent Buddha who knows all her letters— seems like the sanest person in the room.

Andrew is making a sweeping gesture with his arm, something meant to include everyone in the room.

"People," says Tad.

"Family," says Pam.

Ann has come back from the kitchen and sits down on the sofa. "Us," she says.

Andrew smiles and nods.

"Us. Thom-us," says Ann. "Clarence Thomas."

"Yes," says Andrew with a clap. "What was the time on that?"

"Thirty seconds," says Tad.

"Well, I guess he's on the tip of everyone's tongue," says Therese's mother.

"I guess so," says Therese.

"It was interesting to see all those black people from Yale," says Therese's mother. "All sitting there in the Senate caucus room. I'll bet their parents were proud."

Ann did not get into Yale. "What I don't like," she says, "is all these black people who don't like whites. They're so hostile. I see it all the time in law school. It's the blacks, not the whites, who are angry."

"Imagine that," says Ray.

"Yes. Imagine," says Therese. Something bursts in her. "You know what else I don't like? I don't like all these gay men who have gotten just a little too sombre and butch. You know what I

mean? Where is the mincing and *high-spirited* shrieking of yes-
teryear? I say, where is the *gaiety* in gay? It's all so confusing
and inconvenient! You can't tell who's who without a goddam
playbill!" She stands up and looks at Ray. It is time to go. She
lost her judicial temperament hours ago. She fears she is going
to do another pratfall, only this time she will break something.
She will break furnishings. She will break bones. Already she
sees herself carted out on a stretcher, brought toward the airport, and toward home, saying the final words she has to say to
her family, has always had to say to her family. Sounds like
"could cry."

   "Goodbye!"
   "Goodbye!"
   "Goodbye!"
   "Goodbye!"
   "Goodbye!"
   "Goodbye!"

But first Ray must do his charade, which is Confucius. "O.K.
I'm ready," he says, and begins to wander around the living
room in a wild-eyed daze, looking as confused as possible,
groping at the bookcases, placing his palm to his brow. And, in
that moment, Therese thinks how good-looking he is and how
kind, and how she loves nobody else in the world even half as
much.

Kate Wheeler

IMPROVING MY AVERAGE

The prop plane labored up the Andes' blue and white spine, at the mercy of blasts and vacuums. My scrambled eggs jittered in their dish, like the coarse yellow foam that storms leave on a beach. I had no intention of eating them: I was counting cities on my fingers, dividing in my head. After calculating backwards twice, I'd just gotten it straight. Being twelve years old, having lived in eight places, I'd inhabited each location of my childhood for one and four-eighths years, eighteen months, too long.

When I'd arrived where we were now leaving, I was seven and had lived in seven places. I'd been in a state of perfect balance, I now realized, like the Golden Age of Pericles: I couldn't remember having worried about anything. But then my dad's company kept him five years in Terremotos, Perú. In the yellow desert of the north, I grew old enough for first loves—skinny Mike Grady, who could walk on his knees in lotus pose, and the Pacific Ocean, which almost claimed me one day in an undertow. Time stretched out so long in Terremotos, I forgot it was dragging me toward this, the day of departure.

Now we were moving to Cartagena, Colombia, on the bathtub-shallow Caribbean. My father's company had promoted him to manage a plant that extruded polyethylene. I'd be able to see Plasticos Revo across the bay from my own balcony, promised my mother, who'd made a househunting trip a month ago and rented the same house my father's predecessor had lived in.

"I hope we leave it soon," I said meanly when she showed me the picture of the house, pink and modern, with a rubber tree over the garage.

"You jackal, I worked so hard," she said, and burst into tears.

"Eat those eggs," she told me now. "A protein breakfast is the best gift you can give your brain."

Before I could hesitate, my father's eye rolled over onto me, and I heard him clear his throat. "Lila."

I stabbed them, wishing I could throw them out the sealed window for condors to eat.

The plane's silver wing hung over the Cordillera Blanca, perfectly static, as if we weren't really moving. If we crashed, I'd touch snow for the first time. I imagined search parties of *cholos* fanning out over a glacier, chewing coca leaves for endurance. By the time they found us, most of the passengers would be frozen, dreaming their way deeper and deeper into total darkness. Not me—I'd read in Jack London how to bury yourself in a drift and remain alive, insulated by snow itself.

Incas' descendants would adopt me; I'd live the rest of my life on the altiplano, playing a *quena* among stone ruins.

We landed, and Cartagena clapped itself around us like a boiled towel. The Customs official smirked as he ran his hands under my mother's nighties, examined the soles of my U.S.—made saddle shoes for marks of use. He envied us, I knew. Still, I wanted to explain that I'd been born in the jungle in Venezuela, and so wasn't blood-connected with this mortifying mountain of imported goods. Because our main shipment wasn't due for several months, my mother had packed everything from aspirin to bedspreads in fifteen suitcases.

My father's new driver took charge of us outside Customs. His name was Cosme Leña. He was the color of a plum and had no voice, only a kind of hiccup like the catch between sobs. As he gesticulated at the porters, my mother explained that Cosme had had a tracheotomy, and so lacked vocal cords. The operation was performed on the HOPE ship, a fact Cosme was proud of, my mom said, with a minuscule lifting of her eyebrows. I saw the scar in the pit of his throat, darker-purple, thickened skin, like a splash of glaze on ceramic.

Mom and I squeezed in back with five suitcases. Cosme babied the company Fairlane along ruts, through ponds, the thin circle of the wheel stopping then spinning in his big hands. Most of the other cars were sturdier, Jeeps or pickups; I'd have preferred one of them, by far, to our fragile U.S. product.

YANQUI GO HOME, all the walls said.

Cosme hiccupped steadily to my father, and bit by bit I deciphered his words of pure breath. He was trying to get his daughter hired as a maid in our house. She was good, clean, hardworking, religious—a Protestant converted by missionaries from the States, Cosme said, as if this were a bond my father must acknowledge. Alas, Señora Leña had just had their eighth baby, and there was no more room in their humble home. So Estrellita, the oldest at seventeen, must leave.

"Lo pienso, Leña," my father said irritably. I'll think about it.

"Po'a'o," Cosme begged. Please.

We rolled past mildewed coral battlements hung with faded wash. Naked boys pranced, an inky cloud hung over the sea, a white goat was staked at the edge of a soccer field. These new sights made me feel I could be happy here.

"There's your school," my father said as we passed a yellow building.

Our house was pinker than its photo. Meters from the bay, its yard was pitted with land crabs' holes. A young woman stood on the front-door porch, a nylon shopping bag at her feet.

"Uh-oh," I said.

"Who's that?" said my mother, who didn't speak enough Spanish to have deciphered Cosme's proposal.

"I think it's our new maid," I whispered.

She came tilting toward the car. Something was wrong with her, too: her right calf was thinner than her left, and gave her walk a crooked kind of eagerness, the limp throwing her body forward on every other step. She stopped in the shade of the rubber tree and stood there trying to look eligible. I shrank down as my father growled in his throat, preparing to dispel her.

"Polio," pronounced my mother.

"*E'm'ia*," Cosme corrected. *Es mi hija,* she's my daughter.

"Oh, hell, Leña," my father said. "What's she doing here?"

Not polio, Cosme was saying, only a problem of the knee.

"She looks nice," I said, meaning beautiful. Estrellita was the color of a bay horse, with an aquiline nose that made her look like she should be riding on a palanquin.

My father surged out of the car, followed by my mother and Cosme. I slid farther down in the seat and ran my fingernail down the vinyl's textured stripes. When their voices stopped I mustered courage to sit up, terrified I'd see Estrellita prostrate and kissing my father's wingtips, or else humping to the bus stop with her sad bag. But all had been resolved; Estrellita Leña was ours. She was following my dad to the front door; he strode ahead holding the key in front of him like the solution to great problems. Cosme was thanking my mother, clasping his hands and rolling his eyeballs skyward.

My mother nodded sideways for him to start unloading.

"Well, we got a bargain," she said wearily. Inside, she threw herself down on a couch the Martins had left. My mother did not always seem strong enough for her own life.

That night I lay on a buttony, damp-smelling mattress between my favorite sheets. They'd been hanging out on a line this morning and still smelled seared by Terremotos' perpetual sun, but I was far from fooled. Outside, blue and orange crabs circled under the porch light, bubbles clicking from their furry sectioned mouths.

I'd recalculated my life on paper, and happily found that my average went down to sixteen months the minute we landed in Cartagena. As I lay in bed it occurred to me that the new maid had acquired an average, too, this very day. After seventeen years in one house, her life was cut in half by moving in with us. Since for myself I did not calculate changes of house in one city, her case allowed me to savor my own magnanimity.

The next morning I peeked into Estrellita's room while she

was washing walls upstairs. It was freshly painted chalk yellow,
but had a slick cement floor that sloped to a central drain. A
pair of pointy white church pumps sat under the bed, deformed
to the different widths of Estrellita's feet. She also owned a bottle of perfume, a transistor radio, and a hairbrush. My favorite
was the picture tucked into the edge of the mirror. Sinners in a
lake of fire. Their mouths were open screaming for the help of
Jesus, who stood smiling on a blue cloud surrounded by cherubs. The cherubs were bodiless babies' heads with wings, more
like moths than angels.

School wouldn't start for weeks. I met a boy my age at a welcoming party, Walter Nugent, but he'd just come down from the
States and couldn't speak any Spanish, so I wasn't interested in
him. He had one good trick, which was to scrunch his face to
show forceps dents he'd gotten in his temples, being pulled
from the womb in Pittsburgh.

I tried catching lizards in the yard. They were fast and I got
only one; its blue neon tail broke off in my hand while its green
trunk scuttled into a crab's hole. "Grow another tail," I said,
burying the old one under the gladioli.

My head was pounding with the heat. In Terremotos, Mike
Grady and I had had a zoo. We charged half a *sol* admission to
see my iguana, parakeet and scorpions, plus Mike's dog Muffin
(whom we said was a lion), his two dead seasnakes in alcohol,
and his father's saltwater aquarium. No one came, but the zoo
made us happy, until the iguana opened the cage with its hand-
like claw and ran away.

I retreated to the shade of my balcony, where a plastic-wicker
chair had been left by the previous renters. Staring across the
flat, oily bay at the old city, the port, and the pale scientific
turrets of my father's chemical plant, I decided all of life was an
illusion of the senses. The raw salt smell of the breeze was just
molecules hitting my nose. I'd never touch the turrets of my
father's plant, even though I could see them perfectly clearly.

In coming days I learned to put myself in a trance by willing
my finger to rise and also to disobey me and lie still. Sometimes
it stayed paralyzed even when I seriously tried to move it.

I heard the vacuum cleaner stop. A subtle pressure grew against the back of my head—I was being spied on.

Estrellita.

For two days I pretended not to notice.

The diagonals of her back crisscrossed unevenly as she strolled past me and leaned on the balustrade, lifting her pink heels off her plastic sandals.

"*Bonita la suidá*," she observed. Pretty city.

"*Muy*," I said warmly. Very.

She sniffed deeply and fell back on her heels again. I wondered where her thoughts went as she gazed beyond La Popa, the green promontory that bounded the far end of Cartagena. So I asked her.

She shrugged. "*Monte. Finca. Perro rabioso.*" Bush, farm, rabid dog.

I wasn't very surprised when, the next day, she said, "*Ven.*" Come.

I followed her inside, through my own bedroom, out a door that opened from the second floor onto the roof of the garage. She had no trouble hopping onto the waist-high roof of the servants' quarters. We walked to the edge and looked over into a patio nicer than ours. Striped tiles, potted *adorno* and crotons, bentwood rockers, and a green Amazon parrot.

"*Mírala, que blanca,*" Estrellita said. Look how white she is.

"*Verde,*" I disagreed, thinking she meant the parrot.

She tisked and pointed. Higher up. "*Blanca, 'ombé.*"

"*Huy.*" A naked girl was creeping across the floor of the balcony, pale and bumbling as a white puppy. A bamboo screen hid her from all angles except from where we stood.

This was Isis Román, oldest daughter of the Román family. They owned the factory that made five colors of soft drink, red, black, purple, green and orange. Estrellita explained that Isis was sixteen but would never marry because of her mental defect. She'd live all her life as a caterpillar on her parents' balcony.

My mother had mentioned that our neighbors were first cousins: the five important families in Cartagena had pure blood from Spain they couldn't bear to dilute. I tried to explain recessive genes to Estrellita, but she already understood them—God sends bad seeds into the womb to punish parents' sins. Especially, pride. From the fierce look on Estrellita's face, I could tell that Cosme and Señora Leña had already been cast into her private lake of fire. I wondered whether she saw my face there, too, among the unsaved.

Isis Román swiveled her head, rolled sideways, and, moving as slowly as seaweed underwater, displayed her breasts, black bush, and pale underarm tufts. Her gray eyes slipped over us, hot and unfocused as the sky. As her hand crawled down between her legs, a sudden vacuum pulled at my womb and I had to step back from the edge of the roof.

Estrellita said, *"Pobrecita. Ella no sabe na'."* Poor little thing, she doesn't know anything.

Back on the balcony, I asked Estrellita if she herself was engaged. Or, I added, remembering her bad leg, did Cosme want to keep her close to him?

No! She had a fiancé, she said proudly, a truck mechanic named Americo Velarde. They'd be married next year.

"Handsome?" I asked respectfully.

"No." She smiled. "I am the only one who loves Americo."

I was filled with joy. It was so romantic, like Beauty and the Beast. "Why don't you marry him now? Then you wouldn't have to work for us."

"It's to marry that I have to work," she said, explaining that Americo's parents had asked for a cash payment because their son was marrying a cripple. Cosme didn't like Americo, so Estrellita was earning the money herself. She gave half her wages to her parents, half to Senor and Señora Velarde. She'd be paid up by New Year's.

I was so shocked, my ears rang. "That's not fair," I said. "What about Americo?"

"He is helping."

How could true love accept such a bad bargain? I tried not to think about this, but Estrellita visited my balcony daily and talked about everything, especially love, especially Americo. Americo had called her on the phone while my mother was out shopping. Americo liked green mangoes with salt, and the *cum-*

bia was his favorite dance. Nothing could ever divide them. The two of them had already become husband and wife to each other, if I understood what that meant.

I said yes.

She made me taste green mangoes, and brought her transistor up to teach me the *cumbia.* We hardly needed music, for in Cartagena an itching syncopation lived in the air itself. On that big balcony we pursued each other, wriggling our shoulders like lovesick pigeons, burning each other's faces with imaginary candles. The *cumbia* imitates a slaves' courtship in ball and chain, dragging one foot behind the other: it was the perfect dance for Estrellita's lame leg.

"*Soy hombre,*" she'd say, grabbing my waist, I'm a man. Looking up at her noble African face, I failed to imagine any future husband. Mike Grady was too far away, and had somehow become too young.

I tried to teach her the alphabet, in its Spanish version with extra ñ and ll, optional y and w. Copying my letters, she gripped the crayon so tightly she nearly crushed it; her letters came out tall and crooked, mauve and lime-green beings with an animated aspect, like the living hieroglyphs of a spell. But these lessons made both of us uncomfortable, and after two lessons we dropped them to return to hotter topics, love, *cumbia,* and the *radionovela* of four o'clock, "*Amores desesperados.*"

The scion of a rich family falls in love with the housemaid. His parents find out and have her locked in a convent, but he comes with a ladder in the night and springs her. They elope, and live in a penthouse in Bogota. The wicked, rich parents try various stratagems to break up their marriage—abduction, the spreading of evil rumors, sending temptresses to the young husband's place of work.

Estrellita listened raptly to this wild plot: I knew she imagined herself in some glittering gown, on a balcony overlooking the winking lights of the capital, and beset by treachery. Alas, I couldn't be the *novia:* I had no poverty, no lover, and no entrapment to be saved from. Instead, I yearned to be the hero. Eighteen and powerful, a rescuer for Estrellita.

Clearly there was no reason why I was I and Estrellita, Estrellita; therefore, no reason for me to be rich and her to be my servant. But, since I found myself in the position of privilege, I was responsible for helping her.

Saving her would not be easy. Having shared their houses with servants for twelve years, my parents never lost sight of their wallets. Our shipment was delayed, too, so there was nothing in the house to steal and sell. Even my piggybank, with its hoard of Peruvian *soles,* was out at sea in some container ship.

I lay awake each night, plotting and worrying. In order to sleep, I put my hand between my own thighs, imitating Isis Román, the girl who didn't know anything. I loved what I felt, but it was embarrassing to imagine sharing such sensations with another person, especially a man.

First day of school at Teddy Roosevelt. I waited for the bus under a banyan tree with Graciela and Adolfo Román, Isis' sister and brother, and Barbara Murphy, a missionary kid with hard red cheeks and a forehead so shiny it looked like her mother must scrub it every day with Ajax.

Graciela and Barbara were both in my grade, seventh. Graciela was three years too old, because she had trouble with English. She wore a tight lavender dress, mourning for a dead uncle, that folded into three creases of her belly. I could see her body was blocky and abundant, just like Isis'. She right away invited me to her *quinceañera* party, a sort of coming out; but visions of nakedness, hers and her sister's, discomfited me so much that I said my parents didn't let me go to boy-girl parties. And added, for good measure, that she looked like a boiled grape, *una uva hervida.*

Barbara sat next to me on the bus. "You better wear shorts underneath," she warned. "Adolfo was lifting up your skirt from behind with his Coca-Cola yoyo. That's what boys at Roosevelt do. Are you saved?"

What a weirdo: I willed her to vanish. "I don't know."

"If you don't know, you're not, and you're going to hell." Lifting her chin, she said, "I'm a half-orphan. My real dad was a martyr."

He'd been murdered by members of a jungle tribe he'd been

trying to convert. She told me the story in detail, speaking so fast and smoothly it was like she'd memorized a script. Drunken men locked her and her mother into the kitchen and then dragged her father into the bush and chopped him up with machetes. A bachelor missionary was sent to bring Barbara and her mother down the Magdalena River to safety. This man was now Barbara's stepfather; he was the minister at the *Iglesia Bautista Cuadrangular.*

I left a silence of respect, then said, "That's my maid's church. Do you know Estrellita Leña?"

"Yup," Barbara said, and I realized that she was closer to Estrellita than I was, less of a *norteamericana*—only because she'd lived all her life in this one country of Colombia, I reminded myself. Still, I felt inferior.

I let her sit next to me in class even though it meant I might not make any other friends. She was definitely strange, with that shiny forehead and hard blue eyes glittering with conviction; but a saved half-orphan was a powerful being. In the middle of class she got up from her desk, went to the window, looked out, and returned. Mr. Clements frowned, but kept writing on the board about capitalization. Inspired, after recess I raised my hand and asked to go to the bathroom even though I didn't need to. Of course, Mr. Clements had to say yes.

Liberation.

Walking down the breezeway, I looked into the classrooms at the diligent teachers and distracted students, then outward, past the rattling palms, to where a ball of light hung over the green sea.

I wanted to be Barbara. After school, she invited me to the sea wall to look at the black iguanas, and then to ride home together on the public bus. My mother wouldn't mind; in those days Cartagena was as safe as a bathtub.

"Stay away from the edge," Barbara warned. "A barracuda once jumped out and bit off a woman's foot near here."

We admired the iguanas, wet with spray, lying so still and ancient on the reddish coral blocks.

"How do you get saved?" I asked.

"Just ask Christ Jesus into your heart. Knock and it shall be opened."

At home, I lay on my bed with the air conditioner off, so as not to have distracting noise. My heart beat against my ribs, maybe the Lord trying to get in. "Come in," I said, but didn't feel improved. "Give me a sign if I am saved."

Silence pulsed, thick and heavy. Then I heard Estrellita coming upstairs, whistling through her teeth. I'd forgotten about her since this morning. If I'm saved she'll open the door and say hello, I thought, but she passed by.

Maybe, being already saved, she didn't really need me.

I lay there ten minutes before going to find her, down in the patio combing her stiff redbrown hair. She asked me how school was. I said, "Boring. The daughter of Reverend Murphy is in my class."

"*La Barbara,*" Estrellita said, which also means "The Barbarian." I laughed, traitorously.

The next day at school I confessed to Barbara that my conversion hadn't worked.

"You can't throw off sin by your own strength," Barbara explained. "You better come to church."

My mother gave permission easily, saying church would be good for me. "It'll help you think of something larger than yourself." I wanted to tell her I was always thinking about larger things, but I didn't want to sound vain.

I spent Saturday night at Barbara's. The Murphys lived in a converted garage; their biggest possession was an upright piano Eve Murphy pounded out hymns on. No other music was allowed in their home, a fact Barbara was proud of.

I hated Reverend Murphy right away. He was a tall, fat, pale, ugly man who made Barbara and me call him Sir. He stared at me through Eve's Grace as if trying to force my soul into submission; then between bites of meatloaf he asked if I'd ever been to church.

That night, Barbara started teaching me the books of the bible. When I memorized them all I could win a New Testament. The books had a rhythm, like the alphabet's, that could underpin your life: that night, I got as far as Habakkuk.

I asked Barbara what God's view of stealing was, if the stealing was in a good cause—for example, to raise money for a Christian wedding—and I described Estrellita's marriage problem. Barbara said I'd be doing my parents a favor. Wealth turned people into camels, too fat to fit through the eye of Heaven's needle.

In the morning we burst out of the bedroom in pajamas and grilled her mother about breakfast food. "Who made this banana? Who made this egg?"

"Why, God, of course. Silly girls." She was wearing a printed smock that tied down the back, like a hospital gown; her eyes were as mournful as a Cocker Spaniel's, and her secret shone out, plain: she'd loved her first husband, the martyr, but she didn't love the Reverend Murphy.

I heard thunder in the distance as Barbara and I sat down and ate eggs, bananas and toast.

The *Iglesia* was in a humble part of town. Plastic shelf lining had been glued to the windowpanes to imitate stained glass; the bright red, green and yellow light made the room feel even hotter than it was that day, which was still and moist, waiting to storm. The whole congregation was black except the Murphys and me; patches of color glinted on their sweaty chins and cheeks, and shone around their eyes.

Estrellita and Americo had saved seats in the front row for Barbara and me. Americo was less ugly than I'd imagined. But I was disappointed for my vague ideas about him to be shrunk into any single, unexpected form. He was a pale-brown person, shorter than Estrellita, and solid as a pot. His hand rested on the small of her back as lightly as a dove in its nest; when he and Estrellita caught each other's eyes, a kind of light appeared between them, so that I knew that I was really seeing it—two people in love—for the first time.

Why was I not happy? I couldn't even understand where the light was coming from; they were just two ordinary people.

The sermon was about Jonah and the whale. Barbara's stepfather searched the world's oceans with glittering eyes, he stabbed the air with a forefinger to make his point: God's will is a whale that will swallow us if we resist. His pale, wetted hair straggled like seaweed across his noggin. Outside thunder was rumbling. God's voice, the voice of the reason for everything.

The congregation was moaning, *"Si, señor,"* ominously as the sea. In back a woman started speaking loudly in tongues: *Ashmada, Yoi, Verrabazal!* A jumping lightness attacked my ankles, bounced up my thighs into my chest; I was nearly lifted from the ground.

Barbara said excitedly, "Feel the spirit?"

"Make your heart open to Christ," the Reverend Murphy cried. "Humbly say Please, Please, Lord."

I was shaking all over. On both sides, my girl friends squeezed my arms, wanting me to be one with them in Christ.

"Please, Please, Lord," I cried, really trying to open my heart.

"Come down," the Reverend Murphy said. "Come down." I got up and joined a little file of people who were being converted. The aisle was a tunnel; at the end stood the Reverend Murphy with his arms upraised. When it was my turn, he put his hands on the top of my head and prayed for my new life in Christ. His touch made me cringe.

The rain started outside, a sudden heavy rush that dimmed the light inside the church. Behind me the congregation sang, the collection plates began to pass around.

Dear God, I prayed, thank you for saving me. Please help Estrellita and Americo. I couldn't feel anything, or anyone, listening, but I kept on praying anyway.

Some weeks later the principal came to class to announce that the HOPE ship was on its way back around the coast of South America, and would stop again in Cartagena before returning to the United States. Roosevelt students were invited to tour the ship and meet the doctors and nurses.

Desk to desk, Barbara and I made faces at each other. As Christian girls, we were entitled to despise all worldly, adult, pretentious and American things. We called the principal "Caesar" and the school "Babylon"; we stopped people in the street to ask if they believed God made the universe. Of course, everyone said Yes: Colombia is a Catholic country.

At home, I asked my parents if they'd heard about the HOPE ship's return. They had, but were not excited either. They were having their Scotches in the living room.

My mom said, "JFK is too handsome to be trusted."

My father huffed, "He's offending the Latins with his largesse. They hate to feel we're better than they are."

"I'm going to tour the ship and meet the doctors and nurses," I said.

My mother said quickly, "Congratulations! It's a *good* ship. Saved Cosme from throat cancer. God knows why he still smokes cigars."

"He likes them," my father said.

They let me make them second Scotches.

"Cosme's agitating to get his daughter's leg fixed on the ship," my father reported. "I don't know if he can."

"I thought they tried to stick to life and death," my mother said.

"He wants me to make a recommendation," my father said, "for the surgery list."

"Oh, do it, Daddy. Then she can get married." I explained the uses of Estrellita's salary, the payoff to Americo's parents.

"Now that stinks," my father said. "Cosme makes enough money. Revo's the best employer in town. I ought to fire him. That old rat. That old weasel."

"Firing him would only make it worse," my mother said. "It's no skin off your nose, honey. One phone call."

"I'd better ignore the whole thing," my father muttered. "It's not ethical. The company wouldn't like it."

"That poor child," said my mother.

"Daddy, please," I said. "Ple-e-e-ase."

"Oh, hell," my father said, meaning yes. I kissed him extravagantly; at bedtime I modified my prayers, no longer begging God to find money for Estrellita, but to guarantee all the linked events that would get her into surgery.

The HOPE ship was huge, white as a sail by day, lit up festively at night, with its name all in capitals written on both sides. Estrellita spotted it sailing into port while I was at school; she compared it to a nurse's hat. She told me the story of

Cosme's operation, how he'd been full of tubes and said *barbaridades* coming out of the anesthetic.

She was sitting on a chair in the patio, peeling yucca and putting it into an enamel bowl.

"I'm going to tour the HOPE ship," I said, gritting my teeth against Estrellita's disappointment.

"I'm going to tour it, too," she said.

"What?"

She turned her sharp profile to me and shrugged. Her lips curved up slightly, in triumph.

"Come on," I coaxed.

"They're going to cure my knee."

"*¡Qué bien!*" I gushed. "I was praying for you every night." Maybe I was, then, really saved, and God had heard me in some way; I'd understand after I died.

"Americo was praying, too. I owe it to you two."

"And to the *Padre Todopoderoso,*" I said, the All-Powerful Father.

Our eyes shone into each other's. No more bad bargains.

"The truth, I'm afraid," she said. She held her two legs out for comparison, then kicked her right heel against the floor. "It's not so bad. I came out of my mother feet first, that's all. I keep thinking about the scalpel. So sharp." She shuddered. "So much blood."

"Don't worry, you'll be asleep when they do it," I said. "Let's go look at Isis."

Today Isis was dressed in a little sunsuit. When her eyes rolled upward, I waved and jumped up and down to catch her attention. Isis saw, and was intrigued. She sat up and began shaking her wrists excitedly. Then she began hooting like a chimpanzee. Estrellita and I ran away, giggling, just in time to avoid being seen by the Román's maid.

On the day we toured the HOPE ship, Cosme drove me to school. He was grateful to John F. Kennedy, who had saved his life and now was going to remove his daughter's defect. He was grateful to the people of the United States, and to my father, a powerful man, as I must know.

I pretended ignorance. "My father helped you?"

Oh yes. It had been difficult because Estrellita had no grave condition, but Cosme worked for the manager of Plasticos Revo and now Estrellita would be perfect for her new husband. "*E'te'de?*" he said, looking at me with complicity and pride. *Entiende*, do you understand?

I said I understood. "Americo Velarde will love her even more, if that is possible."

Cosme's face clouded. Americo, Americo was a little Indian. Cosme knew a young man who worked for a bank downtown.

"But Estrellita loves Americo," I cried.

Yes, but Estrellita was silly, she didn't know. Now she was saying she was afraid of the knife.

His chuckle axed through all warmth, all confidence. Violently I wished I'd never asked God to get Estrellita on the surgery list. Please, God, forget it, get her off it again, I prayed. Then I realized that I should make prayers general. God might be angry with me for changing my mind. You never knew what might come along with the satisfaction of a specific request.

Please, God, just make it turn out all right.

"Don't make her get the operation," I pleaded with Cosme. "She's beautiful as she is. She works all day, she can dance the *cumbia*, and her children won't be affected."

Silence. Cosme's wide, crumpled baby face was closed up tightly.

The HOPE nurses turned our tongues green with Kool-Aid from the States, the captain showed us the seven layers of paint that lay like icing on all surfaces, and Barbara was hilarious, but I hardly noticed. I had an attack of claustrophobia in the operating room, far below the waterline and inescapable as a tomb. Mr. Clements said seasickness was impossible in port, but still a nurse took me out on deck, where I hung over the railing looking down at the greasy rainbows in Cartagena Bay.

There was no God, really, I thought. Whenever I tried to find him, there was just a hollow feeling at the base of my skull. How could God let the bay get so polluted? How could He let that poor dog die and be floating, rotting, with its entrails coming out? I'd set evil in motion by pretending to believe in Him. If I'd believed perfectly, my prayers would have been answered perfectly. But I'd prayed selfishly, just to get what I wanted, and I'd lied to Barbara about feeling at home in Christ. So anything bad was going to be my fault.

At home, I couldn't find Estrellita. I searched frantically, upstairs and down, in the kitchen and in her room, out on my balcony, and at the Isis-spying place. The cook didn't know, Cosme smoking a cigar in the garage didn't know, my mother didn't know where she was.

An hour later she came in, beaming. She'd been to the little store to buy milk—and! Her voice dropped to a whisper. She'd had a secret meeting with Americo Velarde to talk about her operation, which would be in two days.

Americo was happy that her leg would be fixed. He'd convinced his parents to return some of the money, so now he and Estrellita were thinking about a little house. He told her not to be afraid of the scalpel. He would pray for her all through the operation.

"No," I said. "Your father said he's going to make you marry some bank clerk. Forget the operation—run away and marry Americo!"

I saw Estrellita and Americo flying out over the ocean, holding hands, dressed in white baptismal robes.

She looked surprised. "Don't worry, my father can't make me do anything I don't want to do. I will never marry Ermincio Bastos, certainly not." Her voice dropped. "I can tell all the world, without any shame, that Americo and I have already consummated our union. Then Ermincio Bastos will not want me."

"Yes. How beautiful," I said, somewhat relieved.

"Yes, it was very beautiful." Her smile went inward, like a cat's.

I got up early the next morning to say goodbye and wish her well, but Estrellita was gone. The Fairlane was gone, too: Cosme must have gotten permission to drive his daughter to the ship, and to visit Señora Leña on the way.

I went into Estrellita's little room and sat on the bed. It was just the same as when I'd first peeked into it, except that there was a sharp smell of her recently sleeping body, and the faces of the sinners in her lake of fire seemed mysteriously fewer. It was the coolest hour of the day; a mist redolent of salt and dead dogs rose from the bay and curled into the courtyard.

I sent out my most powerful wish, for it to be my first day in Cartagena again, without anything having happened yet.

All day at school I wished for the operation's success. Not to God, just to whatever there was. Even if there was just a big nothing, I still couldn't help but wish. I asked Barbara to pray, and she did, in Jesus' name.

"We have to have a talk," my mother said the next night.

Her tone of voice told me all but the location: my average was about to improve. I divided quickly. One and three-ninths years. A year and four months.

"Your father's been promoted and we're moving to Bogotá after Christmas. He'll be director of marketing for Venezuela, Colombia and Perú. They haven't named his successor, so don't tell your friends. Isn't it exciting?"

"We'll miss Estrellita's wedding," I said.

"Well," my mother said and sighed. Snakes began to crawl inside my chest. Snakes and worms. My mother's eyes shifted. "You'd better talk to your father."

This was how punishments always began. I approached my father's huge knees. He was reading papers in the Danish chair. "Dad."

He looked up and when he saw it was me, he took off his reading glasses. Presbyopic is the word: he couldn't see small things near him.

When my father spoke, I knew I'd heard the news before, in a dream or in a previous life.

"Honey, there was a problem with the maid's operation." He sounded annoyed.

"We'll miss Estrellita's wedding," I said.

"Well," my mother said and sighed. Snakes began to crawl inside my chest.

A Colombian medical student had performed the operation, not the American surgeon. The student had botched the work so that Estrellita's leg had had to be amputated at the knee. "Cosme was arrested this morning trying to get on the boat with a pistol to kill the guy," my father said. "But I'll bail him out. And I'm paying for an artificial leg. She'll be all right."

"Is she still getting married?"

"I don't know."

"Can I go to her house?"

"No, honey, I don't think it's a good idea. We'll have her come back and see us before we leave."

Ashamed, tiny, filthy, and depressed, I went out to see Isis, but there was only a blue bath towel lying on the balcony. Looking carefully, I saw the terry flattened, like grass where a cow has slept.

If only I could be like Isis, nothing to do except lie in the sun touching myself, all my life on that same balcony. Isis had no average; thinking about Isis' average was like dividing by zero, or trying to imagine God. If I fell off the roof in front of her, she probably wouldn't understand enough to care.

Barbara came to pick me up for church. She walked through the living room like Shadrach in the fiery furnace, inspecting the turquoise sculptured carpet and the objects my parents had looted, like Conquistadores, from each place we'd lived. These things had just arrived, and soon they would disappear into boxes again. They followed us with touching faithfulness, delayed only because they had no life.

Barbara's stepfather had learned from his congregation that Americo and Estrellita were still engaged. I hadn't told my parents, but after the service at *La Iglesia Bautista Cuadrangular*, the Murphys and I were going to visit Estrellita at home. I'd packed some of my stuffed animals to keep her company during her recovery. Surely she'd one day have a baby and need toys for it, too.

So I told myself. But I was horrified, imagining my Teddy sitting on the flat bedclothes where my friend's foot should have been. That morning, I believed that I was evil. I realized I'd never wanted to go to the Leñas' house and see how dark it was, how crowded, Mrs. Leña wringing her hands surrounded by her eight babies—now, with Cosme in jail and Estrellita, I had become a distant stranger.

Every night I'd dreamed about the poor leg living on, a separate life: dancing the *cumbia*, dragging a slave's ball, kicking its heel in the sky, having its own funeral in a coffin drawn by black horses with tufts on their heads, floating in the bay with two dead dogs. When, awake, I tried to think where her leg had gone, something hit me so hard along the top ridge of my head, I couldn't see.

I was glad the Reverend Murphy was coming along to the Leñas', because I had nothing to say. I didn't want to let Estrellita talk to me, either.

She might smile at me bravely, and make it easy for me. She might be glad I came to see her, and then how could I ever leave? How could I bear to know that one day I might be standing on a balcony in Bogotá, like the *novia* in the *radionovela*. Standing there, having forgotten enough about Estrellita, and Americo, and all of Cartagena: forgotten enough to enjoy the lights of the capital spread out at my feet?

Peter Weltner

THE GREEK HEAD

To the memory of George Stambolian

Our world, mine and Charlie's, resembled theirs, Don's and Roger's, only superficially. It was curious that Don and I both managed record stores, though his was twice as large as mine and three times more successful, and that Roger and Charlie were both vice principals at middle schools here in the city; that Roger and I both came from Providence and that Charlie and Donald grew up, if thirty years apart, nonetheless within blocks of one another in San Mateo; that Don and Roger had met in 1946 in a bar located in the same block as the bar in which Charlie and I met twenty-nine years later; and that the first several letters of our pair of last names were the same, Don Ross and Roger White, Charlie Roberts and Sam Whitten. But it was only curious, nothing more. People are constantly taking accidental facts and arranging them into some kind of order, as if to show, in this instance, that the two of us were destined to become friends with the two of them. But that's not how it happened, of course. We saw their "For Rent" sign before someone else, that's all. And, if the truth were told, we didn't really get along all that well, not well enough to be described as truly successful friends.

When an artery in Donald's brain, having apparently already

ballooned, finally exploded, I was at lunch with a guy named Rick whose ad I'd answered—eyes wide open and skeptical, not expecting much. Of course, it turned out he was the one to be disappointed since he had apparently believed, when I'd told him on the phone that I was currently uninvolved, that I'd meant "really." Though we'd agreed nothing would come of it, the meal still lasted too long because I had been trying to justify myself to him and to myself at the same time, attempting to explain that all I had meant to say was that I was unhappy. Nor was I home later when Roger first pounded on our door at a time when I'd told him I'd be sure to be back from work in case he heard anything from the hospital. He had heard something. Donald was dead.

I knew that there was no need for me to feel guilty. It was just a mistake, something bad that happened while I was looking for a way out of my life and not paying attention to much else. Still, if you'd asked me how my life was going then, I'd have answered as Don used to when he was down in the dumps, "In low water." I knew one of us, either Charlie or I, should have made the break and gotten it over with long ago. But neither of us did, perhaps because it's so hard nowadays to be certain whether one is behaving rationally or from fear. Charlie figured I was safe, I figured he was safe, so it was OK. We were all right together. Or that's what we pretended: safe, safe, discontent, and safe.

That's just another way that Roger and Don weren't like us, only seeming the same. They argued all the time, too. But the difference is that they were never afraid. They had never been afraid of anything, not of each other, not of splitting apart, not of the world's opinion of them, certainly not of dying. They understood as well as anyone that nothing was forever. But they endured. They stuck it out anyway. They had become famous for lasting. Thirty-nine years they had been together, thirty-nine years and counting, Roger had said when Charlie and I had helped them celebrate their anniversary right before last Christmas.

It was a familiar number by then, they'd repeated it so often, but all of a sudden it seemed a miracle to me. Their entire lives

were somehow like the one brief moment when Charlie and I
had just become lovers and we'd flown to the Cape to rejoice in
our success. All week long the weather was beautiful, mild. We
rode rented bikes, swam, walked the beaches, strolled the strip,
danced at the Sea Drift, drank too much, ate too much, got too
much sun, made love, were happy, the night sky so clear as we
lay back on the sand that it seemed as if the souls of all our just-
spent seeds' unborn children were blinking to us from the stars.
It didn't last. The first fight after our return to San Francisco
almost destroyed everything. Like pilgrims in search of consola-
tion, we took another trip, this one to Seattle. It worked. When
we got back, we found the apartment, its garden for our use,
too.

The days after Don's death as Roger waited anxiously for
Don's sister Susan to arrive, we could hear him pacing overhead, especially at night. It kept even Charlie awake who, if
tired enough, could easily fall asleep while having sex. In earlier
years, we might have known what to do about Roger, might
have known better how to behave and what to say so that we
might have believed some of it ourselves. But we had given up
speaking about such things or trying to affect the course of grief,
Charlie months before me. Don's was the third death of a friend
in a year that was barely a month old. The other two had been
twenty years or more younger, and their dying had been much
more painful, taken far longer, and been terrible to witness.
Why waste more useless words on Don's death? It had been
easier, much easier, than most. He was almost old. He'd been,
he said, a happy man. Wasn't that enough? Let Roger remember
all of that and quit stomping down on the floor, on our ceiling,
as if it could do any good.

A big and awkward man, Roger seemed to be foraging for
food, the refrigerator door opening and slamming shut over and
over. Or was it only ice he was after? It annoyed us and was
meant to annoy us. I was sure of it. We could hear the anger in
it, expressed as well in the clogs he had apparently exchanged
for his usual soft slippers, an anger directed against us and our
silence, I figured, at our failure to have offered him any comfort,
sham though it might be. It was funny in a way, like the bratty

kid spoiling the party for all the others because he hadn't been invited. For the first time, Roger had to envy us for something more substantial than our relative youth. Unhappy as we were, we still had each other, if we wanted, for a while longer. There was still a party of sorts downstairs, even if it was breaking up. And, momentarily at least, he hated us for having it. I knew he did.

Because of him, we were eating breakfast much earlier than usual. "I didn't know they bothered to carve clogs in a size fifteen," I remarked. "Those things must weigh ten pounds each." It sounded like dumbbells falling in a gym or like furniture dropping.

Charlie said nothing. He was quietly furious. He had just found the new ad I had cut out and boldly circled, and he was refusing to acknowledge it. It didn't puzzle me why I had left it out on the top of the bureau like that, exposed so blatantly under the lamp's light in an otherwise black room as if deliberately to call his attention to it, the way lately he had been calling my attention to the fact that he had masturbated while I was gone by leaving a porno mag or two lying on the night stand top rather than hiding them back in the drawer where he knew I knew he kept them. The previous night I'd been searching for my one pair of black socks in the back of my bureau drawer, thinking I'd need them for the funeral or whatever. But I didn't put everything back in. That was why I was pretending to look for those socks; I was preparing to pay Charlie back for the golden boys he had been fucking in his imagination yesterday afternoon, if it was only in his imagination since Duane had entered the picture. So it went. We were each trying to let the other know he wasn't necessary anymore. We had been trying to tell each other that for a long time. Only in the past we had bothered to be subtler.

Charlie chomped down hard on his toasted bagel and with one hand opened the interior shutters behind the kitchen table. The sky was already a radiantly pure blue, the surprising storm which had sailed through last night having netted up all the junk that usually floats in the air and left in its wake only a few wisps of clouds.

I sipped my coffee. Why does it never taste as good as it smells? That had been Donald's annoying question nearly every morning when we four were in Baja together on a week's vacation five winters ago.

"Which of these shells do you like best, Charlie?" I prodded. "I think this one is probably my favorite." I shoved it over toward him from the pile in the middle of the table which Roger had arranged as a centerpiece, though it had early become unglued. "What do you think?"

He picked the shell up, examined its shape, so much like a dragonfly's wing and nearly as transparent, and tested its firm, sharp edge, like a knife's. His duty done, he tossed it back to join the others, no two alike, Roger had boasted. "It's OK. It's pretty."

"Right," I said and stared back out the window. It had been a dumb question on a lousy topic, the centerpiece itself something we kept on display only to please Roger. I'd hated the foul, variously infested town on the southeastern coast where Don had directed us all because it was supposed to be such a great spot for diving. Charlie, of course, liked it. Ever since, each time I had mentioned anything about it, Charlie scowled at me in exactly the same way, as if he owned this one special mask whose sole purpose was to remind me that my bad time there was no one's fault but my own. But that was like Charlie. The bad times anywhere with anyone were always the other person's fault, and he had designed lots of different scary masks to let us know it. Yet the truth is that Charlie is much better company than I am. Nearly everyone says so. I've told him so many times myself.

I glanced up at the ceiling. "Roger seems to have settled down."

"So it seems. Maybe he's gone to bed." Charlie checked his watch. "Finally." He folded our newspaper and laid it on the table next to my elbow. "Talk to him today, will you? Find out what's going on with him. What did that note say? That Don's sister is to be here at least by tomorrow, didn't it? She's next of kin, for God's sake. Roger's got to have his wits about him, even in this enlightened era. Try to calm him down some."

"Why don't you?"

"Because I'm going to work." He took a last swallow of his yogurt drink and stood up.

"So am I."

"Yeah. But not for four more hours."

"So what? I don't get it. What's the big difference?"

"You don't have to get it. Just do it."

"Why are you avoiding him, Charlie?"

"Why are you?"

"I'm not."

"Like shit you aren't," Charlie said. "You're avoiding Roger every bit as much as I am. And we both know why."

"We do?"

"Oh, cut the crap, Sam. You don't want him to know we're really breaking up this time. I don't either. Not now, not yet. It's that simple."

"Are we?"

"What?"

"Are we really breaking up this time?"

"Of course. Don't be an ass. We've been doing it for months and months. I suppose it's just taken me this long to find the guts to say so. Now all you have to do is to find the guts to admit it." He walked around the table to position himself behind me and bent to kiss the back of my neck. I shivered. "No scenes now. We promised, remember? I've got to go. I've got a lazy teacher to bawl out."

"It's still early," I protested.

"I know," he said and left the room.

I sat in my chair motionless, nearly rigid. Outside our window, the city looked dazed, too, as if it had yet to recover its breath from the blow of the storm's wild punch. Twenty or thirty minutes at least must have passed in silence as the sun strolled over a golden flank of Telegraph Hill. Never had a place seemed more beautiful to me than San Francisco at that moment, until Roger resumed his pacing, the thud, thud, thud, pause, thud, thud, thud, pause and turn as regular and as infuriating as a madman's dance.

So I didn't go up to Roger's. I couldn't yet, I just couldn't do it. I was too angry at everything and at everyone, at Donald for dying and messing things up this badly, at Roger for grieving and carrying on, and most of all at Charlie for having walked out on me before I'd summoned the courage to leave him first. I was furious at all of them for their not having asked me whether this was the way I wanted it or not. And something, maybe it was my heart, was jumping up and down inside of me like Rumpelstiltskin in a rage at having been found out.

To pass the hours before work, I watched two "I Love Lucy" reruns, early ones full of the kind of slapstick and mugging that Charlie hated, and then I took a long, intense shower, soaping my whole body repeatedly to feel the pleasure of washing myself clean over and over again—in the process, however, apparently stripping my pores of all their oil because after I'd dried myself off my skin was like an old man's, like Roger's, old parchment from which all the legible writing had long ago faded.

I stood in front of the mirror, disgusted by my own body, then opened the medicine cabinet door and drenched myself with Charlie's precious baby oil, watching it soak in and bring me back to life like the rush of tide over the body of a beached and dying starfish. It worked. The evidence was that I wasn't so bad off after all. I'd panicked needlessly. There was some semblance of youth left in me, not much perhaps, but enough for a while. Basking in the sunlight piercing through the bathroom window, I almost glowed, the oil covering my body like an unguent that might protect it from the world and time. Before I could dress, however, I had to wipe most of it off with a towel to keep it from seeping into my clothes. So much, I thought, for magic.

I left Roger a note taped to his mailbox, assuring him I'd drop by that night, after I got home. I walked to work. There was still time, lots of time, and the day was too near perfection to lose altogether, the winter's light pure, the views unimpeded for miles, all colors everywhere reduced to either bright blue or stark white, like the earth in pictures taken from the moon. Chinese New Year was to be early this year, apparently. Firecrackers were exploding somewhere up Jones Street and down

Greenwich, too. As I turned to walk up the steps, a cherry bomb exploded behind me.

Don always dreaded these weeks because the noise reminded him of the sounds of battle and especially of the time when he was wounded on Kwajalein. That was practically all he ever mentioned about it, just a little grumbling during the two weeks or so every year when firecrackers burst all around us. The festivities didn't bother Roger though, Don said, because Roger had held a desk job in Honolulu throughout the duration. Don's eyes gleamed as Roger blushed.

As I paused on top of Russian Hill for a couple of minutes, standing in one corner of the park on what Don liked to call "our" hill—meaning his and Roger's, mine and Charlie's—and gazing northward over the bay toward Marin, I remembered his saying how the sky here on such brilliant, weightless days was like the Greek sky he and Roger had seen so often, a strange, oddly suspenseful sky as if some god were just about to step out from it. Constantly in Greece, he said, it came as a shock to discover that eyes so dazzled could see so clearly. He had winked at me, a bright glint in his imp's eyes, touched me briefly but firmly where he knew I wouldn't forget his fingers had been, the running shorts and jock that separated my flesh from his flesh somehow immaterial for the moment, and he walked away, never again to make that sort of advance. Charlie and I had been living downstairs for only six months. I still don't know what sort of claim Donald was staking that morning, if any. But recollecting it, I cried a little for the first time about his being dead, until finally I pulled myself together and hauled ass the rest of the way to the store.

Only later that night, after I'd closed the shop and turned off all the lights except for the one over the counter and gone in the back to use the john, while I was sitting there in the dark without accomplishing very much, did I think of Don again with that sort of clarity, as if he were standing in the flesh by the door, grinning that half-salacious, half-beatific smile of his, like that time he caught me coming out of the shower. I had stomped back into the bathroom and grabbed a huge towel to wrap around my middle.

"Don't you ever knock? What the hell are you doing barging in here like this, Don?" My hands were shaking, I was so mad.

"You're angry," he said calmly and started to whistle "Danny Boy," which he called "Sammy Boy" to irk me.

"Stop it, Don."

He quit, leaned back against the jamb, and crossed his legs at the ankle, looking quite pleased with himself. "Care to join us for dinner tonight?"

"It's late, Don."

"But you haven't eaten?"

"No."

Without moving any part of his body, not even his eyes, he surveyed the room. "And Charlie's not here," he observed.

"He's at some gay political meeting. Get out of here and let me dress, will you?"

"What are you ashamed of, Sammy?"

"Don!"

"Charlie's never minded. But then he has a better sense of fair play. It's only a peek I want, after all." I let the towel fall. "Very nice. Sam, Sam," he clucked, "You think the whole world's out to make you, don't you? That's why you're always so on edge, doll, like some sweet young thing out on the streets alone late at night checking over her shoulder to make sure no one's there. But you'd like someone to be there, wouldn't you? Wouldn't you, Sammy?"

I dressed quickly. "Maybe Charlie and I should move out."

"I thought we were going to be friends, we four."

"I'd hoped so, too, Don."

As he two-fingered a cigarette out of his shirt pocket and lit it, I wanted to beg him to stop, but it was absurd to try. Don would smoke even after he was dead. We all knew that, though he did manage to refrain sometimes, like when we were all driving somewhere together. "Listen to me, lad," he said and drew in a lungful of smoke. "You imagine I'm on the make, don't you? Well, maybe I am in a way. But Roger and I are happy. We've been happy together all these years. And do you know why? Do you know why he's really all I want, old fart that I am?"

"I wish I did," I said honestly enough. "I wish I did know, Don."

"It's because neither of us ever expected more from life than what it gave us, including each other. I mean, Roger was pretty spectacular when I first met him. But so were lots of other men, if you get my drift. We just never wasted any time hoping or waiting for something more or better. We made it work, doll. Do you understand me? Is my message clear? We made it go."

"You're not telling me very much, Don."

"You kids," he said, snickering, gazing down absent-eyed at the ember of his cigarette. "You young pups. You know what? I wouldn't see the world as you kids see it for all the hunks in this town. It wouldn't be worth it. It just makes you all so angry, thinking you can have everything and everyone, because you can't. You never could. It's such an elementary truth. Roger and I, we made do," he stressed once more. "Who believes that's enough anymore?"

"I don't know. Don?"

"What?" He grinned at me, his smile as pure and as enigmatic as any virgin's.

"Please don't do this again."

"Do what?"

"Surprise me."

He chucked my chin. "Dinner's at nine," he called behind him as he strolled out the door, turning back briefly only to disentangle his favorite fraying red cardigan from the latch where it had caught.

It was after ten and I was still thinking about Don by the time I wearily walked in the door of our apartment and switched on the light. Charlie had left a note in an envelope on the mantel, but I didn't want to read it. Instead, I made straight for the kitchen, grabbed a bottle of scotch from the cabinet over the sink, and carried it upstairs.

When Roger opened the door, his appearance shocked me. Why was I so disappointed? What had I imagined, or hoped, I'd find? He looked great, clean shaven, casually dressed but dapper as always, his dark eyes bright and quick as a curious child's, no heavy clogs on his feet after all but only his usual well-shined loafers.

"I could use a drink," I said, offering him the bottle. It was less than half full, but it didn't matter. Roger wasn't much of a drinker, either.

He accepted it. "A hard day, Sam?"

"You could say that. I kept thinking about Don."

Roger smiled down at me sympathetically. If he and Don had ever played good cop/bad cop, Roger would have been the good cop, the pal, the buddy, the one with the smile you could trust until you confessed. I followed him into the kitchen where he filled the glasses with ice cracked from the tray and poured enough scotch on top of it to leave room for only an inch or so of water. He tasted it, grimaced, and pointed back out to the living room where, glass in hand, I pursued him to the window which overlooked the deck and garden with their splendid views of the bay. "What a clear night!" Roger exclaimed.

"Yes," I agreed. "It's swell. Roger?"

"Sam."

"I'm sorry."

"I know you are, Sam." He laid a kindly hand, wide and warm, on my shoulder. "I know you are. Don was cremated today, incidentally. Around noon, I think. We'll sail him out onto the bay in a few days, perhaps Sunday, and sneak him into it, just as he wanted, you and me and Charlie. His family." He withdrew his hand.

I didn't know what to do or to say so I said only, "That'll be fine, Roger."

"Good. Good."

"Roger?"

"Yes?"

"I haven't meant to be avoiding you." When I jerked around to look, he was no longer even pretending to smile, his face creased with a frown like the one teachers use to express disappointment at your failure. "I mean I haven't known what to say. I still don't know what to say."

"Yes," he nodded too eagerly. "It is difficult, isn't it?" He took a sip of his drink. "Come over here," he directed me, indicating the love seat opposite the one he had just flopped into.

A small, restless fire burned in the fireplace to my right. Between us stood a glass-top coffee table covered with the usual art and travel magazines scattered about. But the Greek head sat as always exactly in the center, handsome and proud and serene. I bent over to touch its eyes, as if to keep them from staring up at me.

"You know I wasn't with him when Don stole that," Roger said.

"I know," I said. "You were . . . ," but I stopped myself.

He placed his sweating glass carefully on top of an old *Holiday* and folded his arms across his broad chest like someone with a chill. "Only that strange, wonderful woman who had attached herself to us in Perugia. By the time we reached Rome, Cecille was simply a part of us and our vacation. To this day, I don't understand how it happened. She had broken her leg climbing up to some forbidden monastery high in the Tirol and was on crutches when we met her in that little café. How she had managed to see so much on crutches without our help I never figured out, either. Without a word from either of us, she understood the score right off and never once tried to interfere. In fact, if anyone became jealous, it was us of her. How that woman enjoyed Italy!

"Then, when I got so sick in Rome, Don and Cecille went everywhere together and immediately afterwards told me all about it so I might feel I'd done it all, too, been everywhere, seen everything with them. Nine years later, when Don and I returned to Rome, it was so strange because I did have this powerful sensation I actually had done everything they'd told me about. It was Don who was all the time having to straighten me out. 'No, no,' he'd say, 'Cecille and I told you about this place. You weren't here. You were flat on your back in that miserable pensione, poor guy.'

"He was right, of course. And yet it all really was that vivid. The whole city. Cecille and Don had described everything so perfectly it was like life. It was like having lived the words in a book.'' Roger took another sip from his drink and settled back deeper into the couch's plush cushions, staring into the flickering fire. The apartment was too warm. Don's and Roger's rooms, anywhere they were, were always too warm. Yet they were both big, husky men. ''I miss him, Sam.''

''So do I. So does Charlie,'' I added as an afterthought. ''Already very much.''

''Maybe that first trip was our best,'' he mused. ''We felt so lucky to be alive after the war, especially Donald. It had been terrible, but for us in a way it had been lucky, too, since it had brought us to new worlds and eventually here to San Francisco. I'd just finished at State under the GI Bill. Don had made some money at that original store he'd opened downtown. We were in love. I mean that. We were really in love. We neither of us had ever been to Europe before. It was wonderful.''

I couldn't look at him. ''First trips can be like that,'' I suggested. ''The best. Or the worst. So much is being tested.''

''Tested? Perhaps.'' His eyes seemed fixed on the fire. I could only hope that he, unlike me, wasn't picturing Don's naked body on a pallet sliding into a burning chamber. He had started to cry, very quietly.

''Roger?''

''I'll be all right. In a minute. In a minute. It's just that we hadn't expected it. We thought there would be more time.'' He attempted a smile. ''But I suppose that's only human, always hoping for more time than fate is willing to give you.''

I reached over, picked the Greek head up off its stand, and fondled it in my lap. ''It's very beautiful, one of the most beautiful, sexy heads I've ever seen. It must weigh twenty pounds, Roger.''

''Surely not so much. It's funny, though. We've never weighed it. Think of all the countless things we must have weighed in a lifetime, but we never weighed the head. We shipped it home surrounded by many, many cans of olives that concealed what was placed in sawdust in the center of the box. To fool customs. And it worked. So I only know what it weighed with the olives, not by itself. Don and I were eating those olives for years afterwards,'' he laughed, ''serving them to guests, too, especially in martinis. We saved one can, for good luck. It's still in the cupboard, the last I looked.

"The Italians were digging up heads and other bits and pieces of classical statues, Greek and Roman, all over the place in those days. It was the war. It had disturbed so much earth that practically every back yard or field yielded one antique body part or another. They simply didn't know what to do with them all. Too many living people had lost parts of their own bodies, or their loved ones, for them to care much about bits and pieces of broken statuary. There are times in history, and this was one of them, when art doesn't mean a thing. Not a thing. So some museums were actually littered with fragments of classical sculpture lying around in basements, in courtyards, in gardens, scattered all over floors. Nobody had the time or the money to do anything with it except pile it all together somewhere.

"I'm exaggerating, of course. Still, it was quite easy, Don said, for him and Cecille to steal this one. She was on her crutches, of course, and had to carry a big bag, more like a sack, draped over her shoulders to hold her belongings, like her wallet and all those mysterious women's things that in those days seemed so indispensable. Don simply waited until the coast was clear, decided upon that head there, lifted it off the cluttered table where it lay with other black marble pieces, and dropped it in Cecille's bag. Then they walked calmly out—or rather he walked calmly out, and she somewhat nervously, she reported, hobbled out behind him. Isn't that amazing? You see, Cecille didn't want Don implicated if she were caught. She said she was convinced that she could easily charm her way out of any Italian jail. I imagine she could have.

"It was to be a present to me, for having missed so much. It's funny. I don't recall feeling I'd missed anything at all. And yet if I hadn't been sick, maybe Don wouldn't have gotten the nerve to pull off the heist. Cecille, well, for her it was a game mostly, something to do so that she could prove she could do it. But Don wanted to accomplish something spectacular for me. For us, I mean. No matter what else might happen to us in our life together, we'd have this special thing no one else like us would own. A real Greek head, early fourth century B.C., Cecille said.

Ours, Don's and mine. A work of art for her two Greeks, Cecille said. She loved that phrase. Her two Greeks. Because it was her gift, too, after all, the beautiful thing that remains after everything else has died, she said."

I carefully placed the head back on its stand, the one Don had built for it thirty-five years ago, picked up my drink off the floor, and drained it. "Are you going to be all right? Would you like me to sleep up here tonight? Roger?"

He wiped his eyes. "I must have bored you with that old story."

"Not at all," I protested, though in fact the story had bored me. I couldn't concentrate on it and kept shifting to Charlie, as if he were naked and aroused downstairs in bed. "What did you say, Roger?"

He shook his head. "I said, 'Don't be silly.' I'm fine. Do me a favor tomorrow instead though, will you?"

"Certainly."

"Help me entertain Don's sister. She'll be here around five or so. Come for dinner, why don't you, you and Charlie. Let your assistant handle the store tomorrow night. I'll need to talk to her alone first. But I'd like to spend as little unprotected time with her as possible. She's always blamed me for Donald's problem, as she calls it."

"Blamed you?"

"For making him abnormal or something equally nonsensical. I don't pretend to understand such people. Wouldn't it be marvelous if we actually did have such power? She'll have a fit about the cremation, of course."

"She didn't know?"

"There's a family burial plot outside of San Mateo someplace up in the hills. They all expect Don to lie in it. He said no way. But they didn't believe him. It's strange what some families won't believe, isn't it? I have Don's will to back me up. I've already had to refer to it a couple of times, though I confess I haven't been able to bring myself to read it yet. Don told me the essence of what was in it. That was enough for me."

"You ought to read it," I recommended.

"Yes. Eventually."

"I should go, Roger."

"Thank you, Sam." He stood up and pecked my cheek.

"For what?"

"For conquering your fear at last and coming up. You see, I'm really all right, aren't I? There's no need to be afraid."

"I wasn't afraid."

"And Charlie? He's not afraid either?"

"He'll be up to see you tomorrow, Roger."

"Good." The toe of his shoe poked at the rug. "I guess I'm the odd man out, now, aren't I? Our traveling days together are done."

"I don't see why," I said, though I knew exactly what he meant. "Don wouldn't want your life to stop any more than you would want his to if you had died first," I counseled.

"But I didn't," he said bitterly. "I didn't die first. Good night, Sam." He opened the door for me. "Oh, by the way. What was Charlie doing at home much of the mid-afternoon? Is he sick?"

"I don't know," I said and almost stumbled out.

I lay still dressed on my bed, unable to sleep and impatient with all the night sounds of the city that seemed determined to keep me awake, and I could hear Roger pacing again, more quietly this time, the circle he was making growing smaller as if he were spiraling toward some still center where he and I both might find some rest. The first time I woke up, the light I'd unknowingly left on in the hall, dim as it was, nonetheless nearly blinded me when I opened my startled eyes. After I'd jumped out of bed and switched it off, however, the moon's light bathing the living room was as soothing, as refreshing as the morning sun on those late-summer backpacking treks Charlie and I used to enjoy in the Sierra when we'd hiked high enough to be alone, leaving Roger and Don a couple of thousand feet below, since the rare air wasn't good for Don's heart and Roger was afraid of heights. So it goes. So it went. Later, I would fall behind, too, as afraid as Roger, while Charlie and Don, to all our surprise feeling stronger again as he got older, climbed far above.

My stomach growled, my head ached from hunger, my toes

itched. Propped there on the mantel, Charlie's note seemed not so much to glow in the moon's rays as to be illuminated from within, like a child's night light. For a moment, long enough for me to reach for it, it consoled me and made me feel safe. But then I read it.

> Roses are red,
> Violets are blue,
> I'll be back for the heavy stuff
> When the rent is due.

In the bathroom, I flushed the bits of torn paper down the toilet and tried not to look at myself in the mirror. It was dark enough that I almost succeeded. I didn't look in Charlie's empty drawers or closet, either.

Half stripped of what belonged in it by Charlie, the bedroom began to smell slightly of disinfectant, like a hospital corridor. For a well man, however worried, I had been in too many sick-rooms lately. You can't suppress the smell of death. Clean the walls and floors, the glass, the tiles, the chrome, the sheets and other bedclothes. Take out the bodies. Death still sticks to things. It can't be hidden, any more than old people can conceal the smell of their dying flesh with fragrances or young body-builders can hide it beneath their sweat. The skin always stinks of it, lurking just beneath the surface the way the rain-drenched earth, full of rot, lingers just under the sweet, musty odor of any rose or the taste of a ripe peach. It was there, too, in the absence Charlie had left behind.

For the first time in nearly three days, I heard Roger walk the long way down the hall to their bedroom, tucked back in that part of the house which cut into the hill, for their flat expanded considerably beyond ours. He moved slowly, almost staggering across the floor as if something heavier than the weight of sleep drew him on. A door shut. Then the whole house grew quiet, as if it, like me, had been waiting for Roger to find his way back to bed and rest.

Though the night was chilly, I undressed and walked out onto the deck naked, as Charlie and I would sometimes do to make love on a couple of air mattresses, pretending we were back in the high country. The moon had just slipped out of sight. Directly overhead, an airplane flew, its red warning lights flashing, and banked toward Japan. Early last September, Don and Roger had tried to talk us into going there with them the next summer. Don said he thought he'd almost forgotten enough about the war to enjoy a visit. Roger maintained all he cared about was seeing a real rock garden—not an imported one, since theirs was obviously missing something—but that if he had his way they'd be going to the Dordogne. Charlie jumped at the proposal. I was less certain. I had been promising myself someplace alone with Charlie, though I didn't know why or where.

Now there would be no trips. I hunkered down and gripped the deck's railing with both hands to keep from toppling over, a sudden gust of emotion blowing through me without doing much damage. I wanted to feel sad, I really did. I wanted badly to feel sad about something real, at least about Don's death or Charlie's leaving, if not about all those other deaths and departures that were taking place around me as if daily. I needed to grieve, but I couldn't. Real sadness, I thought, had to be like fierce desire, a thing of the moment, doomed not to last, but nonetheless profound and enduring in its effects. I believed that once Charlie and I had experienced such passion. It hadn't lasted much longer than the first six months, if that long, and yet I thought we could live off it for the rest of our lives. Apparently I had been wrong. We had both been mistaken. But, if I couldn't love him anymore, I wanted at least to feel the sorrow that was supposed to follow his going. Then I could grieve for Don, too, clinging to the memory of each of them as to a lost hope.

I slept poorly, went to work early, left the store early, having put my best clerk in charge for a few days. While waiting downstairs for Susan to arrive, I pictured her as a tall, gaunt woman dressed in severe black, a handsome woman, handsomer than her brother, her hair the same iron gray as his, her eyes dewey, her lips atremble, her fingers still nimble enough, however, to turn the pages of a will with care. As usual, my fantasy was wrong. When, having heard a car turn into the driveway and park, I peeked around our living room curtain, I saw a short, dumpy, henna-rinsed, slightly comical-looking old bag dressed in a white frocklike dress dotted with cute little blue birds. She was so pudgy that she had to use both hands to haul herself up the stairs. Once on the stoop, she stood there panting, the loose skin on her neck quivering like a biddy's wattle, and she repeatedly poked at the buzzer with an uncertain finger. She was still breathing too hard to speak when Roger opened the door for her.

Less than an hour later, Roger stamped down on his floor three times, paused, then pounded down three times more, the usual signal that he and Don were ready for me and Charlie to come up and join their festivities, whatever they were—drinks and dinner, a sample of a just-discovered Burgundy, fresh brochures from their travel agent or a consulate, more recently a new movie on their VCR. They wanted us to share in nearly everything they bought and participate in almost everything they planned because, Don enjoyed saying, they were that rare phenomenon, a one-couple couple and thus truly monogamous.

Neither Charlie nor I ever got around to telling either of them how uneasy that attitude made us. Instead, we simply went along with it, coasting, since we liked them and since they, unlike ourselves, were always so full of plans. Yet Roger's coded stomping on the floor had early on irked us both, perhaps because it sounded too much like an official summons and Charlie and I resented all such commands, all orders, anyone's telling us what to do. Someone's telling somebody, the wrong somebody, what to do was the origin of all the world's revolutions, Charlie remarked one afternoon, glancing up at our throbbing ceiling. I was positive that it was the origin of most of the trouble between Charlie and me. Or maybe Charlie and I just didn't have the patience for the long haul.

Roger clomped down again, this time, however, only twice and with so little force to it, so weakly, that the message it sounded seemed more like a plea than a command. When a few seconds later he met me at his door, he boldly shoved me back down a couple of steps and dramatically shut the door behind him, his pale face as sad as a mime's. He was panting. "Sam, oh Sam," he said. "You wouldn't believe what I've been going through with her." He gestured behind him.

"Try me."

"She's a . . . a . . . a Baptist," he finally managed to say. "Can you believe it, in this day and age? I mean, she believes in it all."

"That spells trouble, Roger," I warned.

"She's already informed me three times that she intends to leave all her money to the church and has recommended at least as often that I do the same, for the good of my soul. Why do I have this feeling that she thinks the sooner I go to perdition the better it will be for everyone? What a gabby woman." Roger wiped his brow with his handkerchief, his eyes blinking too rapidly. "You know what I think? I think that old bat is going to contest the will. I think she believes it's her Christian duty. Christian duty," he spat. "Can you imagine?"

I didn't try to hide my surprise. "She's read it?"

"She's reading it," Roger sighed. "She insisted."

"And what about you? Have you? Have you read it yet, Roger?"

He shook his head nervously. A lock of hair, dirty white like raw cotton, fell over one eye. He pushed it back. A truly handsome man, it occurred to me once more. "I've wanted to, Sam," he said. "Really I have. It's only. . . ."

I tugged coaxingly at the sleeve of his blue dress shirt. "Only what, Roger?"

"I'm not sure. It sounds so silly to say it out loud. I've been afraid, I guess."

I took his hand gently in mine. "Afraid?"

"Of surprises. I didn't want to discover any surprises. Isn't that strange? After all these years, after forty some years of Don's and my having been together one way or another, in good times and bad, I'm still not completely sure of what it is that we were together. And wills are such absolute things. You understand. There's no going back and changing them, is there?" He glanced over my shoulder. "Isn't Charlie coming, too? I had been hoping he'd be here as well. I need all the support I can get."

Though I had been expecting it, the question nonetheless startled me. I pulled my hand back and, awkwardly shifting my body away from his, began to fall backward, grabbing for the railing. Roger caught me by the collar of my shirt and held tight until I regained my balance. "Well," he said. "I suppose that answers that question."

"Does it?"

"Yesterday, wasn't it? Yes, it must have been only yesterday. He was carrying too much out for just a trip. But I suppose I pretended not to notice. Give him a day or two more," Roger advised. "Then, if you don't hear, call him. That's what I always did with Don, the few times he left me. That's what he did with me, the one time I left him. You know where he is?"

"Not really. But I can guess. He's at Duane's, I'd bet anything. Or at some other blond's with muscles you could see rippling through his clothes."

"Maybe. But maybe not. Give him a day or two more. You boys will be fine. A day or two more is all," Roger repeated, gazing down the stairs wistfully, as if he were wishing he were waiting for someone to come back in a day or two more. "That was all that Don ever needed when he got restless. Well." He took a deep breath. "Ready for Susan?"

"No," I said, grinding my index finger into his stomach. He sucked it up tight.

She sat at the dining-room table, her overfed purse resting next to her right elbow, her broad, bulging bottom spreading out over several pillows that lifted her up closer to the document she was reading as she whistled through her teeth, her lips moving to no word's shape, her chubby little fat-girl's legs dangling, shoes kicked off, nearly a foot above the carpet. She licked the point of the pencil and laid it down, smiling as if her best friend had just entered the room. "Why, who's that? How nice, Rog. You didn't mention anything about company coming."

"I'm not company. I'm Sam Whitten," I said, holding out a hand to her. "I live downstairs."

"Why, that's nice, I suppose," she said, ignoring my offered handshake and returning to the will to examine it further. "Let's see. Donald mentioned someone who lived downstairs to me once. From San Mateo, too, he said, over on Thirteenth Street, just two blocks away from where we was born, him and I and our little sis. But it wasn't you. It was . . . ," she paged through the document, "yes, sir, here it is. I remember now. It was Charlie Roberts. Charles Simpson Roberts, it says here. Oh, Donald was full of high praise for this Mr. Roberts. But I guess he must have moved out," she said to me, smiling for all the world as if I were her darling grandchild, "because you live there now. That's what Roger just told me was the case, wasn't it? Wasn't it, Roger? This man lives there now."

"Yes, ma'am," I said, pleasantly enough, I thought. "Charlie Roberts moved out."

"Isn't that just the way of the world?" she said, smiling brightly, as if this were the sunniest thought she had had all day. "Here today, gone tomorrow, what starts in joy, ends in sorrow. You've got to put your trust in the Lord, Sam Whitten. My poor brother Donald didn't, don't you see, and so everything in this foolish document"—here she gave it a shake in the air—"everything in it is Roger this or Roger that except for this Mr. Roberts once and not one mention of Jesus in it at all. Not one. And He's our only salvation. Well. . . ."

" 'Well' what, Susan?" Roger inquired, his voice quivering, though whether from nerves or anger more, I couldn't be sure.

"Well, some things will have to be changed, I reckon." She had begun to hum the big tune from "The Blue Danube."

"Could I fix you a drink?" Roger asked me.

"Nothing alcoholic for me," Susan sang.

"Orange juice?" Roger offered her.

"Fine, fine," Susan smacked. "A glass of cold orange juice would hit the spot."

"A jigger or two of vodka in mine, Roger," I said.

"At least," Roger agreed. Susan wrinkled her pug nose at us.

"How do you spell 'genealogy'?" she quizzed me the second after Roger had left the room.

"What?"

"How do you spell 'genealogy'?"

"G. E. N. E. A. . . ."

"Oh, heck," she said. "Most people spell it with an *o*. Let me ask Roger again. Roger?"

"Yes?" he called back.

"Susan wants you to spell 'genealogy' for her," I said.

"I just did fifteen minutes ago," he said, exasperated.

"Just do it, Rog," I recommended.

"G. E. N. E. O. . . ."

"You see," she said, winking at me.

"I guess I'm not 'most people' then, Susan."

"Well, neither am I. I'm a genealogist," she boasted, pronouncing the *a* with great care. "I have traced my family's history back seven generations."

"Good for you," I said.

"All the way back to Scotland," she said.

Roger marched into the room, drinks on a tray, and sat Susan's down on a coaster next to her purse. She sniffed it to confirm that hers was the one without the alcohol. "We got rights to Texas oil property," she bragged, "if I can ever get my no-good, no-account grandson Dickie interested in it. Little Bernard, my son by my first marriage, he couldn't care less either. One day I'll be sitting pretty and they'll all be coming begging, you wait and see, though I've already been blessed beyond my hopes and dreams, amen." She began to flip back and forth through the will again until she'd found the section she wanted and reread it, humming all the while some tune that sounded remotely like "Stranger in Paradise." "You answer me this, Rog?"

"I'll try, Susan," he said from his seat way across the room near the fireplace. I was standing to his right, straddling the living room and the deck, leaning against the edge of the open glass door, watching her warily.

"What's a Greek head?" she asked, her eyes glued to the words which her fingers repeatedly underlined. "Don't it sound gory?"

I scurried over to the coffee table, put down my glass, and lifted it up to show her, stand and all. "This," I said almost proudly, holding it aloft for a few seconds and then carefully setting it back down again.

"Well, it's his," she said, without having bothered to pay it much attention.

Roger blinked once. Otherwise he didn't flinch, he didn't blanch, he didn't falter in any way. He simply quit breathing. "What?" I said.

"It's his," she said and checked the will again. "That Charles Simpson Roberts. The one from San Mateo I was recollecting Don having mentioned before. Oh, the few times we talked and yet Don always had high words for him, all right," she clicked. "I remember now Don's singing his praises, going on about how lucky he was to have such a fine neighbor. What is it, anyhow? Some kind of old art? It looks broken."

"You're kidding, right?" I said to her. "You can't be serious. I mean, you have to know how valuable this is, don't you?"

"Valuable?" She smiled at me scornfully. "Son, only your soul is valuable. Well," she sighed, as if closing up shop, "I reckon I've seen all of what I came to see. It saddens me to think on it, but I guess poor Donald is burning in hell today. He led a wicked life, and who can question the justice of the Lord? It's my duty now to make sure he gets a decent Christian burial in any case, owing to how he might have repented in the end without our knowing it. My poor brother needs at least that kindness, Roger."

"There's not going to be a burial, Susan," Roger said flatly, moving only his lips and jaw, the rest of him motionless, rigid, purple with anger.

" 'Course there is."

"No, there's not. I had him cremated. Yesterday. In accordance with that will of his you supposedly have just read."

"There's not a word in it," she said. "Not a word about any cremation."

"There must be."

"Not a word. Read it yourself," Susan challenged him.

"Oh, God. Please," Roger exclaimed and covered his face. Susan blandly hummed to herself the melody of the "Emperor's

Waltz," her compact out as she layered more powder on her already overpowdered face.

"We're going to scatter his ashes in the bay, Susan," I informed her, for the nasty fun of it. "Roger and I. In a few days. We're going to take Don's ashes out in a small box and dump them into the currents of the bay. You should come along."

"Please, Sam," Roger muttered, his head still in his hands.

She slid down onto the floor and effortfully bent to pick up her shoes, which she carted over to the love seat to put on. The Greek head caught her eye. "Heathen work. Devil work. We've been warned," she said, dismissing it at a glance. "Mind my words, the Lord chastizes. I don't know why Donald wanted such a thing in his house. Do you know, Roger? It's all so puzzling."

"No," Roger said, shaking his head in a kind of amazement. "No, I don't know." He sat upright again. "You're not staying for dinner, Susan?"

"I think I've changed my mind, Rog." Her shoes back on, she heaved herself up and straightened out her dress, picking at one of the blue birds on its design as if it were a spot she was trying to remove by peeling it off. "You took my brother," she said to no one in particular, certainly not directly to Roger, neither anger nor hatred nor emotion of any other kind in her singsong voice. "And now I can't lay him to rest in that hill where Mom and Daddy and my Frank and our little sister and all the others lie so peaceful. So I guess I'll just drive on back down to Foster City." She checked her tiny gold watch. "It's getting late for a tired old woman like me. You're going to be old, too, even you," she warned me. "It's time for you to be making your case before Jesus."

"Oh, do shut up, Susan," Roger snapped, leaping to his feet.

She chose not to hear him. "You play the piano?" she asked me. She'd wandered back to the dining table to retrieve her purse and seemingly had just noticed the baby grand that stood far to the other side of it.

"No," I said, bewildered. "Why?"

"It would be so sweet to hear a little piano music now," she said. "Donald always did play the piano so sweet, don't you agree, Roger? He could have had a major concert career if he had wanted one. A major concert career. But what did he do instead but waste his God-given talent selling records of other people playing trash. Frittered his life away is what he did. It don't make any sense. I never did hear another human being who could play so sweet."

"You loved Don a lot, didn't you, Susan?" Roger offered.

She was swaying back and forth to some imagined music in her mind. "He was my baby brother. I blame that war. It took him from us and unsettled him and changed his way of think-ing. He had been such a right-thinking boy. And then he was called away to fight and came back to. . . ." She looked around the room, her eyes bleary. ". . . to some other place, and none of us ever saw him again, not really. He would have been better off dead, Daddy said, killed on one of those islands. We all said so. Something bad happened to him that made us wish it. Some-thing did." She'd found her keys. Roger opened the door for her. "Help me down, Roger," she directed, slipping her free arm into his. "These stairs frighten me." Her wandering eyes settled on me for a moment. "What you'd want with that ugly old head is more than I can understand," she said, clutching the railing with her other hand, her purse swinging from the crook in her arm and bumping against her bosom. They had maneuvered almost halfway down. "Why did Don give it to him anyway?"

"He didn't," Roger said.

"My brother was a strange man," Susan said.

"Yes," Roger agreed. But Susan wasn't listening. She had started to hum "Autumn Leaves," her voice pitchless and war-bling, weaving back and forth over the tune like a drunk trying to walk a straight line.

"Well, at least that's over," I said to Roger to console him when, a few minutes later, he joined me out on the deck. The sky was bands of lavender, silver, lace. Then suddenly it was almost night.

"Poor Susan." Roger collapsed into a lawn chair and closed his eyes, his head sinking into his pillow.

"You feel sorry for that dotty old bitch?"

"No." He held his head between his hands as if it were throbbing beyond any relief. "Fix us both another drink, will you, Sam? A real one this time. Something brown, not too translucent, with a kick to it."

When I handed him his, he sat upright to accept it, pulling the back of the lounge up, too.

"So," I said.

"Yes."

"How are you feeling?"

"Peculiar."

"Is that all? Aren't you furious?"

"I don't know," Roger said, stretching out. "I was just thinking about that time on the Hoh River trail when you and I didn't want to cross that ledge and stayed down at Elk Lake and Charlie and Don hiked the rest of the way up to Glacier Meadows by themselves. Remember? How long were they gone? Two days? Three days? I wondered at the time why you were so unpleasant about it. It was hardly the first time they had taken off on their own. But it had never bothered me until I saw how much it was bothering you. So when we got back to the city I asked Don about it."

"And?"

"He said he loved both of you. He loved me first. And then next he loved you, meaning you and Charlie together."

"And?"

"That's all," he said easily.

"That's *all?*"

"It was enough, Sam. I didn't press him any further. Why should I? I was satisfied by what he said. It would have demonstrated a lack of trust to ask any more. You have to have faith, you see. Otherwise, it's no good."

"I see." I squinted out toward Alcatraz where the light had begun to revolve in the gradually thickening dark. I didn't see. "You're kidding yourself, Roger."

"Am I?"

"Admit it. He left the head to Charlie, Roger. He left the head to Charlie."

"Yes." He set his drained glass down on the floor. "As Susan would say, it's puzzling."

"Not to me."

"No, I suppose it isn't to you." He struggled out of the lounge chair, joined me where the deck's stairs led down into the garden, wrapped an arm around my waist, and would not let me pull away. "You know, Sam," he whispered, "Don and I always worried about you and Charlie. You were both very good companions to us, of course. We always enjoyed your company immensely. Our last ten years would have been greatly diminished without it. Yet we found you two to be very strange because, although you were both lovely boys, neither of you seemed to be able to feel anything permanent about the world. I don't know how to explain it, but try to understand that even if Don and Charlie did have some kind of fling together, which I doubt, it can't matter now, don't you see? I mustn't let it. I mustn't have wasted my life."

"Don't let him have it, Roger," I whispered back.

His fingers loosened. "It was mine. It was my gift."

"That's right," I prodded.

"Why would he have to give it away?"

"That's the question, all right."

"To Charlie?" He gazed at me through the shadows, utterly bewildered and dismal.

"To Charlie," I underlined.

"It isn't true," he said quietly.

"You were the one who didn't want to read the will. Why not? Did you know?"

"It isn't true."

"Get rid of it."

"Nothing happened."

"Get rid of it. Get rid of the head. Don't let the bastard have it."

"Nothing happened, I said."

"Sure. Get rid of it. Sink it in the bay with Don."

"Don't turn your anger on me, Sam."

"That's why Charlie moved out three days after Don died. That's why. Why should he stay any longer? His lover was gone."

"Don't, Sam. It's nonsense. Preposterous nonsense."

"Nothing happened," I mocked.

"It didn't. I know it didn't. Don wouldn't. Neither would Charlie."

"I know all about worst fears, kiddo. They always come true. Sacrifice forty years to him and his need to be flattered. See if I care. I only sacrificed ten. What idiots we all are."

"Get out, Sam." Roger had retreated to the glass door and had already pulled it halfway closed. "Now."

I stepped onto the first stair down. "Sure. That's right. Blame it on me. Kill the messenger."

"I mean it, Sam."

"Do you want to give it to him or should I? Some lawyer's going to have to check it all out, you know. Tell him it's gone. Tell him it disappeared. That's the thing to say. Don't let Charlie have it, Roger. It's yours. Get rid of it. Sink it."

"Now, Sam."

"Drown it. What the heck? You couldn't stand to look at it again, could you?"

He slowly shook his head. "No," he said and slid the door all the way closed, backing into the room so that he wouldn't have to notice the Greek head in the place of honor where it had sat for decades.

I lay on our bed, on the guest bed, on the couch in the living room, clutching the dark. Nothing worked. I got up, turned on a lamp, rearranged books from one shelf to another, separating mine from Charlie's. One of them, a hardback Durrell, was Don's. I set it aside, then placed it on the stack with the others that I knew weren't ever mine. Some kind of pain grabbed the back of my neck and yanked on it, like a not-quite-legal wrestling hold just before a fall. I jerked on the lamp's chain to turn it off, nearly stumbling over a pile of paperbacks in the process, and fell against the wall, the cool of its plaster like smooth marble against my face.

In the hall, a sliver of light shone around the perimeter of the closet door. Charlie must have left it on yesterday. He was always leaving lights on somewhere. But why hadn't I noticed it earlier? Maybe he had been back today, too, while I was up at

Roger's, though that was highly unlikely. Why would he have come back here? It didn't matter. Whenever, he had knocked over one of the boxes of letters and postcards we saved there. Or had they spilled out as he searched for one particular card or letter? That couldn't matter either. I might have done it myself, after all, and forgotten.

I picked a handful up. "Our winter was less productive than I had hoped it would be. We have been seduced by the lawn furniture. James studies his law books. The weather is blissful here. And yours?" Another: "Yesterday Delos. Tomorrow Rhodes. Then on to Turkey. Don is exhausted but looks forward to seeing his first camel caravan. So do I. Miss you two. All best." Or another: "The one hurtling off the cliff like Greg L. is mine. The one waiting his turn in the white bikini is Al's. Hi! This island's just what the doctor ordered, guys. It's like no one alive has ever been sick. Al says he could live forever. But what the hey, huh? We've had our fun." One more: "You two have got to be the best tour guides in that crazy town. Thanks for the sack space. That couch is better than my bed back home. Really! Don't apologize about the guest bed's being occupied. Actually, I got in it once. That Tom is wild. Did he tell you? It gets lonely here in Kansas. I wish I could have stayed out there for good. But I guess I'm needed where I am. Needed? Lord! Love ya."

I didn't leave right away. I flipped through several more cards, the pictures on each one like photographs taken by the same uncurious tourist's camera, always aiming for the obvious, for the cliché, so that you'd think the world was everywhere equally dull until you flipped the card over and read the message, only to find out that instead it was merely hopeless and sad. I tossed them all back into the box. Whatever I was going to do, I knew I couldn't stay all night confined by these walls. I was too angry, at Don and Charlie, of course, but at Roger and myself as well, furious at all of us for not being better at life than we were.

I clicked on a light in the bedroom and retrieved from the back of my dresser's top drawer the fragment of the page from the personals I had torn out about a month ago, on which I'd jotted down Rick's number when he called after receiving my letter. When I phoned, Rick was surprised to hear from me again, of course, and cool to the idea at first. But, when I told him that Charlie and I had really split up this time, he agreed to meet me an hour and a half later at a bar we both knew in the Haight just a few blocks from my store. And the thought of seeing him again actually revived my spirits for a while.

I neither changed nor showered as I usually would have. I didn't have to. Since Charlie was gone, there was nothing I needed to shed. Though I hopped on a bus for the middle part of the trip through a risky part of town I didn't feel much like braving in the night, it still took me over an hour to get there. Rick was already in the bar when I arrived, just as I hoped he would be. He didn't seem to recognize me at first, but that was all right because it wasn't recognition I was after. First he said how pissed he'd been about my having lied to him during our first conversation on the phone. But when I explained to him about my life now, not having to lie at all this time, he said he guessed he understood. Then he smiled like a man who knew he had just been lied to again, even if only a little, and who plainly had decided he wouldn't mind. He was used to it. We were all used to it. No big deal.

In the morning, I wandered home slowly and stopped at a travel agent or two to check out their new brochures. There was a special on Catalonia that looked inviting, and another to Tibet which, though still very expensive, promised the ultimate in exoticism, and a third to the Marianas that Don would have avoided at all costs, and a fourth to Great English Gardens, and a fifth for a cruise to Alaska, and a sixth for another through the Panama Canal. All specials. Every place was special, every place on sale. I gathered them all up and carried them home, studying each off and on along the way, wondering what it was that Don and Roger had hoped to find by traveling. If Don knew, he never told us. I would have to ask Roger one of these days, before it was too late. Whatever it was, however, they plainly hadn't discovered it any more than Charlie and I had, because in a way they were even more restless than we were. If Charlie and I needed an occasional strange body, Roger and Don had demanded whole strange new worlds, none of which was ever quite strange enough to hold them there. So maybe it wasn't so surprising that in the end Don had settled for an ordinary faithlessness after all, just like the rest of us.

Back at the house, I knocked on Roger's door to see how he was doing, but he either wasn't home or, mad at me, didn't answer. Sitting on the stoop off the street, I watched the mailman slowly work his way up it, a buckle on the strap of his bag catching the sun and reflecting it brilliantly, like a shiny new silver dollar back when we were kids. Maybe there would be a letter from Charlie. I knew there wouldn't be a letter from him. Yet maybe there would be.

I perched myself eagerly on a higher step for a better view since Charlie had said recently that our new mailman was by far the best looking in the city. When I asked him how he knew, he didn't answer. "There couldn't be much competition," I said, and he responded, "Maybe not, but check him out anyway." OK, for Charlie's sake, I'd check him out. But the letter carrier passed me by, not even delivering any junk mail and carefully avoiding my eyes, as someone accidentally encountering a funeral party will avoid the eyes of the mourners, eager to get on with his business and not wanting to be implicated in their grief, however slightly. As usual, Charlie had been right. He was a babe, his calves and thighs bulging like plates of armor beneath those floppy dull gray trousers they make them wear.

But, because he hadn't opened the gate, come up the walk, mounted the steps, my life would go on just the same, unchanged. So why did each tick of my old windup wristwatch seem dimmer, until at last there were no sounds left at all? No firecrackers bursting, no children's voices from the school playground across the street, no backfires from the truck struggling up Jones Street and spitting black fumes from its tailpipe, no hammering noises from the workmen repairing the roof on the stark Victorian near the corner, though I could see their arms continue to drive in nails, row after row. Although the chill wind off the bay quietly prickled my skin, it did so without once whistling through the gutters. Not hearing anything, not a thing, I sat there, arms wrapped around my knees, and stared happily into the silence, watching it grow steadily brighter as the sky does in mountain valleys long before you see the sun. One of the neighbor's scruffier cats scaled the front railing, slunk along the coping of the wall, pounced, and landed in my lap. I could feel it purr, I could see it meow when I yanked its stubby tail, but that was all.

It wasn't that I had gone deaf. Not for a second was I afraid that I had lost my hearing. I simply had made a choice and without knowing it had chosen silence. As if by magic, I had been able to still the world, especially the raucous world of my own body, and keep it hushed for a while. I stood up, unbuckled my unwanted watch from my wrist, and read it, astonished at the time. Back inside the apartment, I dropped it into the hall wastebasket, grabbed a chair from the kitchen table, set the chair on the deck, sat down, and, wondering if blindness might be equally liberating, stared briefly up at the heavens, the whole sky in flames, all of it, save for the huge white disc at its core, burning with the clear, clean blue translucence of a Bunsen burner. In the back of my eyes, orange and red dots began to swirl and collide, battering one another, but I refused to blink.

"Don't," I could hear Don advise me as if he were actually there. I didn't have to see him to know it was he. I could smell him and his cigarettes, and almost feel his knobby fingers grip my shoulder.

"All right," I consented, though I lowered my eyelids slowly, as if I were gradually letting down shades in a too-sunny room. The bitter, acrid odor of those French cigarettes he liked so much—the ones with the strong Turkish blend of Turkish men's sweaty pits, Roger used to joke, holding his nose—left an aftertaste in my mouth. Then all the city's shrill noises swelled up once more into my ears. It was rush hour already. How had it gotten so late? Hours must have passed. I breathed in deeply, but the air had changed again. Now it mixed dry earth, fetid water, and redwood and cedar chips with a hint of gardenia sweetness and the sour odor of too many neighborhood cats. Another cat, different from the one earlier, bounded into my lap, digging two of its claws into one knee. With a wicked swipe of my arm, I knocked it off. When it hit the brick wall, it squalled like a baby.

"Meditating?" I heard Charlie ask. "Is that what you do when I walk out on you? Sit around and meditate? That and attack cats?" He was standing just inside the sliding doors which I had left open, sweating hard, back pressed flush against the kitchen wall, the sleeve of his sport shirt ripped at the shoulder, exposing a bad bruise.

"Something like that," I said. "Who's been beating up on you, Charlie? Duane?"

"This?" He examined the spot. "I tore it on that new hook in the closet, the one with the sharp point you've been complaining about. Which of course made me lose my footing. Which made me collapse into the corner of that wardrobe of yours. So I fell. Backwards. You mean you didn't hear? You really haven't heard all the racket I've been making? I've been so noisy, chum, I might as well have been building this house all over again."

"You're moving back in then, Charlie?"

"Sure. I figured the point's been made. What the hell, huh?"

"That's nice. What point?"

He flipped something off one finger with his thumb. "The same one as always. You know. The one that says we'd better stick together because anyone else we'd choose would be that much worse. Incidentally, you certainly have been acting strangely for the last couple of hours or so. I figured it was some sort of quiet fit you were throwing for my benefit that we'd have to talk about later."

"Uh-huh. Maybe I don't want you back, Charlie."

"Of course you do, booby," he said, gnawing on a fingernail. "Nobody else would put up with you."

Roger peered over the upstairs railing. "Is that Charlie I hear?" Charlie stepped out onto our deck to offer him a little salute and a click of his heels. "Welcome home, lad. I thought I heard you hard at work down here. I just got back myself," Roger offered as he joined us, "from an important trip. A most important trip. It feels wonderful to be so free of it, I must say, much to my surprise."

"Oh? Where to, Rog?" Charlie said. A swallow landed on the head of the statue of Eros which stood as if to pee in the middle of the birdbath in the middle of the almost dry pond, and it immediately flew off again so that another swallow could pause briefly after it on the same spot which, once the second had departed, was followed by a third. While I waited for the fourth, Roger positioned a white wrought-iron lawn chair at almost exactly ninety degrees to my left, much closer to Charlie.

"So, welcome home," Roger said to him again. Crossing one leg over another, he fixed the crease in his trousers.

"Thanks," Charlie said, blushing. "I'm sorry, Roger. Please forgive me. It was a lousy time for me to have run out on you. I guess I just got scared there for a couple of days. Certain . . . problems between me and Sam came to a boil. I had to go away and think."

"I understand," Roger said. "I really do quite understand." There was a sharp, slightly rusty edge to his voice though. He two-fingered a cigarette from his shirt pocket and lit it. It was one of Don's cigarettes and he lit it with Don's lighter. "Yes, you needn't tell me, I know," he said, acknowledging our stares, "it's an odd time in my life to start so disgraceful a habit. But it comforts me. I thought of it last night after our discussion, Sam, and it comforted me some. There are so many little things that I didn't like about Don which now, of course, I find myself missing. Remember that, you two. Sometimes what you disliked, even hated, is no easier to lose than what you've admired or loved. It makes it no easier to sleep recalling one more than the other."

Charlie reached to pick a pebble from the ground and pitched it into the pond where it hovered, suspended in green scum for several seconds before it sank. "We must clean that soon," Roger suggested, "and buy some new goldfish. It would be nice for the spring."

A brown rat poked its head out of the end of a broken piece of drainpipe and dashed down the retaining wall behind me heading straight for the neighbor's. Below, one cat after another arched its back and hissed. Roger surveyed his garden, which had become almost entirely shadowed by the hill. "We should water tomorrow when it's light enough. We've been neglecting it."

"I will," Charlie promised.

"But early," Roger emphasized, "before the sun is too high."

"Yes," Charlie said. "I know how you like it done, Roger."

Extinguishing one cigarette, Roger lit another. "I don't inhale. I'm afraid to inhale."

"That's good," Charlie said.

"Don always inhaled. Deeply. He did everything deeply. Don Profondo, I called him. Did you know that?"

"Yes. I think so," Charlie said.

"That was Don. If you're going to fight, really fight. If you're going to love, really love. If you're going to smoke, really smoke. So he smoked like a fiend."

"Say. Isn't that one of Don's sweaters you're wearing?" Charlie observed. "I've never known you to wear bright red before, Roger. It looks good on you, really good. You should keep it up. Very sexy."

"Do you think so?" Roger said. "I suppose I have always been too conservative. Don always complained that I was too conservative, that I should take more chances, more risks. And I thought maybe I should put his things to some use. Just a few things, of course. I'll give a lot away. I'm making a list. But I've always liked this old sweater. It's Italian."

"It looks Italian," Charlie said, admiring it some more. "It has that flair."

"But I won't give everything away," Roger insisted.

"No, not everything," Charlie said. "Why should you?"

I shivered. In the shade, the air had become cool and damp. Overhead, several flocks of swallows were flitting this way and that seemingly without direction or purpose, like radarless bats, beating their wings all the more furiously, I surmised, because there was no sense to it.

"Not the Greek head, for instance," Roger said, that dangerous cutting edge returning to his voice. "Not that. I've taken care of that." He took a puff, long, leisurely, and pointed, and would glance neither to his left nor to his right. We were both being told something. Charlie started to speak, hesitated, and looked away uneasily.

"Look behind you," Roger said to Charlie, who sat hunkered on the bricks. "How beautiful even the shabbiest of our westward facades become at sunset. They seem to be clutching at these last rays of light like some miser his gold, just as it's to be taken from him. It's why we go to museums, Don used to say. To get some of that lost gold back, the lost gold of the sun. Don was a wonderful traveler. Well, you know that. You can appreciate that, how well he saw everything. He was the most impartially curious man I've ever known."

"Yes," Charlie acknowledged.

"Don Impavido, Cecille would call him. I've missed her so much these last few days, regretting all the more the rupture that both Don and I felt was nearly unhealable between her and us after she married her second husband, a piously conventional man who couldn't help expressing his disapproval of us in numerous petty ways. Don Intrepido was another of Cecille's names for Donald. I especially liked that. Don Intrepido."

"What about Don Giovanni?" I scoffed.

"What is your problem exactly?" Charlie said to me.

"Hardly," Roger said. "No. Don was no Don Juan. To me he was pure pleasure, a fine lover, but he was no Don Juan and he knew it." The night had blackened the lines on his face and deepened them so that it appeared Roger was wearing a mask which, as he smiled, turned comic, a satyr's mask strangely befitting him.

Charlie had taken a cushion from a deck chair and was leaning back upon it, propped against the pond's brick wall, an unopened six pack next to him. When had he brought the beer out to the garden? What was happening to my ability to observe things? Did all men become handsomer, like Charlie, in the dark of night and shadows? If so, did that explain why Don liked black marble best? Something deep inside of me had finally started to hurt. "Charlie," I called to him. He grinned and pitched a can over to me, carrying another to Roger. I opened mine gingerly, spilling none.

"Rog?" he prompted. "You said you took care of the Greek head. What did you mean, 'took care of it'? Because Don wanted me to. . . ."

"Please," Roger interrupted him, holding his hand up as if to warn him to stop. "Let me finish what I have to say first." With the toe of his shoe, he squashed his cigarette into the ground like a hated snail. "You see, Charlie, I just got around to reading Don's will last night. Sam already knows all about it in a way. I'd been putting it off and putting it off because the prospect of reading it frightened me. You'll know what I mean some day if you're the one that's left. But once his ineffable sister Susan had perused it, I felt compelled to do so myself at once. And of course she was completely wrong about the cremation. There it was, all spelled out quite clearly, just as Don had told me," Roger said to me without taking his primary attention from Charlie. "That woman is either dinghier than I thought or crazed by religion. But about the Greek head, which she had no personal interest in, she was nonetheless exact. And I don't understand it. I simply can't understand it, Charlie. Can you? You do know what I'm talking about, don't you? You must."

Charlie flipped his empty can into the open trash barrel hidden under the upstairs deck. "About the head? I know that Don left it to me to take care of, if that's what you mean. Is there something else I'm supposed to understand, Roger? Because, if there is, I don't. . . ."

"I'll be plainer then. The question is this. Did you or did you not have an affair with Don, as Sam so cruelly insinuated last night? Or is 'insinuate' too benign a word for what you did, Sam? Explain it to me. Why did he leave it to you, Charlie? It was the possession of ours we both loved most, our symbol and his most precious gift to me. Yet he left it to you. Why? I have to ask. I have to ask, Charlie," he pleaded.

"Of course you have to. It's my fault. It's all my fault, Roger," Charlie apologized quietly. "I should have come to you first. Days ago. Right away. You see, Don didn't trust you."

"Didn't trust me? Of course he trusted me. I never gave him the slightest reason not to. . . ."

"I don't mean it in that way, Rog," Charlie said.

"Then how?"

"Yes, how?" I interjected.

"Oh, do be quiet, Sam," Roger said. "You've done enough harm. Please, Charlie. How?"

"He didn't trust you to give it back," Charlie said, casually popping the top on another can and setting it aside to dry his hands off on the front of his shirt. "He told me what he was going to do a couple of years ago, that time he and I went on up to Glacier Meadow and left you guys behind at that lake. He swore me to secrecy, of course, because he knew how you'd resist the idea. Don't you see, Roger? For three and a half decades, Don apparently felt guilty for stealing that thing, for having taken it from its own soil and secluded it here in this house so far away from where it belonged among all those other beautiful things the Greeks had made in Italy. He didn't want you to know, Rog, but he longed to send it back. That was to be my job only because he said you loved it too much. You understand? You loved it too much. So did he, almost as much as you did. That's why he knew he'd never get enough nerve to do it himself. And he wouldn't ask Sam over there because he figured Sam would probably just go ahead and hold onto it, pissed that anyone should have to give anything up. Don said he knew I'd do it if he asked me since he believed I didn't cling to things. I don't think he meant that as a compliment, Roger. It was just something he'd observed, like he knew you'd never read his will until you absolutely had to.

"I have the address and all the instructions written down in my desk at the office at school. I thought I'd lost them, but I found them last evening when I snuck in here while you two were upstairs talking.

"Please don't worry, Roger. It's yours to keep until, well, you know . . . I mean, all this I'm telling you now isn't written out in the will because Don only wanted to make sure it got done some day, that's all. And he thought that meant I'd have to be made the head's legal owner. He knew I'd explain everything to you. It was only that my timing was off, I mean, I should have been here to tell you. Don said he would rest easier knowing that it would find its way home eventually. I promised him I'd see to it. That's all. So," Charlie said, slapping his hands together. "That's the story, Rog. Believe it."

Roger stood up, his back cracking, and walked cautiously toward the stairs like an old man, the gentle breeze after sunset blowing his hair about so that it glittered like sea grass in the moonlight. He reached for the handrail and grabbed it firmly. "I do believe you, Charlie," he said softly. "I believe you and I believe Don. It's so strange. This afternoon, I was so maddened by jealousy, I packed it up in a crate all by myself and drove it to the parcel service, and shipped it back to that museum in Italy. I didn't want you to have it, you see. Better them than you. So I don't blame Sam, despite all his unfortunate insinuations. Not really, no more than Othello could blame Iago. The doubt was in me, the anger was in him, the two matched almost perfectly. That's all.

"Don would be laughing now, that great belly-walloping laugh of his I always found so sexy. He would be enjoying it, the irony of it, I'm sure. It happens only rarely, but sometimes worst things can come to good in the end. It's our one hope. Good night, gentlemen," he said, waving at us both. "I'm very tired all of a sudden. We'll talk more tomorrow?"

"Roger!" I stopped him. "I'm so sorry. I. . . ."

"Yes," he accepted. "Good night. Oh, only one thing more," he said without turning around again. "Did it ever strike you as odd, Charlie, that Don thought the head was his to give back? Well, never mind. Good night once more."

Charlie and I stood opposite one another, waiting, as we had so often waited, for the glass doors above to slide closed. "I'm sorry for so much," I said to him.

"Yes. I know," Charlie said. "So am I." He pointed upstairs. "Our voices carry. We should go inside. Come on inside now, Sam. Come help me finish my unpacking."

The following Sunday, the three of us poured Don's remains into the bay, each taking his turn holding the ciborium-shaped vase as, once the rented boat was safely stabilized, we scattered the ashes and bits of bone into water and wind. The night before, the weather had soured, and it stayed bad all morning, the clouds immediately overhead dirty gray and feathery as a pigeon's wings, the bay's water surging up over the gunwale cold and bitter, the boat rising and falling over and under surprisingly high swells. But none of us was sick. We were too sad to be sick for so little reason.

As we coasted back into the marina, though, the sky cleared and the sun shone brightly once more. All the while we had been on the water, Roger had retained his composure, but the minute both his feet touched land again, he collapsed into Charlie's arms, sobbing. After we'd driven him home, we brought him a brandy in a warmed snifter on a silver tray and talked to him about his plans for a trip to the Dordogne next summer. We offered to go along. He listened politely to our enthusiasm and smiled and said, No, no, no. It wouldn't do. It was time for him to be alone now. He thought he'd sell the house and move to an apartment somewhere out in the Richmond, a smaller place, easier to keep up and closer to his school. He wondered if we'd like to buy the house. But Charlie and I couldn't afford it, we said, and our future together—this came out almost in unison—was simply too much in doubt. Roger smiled, his kind way of acknowledging that he knew better than we how doubtful or sure it was.

Charlie and I helped put him to bed and spent the rest of the afternoon and evening in his apartment looking through photograph albums we'd never seen before which Roger had been reviewing the previous night.

"Let me see that first book again," Charlie said to me. I passed it to him. "You know," he said, studying several early photos, "Don was right. Roger really did look like that Greek head when he was young. What a beauty. And so serene."

"I wonder if he really gave it back," I said, "or whether he only hid it some place where he can look at it whenever he wants to."

"You're joking, right? Of course he did. Of course he sent it back. Roger doesn't lie."

"I wouldn't have," I said. "Don was right about that."

"Me neither," Charlie laughed. "Or maybe I would have. I don't know. I did promise him."

Back in the bedroom, Roger cried out Don's name once, then again. Charlie rushed in to check on him. When he returned to the living room, he was crying a little, his cheeks flushed and damp. "He's still asleep," he said, "all squeezed over on one side of the bed as if Don were still lying next to him. It's good that he's going back to work tomorrow."

"Yes," I said. "Very good. Pass me that album with the green binding, would you, Charlie? Look," I showed him. "We're not in this one either. And this was Baja."

"Let me see," Charlie said, taking the book from me, flipping through the pages himself, as surprised as I had been.

As we moved from album to album again, what unfolded before us with increasing clarity was the joy of Don's and Roger's life together, each trip, each special event, each important occasion carefully documented by the camera, as if to suggest that some day its meaning, not apparent at the time perhaps, would be discovered by people like Charlie and me. And yet Charlie and I seldom showed up in the pictures of the last ten years. We found ourselves in some of them, of course, and it was obvious that Charlie or I had taken many. But we agreed that we thought there should have been more, that we remembered having posed for many more, and wondered in whispers what had happened to them.

C. E. Poverman

THE MAN WHO DIED

Six weeks after what came to be referred to as the incident, Tom
Fields—Doctor Fields—was arrested. He'd just returned home
from a faculty meeting. He was charged by two plainclothes
detectives who read him his Miranda rights. He couldn't believe
it. He was handcuffed and walked out to the unmarked car in
front of his house.

His first glimpse of the county jail was what seemed to be
miles of razor wire gleaming silver on top of a chain link fence.
He was walked from the parking lot into the jail where, on
opening the door, the smell of paint and linoleum and Pinesol
hit him. Several doors were unlocked and relocked behind him
as he was led inside. Papers were processed along the way. The
handcuffs were removed. He was fingerprinted and photo-
graphed. Finally, he stood at a counter with a wire grating, and
there he was directed to empty the contents of his pockets. The
deputy placed his wallet, keys, change, and a penknife in a
brown manila envelope, and wrote his name, the date and time.
He was allowed to keep a quarter for the pay phone across the
room where he called a friend—an attorney with a civil practice
—who said he'd drop everything and get Tom a criminal lawyer.

When he hung up, a deputy took him by the biceps, led him

down a corridor where a block door was unlocked, and Tom
Fields was placed in a cell. As the door closed, he was overwhelmed by the cloy of stale food, a toilet, sweat, and the racket
of a radio and prisoners shouting. He walked to the far wall and
looked through the bars and glass at the desert glaring white in
the sun, then glanced cautiously around at the other prisoners.
He sat down on a metal stool bolted to the tile wall and placed
his elbows on his knees.

Someone said, "Got a cigarette?"

Tom patted his pockets. "No, I don't smoke."

The prisoner said, "The fuck ya check for?"

Tom shrugged. He stared at the floor and started thinking
about the girl but couldn't get her into focus.

His dinner still sat untouched on a tray, when the deputy came
and led him back down the corridor. He again saw his lawyer
waiting for him on the other side of the cell-block door. "Bail's
paid. Let's get out of here." Tom walked toward him, offered his
hand.

Outside, Tom took a deep breath. The mountains were throwing long deepening shadows across the desert. As they walked
toward Levy's car, Michael said, "Did they try to get you to talk
to them when they arrested you?"

Tom shook his head. "No."

"You didn't attempt to explain anything?"

"No, they just took me in."

Levy nodded. "And they Mirandized you—they read you
your rights: 'You have the right to remain silent . . .'?" Tom
nodded. "Okay. Good that you didn't talk." Levy stopped at a
silver BMW. "This one." He glanced back across the parking lot
at the jail. "Not much fun in there."

Tom took another deep breath and got in the car. He knew
Levy was about his age—forty—had seen his name in the paper
for years. They'd once met at a party, but Fields doubted Levy
would remember. Again, he tried to recall the girl. The detectives cited the incident as having taken place five weeks ago,
which he didn't remember, but a close friend of his had been
killed two months ago, and he knew that date. Jim had been

killed riding his bike—he was training for a triathlon—and had been struck by a hit-and-run driver in Marin County. Tom had been away skiing and hadn't heard about the death until ten days after the funeral. By then, all he'd been able to do was make a few phone calls to Jim's parents and ex-wife. Shortly after the death, Fields became vaguely aware that his tongue thickened in his mouth when he tried to speak, his handwriting crossed the paper in an illegible scrawl, and he felt off balance and forgetful. One afternoon, unaware, he ran a red light and came within a moment of being hit. He'd met the girl two days later. He glanced over at Levy—curly blond hair, dark eyes, a boxer's face flushed red in the setting sun. As they drove, he wondered if Levy thought he was guilty of the charges.

Several days after his release on bail, Fields had impulsively driven back to Levy's office without an appointment. He'd been remembering his initial appearance. When his case had been called, Fields stood with Levy and walked to the front of the courtroom. When her name was read as the plaintiff, Susanne Raine, Fields remembered telling her that she had a beautiful name. It was impossible to know if he had actually believed this, but there had been something . . .

Now Fields caught up with Levy in the corridor outside his office. Levy was walking out and Tom fell in beside him. "Michael, look, maybe if I just gave her a call and talked to her, I could straighten things . . ." Levy took his arm.

Outside the courthouse, he turned to face Fields. "Tom, listen to me carefully. A twenty-year-old girl has charged you with kidnapping and sexual abuse. They're serious charges. I know from our conversation that you're confused now—anyone would be under these circumstances—which is one reason you have a lawyer. And I can see you're an emotional guy, anyway." Levy paused. "I've got your statement, the police reports, her statement; we've got a pretty good idea what we're doing. Everything's under control."

Levy's New York accent, his lowered, confiding voice, comforted Tom. Tom was an Easterner, too. Levy put his hand on Tom's shoulder. "Whatever you do, promise me that you will not try to contact Susanne Raine in any way and for any reason." Tom nodded. "Okay. Good. Look, you're exhausted. Just try to get some sleep and put this out of your mind as much as possible. I know it won't be easy, but try." Levy studied him, then patted him on the shoulder. "Got to run. We'll talk." Levy walked quickly across the bricked courtyard.

Tom took off his tie and jacket and slid into his car, baking hot in the February sun. He opened the windows and drove toward the exit. Since the detectives had come to his door two days ago, he hadn't really slept. He'd doze off and then jerk awake, sometimes to the clamor in the jail cell. He'd think about the girl. No matter how hard he tried, he couldn't remember exactly what had happened, though he was sure it was nothing. She'd come to the house. They talked. There'd been some hugging, some rolling on the sofa. She'd left when she'd wanted. They hadn't seen or contacted each other after that.

He hunted up the ticket, dug out his wallet, and paid the attendant, who raised the gate. Tom fumbled his sunglasses off the dash. Levy had reminded Tom—it was in her statement, but Fields had dismissed the conversation—that there had been further contact between himself and the alleged victim. Susanne Raine had called him three weeks later. As they talked, Tom had been able to recall fragments for Levy. She'd started by saying, "Do you know who this is? Do you remember my voice . . . or have you forgotten?" He stalled. "Of course, I remember you." "You do? Oh, good." She'd talked aimlessly, and then out of the blue, "Why did you touch my groin area that day I came to your house?" And he'd been so struck by its clinical sound, he hadn't known what to say. "No answer, huh?" She'd gone on. "Well, I guess you've been very busy." Several times she circled back to a beginning. "Well, how've you been?" Hoping to connect with her, he'd said, "Look . . ." She'd picked up on it. "Susanne. Susanne Raine, the girl from the mall. I knew you didn't remember my name, that's okay, you remember me, and I certainly remember you." Something about her voice and tone were making him nervous. She said, "You didn't remember my name. But now you've got it. Susanne. Hey, that's okay, Tom, I don't hold it against you, but one thing I'd really like to know is why you masturbated against me." He was silent. "You know, as in hump." He really had no idea what she was talking about. Finally, he said, "Susanne, I don't remember anything like that. You came to my house. We hugged. We liked each other. You hugged me. We were affectionate." Then, because he imagined she wanted to hear it, he said, "I thought we'd get together again, but I've been very busy. Maybe we can still do something." She said, "Oh, sure, maybe." Just before they'd gotten off, she went back to the clinical tone, "Tom, I just want to know why you masturbated when I came to your house? Can you give me an answer?" This confirmed to Tom that she was crazy. Excusing himself, he hung up. That had been three weeks ago.

Tom swung into the drive-thru at a Wendy's. Levy said it was a good thing that he hadn't argued with her. And that he had admitted nothing because, Levy told him, the police had been taping the phone call. She said so in her statement. Levy had shown him her statement to the police. This account said they'd met at Thunderbird Mall where she worked part-time at the information counter. Fields asked her for directions, and then they'd started talking. She told him she had the mall job, was a waitress three days a week, and was also a student at the university. He said he was a professor. They'd talked. He'd asked how much her job paid, and told her he thought he could help her find a better job at the university. He left his number and told her to call if she was interested. She said he genuinely seemed to care about her. That's why she called him.

A few days later, she went to meet him at ten in the morning. She was surprised when the address turned out to be his house —she'd thought they were meeting in a university office. Fields greeted her at the front door which opened directly into the living room. He was wearing jeans and a sports shirt. She thought he'd be dressed a little better. She'd dressed as though for a job interview. Skirt. Blouse.

As she'd walked into the living room, she heard him lock the front door behind her. He showed her around the house a bit. The living room, den, kitchen. They looked into a bedroom, but did not go in. He also showed her the garden. He offered her coffee, which she refused, and he remarked on her good figure and overall look of health. She sat on the sofa opposite the French doors which opened out into a backyard garden. He sat down at the other end of the sofa. They talked about everything but the job. They talked about what she was studying. He asked her personal questions about her life; he asked her what she did to keep so physically fit and she said she was a dancer, but that lately she'd been having lower back pain. He told her he'd had some pain in the same area, but had done exercises which helped him. He stood up to demonstrate a few, then suggested she try them. She was hesitant, but he seemed genuinely to care and so she got up and tried several—there were three or four.

When she sat back down, they were closer together. He put his arm around her, told her he thought she was incredibly beautiful, that she really held something for him and she must know that, and he began to hug her. She let him for a minute, mainly because she was surprised and confused and didn't know what to do next. He moved closer. Then somehow, in the way he moved his body, he got her to lie down beside him on the sofa, began to touch her breasts and groin area. She asked him to stop; he went on hugging and touching her. She decided not to struggle, but wait for the right moment to move. He seemed very excited. This went on for a while. Then she felt his excitement peak. It was then that she knew he'd ejaculated. She could feel it in his body. She pushed away and stood up. She walked to the front door, unlocked it, and then asked him if there had ever really been a job. He didn't answer and she left.

As a result of this incident, she said in her statement, she had been depressed, unable to sleep or eat or concentrate. Her stomach had been upset and it had not been possible to have relations with her boyfriend.

Tom leaned out of his window. One more car before he'd reach the drive-thru window. He swallowed. He had no saliva. When he'd finished making his own statement and been shown a typed copy, his first reaction was: is this all that stands between me and her charges? There was so little to the incident. His account was very much like hers, though he knew he had never locked the front door. She was free to go at any time. It was she who had asked to see the house and had not seemed interested in talking about the job. It was true, he had shown her some exercises. When they sat back down on the sofa, they had hugged at the same time. She had kissed him. There had been some affectionate touching, though he couldn't say where. She pushed away once and then started hugging him again. When she pushed away again, she said that he reminded her of an elementary school teacher who had touched her improperly. She had then become very agitated. He tried to talk to her, but she stood up suddenly and seemed confused. She walked to the front door, asked him if there had ever been any job, and before he could answer, she left.

Tom pulled up to the window. The girl handed over the drink, and one of them fumbled the coins. He took a gulp of the iced tea, and then kneeling on the hot pavement, he gathered up his change.

Several days after his arrest, there was a brief article on the front page of the morning paper: "University Professor Indicted for Kidnapping and Sexual Abuse." He had scheduled two student conferences that day; he had a short faculty meeting and later a graduate seminar. He debated, and then decided it was crucial that he do whatever he was supposed to do.

One of the students didn't show for his conference, but students did forget their appointments. The other, a graduate student, whom he considered a friend, appeared at the right time, but just to tell him she had a scheduling conflict and couldn't stay. She gave him a searching look, hesitated, and left abruptly.

In the halls and in the office, the faculty seemed to avoid him. During the meeting, they displayed a reluctant tolerance of his presence. No one said anything about the article in the paper. No one said or intimated they were sure Tom might be innocent of the charges.

That afternoon, the students in his graduate seminar watched him out of a distance and curiosity. No matter what he said or did, he couldn't bring much back from them. He hung on as long as he could and then dismissed the class early. As he

walked from the room, he had no idea how he would finish the
semester.

In the following days, he greeted people, but several didn't
seem to notice him. He developed a preoccupied air when he
was out, acknowledged almost no one, and avoided restaurants;
he began to shop in grocery stores outside his neighborhood.
There was something familiar about this isolation and banish-
ment.

Alone, unable to concentrate on his work, he put his energy
into training for a triathlon which was to take place in Hawaii
late in May. At sunrise, he followed the bike path to the edge of
town where the suburban streets released him, the desert took
him in, and, his shadow elongating across cactus, palo verde,
and mesquite, he peddled hard and fast. Afternoons, he jogged
or swam laps outdoors, the pool an enormous twilit room electric with white sunlight and the plunging arms and legs of
strangers.

Even under the fluorescent lights, Susanne Raine's reddish
blond hair gave off a kind of heat. Tom couldn't keep himself
from looking over at her. The preliminary hearing. She told her
story. Questions were asked and answered. She seemed very
sure of herself. He told his story. More questions were asked.
They stuck to their stories. He wanted to stand up, cross the
room, and ask her why she was doing this to him? At the end of
the hearing, the case was bound over for trial, and Fields entered a plea of innocent. A trial date was set. As she left the
room, she gave him an expressionless look, and Tom caught the
sharp smell of his own nervous sweat. He turned to Levy.
"Jesus Christ, Michael, what does she really want?"

Levy said, "She wants your ass. I'm going to have my investigator check her out—see if she has a psychiatric history—or if
she has a habit of getting herself into these kinds of situations
and bringing charges. We'll see what comes back."

He came awake sweating, took a deep breath, let it out. Her
hair. The way she'd been that day in the mall. She was just

ahead of him, sipping a coke. Sunlight slanting through a sky-
light high overhead. She walked, her toes out, a dancer's walk,
physical health and power in her movements. He got out of
bed, turning on lights as he went. In the living room, his bicycle
leaned against the fireplace; the hardwood floor creaked with
each step. He retraced her path: she looked around, said, "Beautiful house . . . you live here by yourself? You professors really
have the life. Work a few hours a week. Live like this. Is this
your study?" She tipped her head to read book titles. "These
books and articles have your name on them . . . What do you
write about?" Unsure she'd accept it, he said, "Making people
more comfortable when they're sick and scared." And she'd
nodded and said, "That's nice. Noble. Kind. No, really," the flir-
tatious contempt in her voice exciting him.

Fields walked to the French doors. Outside, the softness of the
desert night; he stood in the garden, the mesquite and olive
trees behind him. Near the wall, the prickly pear had bloomed,
yellow flowers glowing in the dark. He looked into the house at
the sofa. He stared at the cushions. He was sure nothing had
really happened, but she'd been so convincing at the hearing.

As the trial date slowly approached and the semester went on,
the students and faculty remained distant. Fields was starting to
realize that even if he was found innocent, his reputation was
already so badly damaged he'd probably be unable to teach or
work in the community again. Some of the time he believed
this; some of the time he wasn't sure. He started looking for jobs
elsewhere.

Levy was a little late. He came in quickly and took off his
jacket, hung it on the back of his chair. He looked for a file and
then stood reading behind his desk, stroking his chin. When he
looked up at Fields, he said, "My investigator has been checking
on Susanne Raine. I've just received the report." Fields waited.
"So who is she? She's a twenty-year-old part-time student who
has a 3.0 average at the university. She's changed her major
three times; her latest is education with a minor in computer
science; she'd been studying dance until recently. She has a boy-

friend . . ." Levy took a breath, puffed one cheek. "I could go on, but the point, I think, is that she's a typical college student." He closed the file. "She has no history of bringing sexual assault charges, nothing psychiatric."

Levy paused. A fountain splashed softly in the courtyard. Levy said, "We're scheduled to go to trial in a few weeks. We've pleaded innocent. I know that it's extremely important to you to be found innocent." Levy toyed with a letter opener. A secretary peered in, closed the door. Levy said, "Listen to me. We take this to trial. There are no witnesses. It's a swearing contest between you and the girl. The jury watches and listens. You invited Raine to your house to a job-related interview that never took place." Fields started to say something. Levy held up his hand. "From a jury's point of view, Tom. Your house, not your office. Maybe for a job that did not exist. Okay, we're in trial. You get up there. You wear a white shirt, blue suit, tie. The jury looks you over. You're forty-one years old, you're six-one, have a good job, a successful career. You're sophisticated, educated. You tell your story. You talked, you showed Ms. Raine a few exercises, there was some hugging, a little of this, a little of that, she left. Okay?

"Then Susanne Raine gets up there. The jury looks at this young, very pretty girl. The D.A. will have her dress the part— something modest, something sweet. Maybe with some good directing she'll stumble through the emotional parts of her testimony. Maybe she'll cry. Who knows. They'll hear she works at a couple of part-time jobs, she's putting herself through school. She'll make a strong impression on a jury. They'll feel sorry for her. The D.A. will get you up there on the stand and ask you some questions which will make you look bad no matter how you answer." Levy swung in his chair, faced Fields. He leaned on his desk. "Tom, I personally believe you are guilty of nothing more than very bad judgement here. Really. They have a poor case. The kidnapping charges are a joke. But juries are completely unpredictable and you're exposing yourself to a lot of jail time. As your lawyer, I recommend that you plead no contest. You're taking an enormous risk bringing this to trial." Fields started to speak, but Levy put up his hand. "Tom, please.

Don't give me an answer now, but think it over carefully. Will you do that?" Fields stared out the window. Levy said, "I've seen juries convict people for less."

A very small part of Fields was marginally aware he'd done exactly what Susanne Raine had accused him of, but hadn't there been the way she'd guided and held his wrist as he'd placed her coffee on the table, something about the way she'd brushed his shoulder as she sat down? And then, too, wasn't there her look of flirtation and hard contempt which said, Try me; the way she'd moved against him when he did; yes, she'd pulled back, but only after she'd fit herself to him, moved against him; and hadn't she still been saying, Try me? It was nothing like the charges. Kidnapping. Sexual assault. Neither had really happened. That's what Tom remembered.

Fields requested and received permission to take a formal leave of absence from the university, put his house up for sale, and accepted a position back East, which was in the same town where he had grown up. Ten days before he was scheduled to go to trial, he flew out to Hawaii for the triathlon. He knew he wasn't really ready, but the thought of not entering seemed worse. Six hundred and forty-one had entered, four hundred and twelve finished, and Tom Fields finished one hundred and seventy-one—his best time.

The next morning, he rose and slowly walked across the hotel room to the balcony and looked over the palms at the ocean and sea mist thrown up by the distant surf. Hilo. He could still feel the rise and fall of his body in the swells as he'd come ashore, his skin crusted with salt as he pedaled his bicycle. No matter how hard he tried, he could not remember anything happening between himself and the girl. But the fact that he couldn't remember had slowly made him come to doubt himself. Susanne Raine had been so sure of herself at the preliminary hearing. What if the jury didn't believe him? He sat stiffly on the bed and picked up the phone. Reaching Levy in his office, he asked him to plead no contest.

When he returned, Levy told him that although it still hadn't been completely worked out, he thought that in return for

Fields' plea of no contest, Levy could have the kidnapping and sexual assault charges reduced to one charge of sexual assault—a misdemeanor.

As part of his change of plea, he answered a request from the Adult Probation Department to meet with one of their investigators and assist in the preparation of a presentence report. As he waited on the fifth floor, cold in the overly air-conditioned room, he stared through the tinted glass at the cloudless blue sky of the desert, the hard edges of the distant mountains. He hated refrigeration. It made his flesh feel as though it was just meat strung on bones. Northern winters were one of the reasons he had come to the desert.

A woman walked toward him and introduced herself. She was tall and slim, almost as tall as he was. He followed her into her office. As she moved behind her desk, she indicated he take the chair in front. Behind her, the blue sky, the mountains from a different angle. She explained that she was the investigator in charge of his presentence report and that she was going to ask him questions and take his social history, a phrase which momentarily preoccupied him. She had a file open on the blotter in front of her.

She clicked on a hand-sized tape recorder: Jean Davis, investigator; she stated his name, the time and date, the case number, the superior court judge in charge of the case, the victim's name, and then placed the tape recorder on the desk between them. Tom Fields noticed that she wore no wedding ring, thought that she had beautiful hands. He saw a framed Kodak of a boy, maybe eight or ten, who was grinning and holding up a trout and felt a sudden rise of emotion. He looked away. Sure she was divorced; he couldn't keep himself from seeing her, the boy, himself—the three of them—together at some future time. He saw them by a trout stream. He looked at the floor. He knew that as an investigator her evaluation would influence what was done with him.

With several long, self-conscious pauses, he began by responding to her questions about his parents and childhood. As Tom Fields progressed, he became acutely aware that he was coming to something. He talked about his one younger brother, a lawyer, now married and with two children; an ambitious father who was a prosperous businessman; and then his mother, a career woman, a set designer. They'd lived in Connecticut; his parents commuted into New York and were so busy with their successful careers that he and his brother were mostly raised by a grandmother. He saw his parents holidays, summers, and weekends. He mentioned that he came to realize in his twenties that his father was an alcoholic who often verbally abused and demeaned him. Though he was the captain of his basketball and baseball teams at a New England prep school, his father never once came to see him play.

He went on to talk about college; an early marriage; an out-of-college job as a salesman which he had found pointless and demeaning; a stint in the army—he'd avoided Vietnam; another job as a salesman; a growing sense of purposelessness; and the birth of his son. He gazed out the window, felt something begin to hollow in himself. The tape recorder clicked. The investigator turned over the cassette, clicked it on, and nodded, go ahead.

After a long uncertain pause, he said that his parents were no longer living. His father had died in his sleep two years ago. It had been seventeen years since his mother had died of cancer. He felt the hollowing in him widen, deepen. He said that his mother's death was the turning point in his life. He stared at the cluster of microphone holes. "After seeing her humiliating death in what was supposed to be one of the best hospitals, I promised myself I'd change the nature of dying in this country." He went on now to talk about getting a Ph.D. in Public Health, going to England to study their Hospice program on a National Science Foundation Grant.

When he had regained control of his voice, he started giving the investigator an even, measured account of his mother's death. His mother was still young—in her late forties. She'd had a mastectomy, followed by chemotherapy, lost her hair, but had kept up her spirits. She seemed to be recovering when an examination revealed the cancer had metastasized into her stomach and lungs. She went back into the hospital.

The cassette clicked to an end. The investigator glanced at her watch and stood. Fields looked out the window. The mountains had taken on definition and were starting to cast long purple shadows in the distance. She asked him if he wanted coffee, he shook his head no, perhaps water. She returned with coffee for herself, placed a plastic cup of water in front of him. The air conditioning made him ache. She replaced the cassette, clicked it on. He resumed speaking in a shaky voice.

Realizing it was to be his last chance with his mother, he spent hours by her bed, talking to her, holding her hand, reassuring her, telling her that he loved her. Everything that happened in those days imprinted itself on him. He noticed that as long as he was touching his mother—a hand, an arm—that her pain was eased. The sound of his voice, too, calmed her. When doctors came into her room—they rarely came alone, but usually in twos and threes—they stood back, almost never touched her, averted their eyes, and left quickly. His mother and his family were never asked anything about what might be wanted.

What he remembered most clearly was that when the windows were darkening with oncoming night, his mother, knowing he would have to leave, grew restless, tossing and turning in the bed. And when visiting hours were over, and he let go of her hand, she would get a wild, abandoned look in her eyes, and start to moan with pain. The hospital administration refused his request to sleep in an adjoining room. As he walked toward the elevator, he could hear her begin to howl.

Mornings, as he stepped into the hall, he heard her begging for painkillers, and the nurse explaining patiently as if to a child that she would have to wait, just another forty minutes, that they couldn't deviate from their schedule. Some mornings he helped the nurse lift his mother and wondered at how light her body was becoming.

He went silent, noticed the sunlight had moved across the investigator's desk. He followed a series of images. Every night he walks away from the hospital and across the street to a parking lot which is piled with black snow. The air is cold, smells of soot. He goes home to his wife and young son where they live on the second floor of a duplex. He sees the rooms, sees his wife waiting at the kitchen table, his son playing on the floor, sees the furniture in the different rooms, the double bed in the shadows. There is silvery condensation from their breathing on the windows. One night he gets into his car to go home, but cannot turn the key; he feels the hospital at his back, his apartment waiting. He gets out of the car and walks to a nearby bar. The bar is warm and quiet, the lights low; he takes a stool and has a beer, another beer, a shot, then notices someone, a girl who works at a desk in the hospital. Recognizing him, she nods, they slide down several stools. Later, when they walk out together, it is sleeting, the trees and bare branches are encased with ice, the streets glazed. As they step off the curb, a car comes down the street in a sideslip, the driver motionless, and passes through a red light. Steadying each other, they walk toward her car, which is frozen in ice. They begin to chip at the lock with keys. From inside, the parked cars and distant lights are formless shapes through the iced glass. They turn to each other, kiss, and start pulling at each other's clothes.

After a long silence, Fields spoke. He said that his mother died six weeks after she'd returned to the hospital. She died sometime after evening visiting hours ended and the next morning. He walked into her room to find the bed empty, an orderly tucking in fresh sheets. When Fields tried to find out if someone had been with her when she died, he could get no answers.

He gazed at the Kodak of the boy with the trout. He remained silent. He'd loved his wife, but couldn't go home to her. There had been dozens of brief sexual encounters, which he could barely remember, as if the women were met and embraced while sleepwalking, and after two years his wife had divorced him. He'd seen his son each summer. He was a junior in college now.

The investigator glanced at her watch and clicked off the tape.

At the second interview a few weeks later, she was asking Fields about a newspaper article. There was a picture of him in a suit and tie. He was smiling. His cheeks were hollow. It went back twelve years and referred to the first major field study he'd undertaken after returning from his hospice research in England. The article was titled "The Man Who Died," and described how Fields had faked cancer. To do so, he'd lost twenty pounds, had a biopsy scar incised on his neck, and shaved his head to simulate hair loss from chemotherapy; he'd had ultraviolet burns on his abdomen to simulate radiation burns, and i.v. marks in his arm. Unshaven and unshowered, diagnosed as having terminal cancer, he'd been admitted to the surgical ward of a large city hospital. Only two of the most senior administrators knew what he was doing. Within forty-eight hours of being admitted, he'd developed real symptoms—pain, vomiting, nausea, and listlessness. Afraid that painkillers would dull his ability to observe, he'd remained in this state in the ward for two weeks. He'd told the investigator that there he had confirmed everything he had observed during his mother's death six years before. In their daily visits, the doctors had avoided eye contact, stood at a distance from the patient, and spent less than five minutes per visit with him. He had gone on to write up his findings and recommendations; many had been put into practice. Several well-known thanatologists had worried about the long-term effects of such an experiment on his psyche, but Fields had said in the article and repeated now that he couldn't let things like that stop him. His supporters had praised the study as brilliant, though dangerous to his personal well-being. His detractors had called it a morbid stunt. The article had concluded with Fields being quoted as saying, "The dying teach us to live. They have finally dropped their masks and see life as it is."

Fields could see the investigator had underlined the phrase *dropped their masks*. She swivelled in her chair once. He stared at her beautiful hands. Fields waited. She seemed to debate, then turned the article over and went on.

At the end of the interview, she asked him about his plans, and he said he hoped to go on with his work. He hesitated, then asked how her report would be used. She closed the file and said that all of this information would go to the Superior Court Judge in charge of his case. "If you have questions, your lawyer is the person to talk to."

·   ·   ·

His house sold quickly. He took a job back East at the end of the summer. His mother had left him a house on some land in the country and in August he moved in. He walked across the fields, remembering how when he was a boy the trail to the pond had seemed infinite and mysterious. In cleaning out the house, kneeling in the corner of a second-floor bedroom where he and his brother had slept, his head at the windowsill, he stopped. Something had happened in this room with his mother years ago. She'd spanked him for something his brother had done and nothing he'd said could convince her it wasn't him. She'd held him here. His head not quite reaching the window. The sudden terror of her taking hold of him. He stood slowly with the dustpan carefully poised, looked out across the fields to the woods, his weight off balance where the floor had settled. Outside, it was raining beneath a white sky.

Levy was on the phone. "I just want to keep you up to date. You've gotten some great letters of support from various professional people around the country. And one man in particular wrote how you'd helped his father die peacefully—calmed him for days, refused any fee. But you also have damaging letters. One woman wrote that she knew of several women who had gotten involved with you, but were too ashamed to come forward afterward. Another wrote of being drawn in, but asking around before she got involved; she said she found out that you had a reputation for collecting young women. I'm quoting phrases from the letters. These aren't my words." Levy paused. "Your good letters should far outweigh anything negative—it's a first offense and the charge is down to a misdemeanor, but I want you to be informed."

In early November he returned to the desert for sentencing. As Tom stepped off the plane, he felt the blue sky open over him, the white light of fall, and realized he'd been aching for this light without knowing it. The next morning, he met Levy at his office, and they went to court together. The maximum jail sentence for the misdemeanor could have been four months, but the Superior Court Judge said that considering the many good things Fields had done, a jail sentence seemed pointless. The judge gave him a year's probation, a fine of fifteen hundred dollars and ordered him to undergo counselling.

The next morning his picture appeared in the newspaper. Taken from the side, it showed him in a dark suit, with close-cropped hair, and a marathoner's hollow cheeks. He was staring straight ahead with no expression. The caption was: *Thomas Fields awaits sentencing in Superior Court.* Later, when he went to his department to pick up a box of his books which had been left behind, he saw two faculty members leaning over the picture. Tom Fields heard one of them remark that it was the only time he'd ever seen Fields look completely at peace.

Jennifer Egan

PUERTO VALLARTA

On their last day in Puerto Vallarta, the fathers rented horses. Ellen's father let her come along, though she was only eleven and hadn't ridden before. She stayed close to his side, staring at the tin shacks and rows of hobbled corn along the back streets. Her father drank wine from a pig-bladder pouch and gave her a sip when she asked. It was sour and hot. He bought her a sombrero embroidered with green and pink flowers, and placed it carefully over her head. Gradually, they drifted apart from the others.

Ellen was rarely alone with her father. She and her parents had joined two other families in Mexico, and for ten days had descended in large, whooping groups over local cafés and beaches. Her father told jokes and chose restaurants, whatever people wanted. He was Master of Ceremonies.

"Aren't we meeting Mom for lunch?" Ellen asked when the two of them reached a strip of pressed, pale dirt leading out of town.

Her father nodded. "Want to turn around?"

Slowly, Ellen shook her head.

"Me either," her father said.

He leaned close to Ellen, surrounding her with a fresh, wet smell like cut grass. Then he set his watch back. It took an instant, a twirl of the tiny hands, and they were free. Ellen felt a thrill of mischief, and a nervous grin split her face. She did not think of her mother, only of a hurdle she and her father had leapt together. As they rode on, she stared greedily at each dry bush and blotched, scampering pig.

"When I was young," her father said, staring at the horizon, "I bought a motorcycle and rode around Europe for months."

Ellen had never heard this before. "Was it fun?" she asked.

"I lived like a maniac."

She paused, unsure if this was good or bad. "Was it fun?" she asked again.

"Fun. Was it fun." He stared across the miles of dead grass and shook his head. "It was the best time of my life."

Ellen grew suddenly shy. She followed her father's gaze to the horizon, where faded earth nudged a faded sky. It looked like the edge of something hidden, a place her father alone had explored.

"Come on," she said, kicking the shaggy sides of her pony. As it stamped into the hot, dry wind she felt a longing never to go back.

"You're a hooligan," her father laughed when he'd caught up to her.

"I'm a maniac," Ellen said.

The sun was low when they finally returned to the beach. Ellen's mother, Vivian, waited on the cooling sand. When she saw them she jumped to her feet. "Thank God," she cried. "I thought you'd been robbed or something."

"This goddamn watch," Ellen's father said. "I swear it's running backwards."

"Well, your lunches are here if you want them," Vivian said. "Then I guess we'd better pack."

Ellen sank onto the sand and began eating frantically. The sandwiches were warm from hours of heat. Her mother didn't ask where Ellen and her father had been, she just stared across the water. It was the last day of their vacation.

"I'm sorry, Mom," Ellen said through a mouthful of food. "I'm sorry you were by yourself."

Her father cleared his throat and stood up.

Vivian looked at Ellen curiously. "Relax," she said. "What could you have done?"

In the five years since that trip, there had been no time for family vacations; Ellen's father traveled too much on business. This year he was selling franchises for Tommy's, a lobster restaurant in downtown Detroit. "They use real butter—sweet butter," he would tell prospective investors. "Quality like that you can't find nowadays." Ellen imagined sometimes that Tommy was the name of his son from an earlier marriage, some young prodigy living in another state.

At one time Vivian had gone with him on his trips. Lately she stayed home, though, conditioning her hair and soaking her Boston ferns in the kitchen sink. She grew thin, and reminisced about their trips.

"I was almost killed in Jamaica," she said at breakfast. "Your dad swam away from our boat and a wind came. I started sailing out to sea."

She spoke with the urgency of a first telling, though Ellen had heard the story many times.

"What a nightmare," her father said, looking up from his paper. "You were going so fast I couldn't catch up. I was splashing around, screaming how to turn the boat, but you couldn't hear me."

"So what happened?" Ellen cried, caught by the mood of the story.

"I jumped off," her mother said. "I swam back to your father. The boat kept going." She was washing apples in the kitchen sink. Now she stopped, still holding the colander under the running faucet, and turned to her husband. Ellen's parents looked at one another, and Ellen felt a current of something between them which startled her.

After a moment they looked away. Her mother shook the colander under the water. Ellen heard apples bumping against its sides. Her father put on his coat, shaking the sleeves gently over his arms. He was leaving for the airport, catching a plane to Australia.

"I have an idea," he said, kissing them each goodbye. "Easter's six weeks away. We'll go back to Puerto Vallarta."

While her father was in Australia, Ellen went with her friend Renata to a Mexican restaurant in Glencoe. It was a train ride outside Chicago, but Renata's brother Eric was a bartender there, and had promised to serve them alcohol. Ellen had never been to a bar before. She ordered a rum cocktail crowded with small umbrellas and leaned back, crossing her legs in a way she hoped was sophisticated. Then, at a corner table half-hidden by a ficus, Ellen saw her father.

She sat very still, lips on her straw, and tried to make sense of this. He had left for Australia six days ago, and was not due back for four more. He sat with another man and two women, one of whom wore the striped tennis sweater Ellen had given her father last Christmas. The woman had on salmon-colored lipstick. Her hand rested on Ellen's father's shoulder.

Ellen carefully set down her glass. She blinked at her smeared reflection in the strip of brass that ran along the bar, then looked back at her father. He had a large, vivid face, shaped like the spade on a playing card. His eyes were gray as fish scales. Ellen was struck by how handsome he looked—handsome the way strangers are, people on buses or in the supermarket. A sharp, metallic taste filled her mouth. Her father was handsome, a handsome man in a restaurant surrounded by other handsome people who were his friends. He talked, he moved his hands, and as Ellen watched she began to feel that she herself had no right to be here. He belonged wherever he was.

When the group stood up she swiveled toward the bar and hunched over her drink. Renata had gone to the bathroom, and Eric was washing glasses at the sink. Ellen heard her father's loud laugh behind her, and was overcome with a sudden, dreamlike calm, as if moments from now she would realize that none of this had happened. A car pulled up to the restaurant. There were shoes on the pavement, laughter, shutting doors. When the left rear door stuck, Ellen knew the car was her father's. Six days ago he'd driven that car to the airport, and Ellen had waved goodbye to him through the tinted windshield.

When she heard nothing but silence, Ellen slid from her stool and went outside the restaurant. She was panting, and her heartbeat made her dizzy. It was dusk. A curved driveway arched toward the door of the restaurant, and beyond it sprawled the wide suburban parking lot. Ellen looked across it. She felt a pain somewhere inside her, but couldn't find its source. She stared at the passing cars, the pale moon rising over the asphalt. "Where does it hurt?" her mother would ask. "Where does it hurt the most?" It hurt everywhere, she thought. It didn't hurt enough.

Ellen searched the frail rim of trees around the lot, the sky soaked in dusk. Everything looked wrong to her, garish and soiled. Two hours ago, she and Renata had skipped across this lot, running their hands along cars and loudly debating what drinks they should order: Martinis? Bloody Marys? Piña coladas? It seemed an ancient memory now, a scene from her childhood. Ellen wanted nothing more than to pick up where that memory had ended, to go back inside and burrow in the company of Eric and Renata. They hadn't seen her father, they had no idea. It was almost like not having seen him herself.

During the ride back to Chicago, Ellen rocked against the seat of Eric's car, impatient to throw herself in her mother's arms and be soothed. Her mother had long, cool hands and hair like a lioness. She was the most comforting person on earth.

Ellen found her mother seated on the living-room floor, her hair in a scarf. She had the dreamy look she often wore after spending several hours by herself.

"I'm rearranging," she said. "Dusting."

Around her lay things she had bought on her various trips: inlaid wood chests, cornhusk dolls, animals carved from ivory. In a glass dish were the colored marble eggs she had bought with her husband in Florence. Ellen felt a nervous fluttering under her ribs.

"I've lost perspective," her mother said. "Can you see any difference?"

Ellen wished she were back at the age when she would howl shamelessly while her mother used a tweezer to pick bits of gravel from her skinned knees. Her mother looked as frail to her now, as easy to shatter, as the blown-glass vase she was holding.

"Mom," Ellen said.

Vivian looked up. The room was very still. Ellen felt the weight of the old house, its dense curtains and clean, swept kitchen. Her mother's world was reliable, steadfast, decent. The fun was elsewhere.

"What is it?" her mother asked.

Ellen sank to the floor and lifted a crimson egg from the dish. She felt a ghastly power, the kind she felt sometimes when using a knife or scissors. Once while she was chopping celery she had glanced at her mother's pale arm and thought with horror of how easily she might cut the soft skin. She had pictured the bright stripe of blood, her mother's look of surprise and pain. She had tortured herself with these thoughts for several moments before putting down the knife and wrapping her mother tightly in her arms. As she hugged, Vivian had begun to laugh. "Such affection," she'd said. "What have I done to deserve this?"

"Oh, your father called tonight," she said now. "From Sydney. He sends a kiss."

Ellen stared at her. "How's he doing?" she managed to ask.

"Lonely," said her mother. "At least the weather's good."

Ellen leaned back against her hands. She watched the long cords of her mother's neck, the fragile blade of her chin, and was suddenly furious at Vivian for letting herself be fooled, for knowing less than Ellen did. "How come you don't go with him anymore?" Ellen demanded.

Vivian shrugged. "He's busy." She polished another egg, then looked back at Ellen. "What makes you ask?"

Ellen felt a surge of guilt, as if she and her father were in this thing together. She avoided her mother's eyes. "I think it's Tommy's," she said. "I think it keeps him busy."

"Exactly," her mother said.

Ellen's father brought her a glass paperweight shaped like a kangaroo and a T-shirt which said SYDNEY. She felt senseless, giddy relief as he talked about the vineyards he had seen, their blond dirt and acrid smell of ripeness. That night at the Mexican restaurant was something separate, something cordoned off. It made no difference. She thought about it constantly.

Ellen and her parents flew to Puerto Vallarta two days before Easter. They rented a small house outside of town, where flowers poured from the cliffs in a bright, clotted rush. Their first morning they sat on the terrace, eating sweet Mexican rolls and drinking coffee.

"Remember Bo Horgan?" her father said. "He's building some condos up the hill. I should take a look, the poor guy."

Her mother rolled her eyes. "Bo Horgan," she said. "I think I'll meet you in town."

Ellen watched her father. She watched him constantly now, searching for signs of restlessness or boredom. Often his eyes had the fractured, glossy look of something repaired with too much glue. He would glance at his watch as though tracking events somewhere else. Ellen felt a continual need to distract him, to hold his attention.

"I'll go with you," she said.

"It's hot up there, Squirrel."

"So?"

Her parents exchanged looks of surprise. Ellen felt her mother's gaze, the soft eyes in a face as rigid and spare as a kitchen table. She could still remember a time when her mother would lie in bed on weekends with a cup of cocoa, eating croissants Ellen's father brought from the French bakery. He would rest his head on Vivian's stomach and protest that she was dropping crumbs in his eyes. "Oh hush," she would say, licking her fingers one at a time. But she wasn't like that now. She was a person who got left in other people's wakes.

Ellen and her father drove up the mountain road in a rattling jeep. His elbow pointed out the window. Ellen pointed her own the same way. She kept her eyes on the wet curl of growth which sprang from the red dirt. Beside them, cliffs dropped straight to the sea.

"Am I a lot like Mom?" she asked.

"In some ways," he said. "Although you've got my adventurous streak, that's a difference." He drove with one finger on the wheel, making it look easy. When Ellen learned to drive this year, she would drive like that.

"Could get you into trouble," he added, grinning.

Ellen smiled at the wind, letting its hot blast dry her lips and teeth. "I hope so," she said.

Bo Horgan had a greasy, cream-colored beard and the sort of skin that can only grow more red. He picked his way toward them over mounds of steaming earth. Skeleton houses dotted the land: fresh blond planks shimmering in the midday sun. A bulldozer smeared the air with its heat.

"I didn't know you had a daughter," Bo said, pouring them each a vodka at a flimsy outdoor table.

Ellen's father chuckled. "I keep her hidden."

"No wonder," Bo said, winking at Ellen as he handed her a glass. He gave off a meaty smell, as if the sun had partially cooked him. The heat soaked Ellen's dark hair, making her feel almost faint.

"You may want to skip the booze, Squirrel," her father said.

He watched as she lifted her glass. Ellen sensed that he was nervous, and felt a rare, tenuous power over him. She took a large sip. "Delicious," she lied.

Her father smiled uneasily and looked at his watch. "We're in and out of here," he said.

"Relax," Bo told him. "Hang around a little."

He topped off Ellen's glass, filling it so high that the vodka spilled on her fingers when she tried to lift it. She and Ed toasted and drank. Vodka fumes flooded her throat, nearly gagging her. Ellen was desperate to keep the tiny edge she'd gained on her father, no matter what it took. He watched her, shifting in his seat.

"How go the legal battles, Horgan?" he asked.

Bo sighed. "About the same. Only the lawyers win."

Ellen took another sip. It brought tears to her eyes.

"Look at this," Bo said, watching Ellen with surprise. "Chip off the old block."

Her father laughed weakly. "Christ, let's hope not," he said.

When it became too hot to sit still, Bo took them on a tour of his construction site. Ellen was barely able to keep her balance as they padded over the hot, soft earth.

"Take my arm, Squirrel," her father said, watching her with concern. Ellen could see he was anxious to get away. She asked every question she could think of, drawing out the visit.

Finally they reached the Jeep. Bo's face was scarlet, running with sweat. He looked on the verge of collapse. Ellen felt a sudden great affection for this harmless, clownish man who had been her accomplice. She was sorry to leave him. When the men had shaken hands, she kissed Bo goodbye on the lips.

Her father gripped the wheel with both hands as they headed back down the mountain. "I don't think vodka at noon is such a good idea, Squirrel," he said. He spoke in an easy, joking way, but he wasn't smiling.

"You drank," Ellen said, letting her head loll against the seat. "You drink a lot."

"Your mother's not going to like it."

"Are we telling her?"

He glanced at Ellen, then back at the road. "Well no," he said. "I guess we'd better not."

Ellen watched the ocean for a while, her head spinning. "What are Bo's legal battles?" she asked.

Her father explained that Bo had owned a company in Chicago which went bankrupt three years before. Now he was being sued by his former employees.

"Is he guilty?" Ellen asked.

Her father hesitated. "He lied too much," he said. "If he'd told some truth and let the pressure off, he'd be in a lot less trouble now."

Ellen wondered if this meant he was guilty or not.

"He should've told just enough to win people over," her father said. "Enough to look honest."

Ellen nodded in silence.

"As little as possible, but something."

"I see."

"If you have to lie you're already in danger."

They rode in silence. Just outside of town Ellen turned to her father, raising her voice above the engine. "Dad," she said, "have you gone out with anyone else while you and Mom have been married?"

His small, gray eyes were fastened to the road. "Of course not," he said.

"If the answer was yes would you tell me?"

Her father sighed. "No, Squirrel," he said. "I probably wouldn't."

"Well," Ellen said, pleased by the calm in her voice, "then you'd be in a dangerous spot."

Ellen's mother was not at the café where they had arranged to meet. Her father put his hands in his pockets and stared at the breaking waves, which were crowded with the bobbing heads of children. Then he looked at his watch. "We're late," he said.

They sat without speaking. Her father ordered a beer and drank it quickly. He cracked his knuckles one by one. "Let's take a look around," he said.

The streets were crowded with Mexican families celebrating the holiday. There were women in black dresses made of cotton, girls whose thin, dusty legs teetered over high heels as they trod the mud streets. The air smelled of bitter Mexican beer.

Ellen's father stayed close to her as they wove through the crowds. He would crane his neck to look for her mother, then glance quickly back at Ellen. Ellen began to wander more often from his side, peering with sudden interest into the windows of shops while her father rushed to retrieve her.

Finally he put his arm around her, cupping her shoulder in his palm. His hand was large and warm, and Ellen relaxed in the safety of his grip. She steered him into a sweet shop, where he bought her coffee ice cream on a heat-softened cone. In a silversmith's window, a pair of turquoise earrings caught her eye.

"Better wait till we get home before you put these on," her

father said, chuckling as he counted out the bills. "They're pretty flashy."

Ellen smiled sweetly and slipped the earrings on.

So much attention from her father was exhausting, and she felt a giddy tremor rising from her stomach. She tossed her head so the earrings bumped her cheek. She looked for her mother, hoping not to find her.

Finally they stopped. Her father shielded his eyes and turned in a full circle, staring over the crowds. A group of children scampered past, dragging a blue, donkey-shaped piñata through the dust. Young men leaned in doorways and wandered in restless groups. Ellen noticed some of them watching her, and was conscious of her thin, bare arms, the tiny hairs on her thighs.

"I have an idea," her father said. "I'll ask the guy in that shop if he's seen her. It's the kind of place she likes." He pointed to a store which sold clay jugs sprinkled with a thin, clear glaze like sugared water. Beyond it, several men in bare feet and hats lounged against a wall.

"I'll wait here," Ellen said.

"Come on, Squirrel. It'll take a second." He took her elbow, but Ellen pulled away.

"I'll wait," she insisted, flushing to the neck.

Her father's eyes darted along the street. "Just don't move," he said, jogging toward the shop. "I mean it, Squirrel. You stay put."

The moment he was gone, Ellen moved closer to the men by the wall. A few shielded their eyes to look up at her. They were squatting in the dust, passing a bottle around. She stood before them with one leg bent, staring at the exhausted plaster between their shoulders. Her heart was beating fast. She glanced back at the shop to make sure her father hadn't reappeared. His Spanish was poor; the conversation would take a while. Her own mischief struck her as irrepressibly funny, and she gritted her teeth to keep from laughing.

They were young men, smooth-faced and a little shy. They spoke to her in Spanish, but Ellen smiled and shrugged her helplessness. They laughed, shaking their heads, and Ellen saw herself: a thin girl of sixteen with long strands of dark hair, resisting the flow of traffic to stand before these men in silence. It was a senseless, hilarious sight. She felt like crying.

One of the men slowly rose to his feet and came toward her. "*Hola, chica,*" he said.

Ellen smiled at him. She felt as though some force were acting on her, making her breathless and dizzy. "*Hola,*" she said, extending her hand toward the man as if she had just been introduced.

The man's fingers tightened around her own. Ellen tried to slide from his grip, but he clung so hard it hurt. He was grinning at her. Ellen felt the pulse of his hand, the layer of sweat gathering between his skin and hers. She found herself grinning helplessly back, transfixed by the danger. The other men called and clapped, stamping their feet on the dirt. The music seemed louder. The man who held her wrist began to pull her down the street.

She heard running behind her, the sound of her father's shouts. He pushed the man away, knocking him into the dust. The man landed in a roll, and when Ellen's father followed him, he sprang to his feet, poised in a crouch. He was holding a knife, pointing its long blade straight at Ellen's father's chest. Her father froze. A whimper rose in Ellen's throat, and he turned at the sound. The man with the knife slipped into the throng.

Ellen's father grabbed her arm and pulled her against him so hard that her head knocked the bones of his chest. She found that she was crying; the sobs were effortless as laughter. The sweet tastes of vodka and ice cream hung at the back of her throat, and she gulped them down. Her father stroked her hair. Through his ribs Ellen felt the urgent beating of his heart. It filled her with relief, as if it were this precise sound she'd been waiting for all her life.

Ellen's mother wandered from an alley. She was walking slowly, carrying packages wrapped in paper. Wedged in a cone of newsprint was a bouquet of crêpe flowers: dry, colored petals fastened together with wire.

"Vivian," Ellen's father cried, letting her go. "Christ, we've gone crazy looking for you."

"You were late," Vivian said, looking rather pleased. "I got sick of waiting."

He shook his head, breathing hard. "Keeping up with you two is some job."

"Oh?" She smiled. "Maybe you're out of practice."

Ellen's father put an arm around each of them and headed toward the beach. He held tightly, and it seemed to Ellen that he cared more for them now, at this moment, than he had in a long time. He was scared. She could not remember seeing him scared before.

He led them to a restaurant near the beach. A virulent sun lay close to the horizon, and the air felt steamy and dense. Ellen's father leaned back and clasped his hands behind his head. Then he flattened them on the table and spread the fingers.

"I've got a confession to make," he said. "I've had an affair. One. In eighteen years of marriage."

They stared at him. He was folding and unfolding his napkin. The cloth shook in his fingers. He looked up suddenly, before Ellen could look away, and their eyes locked.

"Five years ago," he said, speaking directly at Ellen. "In Kansas City, Missouri. A salesgirl I met on her lunch break."

Ellen looked at her woven place mat and listened to her heart. It bumped in a scary, irregular way, and she wondered if she were old enough to have a heart attack. Her mother sat up straight.

"Why in God's name are you saying this now?" she asked.

He didn't answer. His eyes were still on Ellen, as if awaiting some sign from her. She thought of the day five years ago when he'd moved the hands of his watch, her delight at being part of the conspiracy. She looked at him now: handsome, grave, penitent. His hands were shaking. Going along would be so easy; she'd been following him for weeks.

"He's lying," she said.

Her mother's lips parted. Light shone along the bottoms of her teeth.

Ellen stood up. "Lying," she said again, letting the word rise from her mouth like a bubble. "He never went to Australia. I saw him in a restaurant with a girl."

She glanced at her father and saw his mouth ringed with white. Without another word she turned and walked toward the sea, letting the breeze fill her ears and block out every other sound. The water was rough, and its frothy edge bubbled over her feet. Ellen took a few more steps until the churning water scrubbed her shins, then her thighs. She had an urge to swim in her clothes, to feel the fabrics float around her in the warm tide.

Slowly she moved forward, letting the water cover her by degrees. Then a wave reared in front of her and Ellen dove into it. There was a hard, salty blow to her head and then she was beyond the breaking surf.

Several minutes later, she saw her mother on the beach. Ellen called to her and waved her arms, expecting to be ordered ashore immediately. Instead, Vivian moved closer to the water, keeping her eyes on Ellen. She stepped into the waves with great care, as if fearful that sharp things might be hidden in the sand. Soon the rim of her dress floated around her waist. Standing that way, she looked like a girl, and Ellen was struck by the thought that her mother had once been her own age. She saw this now in the fine, pale bones of her face, in the wet hair sticking to her head.

"Swim," Ellen called to her.

Vivian hesitated, then pushed off. She swam in the smooth, even crawl she used for laps in a pool. The waves jostled her, upsetting the neat strokes.

When she finally reached Ellen, her eyebrows were raised in a look of prolonged amazement. Her head seemed tiny in its slick coating of hair.

"We've lost our minds," she said with a high, nervous laugh.

Ellen was aware of not thinking about her father, and this gave her a fragile sense of freedom.

Her mother treaded water, looking up at the sky. Suddenly she turned to Ellen and grasped her hand underwater. Ellen felt her mother grow perfectly still. After a moment Vivian let go and began swimming back. Ellen followed.

A wave washed them in, and Ellen found herself sprawled

beside her mother on the sand. Her father was nowhere in sight. Vivian's frail, bent limbs showed through her wet dress. Ellen looked down at her own Mexican shirt and saw that its bright pinks and greens had drained away. A sudden despair overwhelmed her. She buried her feet in the sand and grasped a damp, gritty handful in each fist. She had an urge to put some in her mouth and suck the coarse grains.

"What's going to happen?" she asked, ashamed of the tremor in her voice.

Vivian was kneeling, shivering a little. She put an arm around Ellen's shoulders. "We're going back to the house to dry off," she said. "That's what."

She pulled her daughter to her feet, surprising Ellen with the strength of her arms. Ellen leaned against her, allowing herself to be led through the sand. "And after that," her mother said, holding Ellen tightly, "we're getting out of this."

Charles Johnson

KWOON

David Lewis' martial-arts *kwoon* was in a South Side Chicago neighborhood so rough he nearly had to fight to reach the door. Previously, it had been a dry cleaner's, then a small Thai restaurant, and although he Lysol-scrubbed the buckled linoleum floors and burned jade incense for the Buddha before each class, the studio was a blend of pungent odors, the smell of starched shirts and the tang of cinnamon pastries riding alongside the sharp smell of male sweat from nightly workouts. For five months, David had bivouacked on the back-room floor after his students left, not minding the clank of presses from the print shop next door, the noisy garage across the street or even the two-grand bank loan needed to renovate three rooms with low ceilings and leaky pipes overhead. This was his place, earned after ten years of training in San Francisco and his promotion to the hard-won title of *sifu*.

As his customers grunted through Tuesday-night warm-up exercises, then drills with Elizabeth, his senior student (she'd been a dancer and still had the elasticity of Gumby), David stood off to one side to watch, feeling the force of their *kiais* vibrate in the cavity of his chest, interrupting them only to correct a student's stance. On the whole, his students were a hopeless bunch, a Franciscan test of his patience. Some came to class on drugs; one, Wendell Miller, a retired cook trying to recapture his youth, was the obligatory senior citizen; a few were high school dropouts, orange-haired punks who played in rock bands with names like Plastic Anus. But David did not despair. He believed he was duty bound to lead them, like the Pied Piper, from Sylvester Stallone movies to a real understanding of the martial arts as a way that prepared the young, through discipline and large doses of humility, to be of use to themselves and others. Accordingly, his sheet of rules said no high school student could be promoted unless he kept a B average, and no dropouts were allowed through the door until they signed up for their G.E.D. exam; if they got straight A's, he took them to dinner. Anyone caught fighting outside his school was suspended. David had been something of a punk himself a decade earlier, pushing nose candy in Palo Alto, living on barbiturates and beer before his own teacher helped him see, to David's surprise, that in his spirit he had resources greater than anything in the world outside. The master's picture was just inside the door, so all could bow to him when they entered David's school. Spreading the style was his rationale for moving to the Midwest, but the hidden agenda, David believed, was an inward training that would make the need for conflict fall away like a chrysalis. If nothing else, he could make their workouts so tiring none of his students would have any energy left for getting into trouble.

Except, he thought, for Ed Morgan.

He was an older man, maybe 40, with a bald spot and razor burns that ran from just below his ears to his throat. This was his second night at the studio, but David realized Morgan knew the calisthenics routine and basic punching drills cold. He'd been in other schools. Any fool could see that, which meant the new student had lied on his application about having no formal training. Unlike David's regular students, who wore the traditional white Chinese T-shirt and black trousers, Morgan had changed into a butternut running suit with black stripes on the sleeves and pants legs. David had told him to buy a uniform the week before, during his brief interview. Morgan refused. And David dropped the matter, noticing that Morgan had pecs and forearms like Popeye. His triceps could have been lifted right off

Marvin Hagler. He was thick as a tree, even top-heavy, in David's opinion, and he stood half a head taller than the other students. He didn't *have* a suit to fit Morgan. And Morgan moved so fluidly David caught himself frowning, a little frightened, for it was as though the properties of water and rock had come together in one creature. Then he snapped himself back, laughed at his silliness, looked at the clock—only half an hour of class remained—then clapped his hands loudly. He popped his fingers on his left hand, then his right, as his students, eager for his advice, turned to face him.

"We should do a little sparring now. Pair up with somebody your size. Elizabeth, you work with the new students."

"*Sifu?*"

It was Ed Morgan.

David paused, both lips pressed together.

"If you don't mind, I'd like to spar with you."

One of David's younger students, Toughie, a Filipino boy with a falcon emblazoned on his arm, elbowed his partner, who wore his hair in a stiff Mohawk, and both said, "Uh-oh." David felt his body flush hot, sweat suddenly on his palms like a sprinkling of salt water, though there was no whiff of a challenge, no disrespect in Morgan's voice. His speech, in fact, was as soft and gently syllabled as a singer's. David tried to laugh:

"You sure you want to try me?"

"Please." Morgan bowed his head, which might have seemed self-effacing had he not been so tall and still looking down at David's crown. "It would be a privilege."

Rather than spar, his students scrambled back, nearly falling over themselves to form a circle, as if to ring two gun fighters from opposite ends of town. David kept the slightest of smiles on his lips, even when his mouth tired, to give the impression of masterful indifference—he was, after all, *sifu* here, wasn't he? A little sparring would do him good. Wouldn't it? Especially with a man the size of Morgan. Loosen him up, so to speak.

He flipped his red sash behind him and stepped lower into a cat stance, his weight on his rear leg, his lead foot light and lifted slightly, ready to whip forward when Morgan moved into range.

Morgan was not so obliging. He circled left, away from David's lead leg, then did a half step of broken rhythm to confuse David's sense of distance, and then, before he could change stances, flicked a jab at David's jaw. If his students were surprised, David didn't know, for the room fell away instantly, dissolving as his adrenaline rose and his concentration closed out everything but Morgan—he always needed to get hit once before he got serious—and only he and the other existed, both in motion but pulled out of time, the moment flickerish, fibrous and strangely two-dimensional, yet all too familiar to fighters, perhaps to men falling from heights, to motorists microseconds before a head-on collision, these minutes a spinning mosaic of crescent kicks, back fists and flurry punches that, on David's side, failed. All his techniques fell short of Morgan, who, like a shadow—or Mephistopheles—simply dematerialized before they arrived.

The older man shifted from boxing to *wu*-style *ta'i chi Chuan*. From this he flowed into *pa kua*, then Korean karate: style after style, a blending of a dozen cultures and histories in one blink of an eye after another. With one move, he tore away David's sash. Then he called out each move in Mandarin as he dropped it on David, bomb after bomb, as if this were only an exhibition exercise.

On David's face, blossoms of blood opened like orchids. He knew he was being hurt; two ribs felt broken, but he wasn't sure. He thanked God for endorphins—a body's natural painkiller. He'd not touched Morgan once. Outclassed as he was, all he could do was ward him off, stay out of his way—then not even that when a fist the size of a cantaloupe crashed straight down, driving David to the floor, his ears ringing then, and legs outstretched like a doll's. He wanted to stay down forever but sprang to his feet, sweat stinging his eyes, to salvage one scrap of dignity. He found himself facing the wrong way. Morgan was behind him, his hands on his hips, his head thrown back. Two of David's students laughed.

It was Elizabeth who pressed her sweat-moistened towel under David's bloody nose. Morgan's feet came together. He wasn't even winded. "Thank you, *Sifu*." Mockery, David thought, but his head banged too badly to be sure. The room was still behind heat waves, though sounds were coming back, and now he could distinguish one student from another. His sense of clock time returned. He said, "You're a good fighter, Ed."

Toughie whispered, "No shit, *bwana*."

The room suddenly leaned vertiginously to David's left; he bent his knees a little to steady his balance. "But you're still a beginner in this system." Weakly, he lifted his hand, then let it fall. "Go on with class. Elizabeth, give everybody a new lesson."

"David, I think class is over now."

Over? He thought he knew what that meant. "I guess so. Bow to the master."

His students bowed to the portrait of the school's founder.

"Now to each other."

Again, they bowed, but this time to Morgan.

"Class dismissed."

Some of his students were whooping, slapping Morgan on his back as they made their way to the hallway in back to change. Elizabeth, the only female, stayed behind to let them shower and dress. Both she and the youngest student, Mark, a middle school boy with skin as smooth and pale as a girl's, looked bewildered, uncertain what this drubbing meant.

David limped back to his office, which also was his bedroom, separated from the main room only by a curtain. There, he kept equipment: free weights, a heavy bag on which he'd taped a snapshot of himself—for who else did he need to conquer?—and the rowing machine Elizabeth avoided, calling it Instant Abortion. He sat down for a few seconds at his unvarnished kneehole desk bought cheap at a Salvation Army outlet, then rolled onto the floor, wondering what he'd done wrong. Would another *sifu*, more seasoned, simply have refused to spar with a self-styled beginner?

After a few minutes, he heard them leaving, a couple of students begging Morgan to teach them, and really, this was too much to bear. David, holding his side, his head pulled in, limped back out. "Ed," he coughed, then recovered. "Can I talk to you?"

Morgan checked his watch, a diamond-studded thing that doubled as a stop watch and a thermometer, and probably even monitored his pulse. Half its cost would pay the studio's rent for a year. He dressed well, David saw. Like a retired champion, everything tailored, nothing off the rack. "I've got an appointment, *Sifu*. Maybe later, OK?"

A little dazed, David, swallowing the rest of what he wanted to say, gave a headshake. "OK."

Just before the door slammed, he heard another boy say, "Lewis ain't no fighter, man. He's a dancer." He lay down again in his office, too sore to shower, every muscle tender, strung tight as catgut, searching with the tip of his tongue for broken teeth.

As he was stuffing toilet paper into his right nostril to stop the bleeding, Elizabeth, dressed now in high boots and a baggy coat and slacks, stepped behind the curtain. She'd replaced her contacts with owl-frame glasses that made her look spinsterish. "I'm sorry—he was wrong to do that."

"You mean win?"

"It wasn't supposed to be a real fight! He tricked you. Anyone can score, like he did, if they throw out all the rules."

"Tell him that." Wincing, he rubbed his shoulder. "Do you think anybody will come back on Thursday?" She did not answer. "Do you think I should close the school?" David laughed, bleakly. "Or just leave town?"

"David, you're a good teacher. A *sifu* doesn't always have to win, does he? It's not about winning, is it?"

No sooner had she said this than the answer rose between them. Could you be a doctor whose every patient died? A credible mathematician who couldn't count? By the way the world and, more important, his students reckoned things, he was a fraud. Elizabeth hitched the strap on her workout bag, which was big enough for both of them to climb into, higher on her shoulder. "Do you want me to stick around?"

"No."

"You going to put something on that eye?"

Through the eye Morgan hadn't closed, she looked flattened, like a coin, her skin flushed and her hair faintly damp after a

workout, so lovely David wanted to fall against her, blend with
her—disappear. Only, it would hurt now to touch or be
touched. And, unlike some teachers he knew, his policy was to
take whatever he felt for a student—the erotic electricity that
sometimes arose—and transform it into harder teaching, more
time spent on giving them their money's worth. Besides, he was
always broke; his street clothes were old enough to be in elementary school: a 30-year-old man no better educated than
Toughie or Mark, who'd concentrated on shop in high school.
Elizabeth was another story: a working mother, a secretary on
the staff at the University of Illinois at Chicago, surrounded all
day by professors who looked young enough to be graduate
students. A job sweet as this, from David's level, seemed high-
toned and secure. What could he offer Elizabeth? Anyway, this
might be the last night he saw her, if she left with the others,
and who could blame her? He studied her hair, how it fell onyx-
black and abundant, like some kind of blessing over and under
her collar, which forced Elizabeth into the unconscious habit of
tilting her head just so and flicking it back with her fingers, a
gesture of such natural grace it made his chest ache. She was so
much lovelier than she knew. To his surprise, a line from *Psalms*
came to him, "I will praise thee, for I am fearfully and wonderfully made." Whoever wrote that, he thought, meant it for
her.

He looked away. "Go on home."

"We're having class on Thursday?"

"You paid until the end of the month, didn't you?"

"I paid for six months, remember?"

He did—she was literally the one who kept the light bill paid.
"Then we'll have class."

All that night and half the next day David stayed horizontal,
hating Morgan. Hating himself more. It took him hours to stop
shaking. That night it rained. He fended off sleep, listening to
the patter with his full attention, hoping its music might have
something to tell him. Twice he belched up blood, then a paste
of phlegm and hamburger pulp. Jesus, he thought, distantly, I'm
sick. By nightfall, he was able to sit awhile and take a little soup,
but he could not stand. Both his legs ballooned so tightly in his

trousers he had to cut the cloth with scissors and peel it off like strips of bacon. Parts of his body were burning, refusing to obey him. He reached into his desk drawer for Morgan's application and saw straightaway that Ed Morgan couldn't spell. David smiled ruefully, looking for more faults. Morgan listed his address in Skokie, his occupation as a merchant marine, and provided no next of kin to call in case of emergencies.

That was all, and David for the life of him could not see that night, or the following morning, how he could face anyone in the studio again. Painfully, he remembered his promotion a year earlier. His teacher had held a ceremonial Buddhist candle, the only light in his darkened living room in a house near the Mission District barely bigger than a shed. David, kneeling, held a candle, too. "The light that was given to me," said his teacher, repeating an invocation two centuries old, "I now give to you." He touched his flame to the wick of David's candle, passing the light, and David's eyes burned with tears. For the first time in his life, he felt connected to cultures and people he'd never seen —to traditions larger than himself.

His high school instructors had dismissed him as unteachable. Were they right? David wondered. Was he made of wood too flimsy ever to amount to anything? Suddenly, he hated those teachers, as well as the ones at Elizabeth's school, but only for a time, hatred being so sharp an emotion, like the business end of a bali-song knife, he could never hang on to it for long—perhaps that was why he failed as a fighter—and soon he felt nothing, only numbness. As from a great distance, he watched himself sponge-bathe in the sink, dress himself slowly and prepare for Thursday's class, the actions previously fueled by desire, by concern over consequences, by fear of outcome, replaced now by something he could not properly name, as if a costly operation once powered by coal had reverted overnight to the water wheel.

When six o'clock came and only Mark, Wendell and Elizabeth showed, David telephoned a few students, learning from parents, roommates and live-in lovers that none were home. With Morgan, he suspected. So that's who he called next.

"Sure," said Morgan. "A couple are here. They just wanted to talk."

"They're missing class."

"I didn't ask them to come."

Quietly, David drew breath deeply just to see if he could. It hurt, so he stopped, letting his wind stay shallow, swirling at the top of his lungs. He pulled a piece of dead skin off his hand. "Are you coming back?"

"I don't see much point in that, do you?"

In the background he could hear voices, a television and beer cans being opened. "You've fought professionally, haven't you?"

"That was a long time ago—overseas. Won two, lost two, then I quit," said Morgan. "It doesn't count for much."

"Did you teach?"

"Here and there. Listen," he said, "why did you call?"

"Why did you en*roll?*"

"I've been out of training. I wanted to see how much I remembered. What do you want me to say? I won't come back, all right? What do you want from me, Lewis?"

He did not know. He felt the stillness of his studio, a similar stillness in himself, and sat quiet so long he could have been posing for a portrait. Then:

"You paid for a week in advance. I owe you another lesson."

Morgan snorted. "In what—Chinese ballet?"

"Fighting," said David. "A private lesson in *budo.* I'll keep the studio open until you get here." And then he hung up.

Morgan circled the block four times before finding a parking space across from Lewis' school. Why hurry? Ten, maybe 15 minutes he waited, watching the open door, wondering what the boy (and he was a boy to Morgan's eye) wanted. He'd known too many kids like this one. They took a few classes, promoted themselves to seventh *dan,* then opened a storefront *dojo* that was no better than a private stage, a theater for the ego, a place where they could play out fantasies of success denied them on the street, in school, in dead-end jobs. They were phony, Morgan thought, like almost everything in the modern world, which was a subject he could spend hours deriding, though he seldom did, his complaints now being tiresome even to his own ears. *Losers,* he thought, who strutted around in fancy Oriental costumes, refusing to spar or show their skill. "Too advanced for beginners," they claimed, or, "My *sensei* made me promise not to show that to anyone." Hogwash. He could see through that shit. All over America he'd seen them, and India, too, where they weren't called fakirs for nothing. And they'd made him suffer. They made him pay for the "privilege" of their teachings. In 20 years as a merchant marine, he'd been in as many schools in Europe, Japan, Korea and Hong Kong, submitting himself to the lunacy of illiterate fak(e)irs—men who claimed they could slay an opponent with their breath or *ch'i*—and simply because his hunger to learn was insatiable. So he had no rank anywhere. He could tolerate no "master's" posturing long enough to ingratiate himself into the inner circles of any school—though 80 percent of these fly-by-night *dojos* bottomed out inside a year. And, hell, he was a bilge rat, never in any port long enough to move up in rank. Still, he had killed men. It was depressingly easy. Killed them in back alleys in Tokyo with blows so crude no master would include such inelegant means among "traditional" techniques.

More hogwash, thought Morgan. He'd probably done the boy good by exposing him. His own collarbones had been broken twice, each leg three times, all but two fingers smashed, and his nose reshaped so often he couldn't remember its original contours. On wet nights, he had trouble breathing. But why complain? You couldn't make an omelet without breaking a few eggs.

And yet, Morgan thought, squinting at the door of the school, there was a side to Lewis he'd liked. At first, he had felt comfortable, as if he had at last found the *kwoon* he'd been looking for. True, Lewis had come on way too cocky when asked to spar, but what could you expect when he was hardly older than the high school kids he was teaching? And maybe teaching them well, if he was really going by that list of rules he handed

out to beginners. And it wasn't so much that Lewis was a bad
fighter, only that he, Morgan, was about five times better because whatever he lacked now in middle age—flexibility and
youth's fast reflexes—he more than made up for in size and
experience, which was a polite word for dirty tricks. Give Lewis
a few more years, a little more coaching in the combat strategies
Morgan could show him, and he might become a champion.

But who did he think he was fooling? Things never worked
out that way. There was always too much ego in it. Something
every *sifu* figured he had to protect, or save face about. A lesson
in *budo?* Christ, he'd nearly killed this kid, and there he was,
barking on the telephone like Saddam Hussein before the bombing started, even begging for the ground war to begin. And that
was just all right, if a showdown—a duel—was what he
wanted. Morgan set his jaw and stepped onto the pavement of
the parking lot. However things went down, he decided, the
consequences would be on Lewis—it would be *his* call.

Locking his car, then double-checking each door (this was a
rough neighborhood, even by Morgan's standards), he crossed
the street, carrying his workout bag under his arm, the last
threads of smog-filtered twilight fading into darkness, making
the door of the *kwoon* a bright portal chiseled from blocks of
glass and cement. A few feet from the entrance, he heard voices.
Three students had shown. Most of the class had not. The two
who had visited him weren't there. He'd lectured them on his
experience of strangling an assailant in Kyoto, and Toughie had
gone quiet, looked edgy (fighting didn't seem like fun then) and
uneasy. Finally, they left, which was fine with Morgan. He
didn't want followers. Sycophants made him sick. All he
wanted was a teacher he could respect.

Inside the school's foyer, he stopped, his eyes tracking the
room. He never entered closed spaces too quickly or walked
near corners or doorways on the street. Toward the rear, by a
rack filled with halberds and single-edged broadswords, a girl
about five, with piles of ebony hair and blue eyes like splinters
of the sky, was reading a dog-eared copy of *The Cat in the Hat.*
This would be the child of the class leader, he thought, bowing

quickly at the portrait of the school's founder. But why bring her here? It cemented his contempt for this place, more a day-care center than a *kwoon*. Still, he bowed a second time to the founder. Him he respected. Where were such grand old stylists when you needed them? He did not see Lewis, or any other student until, passing the curtained office, Morgan whiffed food cooking on a hot plate and, parting the curtain slightly, he saw Wendell, who would never in this life learn to fight, stirring and seasoning a pot of couscous. He looked like that children's toy, Mr. Potato Head. Morgan wondered, Why did David Lewis encourage the man? Just to take his money? He passed on, feeling his tread shake the floor, into the narrow hall where a few hooks hung for clothing, and found Elizabeth with her left foot on a low bench, lacing the wrestling shoes she wore for working out.

"Excuse me," he said. "I'll wait until you're finished."

Their eyes caught for a moment.

"I'm done now." She kicked her bag under the bench, squeezed past Morgan by flattening herself to the wall, as if he had a disease, then spun round at the entrance and looked squarely at him. "You know something?"

"What?"

"You're wrong. Just *wrong*."

"I don't know what you're talking about."

"The hell you don't! David may not be the fighter, the killer, you are, but he *is* one of the best teachers in this system."

Morgan smirked. "Those who can't do, teach, eh?"

She burned a look of such hatred at Morgan he turned his eyes away. When he looked back, she was gone. He sighed. He'd seen that look on so many faces, yellow, black and white, after he'd punched them in. It hardly mattered anymore. Quietly, he suited up, stretched his arms wide and padded barefoot back onto the main floor, prepared to finish this, if that was what Lewis wanted, for why else would he call?

But at first he could not catch sight of the boy. The others were standing around him in a circle, chatting, oddly like chess pieces shielding an endangered king. His movements were jerky and Chaplinesque, one arm around Elizabeth, the other braced on Wendell's shoulder. Without them, he could not walk until his bruised ankles healed. He was temporarily blind in one blackened, beefed-over eye. And since he could not tie his own sash, Mark was doing it for him. None of them noticed Morgan, but in the school's weak light, he could see blue welts he'd raised like crops on Lewis' cheeks and chest. That, and something else. The hands of the others rested on Lewis' shoulder, his back, as if he belonged to them, no matter what he did or didn't do. Weak as Lewis looked now, even the old cook Wendell could blow him over, and somehow it didn't matter if he was beaten every round, or missed class, or died. The others were the *kwoon*. It wasn't his school. It was theirs. Maybe brought together by the boy, Morgan thought, but now a separate thing living beyond him. To prove the system, the teaching here, false, he would have to strike down every one of them. And still he would have touched nothing.

"Ed," Lewis said, looking over Mark's shoulder. "When we were sparring, I saw mistakes in your form, things someone better than me might take advantage of. I'd like to correct them, if you're ready."

"What things?" His head snapped back. "What mistakes?"

"I can't match your reach," said Lewis, "but someone who could, getting inside your guard, would go for your groin or knee. It's the way you stand, probably a blend of a couple of styles you learned somewhere. But they don't work together. If you do this," he added, torquing his leg slightly so that his thigh guarded his groin, "the problem is solved."

"Is that why you called me?"

"No, there's another reason."

Morgan tensed; he should have known. "You do some warm-up exercises we've never seen. I like them. I want you to lead class tonight, if that's OK, so the others can learn them, too." Then he laughed. "I think I should warm the bench tonight."

Before he could reply, Lewis limped off, leaning on Mark, who led him back to his office. The two others waited for direction from Morgan. For a moment, he shifted his weight uncertainly from his right foot to his left, pausing until his tensed shoulders relaxed and the tight fingers on his right hand, coiled into a fist, opened. Then he pivoted toward the portrait of the founder. "Bow to the master." They bowed. "Now to our teacher." They did so, bowing toward the curtained room, with Morgan, a big man, bending deepest of all.

Linda Svendsen

THE EDGER MAN

When I was thirty-four years old, with two young children, I moved across the river to live in quiet, more affordable Brooklyn. I was twice intimate with failures that seemed, at the time, irredeemable. I had earned my Master's in anthropology, somehow assuming I would live my life in a tent on the tip of someplace in Africa, but due to a variety of circumstance and choice, I was teaching ESL—English as a Second Language—to Arab and Japanese businessmen in midtown. And, not willingly, I was divorced, even though I understood it was for the best.

I spent a lot of time thinking about love. Sometimes about how I had failed to sustain, or perhaps inspire, it in my marriage. Sometimes about how humans are born into this world without the ongoing promise of it from parents, or persons unknown the future holds. About how, if they were not loved, would they learn? Before our children were born, I had loved Bill, my husband, with a love like a Mack truck speeding, and when Graham and then Jane arrived, I discovered a love necessary and dense as air. I often could not believe the deep pleasure I felt watching their dumbest actions—Graham leaning like a tired old man on his left elbow and brushing his teeth; or hearing them root for the Mets and bandying lingo like choke, balk, strike, Strawberry; or how Jane sucked the butter out of her cob of corn.

We didn't belong there. I would have liked to move back west where we were born and start our lives all over again. I wanted my children to grow up in a place where they could play hide-and-seek in a yard until dark, and walk to school under the sway of tall green trees rather than stepping around souls laying themselves down to die a bit more each day. But since I wanted my children to know, and be known by, their father, for better for worse, to be loved, I stayed.

Where I was raised out by the Pacific, every other child's father worked at the sawmill. They were sawyers, boom men, or new on the green chain. Mine was an edger man. First up at a logging camp near Desolation Sound where he sawed cedars centuries old. Then, after he was enchanted by my mother June, music, and her three children, and wed them, he wound up in Vancouver at Pacific Pine. There he cut cants. Mum was forty, he was pushing fifty, and in next to no time, a year, I appeared. He was taken, often, for my grandfather.

Back in 1960, Sundays were for family. We rented a boat at Lost Lagoon and rowed around the fountain in the rain, while Humphrey (Dad to me) recited a poem from his London boyhood,

> It was midnight on the ocean
> Not a streetcar was in sight
> The sun was shining brightly
> And it rained all day that night.

I dangled my hand in the water, dwelling on that rhyme for the longest time. My mother mentioned that sitting in a damp boat on a wet lake, listening to nonsense, wasn't her idea of entertainment.

And we drove all the way to the United States to ride the Octopus and roller skate outdoors, past the border town of Blaine, to Birch Bay, where fun was loud, and colors so rude and bright they slammed my eyes. Mum begged Dad to join her for a cold beer on tap, since taverns were open Sundays serving throngs of pagan Canadians, and he squinted and said he only imbibed if someone died. Ray tuned his guitar under a totem pole. Irene and Joyce, eighteen and sixteen, marched the beach in their striped Bermuda shorts.

I followed. "Supposed to watch me."

"So we are," Joyce said and they took off, kicking up mouthfuls of sand, then turned and walked backwards and waved interminably like the hillbillies.

"I see," Irene's small voice carried, "you."

I bent over and wiggled, but when I looked between my knees, they were upside down and disappearing.

On the way home, Ray and my sisters laughed so much the back seat seemed like a faraway, jolly country. Ray whispered dirty book jokes ("Ever read *Russian Passion?* By Natasha Bitaballoff?"), that made Mum look away out the open window and snicker.

I sat wedged between her and my father. She reached over my straw-hatted head, scratched his neck, and said, "Cat got your tongue, Humphrey?" and in his calm, logical tone he said he was trying to digest his dinner. She patted my bare leg, "Cold?," and her hand travelled back to hold the purse in her lap.

When I whined to climb into the back seat, Ray reminded everyone I hadn't got my rabies shot yet, which made the girls hoot. Inspired, I lied that I had, and then my father spoke up, "Enough back there. Unless you want to become pedestrians," and the car was one again, united by quiet. We even passed stiff dead deer without adding to the count.

There was another Sunday when Dad ended up taking only me. This was after the arguments between Mum and him had begun, and she'd started taking the other three children to matinees and staying out for supper.

We went in the car. He didn't talk. I lay across the back seat of the Chev and stared at the back of his bald head, and at the thatch of black hair inside his ear. He parked, and we got out and walked toward the bright lumber right on the river. The heady scent of wet cedar was in the wind. Dad pointed to a sign and said, "Pacific—?"

"Pine," I answered. Dad believed I'd inherited his brains and always found ways to prove this.

"This is where I work," he said. "Your father is first edger man."

We walked up a steep wooden staircase and stepped inside. The sawmill stretched like a very long shack, big and dark, without rooms. The windows were without glass. When I looked out, I saw the river in the rain, and it seemed as if the mill had come unmoored, and that we were floating down and out to the saltchuck. Our four legs strode into light, out of step, and back into dark, past a picture of Smokey the Bear, his back to black trees and wild white fire.

He told me the forests of Europe were shrinking, and that their trees had stopped growing, cut short, scorched by war. Our trees were among the tallest on the planet, so tall their ends couldn't be seen. Widowmakers he called them. Heartwood, the inside of a tree, was dead. Sapwood, the outside, was alive. To cut a tree down, he kept the saw in the same place. The tree wasn't going anywhere. Sooner or later, it fell. He looked for points of crooks, or whorls of knots. He made an undercut. He talked about knaps, knars, stumps and spars, and about all sorts of saws—bull, hula, muley, whip and chain.

I didn't understand any of this, but I listened. He always talked to me as if I knew exactly what he was going on about— how he'd found an ingenious way to repair the lawn mower, or the principle of a V-8 engine. Sometimes he realized he was speaking over my head, and he looked down at me with serious regard and said, "Adele? Are you *still* a child?" as if I were taking an extraordinarily long time to mature.

The other end of the mill jutted over the river. It was wide open, without a wall, and below us booms of logs bobbed like long crocodiles. Dad put one hand on the railing and looked down. "Stinkwood," he said. "Hemlock."

I stood beside my father with my hand in his big one. Sometimes he let me bite tiny slivers of wood out of his hand. I felt a longing deep inside, but didn't know for what. I felt light as sawdust in a palm, as if I could be blown away at any moment.

On the walk back, Dad stopped to explain his machine, the

edger. He had taken his pen out and was drawing a diagram, and before I was even conscious of what I intended, I bolted away down the aisle, off balance in my rubber boots, and ducked down inside a booth. I waited, wild inside.

It only took a few seconds. "Adele." He was piqued. "Don't be an idiot. A sawmill is dangerous. It is not the place for a child to play."

I laughed.

I heard his slow, steady tread. He was close. I caught a glimpse of his red plaid shirt coming even with me, and then he stood still. We were both quiet for the longest time. Outside a seagull cried like a cat. I stuck out my foot. "Warm," I whispered.

He was looking right at it, my foot, and then suddenly gazed directly over my head, past me, and quickly away, as if he hadn't even sensed me. He continued on, nonchalant. He kept going. "Dad?" I called out. He picked up his pace. "Dad?" I said again. "Cold, you're getting cold." I waited, and then didn't hear him anymore. I got up, shaking off flakes of sawdust. At the far end, he was turning to descend the stairs. He wasn't looking back. My heart hopped like a small bird in my chest. I wanted to be found. The whole point of hiding was to be found.

We left with just our clothes. The new house was empty, without an upstairs or curtains. If you opened a door in the kitchen, an ironing board fell and stuck out like a sick tongue. I was finally allowed a pet, a comatose turtle.

Mum saw quite a bit of Robert, who didn't stay with us but always seemed to be underfoot. Meals became more exciting because he was a little deaf and tremendously loud. He bought a movie camera at a police auction and at the break of day, we burned under a blazing bar of light, eating breakfast, our names spelled in Alphabets on spoons. His hair was slicked back and shiny black. He always seemed to be kissing Mum or rubbing her feet, and he did that loudly too. He called her Beauty.

I still didn't miss my father at all. I met children my age who all seemed to have drawbacks—cry-baby, eczema, boring, pretty and always got picked to be princess. I often walked my turtle, wishing it were a dog. I spent most of my days exploring the field across the street, wild with clover and buttercups, full of garter snakes, puddles, prickles, and mad driven bees. I buried dead birds and made crosses of small white rocks. This was my hobby.

Nights, I kneeled in front of the television set and changed channels for Ray, who said his wrist needed a rest. Or sometimes, after my bath, if it was a balmy, warm evening, and nobody appeared at my bed to read a story, I wandered outside in my pajamas and watched Mum and Robert listen to a Mounties baseball game on the radio. They sat on the same side of the picnic table he'd built. He deciphered the plays for Mum, who seemed morally perturbed by runners stealing, and wondered why they weren't pleased with the base they'd already reached. Sometimes Robert let on he knew I was there.

"Started counting the stars yet, Delbert?" Robert would say over his shoulder. "Because I'm going to ask you. I'm going to ask you how many there are."

"She can't count that high," Mum said protectively. "How high can you go?" Mum asked me.

"I'll check in the *Sun* tomorrow and see how many stars were out tonight. So you better start counting, Delbert."

"Don't call her Delbert, Robert."

"Wakey wakey, Delbert."

I would mumble a number, eight, or my favorite, ninety-nine, and Mum give a frilly laugh, Robert add something encouraging, and then they would forget I was there again. Some nights they listened to string music with sad singers, Judy Garland, Peggy Lee, and got all worked up about their divorces. By the end of summer, before I began grade one, the main topic was the detective hired to watch our house, and whose spouse was paying, or were my Dad and Robert's wife in cahoots?

There were sudden new rules. Venetian blinds were kept drawn, even during a cloudy day, and Robert parked a block up the hill, and rang the front doorbell before barging in whenever he wanted. Joyce was not allowed to linger necking in her boyfriend Eric's Zephyr; she had to drive away to hell and gone.

One night I woke up, looked out the window, and thought I saw him standing on the lawn just staring at me. I roused Ray. He said, "You're cruising for a bruising," but finally got up, and went back with me to the living room, and pried open the blinds. His hand shook, then he made it shake more, and I laughed. "Nobody," he said. Then I had to get him a frosty Molson's. He gave me sips and let me watch part of a war epic with him, to calm down.

The next time I got scared, Ray wasn't home, and I crawled in with Mum without telling why. I didn't want to worry her. "Who's that?" she said perkily. "My Mince Pie?" Then I placed my frozen feet on her hot calves, and she said, "Go to sleep, Mince."

"I can't."

She pushed my pajama top up to my neck and played piano on my back, any song I wanted, "Away in a Manger," "Wonderful Wonderful Copenhagen," anything, and I heard it in her fingertips, in that soft force.

I didn't see my father again until I was ten years old and he came to pick me up to go ice-skating at Queen's Park rink. The divorce suit was final; he'd lost custody and been granted access every second Saturday. He was close to sixty. Mum shooed me out the door with a banana. She also handed me a dime, "For if there's a snit."

He waited in the green Chev, and wore the same outfit he was wearing the last time I remembered seeing him, Stanley Park Sunday clothes: a hat with a small red feather, herringbone jacket, blue tie with fish lures, solid blue shirt. He looked business as usual: slow, logical. He didn't seem mean, the goon who'd bled Mum by making her pay lawyers' holidays for years. He leaned over, opened the door, and said to keep the window down on my side; the muffler was on the blink and I could be poisoned by carbon monoxide. He meant to fix it someday. Once he turned onto Kingsway, he said, "Incidentally, do you recollect the rhyme?"

"No," I said.

"Oh." He looked away. "When you were young," he said,

"you used to get frightfully upset and say, 'How could there be a streetcar on the ocean, Daddy?' You took it quite literally." He seemed saddened by my unreliable memory.

"Oh," I said. My legs were getting damp from the rain slicing in the open window, but I didn't shove over.

He inquired after "the Armstrongs"; I told him Joyce had eloped with Eric, and Irene married Peter—the Belgian boy from down the lane—and Ray was Casanova. I took it upon myself to inform him I was in grade five and got straight B's.

At the rink, they played rock and roll. "Nigger music," Dad announced, then moved overly briskly in the thick of a pack of hunched boys. I hugged the side every few feet. The only way I knew to brake was to slam into the wood. The ice was strewn with teenagers, the normal sort and a mentally retarded bunch. One of them took over the penalty box, pounded his mitts together, and screamed "Santa" each time Dad whizzed by, until he was given a needle.

The light dimmed for the couples-only, a ballad with lots of violin and philosophy. Dad stopped with a crisp *shmoosh*. Shaved ice skimmed off his blade. He stuck out a hand.

"But it's *couples*."

"We pass," he said, out of breath, "muster."

I took skittery steps to keep up, then let myself be towed. A rink-rat passed and said, "Who's holding up who?" Meanwhile Dad said the only time he'd skied, he'd enjoyed it immensely, so much so he swore never to do it again. He mentioned Wormwood Scrubs in London, England, and about how if he didn't eat all his dinner, his psychotic mother sent him over to sit on the prison steps. The song seemed to go on for a complete century or two.

At Hudson's Bay on the way home, he bought me Barbie's "Tennis, Anyone?" outfit and a young-adult biography of Mary, Queen of Scots, which I started to read right away. We ate supper at the White Spot and dined in the car with a tray up to our necks. He inevitably brought up Robert, whom he blamed for the break-up of the marriage and the loss of his family. He told me Wily Kiely wasn't the first boyfriend that the adulteress had gotten chummy with. I didn't believe it. "My mother's not an adulteress," I said. "She said she would have left you whether Robert moseyed along or not."

Dad kept chewing. He looked straight ahead. He said, "I don't believe that for one instant." He thought of Mum as a wayward child, without will or common sense, lured away.

"You weren't affectionate she said."

He spoke perfunctorily. "That is simply not true." He took a sip of his tea. "Did you know that your mother, like my own mother, thought I was to blame for everything? If it was raining, she would attribute that to some malicious wish on my part."

When we ended up back at Mum's, I got out of the old Chev, didn't answer his farewell and, arms full of the day's loot, walked into the house and slammed the door. Nobody was home anyway. I went to my room and read the beheading section.

I knew my mother hadn't loved him, not the way she'd loved Ray, Irene and Joyce's dad. She still missed their father. She braided my hair into two tight twigs before school one morning and said she had dreamed again about the original Ray, Ray Senior. "I didn't want to wake up," she said. "It seemed so real. I just wanted to talk with him some more. God, he looked well."

"Did you ever love my Dad?" I asked. I knew he still loved her in his way. He didn't date other old ladies; he lived like a hermit.

"I wanted to," she said. "I tried."

After one of my regular Saturday arguments with Humphrey, I pictured him driving home in his car—tired after the heavy meal and movies, discouraged after our row—and saw him falling asleep at the wheel. Switching lanes without signaling, which was his habit, and being in a car accident and dying, and all this without ever being loved. By his mother or mine. I went into the kitchen, picked up the phone, dialed, and heard it ring, over and over, my eye on the clock, and thought *he should be home by now, this is enough time*. I started to pray. "Please let him be all right. Let him get home O.K. Let him answer the phone," until I heard the click, and his calm, annoying voice say, "Hullo." I hung up.

. . .

Mum and Robert's honeymoon consisted of a two-week cruise to Anchorage: Mum was playing the Hammond organ happy hours, and Robert was master of ceremonies and *maracas*. He kept time, those little beans stinging the beat. Mum had figured on taking me along but Robert alarmed her with talk of icebergs.

I didn't want to stay at Dad's. His house was filthy. Mum and Irene had put up wallpaper after I was born—a pattern of hundreds of the same little Mexican boy feeding chickens—and his smiles and *sombreros* and hens were lost under thick dark soot. The hook for my Jolly Jumper still hung in the hall. He watched PBS on an old, boxy, black-and-white television in the kitchen, with his feet up on the coal hopper. After his retirement, he did odd jobs—mowing people's lawns, chopping and stacking wood.

When he inquired after the "wedding event," I didn't know what to say. I told him about Groucho, our Corgi, sprung from the basement of our new split-level home, slurping up drinks left by folding chairs outside on the patio. He'd gotten sloshed and I'd spent the next day by his basket, holding his paw through the hangover. I didn't tell him about Robert's tearful toast to the bride, which had a female guest writing his words down on a drink napkin; I didn't tell him how snug and right Mum and Robert looked dancing together. My father didn't ask anymore about it.

Our last night together, we went to an opera. I'd never been to one before, although he'd always wanted to take me. This was a big city touring company, condescending to play their extravaganza in the provinces en route to Seattle and San Francisco. I wore what I'd worn to Mum's wedding. Dad dressed up. He'd shrunk in recent years, so his frayed trouser cuffs tickled the ground, and the herringbone jacket seemed huge, but the shirt and light blue tie Mum had picked out for me to give him that Christmas fit fine. "All you need to know," Dad said, "is that everybody kicks the bucket, and sings an horrendously long time while doing so."

It was *Tosca*. I didn't understand a word, but the music was shockingly beautiful. Towards the end of Act I, there was a scene at the fount of the church. It built slowly, with organ, and the chorus kneeling, crossing themselves, singing Latin mass until they were in full voice, with cannons blasting, bells pealing wildly, and the heralding of trumpets. I felt enraptured. The music was the texture of rich velvet. Then I heard his noisy breathing. My father's shoulders shook and tears poured down his face and dripped onto his jacket.

I poked him in the side. "Dad," I said. "Your nose is running."

He didn't have a handkerchief, and I didn't have tissues, and he had to wipe his nose on his jacket sleeve. Somebody behind us passed along a starched white one, saying, "Keep it. You'll need it later." As Scarpia kneeled, almost humble, and confessed that his passion had made him forget God, Dad wiped his face. He shook his head in bewilderment at himself. "And not a soul has died," he said.

At the intermission, I told him if he was going to bawl like that, I would leave him and watch from standing room. He promised he wouldn't exhibit that behavior again and he didn't. Everyone else was, even I, and he sat there, his chin propped in his right hand, with bright dry eyes.

I completed grades eleven and twelve in one year, went away to school in the east, to U. of T., the University of Toronto, for a traumatic semester, then returned to British Columbia and majored in cultural anthropology. After my bachelor's, I forged ahead with graduate work and lived in the Arctic for a winter researching my thesis. A plane flew into the village once every two weeks with mail and supplies. Mum wrote with news of disasters and siblings, getting her hair done, and the new dog's bad breath. I didn't hear once from my father.

I boarded in the little village of Igloolik, high above Hudson Bay, with an Inuit couple, Abel and Molly Pawlangtuk. They had lost their three children: by drowning, by exposure, by birth, strangled by the cord. They joked around and called me "nanook," and "white daughter." I had my own room in their generic government house, sometimes ate meals with them—frozen caribou brought down from our roof, or tasty narwhal guts—and was free to come and go.

I was studying the effects of Christianity on the Inuit belief in shamanism, so I spent a lot of time at masses and evensong, and at teas with parishioners. I also attended faith-healing missions, watching locals faint, Pentecostals speak in tongues, and the blind point to the flickering flame of a candle, seeing the light for the first time. I asked a lot of questions about their conception of God. What did He look like? Describe Jesus. What did shamans do and where did they go? Were there any shamans living in the village now?

I also, unethically, dated a shaman. Dated wasn't the word; we were lovers. He was far older than me, although I never learned his true age, and his skin was soft and smoother than mine. When we came in from a walk on ice, he pulled off my high-tech mitts, lifted up his parka, and pressed my hands to his abdomen. He licked my lashes and ate the ice off my brows. He shot our food. He took good care of me. Since it was night a fair chunk of the day, we spent a lot of time in his bed under bear-skins. My body had never been healthier, leaner, more exercised, more loved. Before we fell asleep, he said, *"Igluksak."*

"Snow you can build with."

"Aput."

"Snow just lying on the ground."

"Piqtuq."

"Snow blown through the air during a blizzard."

"Ganik."

"Falling snow."

"Mauya."

"Mauya is soft, deep *sotto sotto* snow." I kissed him everywhere. "For lying down and making angels." I learned the meaning of *quviannikumuit*. To feel deeply happy. *Nuannarpoq*. To take extravagant pleasure in being alive.

Then one day I woke up feeling guilty about him and quickly ended it. He left the village soon after, and nobody knew where he'd gone. Many villagers thought he'd turned himself into a polar bear and flown away, but nobody publicly admitted to the old beliefs.

After the winter solstice, when the sun no longer appeared, I grew quite depressed. I didn't want to get out of bed, and stayed under the caribou, listening on my recorder to tapes of the Talking Heads, *La Boheme* or Dire Straits. I could not work. I walked with Molly through the village, down to the shore, where life seemed to be gradations of white and gray, and boats were packed off ice, and dogs were tied up, howling, below roofs holding carcasses of seal. I was living alone on a new planet. Abel said it was cabin fever. The government nurse prescribed an antidepressant, which I didn't take, and handed me a stack of old *People*'s. The Catholic priest visited, though aware I was an atheist, and held my hand while we read prayers aloud together. Then he suggested I go home for a breather. I wasn't sure where home was anymore.

Flying south took fifteen hours, three flights. I remember the jolt of joy when the treeline appeared, dark, a five o'clock stubble on the face of the blank earth. Timber.

A year later, my father flew to New York for my sudden, small wedding. It was his first trip on a plane and he was terrified. In fact, he had not planned to attend the ceremony; he'd wanted to send my mother as she and Robert were strapped. But Robert was in the hospital with a hernia and Mum wouldn't budge from his bedside. I prepped my fiance. "Dad's a Brit Canuck. Jewish means Motel the Tailor. He doesn't know we're expecting." In fact, nobody but us knew about the wee one. We were marrying so that Bill would be able to support us by securing lucrative scientific drudgery with the Canadian government up north.

At LaGuardia, my father was already deep in conversation with a shabbily dressed woman. Actually, he was similarly attired. People gave them looks. I embraced him—shorter, frail, afloat in his shirt—and when he started to introduce us, tugged him aside. "Dad, that's a bag lady."

"Is that so?" he said, not registering. "She was relating an interesting tale about her involvement with your Jewish mayor."

A troupe of teen ballerinas giraffed by. "The bunheads are coming," the bag lady said. "Pay attention. Bunheads."

"And what exactly are the bunheads?" Dad asked as a porter hustled us along. His balance was poor and he couldn't negotiate the multitude, but shook off my arm. I slowed and we caught up to his medieval suitcase at the curb.

Bill squealed up in the car. "Mr. Nordstrom," he said. "Motel the physicist." My father warmed to him and started telling about the bag lady and Mayor Koch, whom he seemed to think Bill might know, or be related to.

It was an intimate wedding—us. The Justice of the Peace informed my father he wouldn't be asking, "Who gives this woman?," and Dad said I'd not officially been his to donate to the fray since 1964.

We dined at a semi-pompous Hicksville restaurant with valet parking. There were paintings of fox hunts and a zoo of over-dressed drinkers on the terrace. It turned out they were another wedding soaking up the open bar. Our waiter told us it was the bride's second go-round at this venue. When she bore down upon the *chuppah*, Dad craned for a view. Her gown was fifties, long, low-cut. "A magnificent specimen," Dad said, then Bill stood up and ogled, too.

From there we drove to a motor inn at Elmhurst, Queens, the international crossroads of the world and close to both airports. Bill checked us in and ordered double wake-up calls. In the elevator, he shook my father's hand. "Thanks, Dad," he said, "for raising a specimen."

"Oh, you're welcome," Dad said. "Although I don't think I had much to do with it."

Bill got out and I helped my father to his room, floors above ours. "Did I hear correctly?" he said. "Did your rabbi call me Dad?"

"You heard," I said. I flopped in a chair. We were leaving the next day for low season in Negril, courtesy of Dad, and he was flying back to Vancouver. "You didn't have to come," I said.

"Oh, I wouldn't have missed it for the world." He eased himself down onto the bed.

"How's your jet lag?"

"Don't have it." He looked exhausted. "Let's see. It would be nine p.m. back in Vancouver. Do you think perhaps you should call your mother? She might be worried."

I shook my head no. Outside, the traffic from Manhattan snarled by, someone with a horn playing "La Cucaracha," which irritated me.

"That's 'La Cucaracha,' isn't it?" Dad said. In admiration, he added, "They do seem to have *everything* in the States."

I turned on the air-conditioning and we listened to it. Here I was on my wedding night with my father, sitting on a bed, possibly a vibrating one, in a Queens motel.

"Marriage," Dad said, "as I'm sure you've learned during your extensive and, need I add, expensive schooling, is life's most difficult proposition."

"There are no happy marriages," I said. "Only unexamined ones."

"Who says that?"

"Me," I said.

The phone rang. Dad was delighted. "Now who would be paging me *here*?" He answered it and looked confused for a second. "There's no Mrs. Stein on these premises," he said. "You've got the wrong number."

"Dad," I said. "That's me now."

Somewhat embarrassed, he passed the receiver, then bent to pore over the Spanish instructions for the vibrating bed.

"Room service?" It was Bill on the line. He'd obviously popped the champagne. "Hurry up. Send down a hot goy girl or I'm at the bar."

"Great," I said, ticked. "Go to hell." I hung up, breathed, smiled, and said to my father, "I'm going now."

"So soon?"

"Dad," I said. "It's my wedding night. I'm the bride. It's the big day. The big deal."

His hand gripped the headboard and he pulled himself up

onto his feet. We trod over to the door. I smelled the wood smoke caught in his jacket, the odor of home. A burglar had recently broken into his old house; Dad had been in bed, engrossed in a book on British Columbian shipwrecks, and hadn't heard the window below shatter. Nothing was taken. Nothing to take. The police figured it was some soul seeking a roof to sleep under, who thought the house abandoned.

We hugged long and couldn't quite let go of each other. He did not talk. Neither did I. It crossed my mind that I was holding my baby, his only grandchild, against him. But I did not speak up and tell him what was hidden inside. I let go of him. "So long," I said. "Time to fly."

"Oh," he said. "It is getting late."

"Yes," I said. "It is." I backed out. "O.K. Bye. Safe trip."

I pulled the metal door shut behind me. I heard him finally bolt it. Then after three tries, it was gently chained.

Daniel Stern

A HUNGER ARTIST BY FRANZ KAFKA: A STORY

We don't have time enough to be ourselves.
All we have time for is to be happy.

—Camus

We don't have time enough to be ourselves or to be happy. All we have time enough for is our work. And not enough for that. That's what counts!

—Brandauer

Brandauer had Tuna Fish for lunch every day of the nine years I knew him. Sometimes on rye toast, sometimes on white bread, sometimes with a Coke, sometimes with a small glass of milk. Not a full-size glass: the half sizes kids drink from. It took him about twelve minutes and he was ready to go back to work.

We met the year my second book was published—the one written with vanishing ink. I was also working as a rep for a production company which specialized in the fancy avant-garde commercials which were then in style. That was the year applause began to come to Brandauer, late and sudden. When it grew to a crescendo a few years later, while nothing much was happening in what we laughingly called my literary career, he felt a statement was called for. "Don't get too excited," he said. "And don't envy me. Coming at this time in my life, these honors are like rocks falling on my head." He was fifty-six, tall and lean as a panther. A grizzled Jewish Panther of the writing jungle. I didn't believe his disclaimer then; nobody did. Later it was another matter.

This late-bloomed success was the main reason we met. Brandauer had come out of his cage, for a time. This never-photographed, never-interviewed, slowly famous, invisible comic artist of rigor and denial had actually agreed to teach a course at a Creative Writing Workshop. And, as if one wonder were not enough, he also agreed to be interviewed.

The setting for these extraordinary events was to be a small but serious Writers Conference near Seattle. Having been tapped by *The Paris Review* to do the long-refused interview, I sat in on his class. The fortunate few were early, without doubt a first for *them*, notebooks out, necks craned upwards—Brandauer was six feet tall and thin and looked a little like Abraham Lincoln if Abraham Lincoln had been of eastern European Jewish descent.

Everyone sitting around the long oval table waited, watching this man who had emerged from a dozen years at hard labor in solitary confinement, five in the Sheepshead Bay section of Brooklyn and seven in Genoa, Italy, learning, as one critic wrote, to make sentences walk, dance and sing. There were three well-documented years in France, as well, where he'd lived in a stone house on a hill in a tiny perched village near Avignon. But there too he had mostly stayed in his stone room, performing his self-appointed task as the ballet master of the modern English sentence.

That's right—no wife, no children, all sorts of friends, but no family who could claim time away from his mission. Or so everyone thought at the time. Given this well-publicized first surfacing, the class's expectations were naturally high. If Brandauer knew this, he wasn't letting on. He picked up the small, green-covered book of stories by Kafka and began to read: " 'A Hunger Artist,' a story by Franz Kafka. *During these last decades the interest in professional fasting has markedly diminished . . . At one time the whole town took a lively interest in the Hunger Artist. It used to pay very well to stage such great performances under one's own management, but today that is quite impossible. We live in a different world now.*" In a short time it became terribly and comically clear that all Brandauer would teach, in what was advertised as his Creative Writing Workshop, was one fourteen-page story by Kafka. No student self-expression, no handing in of manuscripts to be criticized by the classmates, no memorialized encouraging comments scribbled in the margins by the Master.

What he did give to the students was an eloquent overview of a story about a man whose art was fasting; who practiced it in a cage, setting world records for taking little food sometimes, no food other times, for days, weeks and finally many years—on his own and later in a circus. For a time, since the art of fasting itself had a large audience, he was famous, successful—even as his ribs stuck through his skin. Later, the art falls out of fashion and the hunger artist dies, by now, utterly forgotten. Into his cage they put a young panther; they bring him the food he likes . . . *and the joy of life streamed with such ardent passion from his throat . . .*"

The kids were stunned. When Brandauer read the end in which the dying Hunger Artist whispers to the Overseer that the audience should not admire his fasting . . . *Because I have to fast, I can't help it.* And explains, finally, *Because* . . . and here Brandauer hunched down and spoke the Artist's last words in a hoarse whisper, . . . *I couldn't find the food I liked. If I had found it, believe me, I should have made no fuss and stuffed myself like you or anyone else.*

He was a smash. The young people all around me were applauding, thrilled. They had clearly forgotten, in the excitement of the moment, that Brandauer had not even read a story of his own, let alone one of theirs; had not told them how they should write or even how he wrote, himself, except by implication. It was a subtle, allusive, brilliant performance. Several faculty members had invited themselves in, stood in the back, and they were going wild, too. The single exception was the striking young woman who sat next to me, shoving impatient hands through her long red hair. She never took her eyes off Brandauer. Either she was extraordinarily fair or her exquisite face was pale with some emotion I couldn't figure out. Actually, she looked the way people in books might look when "pale with anger."

While she stared at him and I stared at her, Brandauer made

it clear but not pleasant to the students that *all* he would deal with was the way the story was made. No fancy hermaneutics; just how something is made.

"Look how Kafka has the audience *itself* take an active part in the Hunger Artist's dramatic fasting presentation. There are casual onlookers in front of his cage, but there are also *relays of permanent watchers selected by the public—usually butchers,* Kafka tells us—and they are to watch to make sure the Artist doesn't have some resource to secret nourishment. With two words, *usually butchers,* Kafka introduces humor into this grim business."

"Critics," one student called out.

Brandauer paused; he patted a pencil against the wire frame of his eyeglasses. He did not look at the waiting student. He smiled, as at a private joke. Then he proceeded: "Later, however," he said, "just before the end, not only is he not being scrutinized, but no one even notices the starving Hunger Artist; he's hidden beneath layers of straw, until an Overseer notices what seems to be an empty cage and pokes around until he discovers the artist almost dead from his fast." So much for interpretations and analogies.

Brandauer must have sensed the restlessness, almost a confusion in the air. "This is the way we will work, here," he said, bending over the table on which lay the text. Tall and skinny he arched his back, one half of a pair of parentheses, and explained that the only way he knew to learn to write was to read. So, in the remaining sessions they would read and reread and reread again this small story by Kafka. "We will reinvent this strange little story by one of the strangest writers who ever lived—and then you'll go on to invent your own, that's what counts. I'm sorry if you expected more or different. I can't give more or different. This is the only way I know." It was the first time I heard that phrase from him—"that's what counts." It was not the last.

Outside, on the slippery steps of the conference hall, Brandauer and I made arrangements to meet for the interview. The inevitable Seattle drizzle huddled us under umbrellas. I scribbled his address.

"Come at four. We'll do two hours, then I've invited some people for dinner."

"I'll bring the wine."

"Don't bring anything. I have a bottle."

Suddenly there was a presence between our two umbrellas. The young girl with the angry gaze, my classroom neighbor, stood there. She had forgotten her umbrella but had brought the gaze, intact.

"Professor Brandauer . . ." she said.

"*Mister*," he said. "I don't profess anything. I'm just a writer."

She pushed a bundle of manuscripts towards him. It was dauntingly large enough to be secured by a fat rubber band. Water streamed down her forehead past large blue, unblinking eyes. I couldn't help thinking she looked like a water nymph in some Bernini fountain in Rome; a beauty.

"Can I lend you my umbrella," Brandauer said, an old-fashioned gentleman. He was carefully not looking at the papers she held.

"No," she said. "You can read my stories."

"They're going to be soaking wet." He moved to bring her into the protected circle but she moved away, impatient.

"I came up from Newport News . . ." She paused as if searching for the strongest argument she could make. Indeed, I would have guessed even further south than Virginia, going by the music below the rage in the words. ". . . just to get your comments on my stories."

"You heard what I . . ."

"*This is my life*, Mister Brandauer," she said. "I have read everything you've . . ."

"Only four books," he murmured. But anger had made her deaf to Brandauer's mild irony.

". . . and I didn't come all this soaking way to hear what's his name. I came to hear what you think about my—my—" I was afraid she was going to say her life, again; I'd seen Brandauer sort of wince the first time.

"What's *your* name," Brandauer said.

"Penelope Anne Golden. You *will* read me, then."

I was impressed by the "read me." She couldn't have been more than twenty-four and she already felt there was a "me" to read.

"It wouldn't be f-f-f-fair to the others. Th-th-th-that's what counts."

It was the first time I'd heard him stammer. He owned one; but like the rest of his inventory, he used it sparingly.

"I don't give a damn about the others," Penelope Anne Golden said. "I came here for you!" She licked the rain from her lips while her stone glance stayed on Brandauer's face.

"Miss Golden, you don't understand . . ."

"*I don't have to*," she said and backing off a little, threw the rubber-band–bound sheaf of papers at Brandauer. She threw it underhand, a softball throw and Brandauer had to drop his umbrella to catch it. He stood there, like a statue of himself, Penelope Anne Golden's life in his hands, rain blinding his eyeglasses.

What I remember most about that first evening at the tiny apartment Brandauer had rented in downtown Seattle was how lavishly we three dinner guests poured out conversation, laughter and information. The other two were two professors of American Studies—married to each other and to Brandauer's work. We shared the subtle feeling of being the three people in the world, that night, privileged to be in the presence. I entertained us all with a re-creation of the scene in the rain with the lovely southern rebel. That started a sort of anarchic evening of excessive laughter and noisy talk; not the sort of wildness Brandauer was used to.

Before the others arrived, he had carefully measured out his steps around the little folding table, setting down the napkins, measuring the distance between knife and plate, neatly parsing out everything else: the wine in the small, over-decorated, hardware-store glasses, the lean anecdotes he told, the Chicken Casserole he'd cooked, the portion sizes just enough, no more, no less.

He was so serious! When he joined in the joke telling with a story about a Japanese businessman returning home from a trip to an unfaithful wife who had slept with a Jewish man, we laughed and Brandauer laughed. But by departing for a moment from his habitual grave bearing, he gave the joking weight. He was like a Japanese visitor, without the language, trying to join in a lightheartedness he did not quite understand but longed to experience.

During dinner he continued to measure out the food and wine as if we were marooned on a desert island and had to be sure to make the rations last. He'd told me, "I have a bottle" and that's exactly what he had, one bottle of wine for the four of us, not a drop more. You felt he didn't understand why anyone would want more than was enough. And what was enough was clear. His conversation, too, was carefully proportioned—he spoke in short, clear, ironic phrases with not one stammer. And, at one point, when the laughter and noisy commentary got out of hand, loud and boisterous, Brandauer pounded his hand on the table for quiet. A God of large and small universes, he was accustomed to being able to control them; a master of where to place the period, he got his quiet along with a certain astonishment.

About halfway through the interview session before dinner, he suddenly said, "That girl . . . what did you think?"

"I think you're on the spot," I said. "You and Kafka, both. She's one of those tough southern cookies. She expected personal attention and you gave her Kafka."

"I like her intensity," he said. And he quoted Yeats to me— something about lust and rage attending old age . . . I said, "How old are you?"

"How much do you weigh?" he said. He'd watched me settle and resettle myself on the couch as I fiddled with the tape recorder. He watched everybody and everything, better at asking than answering questions.

"Too damned much."

And I told him how my second marriage had broken up because in one of my cycles of voracious overeating, I had reached over to my wife's plate, at the Peking Gardens, and started eating from it. Everyone else at the table thought it was mildly amusing, a weird little action. To *her* it meant the marriage was over, it meant I didn't give a damn about anybody or anything except my own hopeless hungers.

"Second wife? You're pretty young."

"I'm on my third."

"Sounds like courses in a meal."

"This is my life we're talking, here," I said. "Don't turn it into another Brandauer metaphor."

"*My life*," he murmured. "That's what Penelope Anne said. Everybody seems to have this *life* they own." He said it mournfully. I didn't know him well enough to say, it wasn't like a car you bought or didn't buy—that he, too, must own a life. But it wasn't that clear.

We finished the interview a few days later and I left Seattle to go back to New York, looking for my next job and some fresh ways to patch up the various tears my marriage had developed. I left without finding out what happened to Penelope Anne Golden and her rain-soaked plea for personal literary attention.

I did not see Brandauer again for a year and a half. He was back in his lair, making sentences with which to make stories and making stories in which to nest his sentences. I was busy running around looking for some happiness. I was always able to find *some*, so I could never either renounce the habit or conquer it. I started a magazine designed to appeal to the restless paperback publishing industry, for a time, then did Public Relations for a Ballet Company that spun off from the American Ballet Theater. You get the idea; things that kept me busy but could never be confused with a real career.

Brandauer wrote a letter: "I read your first novel *Skydancer*. It is strongly imagined and seriously comic—but is insufficiently crafted so the spirit dies halfway through, leaving the reader with a big chunk of inanimate flesh to deal with. Perhaps you are too scattered to give your craft enough attention. All these different activities." He closed his unexpected letter with a typical Brandauer trick: two quotations without their sources. *Don't forget*, he wrote, "*Life isn't everything.*" *And in any case*, "*It's best seen through a single window.*" *This last—that's what counts.*

What the hell did he want? He certainly did not think I could follow him into the compression of despairing images into wildly comic characters which, during these next years, made him as famous as Beckett or Malamud—to whom, along with Kafka, he was most often compared. Or into his solitude to become a saint of art. Him and his "that's what counts"—counting up our everlasting pluses and minuses. And what the hell would he do with the sum if he finally arrived at it? In the language of his youth his speed was seventy-eight, mine was thirty-three and a third and often a whirring, laser-spun CD. But I loved his songs. My affection was not unrequited: He invited me to join him at a Writer's Conference at the University of Arizona in June.

I arrived in Tucson by a series of disastrously late planes. Which is why I missed Brandauer's class and drove up to find him standing, surrounded by students in a shimmer of sunshine. I got out of my car and a wall of shaking heat hit my face. Brandauer was the only one who wore a jacket and tie, and he sweated passionately everywhere you could see: his shirt collar wet and limp, his blue tie smeared and wet, his handkerchief mopping eyes and half-bald forehead.

The group thinned out and there was Brandauer with the Angry Young Woman of a year ago: Penelope Whatever-her-name-was. It was the Seattle tableau all over, but instead of rain a monstrous, debilitating fried egg of a sun.

I was so startled to see her that I slowed my approach. I watched them through a shimmering horizon-haze of crackling, dry heat. It was like a mirage must be, except it didn't look pleasant.

"You're just changing names and places, Penny," I heard Brandauer say. "Sometimes the imagination needs a push."

My God, I thought in that hallucinatory hot wind, a year later and they're still arguing. Though I did note the "Penny." The argument, and who knew what else, had become personal.

"*You* need a push," she said. "Get you out of your damned Kafka-land."

They began to walk. I followed, not wanting to interrupt.

"I'm not telling you how or what to do. But a series of sexual encounters do not make a work of fiction."

"That's because I'm a woman. How about D. H. Lawrence?"

"How about sitting in the shade? I'm fainting from the heat."

"Pricks are okay but Cunts are not proper literary material, is that it?" It was the precise moment to interrupt. Now or never and just in time. Between the two of us we got Brandauer into my air-conditioned Toyota. Tucson in June at 11:30 AM: Heat stroke was not unthinkable. We put him to bed in the air-conditioned studio apartment rented for him by the university.

"I should never have come out," he said. "I can't handle you p-p-p-p-people."

I was surprised, again, by the stammer; surprised, too, that he included *me* in his soft, exhausted impeachment.

"Okay," Penny said. "He's right." She paused to soak up her second margarita. "My youth is so full of weird sex stuff that I can't make head or tail out of it. But writing stories is the only way I know to get it all straight—if I don't then I'm cooked."

"Right now, *he's* cooked," I said. "And what do you mean your youth?"

"I'm twenty-four, honey. In Virginia twenty-four is a mature woman." It came out *woeman*. And, in spite of that lovely, lofty white brow and bright red lips, her "honey" was so strongly flavored it shriveled my scrotum.

I took refuge in questions of fact. "How did you get Brandauer to comment on your stories? He was so firm about what he would and wouldn't do in the class."

"He insisted I drop out of the class," Penny said. "Dis-en-roll."

I swear I had guessed the answer in advance; I was getting to know Brandauer in spite of himself.

"It was the only way to be fair to the others, he said. I became an auditor and he'd read my stories and go over them with me over lunch."

"Tuna Fish," I said. "Every day."

"How did you know?"

"So you won."

"I lost," she said miserably. "I wanted to exorcise my crazy adolescence by turning it into fiction. He poisoned my hope."

She was something. No one I knew but Penny could have said, with a straight face, *He poisoned my hope.* She rummaged in a giant tote bag and out came a notebook. "Here's what he said— it was so awful I had to write it down." She read, like a school-girl reciting a lesson, *Art is not ecology. We don't need to conserve the life you've lived and lost—we need a new life from you . . . one you can imagine but probably can't have. We want imagination not biography. That's what counts.*

She threw the book down and then surprised me by dropping her head on her folded arms. For a full minute she wept. I didn't know what to do so I reached across the table and touched her cheek. My hand came away wet. It felt too intimate. But it stopped the flood. She flared up again: "So I said, *How about Proust?* And he said, *How about you?*"

"Why do you care what he thinks so much?" I said hope-lessly.

"Because he knows. You know how he's always saying about this or that—that's what counts? Well, sometimes I think he re-ally knows what counts, that he has that gift. I didn't mean what I said about Pricks and Cunts and all that. He's not full of shit. He may be the only one who's not." Over a Tex-Mex din-ner ordered on impulse I tried to distract her. No use.

"How do you make a living in between Brandauer en-counters?" I asked.

"Sell books in a little store downtown Newport News. That's where I first found him."

"Him?"

"His books. When I heard he was going to teach—I grabbed my stories and lit out for the territory. But he wouldn't teach. Just talk about this one crazy story." She poured a ton of ketchup over everything and laughed. "Dug my own grave," she said. "You're a kind man to listen to my troubles." She spoke with that formal prose southerners seem to be born with.

Later we were less formal. I was too close to her, and she was a melange of smells; some kind of flowery perfume on her neck, fragrant gin on her breath and ketchup on her fingers. Also, the wide blue eyes made things pretty skittish. Except for Brandauer. We'd made the mistake of calling to make sure he wasn't dead of heat stroke. He wasn't, but then he knew Penny and I were together and it smelled like a betrayal. The night's mission was aborted.

Already I could hear him saying: *"Her eyes—you wanted to make love to her because of her wide, beautiful eyes—is that a person, a human being, their eyes, wide or close together? A human being as parts?"* The Brandauer eye went right to the heart of things. Butcher of values, he left no fat on issues—only the hearts of matters were good enough for him to sell. He respected his customers. Okay, call them his readers. Call them the audience.

Finally, I understood Brandauer's exasperated stammering wrap-up of Penny and me: *I should never have left. I can't handle you p-p-p-p-people* . . . I didn't like it, but I understood it. Coming out into the world had left the poor bastard open to everybody from Penny and her all-important "life" to writing groupies from all over. There was one young man whose name had been Wilbur Jonas until he became a convert to Orthodox Judaism. He changed his name to Chaim and brought his unfinished novel all the way from the wealth of Shaker Heights, Cleveland, by bus, to Fargo, North Dakota, to hear Brandauer talk about "A Hunger Artist." He had converted from Jewish Middle-class Agnosticism to Orthodoxy. His beard was so long he looked like his own great-grandfather. Brandauer gave him special attention. He treated him as if he were some sort of sacred monster.

We were *all* his problems. I who wanted to devour all the life and time there was, and was unable to learn the mysterious Brandauer alchemy of making caterpillars out of butterflies, questions out of answers; Chaim, who wanted to find the Talmudic tradition in new fiction; Penny and the other Pennys who were busy with the sacred matters of personal experience which drew his contempt.

Sometimes I got sick of him.

"What's so special about your buddy the shtetl kid," I said, irritated. "The Rabbi Nachman of Cleveland. He wouldn't even eat your Tuna Fish, brought his own food? *You* don't believe that stuff," I said. "Why do you give that kid so much leeway?"

"I like Chaim," he said. "I like his choice of names. It affirms Life."

I shrugged. "He wants to bomb Arabs. Some affirmer of life."

"He's fervent," Brandauer said. "That's what counts."

Those years of his coming out were my pendulum years. I swung like a pendulum from Diet Centers to eating binges, from reducing farms to Food City, no doubt making a shambles of my endocrinological system. Jobs were the same. Like Tarzan on his vines I swung my way through the jungle of employment, never staying put very long.

Women, too, were included in this cycle of appetites. At least two of them had wonderfully adhesive skin, that is they stuck to my life. Others had skin as smooth as a mind without memory and soon became part of the past. One of them, Sybil, became my fourth wife. I wanted Brandauer to be the Best Man but I was afraid he already was, and skipped the invitation.

One November, at a conference in Fargo, North Dakota, Brandauer told me, "You're a feverish man. A cooler temperature would be more productive." I allowed myself an intimate moment with the Master.

"The fever is not the problem," I said. And I tried to make him understand how it was always the matter at hand, whatever it was, which heated me up—a lovely woman who promised understanding and pleasure, not necessarily in that order; a *poulet à l'estragon avec moutarde et endives;* and that fine literary moment when the word *and* joins the actions of two characters perfectly. All were equal in me.

Brandauer gazed at me in spectacled despair. His silhouette seemed more fragile than ever; his cheeks were sinking inwards, signs of age or loss of weight, I couldn't tell.

"That's only good for somebody who's going to live forever," he said. "I haven't met one yet. The rest of us have to choose."

"How about a walk," I said, desperately.

"This is North Dakota. It's five degrees outside."

"Ah," I said. "Yes. As usual I forgot."

The following summer we met at the Bennington Conference.

I was in my brief phase of smoking good cigars—delicious, slow-smoking, fragrant Panatelas made by Upmann in Havana, shipped, legally, to Switzerland to a man named Gross, who then shipped them to me, illegally, in a box marked *Swiss Cigars: Gift Under Twenty-five Dollars.*

"Is it worth all that trouble," Brandauer asked.

"Absolutely."

"I think maybe the trouble is part of the pleasure. It makes a big deal out of a small joy."

To throw him off the scent I told him about Hemingway's comment that you had to plan your pleasures, work at them, otherwise they wouldn't happen. Everything else will happen anyway, work, obligations, but not pleasures, unless you planned for them.

I leaned back satisfied with having scored. Brandauer stood up, said, "It goes vice versa, too," and went home to his desk. As if to prove him right, I wasted that entire day in pointless phone calls, switching vacation plans, while he wrote a page and a half.

A couple of years later I was asked to fill in at the last minute, at a winter Conference in Boulder, Colorado. I was working at a new job: Writer/Producer of trailers for Monster Movies. You know, bite-sized smorgasbords designed to make children and certain minority groups—the primary monster-lovers—hungry for the movie itself. I needed the money to pay for Alimony. The Divorce from Sybil had turned into the usual horror movie and I'd put on thirty pounds out of misery.

But Brandauer was going to be in Boulder, so I cleared my schedule. When I arrived, there he was, small, green-covered Modern Library edition of the *Selected Kafka* stories in hand.

In the interim he had won the Pulitzer Prize for his *Collected Stories* and a National Book Award for a new novel. The novels were getting shorter and shorter. You could hardly tell them from the stories, which were also getting smaller. I was eager to see him. But more eager to have *him* see *me*. I'd just dropped forty-seven pounds at the Pritikin Center in Florida. It had cost all my extra cash—but I was proud of the exhibition of will.

There was a foot of snow everywhere. We met for lunch in some Western Inn-type place with a fireplace, and a moosehead on the wall. They featured Steaks and Venison, but I knew what Brandauer was up for. I took perverse pleasure in ordering even less. What's less than Tuna Fish on white toast and a cup of black coffee? It wasn't easy, but I scrounged up an assorted vegetable plate. That got his attention. But he made no comment.

"I brought you a present," I told him. "It's a poem. I wrote it on eight hundred calories a day, at Pritikin. It's called: 'The Hunger Artist.' "

It was a long son of a bitch but he seemed to pay special attention to the last two stanzas.

> *Out of the fleshly fabrication*
> *Appears an honesty of skin.*
> *In the hungry, human situation*
> *The gotten grace is always thin.*

> *The body less than fills the eye,*
> *The flesh, a tissue shield.*
> *Bare bones beneath a cannibal sky:*
> *Shape is fate revealed.*

"It's not 'The Hunger Artist,' it's 'A Hunger Artist.' " He folded the gift-poem carefully in four parts and put it in his wallet. "The article is crucial. He's a special case."

Not a word about my poem, a poem as personal to me as my gut.

We stormed the snow, a blast of white wind in our faces, and walked to the parking lot. I had to shout to be heard.

"Okay," I said, off-balance as only he could throw me off, *"The—A—*My God . . . I've heard you read that story in eight cities to students dying to learn how to write their own stories . . ."

"Are you finished with your new book?"

"No—I've been gearing up for this new job. And the divorce took it out of me."

"Ah," he said. There was nothing more devastating than a Brandauer "Ah."

"Do you like making these commercials you work at?"

As if confessing something shameful, I said: "I do, yes. It's fun, it's easy and it's good money."

He fiddled with the lock to his car.

"It may be frozen," I said. "Let me try."

He paused a long time and said, "I could never handle the world the way you do." This did not sound as if he admired me for it, believe me. Irritably, I said, "I think *you* do it much better. The world handles me, not vice versa. I'm always playing catch-up with money and women."

"Thanks for the poem," he said.

Before I could reply with something properly bitter, the snowy shape of Penelope Anne Golden made its way through a blast of white wet. She wore a hooded parka; the hood made her look like one of those figures in a medieval print: All she needed was a scythe.

I figured we were finished so I backed away as she approached. I watched them from the safety of my warming car. She was gesticulating wildly, Brandauer stood there like a prisoner being accused of various crimes. Every few moments he shrugged. I don't think he said anything. Clearly, he still had not treated her "life" the way she wished.

I started the car and Penelope was standing outside knocking on the window. She spat a mouthful of snow at me. When I rolled the window down she stuck her sweet snowy face in and kissed me. It was an angry kiss, more like a bite.

"Do y'all want to make love to me?" she asked.

It was such a crazed moment that I thought the "y'all" meant both of us—me and poor soaked Brandauer hunching himself into his Volkswagen. But it was nothing so fancy. He must have said something about her stories that got her southern rage going and I was handy. Her mouth had a soft, wet give that was tempting. But over her shoulder I saw Brandauer struggling to start his frozen car and all I could do was shake my head from side to side.

"Fuck you," she said and stumbled away in the snow.

The next day, in class, Brandauer read the last line of my poem: *Shape is fate revealed.*

"What the hell was that?" I said, afterwards.

"It seemed appropriate."

"You're too damned appropriate, Brandauer," I said. "That line makes no sense without the rest of the poem."

"Too bad," he said. "You gave it to me. It's mine now. And I gave it to the class. Remember it's *A* not *The*. By the way, you look terrific with your new shape. Maybe now you can make do with less all around."

I said nothing about yesterday's craziness in the snow with Penelope. He said even less.

A few months later *Time* magazine got wind of Brandauer's cross-country number. It was oddball enough to get their attention. This shy master suddenly zipping around the country teaching writing students using only a fourteen-page story about a strange custom of fasting as an art form. And, of course, Kafka was the perfect writer to refer to without having to read him. Everybody knows what you mean when you talk about Kafka, don't they?

When they called me, the researcher said they'd gotten my name from a Ms. Penelope Anne Golden. I thought, She doesn't know the rules of the game, and I eased them off the phone. Naturally they confused Brandauer with the Hunger Artist in the story. And naturally they called it *The* Hunger Artist, losing Brandauer's precious *A*.

Reading the piece made me think about our singular friendship. What a match! Brandauer owned a natural dignity and carried himself with such care that it bordered on the mysterious. He had the patience of someone enrolled in a religious order for life whose faith had never been shaken. Myself, I had a gift for clowning and an attention span of about a minute and a half. He was at home with order; I was companion to confusion. His arena of pleasures was narrow, carefully attended to. Mine was indiscriminate, loose (with significant exceptions such as ignoring Penelope Anne's sexual invitation). And, strangest of all, he insisted on taking me seriously; something I could never quite manage. We were a comic pairing, a Mutt and Jeff of the writing life.

The comedy ended abruptly in Miami. There was a woman at his bedside, tall, European looking, her dress a little too long, all in gray. She fluttered off the instant I arrived.

". . . who told you . . . ?"

"Don't talk."

"Isn't it crazy dying *here?* Did you see those foolish-looking palm trees on the way from the airport? This is not a serious place."

He was bringing his own seriousness with him, hooked up to all the usual hi-tech medical paraphernalia, a Frankenstein monster of unexpected disaster.

"The food is terrible here."

"Hospitals," I said stupidly.

"It's Tuna Fish every day for lunch. Awful."

He didn't seem to know he was making his own deathbed comedy. Maybe they gave him Tuna Fish because someone told them it was his lifelong lunch.

Brandauer gestured for me to bend closer. His chest wind was not blowing with its usual strength.

"Chaim . . ."

"No, I'm . . ."

"I know, I know." He was irritated at his lapse—confusing me with his Orthodox Jewish disciple. He wanted order, as usual, not confusion.

"I envy the p-p-p-p-p- . . ." It was the longest, most painful stammer I'd ever heard from him. I waited while he struggled. Finally the word arrived: ". . . panther!" We were back to topic A. Or topic K. Relieved and exhausted by the effort he added, "I envy him—just a little," and sneaked in a quick little smile. "That girl, Penelope . . . you slept with her?"

"No," I said too quickly.

"Ah," he said. "Too bad."

. . .

I was starved. In the gray hospital cafeteria I drank some chemical coffee and ate a cardboard croissant. The pale bird of a
woman who had been at Brandauer's bedside sat down next to
me.

"No intrusion meant," she said. "But you're a friend of my
husband's, are you not?"

She spoke with a foreign accent and sounded like a transla-
tion and that was how I learned the whole secret subtext of
Brandauer's story, a wife and a son kept hidden in Italy all
those years. Her name was Francesca and her son was Mauro.
She was content, she quickly made it clear, to be Brandauer's
background story. Her son had been left with friends in Genoa.
But she'd sought me out because she wanted the world to know
that her husband was honest and responsible and had always
taken care of them even during his long absences.

"What can I do?" I asked.

What came through at last was that, to her, I was Brandauer's
friend the journalist. He must have shown her the Interview in
The Paris Review, so many years ago.

"Tell me," I said, "did he have this heart problem for a long
time?"

"He found out about nine years ago," she said. "His whole
family had the heart—but his started then."

"I see." I don't know what I saw, but nine years ago was
when he'd left his little room to start teaching.

"And you will tell how he was good and a good father, too.
Not just a writer. You will write about this for the world."

I was too exhausted to set her straight, too miserable at how
awfully ill, white of face and starved Brandauer looked. Yes, I
would tell the whole world, I said, I would tell how fine and
honest he was. What the hell! The comedy of misunderstanding
had begun with a generation of students excitedly greeting
Brandauer and, instead, getting Kafka. Let it end—if it was ending—with a redundant, foolish promise. I had no means of addressing any large public to tell them about this man who was,
indeed, so fine and honest that he sometimes seemed a visitor
from a different place. She kissed me on the cheek and left an
odor of dried flowers, vaguely foreign.

. . .

"What I couldn't tell Penny was . . ." He started on this as soon as I was at his bedside again, as if we'd been talking all along. ". . . she couldn't see it . . . that putting it together was the main thing . . . all the big chunks of life she had . . . all the struggles, the pleasures . . . you need a line, I told her . . . a line of words . . . just like a poet you need a line . . . then the people and the lives and what they do to each other . . . then they can go into the line and find their beat . . . But . . ."

"Listen," I said. "How do you feel? Do you want the nurse?"

I waited. He seemed to have forgotten I was there. Then, very softly:

". . . *Enough . . . and not one bit more. That's what counts.*" He laughed. It was like a cough with an edge of amusement. "*And then, even a little less.*"

"Isn't that what you've been telling *me* all this time?" I felt like an idiot dealing myself in. It seemed to me that he nodded.

"But don't forget," I said. "For the panther, enough is a whole lot of bloody meat."

Brandauer smiled. "Did I tell you how I envied the p-p-p-p- . . ."

This time I interrupted and supplied the word. "Yes, the panther," I said. It sounded impatient and mean spirited. I felt badly that I had not let him finish his own stammer and I began a burst of words. "I've always loved the double ending: when the Hunger Artist dies after whispering that the public should not admire him: . . . *I have to fast, I can't help it. . . . I couldn't find the food I liked. If I had found it, believe me, I would have made no fuss and stuffed myself like you or anyone else . . .*" I was weirdly proud at being able to quote so much from memory. Foolishly, as if that meant I understood it, understood Brandauer, our confused friendship, my eternally unfinished life.

"Then they clear out the cage," I went on, "And put in the young panther. *The food he liked was brought to him without hesitation by the attendants . . . his noble body, furnished almost to the bursting point with all that it needed seemed to carry freedom around with it, too . . ."* I was quoting more and more, in desperation, watching Brandauer fade away from me on the rumpled pillow. After all the years of his classes it was like a final examination I'd suddenly set for myself. I spoke the ending.

"Somewhere in his jaws it seemed to lurk; and the joy of life streamed with such ardent passion from his throat that for the onlookers it was not easy to stand the shock of it. But they braced themselves, crowded round the cage and did not want ever to move away."

"Bravo, my friend," Brandauer said, although I'd done nothing more than quote the published ending. Perhaps I'd passed.

"I wonder," he said, "if panthers have heart attacks . . . all that red meat . . ." At the corner of my eye I saw his wife start to move towards us.

"Listen," he said, already fainter.

"Yes . . ."

"That thing you wrote—the gift—a poem about dieting . . ."

"Yes."

"Well," Brandauer paused and a shadow of an old smile showed up on his lips. "It doesn't matter so much what you eat," he said. *"What matters is what eats you. That's what . . ."* Apparently he could not manage the last *counts;* the last summation left hanging in the empty hospital air. He grew silent and the silence became sleep and the sleep became death but not until the next morning while I was turning my rented Ford onto its side at the entrance to the freeway.

"What did he mean, that stuff about the Panther?" Penny asked.

"Who, Kafka?" I was in a teasing mood. My ribs had stopped aching, though they were still strapped. The cuts on my forehead had healed. I'd survived.

"Brandauer, I mean," she said. "You know damned well."

"I think the talk about the Panther was for himself," I told her. "There was something else for you and a few things for me."

She laughed. Not an angry note in her scale these days. "He's preaching at me from beyond the you-know-what."

"Talking, maybe—preaching, no!"

I was determined to be serious for as long as possible, determined to hold out for as long as possible against the white dress, the soft skin, the shining pearls sliding across the summer suntan, the sweet citrus scent of perfume. I told her what Brandauer had said about the trick of just enough and no more —about the line of words, though I couldn't get it exactly as he'd said it.

We were in Middletown, Connecticut in July, a hot and sticky time in the Connecticut River Valley. The Wesleyan Writer's Conference, like so many, was scheduled for a hellish time of the year. I'd called her to deliver Brandauer's message and to ask her if she was still coming to the Conference even though our original reason for enrolling was now cremated, the ashes buried in a cemetery in Italy.

And here we were, wearing our name tags but skipping the standard get-acquainted cocktail party in favor of our own dinner. We sat at the bar waiting for a table and I told her about the accident, about the turbaned Doctor Singh at the Emergency Room, about how he had ignored my Brandauer grief and blamed the crash on vertigo and weakness due to my crazy up-and-down dieting.

Tonight, I said, was definitely to be up. The place I'd picked was famous for its lamb, its fresh vegetables and its strawberry soufflé dessert which had to be ordered hours before dinner. I'd done that and with it a rich '79 Chateau LaLagune.

"No Hunger Artist you," Penny said. "Do you think he knew you'd hunt me up and deliver his last words?"

"I don't know. He didn't have too much breath left and he knew it. He was just getting all sorts of stuff out. Last Chance Saloon stuff."

"I kept thinking he'd drop that damned story. Pay attention to something else. It doesn't matter anymore." She laughed. "God, we fought it out in rain and heat and snow."

"What *were* you two fighting about?"

"I thought I knew—I wanted him to pay attention to me and my life—my love affairs in purple prose . . . yes, I know that's what they were, now . . . I wanted him to love my stories as if they were parts of my body, of my self. Then, when that didn't happen and he stuck to his guns about making me imagine everything as if it was new, then I wanted him to love me and my body as if we were my writing. But he wouldn't do that, either. All he would do was tell me to cool out my prose, cool out my life . . . cool . . . God!"

"Was that about when you asked me if I wanted to make love to you in a blizzard in North Dakota or somewhere? I figured that for a ricochet."

"Did I do that?" It was the first time I'd ever seen the southern steamroller embarrassed. I did not remind her about the "Fuck you" that had followed. "I was so pissed off I told *Time* magazine all sorts of bullshit about him."

"I noticed."

"There's too much air-conditioning in here," she said. But the maître d' quickly rescued her from embarrassment and chill.

Dinner was phenomenal—the lamb pink and juicy and the soufflé hot and runny. Her big theory came out over the coffee.

"If you hadn't called me I would have dug *you* up."

"Oh?"

"I had to tell you what I'd figured out about Brandauer. When I found out about the heart attack it threw me. When I stopped crying I read the full obit and a light bulb went off." She leaned over the debris of dinner, intent in the old way, almost angry again. *"He knew he was going to die,"* she said. "The paper said he'd had a history of heart trouble for almost a decade. It explains everything."

She was in no mood for my interruption or disclaimer. "His picking that particular story and living the way he did, the way he gave only the minimum necessary to life, and *everything* to writing."

"Because he knew his clock was ticking so fast, you mean?"

"Don't forget," she said solemnly, "The only piece that you could call furniture in the Hunger Artist's cage was a clock."

"My God," I said. "You're picking up where he left off."

"That's why Brandauer kept teaching that story. It was his anthem." She wiped some pink from her lips, soufflé or lipstick I couldn't tell.

"That's not all," she said.

"Hold it," I said. "He could just as easily have gone the other way. You know—live all you can—that Henry James stuff . . . seize the *carpe* . . . *carpe* the *diem* . . ."

"Ha, ha," she said. "Listen, I've got something I want to read to you." I'd never read or heard anything she'd written. She pulled out some crumpled papers and over the coffee cups and bread crumbs she read this:

Krakauer: a story

Word was out that Krakauer was leaving his cage. After fourteen years of writing private astonishments, he was going into the public world to teach. This was an event worthy of comment in media as disparate as *The New York Times Magazine* (with its oddly inappropriate ads of young women in their sensual underwear) and *Critical Inquiry,* with its puritanically ordered columns of dense text.

Would he teach hermaneutics and literature—the Real Stuff— or just Creative Writing, the Fake Stuff? Would he be skinny, emaciated from years of isolation in Genoa, making and remaking sentences, *The New York Times* wondered? Would he be distracted from the larger concerns of The Academy by the sophomoric demands of students, *Critical Inquiry* wondered?

On a spring day in Seattle, the mystery was dispelled. That first morning Krakauer met with a crowded class of students still wet behind the ears with Seattle rain.

"I will not read any student's stories," he announced, this wraith from the lost land of language. "Instead, I will read 'A Hunger Artist by Franz Kafka.' "

Muted exclamations of pain and thwarted personal ambition. One pale young woman felt her chance at a new life slipping away.

Krakauer was firm. He began to read . . .

It was too damned good; the sentences supple and simple. Better than what I've written here. Tougher, more condensed, cooler; less tangled with the ego of a narrative voice.

"Hey," I said. "I haven't read your other stuff. But you seem to have cooled out. It's very strong, so far."

"I know," she said folding the papers back into her bag. "It's just the beginning."

I decided that such an expansive dinner deserved a cigar and we moved to the terrace.

"Do you mind if I smoke this?"

"Go on. My Daddy smoked cigars."

I touched Penny's cheek and rubbed my hand gently downwards, to see if anything had changed between us. She closed those enormous eyes for a flick of the lids. Her tongue licked a raspberry seed from her upper lip. A tick of time but it told me enough.

"Well," I said. "I guess it's just us, now."

A long sigh, then a grin. "I miss him," she said. "Even more than when he was here."

Melancholy laughter from both of us.

I put my arm around her shoulder and she collapsed against me. I had a story to finish on my desk, that night. It could wait.

In the morning I woke with my head on Penny's gently moving stomach. I felt satisfied and hungry and strange. The night before we'd been a kind of solution for each other. Now it was morning and we could start the natural process of becoming problems for each other. What would we do now with our bodies, our minds, our stories? How would we deal with each other —our anxieties, our appetites? *It doesn't matter what you eat . . . It matters what eats you . . . That's what . . .*

Penny stirred. She got up and went to the bathroom. When she came out I watched her while she performed a morning stretch, warm and lean. Conventional southern young woman that she was, she'd worn a white nightgown to bed, like a bride. The sun shone behind her through the bathroom window and I saw her shape revealed through the fabric of her nightgown, her parted legs an elegant *V* with curly pubic hair, perfectly clear, infinitely mysterious. My desire for her was urgent and stupid, without thought. I had no wish to read her stories, to encounter previous lovers. I wanted to be Opus One. I made love to her as if I wanted to get her inside myself, not the other way around. The exertion stung my strapped ribs and reminded me of my brush with highway death following my final brush with Brandauer. But holding Penny afterwards made me feel safe for the moment. I noticed, for the first time, that her right eye sort of wandered. Fresh details; she would be my newest unfinished story.

Immediately after, she was back at her idée fixe. She sat up straight. "Now, in the morning light," she said, "do you see how it explains everything? He *knew* he was going to die."

I kissed her lips; a faint flavor of raspberry from the night before. "You mean unlike the rest of us."

"Come on. You know what I mean."

"No," I said, implacable, remembering the jaws of the Panther.

Josephine Jacobsen

THE PIER–GLASS

Now that it's behind me, I remember the Regency real pleasantly, but I wouldn't go back there. I don't know why. I suppose because things I hadn't any responsibility for caused me a
sort of strain. I always like things to work out well—when they
don't, I'm the type that feels upset. Ever since I was a small
child I wanted things to go right and was upset when they
didn't. Some people just don't seem to care, if it's not their toe
stepped on.

The Regency was the only real hotel on the island. Guests'
houses like the Hibiscus or the Morne Rouge seem to me more
like boarding houses—no organization, no entertainment at
night. Not that the Regency is that full of laughs, either. A couple of nights a week, a steel band, which, as far as I'm concerned, is pretty much a good loud racket, crab races once a
week, and a beach-barbecue on Sunday night. The beach thing
is pretty—I'll say that, especially if there's a moon, but in the
sand there're all these little tiny ants that can bite something
fierce. Well, that's the Regency.

That whole matter about Cecilene was something that needn't
ever have happened in the first place. What she did really was
outrageous. Mr. Rufus said he had never experienced anything

like it, and he's been in the hotel business almost twenty years. He must be about the same age as my ex, Mr. Hadley, but Mr. Hadley never kept himself up in the way Mr. Rufus has. I'm not absolutely sure about his hair, but there's lots of it (which is more than you could say the last time I saw Mr. Hadley), and it *looks* perfectly natural.

We got on just beautifully, and frankly, I think that could have progressed farther. But I'm pretty sure that anyone who marries Mr. Rufus (he's a widower) will never have ready money equal to my alimony—and it's perfectly typical of Mr. Hadley that that stops the minute I put on a ring and say "I do."

The whole silly thing started one morning when I was on my way to the beach. I say on my way, but actually I hadn't gotten even as far as the Regency station wagon, which ran us down there at ten-thirty and picked us up at twelve-thirty.

The Regency had a very pretty sort of open-air lounge. There's a fountain place, with goldfish in a little pool, and big tubs of hibiscus, and over the columns there is bougainvillea, which is all over the place anyway. It's a very pretty type of lounge, and the staff is all in little red jackets, etc., and with the tile floor and all, it makes a very colorful picture. After having driven all over the island (not that I drive myself in those types of left-hand-drive islands) and seeing the propped-up shacks— with enough dogs and children under them to make you dizzy —people like the staff come from, it must look like Hollywood itself to them.

*Any*way, I had gotten almost as far as the front desk and could see the station wagon half full, when I remembered what I'd forgotten—my beach bag. It was an awful nuisance to go way back, especially with a number of the clientele, including cross old Mr. Ferguson, waiting; but that beach bag had everything whatsoever in it—suncream, towels, sunglasses, paperback—well, I won't go on and on, but you can imagine the morning without it. So back I went. My room was 21—I'm surprised I remember it so well after all the numbers this winter— and there was a sort of straw matting on the hall floor, so you never could hear anybody until they were right at the door.

I opened my door and walked in and I couldn't believe what I saw. I can see it right this minute.

There was a tall mirror by the left-hand wall—one of those in a big standing frame Mr. Rufus told me was a pier glass. The sun, which is really red hot in the middle of the morning, was just pouring in and hitting the mirror—you could hardly look at it. But I looked again, all right, because at first I thought there were two women in the room.

Cecilene was standing right in front of the glass, and she had her right hand stuck out at the end of her arm and was jerking it back and forth like she was flashing a light. And indeed she was, and so was what I had thought was another girl, only she was in the mirror. They looked like twins, but before I thought that, I saw the flash on their fingers was my blue diamond and ruby ring. It was on Cecilene's third finger.

There were so many shiny things it was really peculiar—the ring on her finger and the ring in the mirror, and the white teeth in that couple of dark faces. At this point, I was in the mirror, too.

Well.

Cecilene was the girl that did my room—made the beds, vacuumed, did the bathroom, and turned down the bed at night. We got on just fine, and I will say she was an exceptionally pretty girl, in spite of the color. She had good teeth and one of those great big smiles, and a nice full trim figure. It took me a while to get her name. The locals have a lot of these fancy names—Adrian and Robin, and Geoffry, and Evelyn for men, for heaven's sake. After I got to know her, and commented on her name, she tells me her daddy wanted a boy and was going to name him *Cecil.*

Well. I don't know which of the two of us was the most surprised. She must have been sure I was on my way to the beach, and I hardly expected her to be waving around my diamond and ruby ring.

She clapped both hands to her mouth like she had screamed without meaning to, and then some big tears popped out of her eyes and ran all over her knuckles. She started tugging at the ring, which came off easy, she having thin fingers, and she laid it really carefully on the glass top of the bureau and began saying, "I was only looking! I was only looking! I was only looking!" She must have said it fully ten times in one minute, while I just stood there looking at *her.*

Then she dropped down on her *knees,* of all things—these people like to be very dramatic. "I just want to see, just to look! Just for then! Just for then! I never see it before!"

Well, of course she hadn't seen it, not being around when I wore it. I always lock my stuff up, naturally, but that night I had come in really late from the Regency bar, where I'd been having a very interesting talk with Mr. Rufus (what you can't learn from a hotelier's experience!), and I hadn't noticed that ring left out.

"For heaven's sake," I said. "Cut out that nonsense. It won't do you the least bit of good."

She jumped up, and for a minute I really thought she was going to run away.

"You realize," I said to her, "what you've done—taken one of my most valuable pieces of jewelry. Naturally, I have to report this."

"Oh, no no no no no!" She seemed to think that the more often she said something, the better off she'd be. "Don't tell Mr. Rufus! Please, no no no, you don't tell Mr. Rufus!"

Well, it went on like that, back and forth. I'm a very, very good-natured woman, and I don't like hassles, and the girl had been extra polite and obliging, nothing too much trouble. She'd ironed some things for me, and even cleaned some of my shoes that had gotten tar on them, and told me all about her grandmother that she lived with. She called her "my Grand."

I began to think that maybe she *had* just tried on the ring—the kind of thing I bet they do with a scarf or a jacket when no one's around. It was going to be a headache if there was a real rumpus, and I might get one of those uppity, disagreeable kind. And you always feel good when you can do a good deed. I made up my mind I'd let it go. Boy, I don't leave my jewelry laying around like that, so it would be a one-time thing.

But I wasn't going to give her the satisfaction that quick, so I told her she had done a very bad thing behind my back, and

Mr. Rufus should certainly know about it, but I would think it over.

She started all over again about being an honest girl, and all she had wanted, etc., but I told her I was holding up the station wagon, and to go about her business, and I dropped the ring in my jewelry case and locked it, and put the key in my wallet in my beach bag. Her face was so puffy at that point that I wondered what the next-door neighbors would think—a cross old couple who never went to the beach and never wore suitable outfits.

Well, the next morning she came to my door before I had even had my beach robe on, and it was more of the same—how she just wanted to see herself in the mirror with the ring on, what an honest girl, etc., etc.

I told her I *chose* to believe her. She would have it that I promise her never to tell Mr. Rufus. I thought that was undignified and said I wouldn't promise, but then we got into the same thing all over again, and finally (I'd made up my mind the day before anyway) I said all right, and you'd think she'd hit the lottery. Actually, it paid off in spades—there was nothing she wouldn't do, and I really believe she wanted to do the things, because I'd already promised, and she took it really seriously and told me God would reward me, and her Grand would pray for me.

A few days after this she brought me some flying fish, which I had complained about not having. I asked her what on earth was I going to do with a bunch of raw fish, and she said she knew the chef, and that he'd cook them specially for me, and he did, and I had them for dinner that night, and they were perfectly delicious. A few days later, she comes in with three red arum lilies from her Grand's "garden." They are showy but so slick and shiny they never look genuine to me. The next week she brings me some *shells*, for heaven's sake. They were unusual —our beach near the Regency isn't a shell beach—just little bits and pieces. I asked her where she found them, and she told me her Grand walks the whole length of the beach every day. "Why?" I asked her, and it turned out her Grand was one of those old ladies who peddle things on the beach: little baskets covered with shells, and palm frond hats, and sometimes fruit from a basket on their heads (which most people couldn't balance if their life depended on it). It turned out her Grand made candy she peddled, though I can't imagine who bought it, what with the hygiene conditions. She was very high on her Grand being ninety-three, as if she'd won some sort of race. Their ages are confusing. Later after I found out her father and mother were both dead, it seemed as though the old lady must be her great Grand. She never talked to me about her father.

It was about that time I began thinking I would leave the island for the end of the winter and go to some place with more to offer in the way of recreation—maybe Trinidad, or even Caracas. My friendship with Mr. Rufus had gone about as far as I wished. He was getting rather restless, and I certainly wasn't going any further in the relationship. Most of the other guests were rather elderly, or were couples, or had unfriendly natures. One couple I liked from Minneapolis, lovely, refined people, had gone on to Caracas, and that made me think about it.

I went to the beach that morning undecided—that is, between Trinidad and Caracas—and that was the morning I finally saw Cecilene's Grand. I never would have known, but just as we were getting out of the beach wagon and Geoffry was getting out the beach chairs and cushions, he said, "There go Cecilene's Grand. She there, just passing."

For ninety-three, I suppose she wasn't too bad, but Lord, she looked a hundred. She had a cotton piece tied over her head under her basket—I bet she was bald—and her face was so wrinkled it looked pleated and put me in mind of one of those Fortuné dresses. I would have said something to her, but by the time I got out, she had plodded on up the beach. She was so bent over she might have been looking for those shells, though there weren't any near there, and even though she was walking on the slick part of the beach near the tide, she wasn't making much time.

Well, I spent the rest of the morning deciding what I was going to do.

There were only five in our group—a German couple who couldn't speak a word of English and a disagreeable woman from Cape Cod who always had her nose stuck in a book whenever you saw her. It seems to me if she wants to read she should do it at home. I decided to speak to Mr. Rufus that afternoon. And in a way, it pleased me how he took on. When he had pinned me down, that I could enjoy a little more exciting nightlife than steel bands and seeing crabs race, he said that he'd like me to meet some business friends of his, and he'd like to give me a special little dinner party on Saturday night. He said we could have it on the outside terrace, where it wasn't sandy. I made up my mind that it would change my plans, but I was intrigued. You never can tell.

I was really curious to know what the friends would be like. I was sure they would be refined people, but they might all be couples.

The general dress at the Regency didn't have too much to be said for it. You couldn't come into the dining room, even for breakfast, in beachwear, and that was about it. After the first night, I had let my really formal eveningwear hang right there in the closet.

But I really thought, after Mr. Rufus told me, that this came under special occasions, and I made up my mind to wear the form-fitting black satin with the blue sequin appliqué, and just my diamond heart as ornament. That heart had been my engagement gift from Mr. Hadley. That heart meant a lot to me; those diamonds were gorgeous.

That was really where the last part of the thing started.

I hadn't worn my diamond heart once, and this night I didn't get it out until I'd done my face, put on my hose and my slippers, and stepped into my dress, which, I will say, looked stunning. Thank God, it zipped up on the side.

Well, I did not get my diamond heart out because it was not there. I couldn't believe it. I kept turning things over—the jewel box has three little drawers. But. It. Was. Not. There.

I knew perfectly well I had brought it, because I had gone back and forth in my mind about whether to bring it at all, and then decided at the last minute, yes, because after all, you never know. And the very minute I realized it wasn't there, I realized where it was. Cecilene had it, and there was absolutely no doubt about that. Not one other human being had been in that room. There was absolutely no way around it. I kept the thing locked up, but admit I am sometimes a careless person late in the evening, as I was when I'd left out my blue diamond and ruby ring. But I remember perfectly the moment I decided to bring that diamond heart after all.

I guess the main thing I felt was furious. I felt like a fool. Here I'd caught the girl with my ring, and now she'd picked out the single most valuable thing Mr. Hadley had given me and walked off with it. I really couldn't get my breath for being so angry. It *would* be the diamond heart—just the sort of thing Cecilene would choose, with her dramatizing.

Well, I really couldn't get my breath for anger. And here I was, due at a dinner party in ten minutes.

I couldn't think about what to do. If I called Mr. Rufus right that minute, he would be so upset it would ruin the whole dinner party, the whole thing would go sour, and we wouldn't have a chance to discuss it. I might not be staying much longer, but one thing I do know about a fine hotelier is that he does not care to have thefts by his employees discussed in public. On the other hand, I doubted I could swallow food, and I'd have to detain Mr. Rufus afterward, which might be suspicious. Well, what I did was phone him right that minute—and I really controlled myself very well—and I said I wanted to have a word with him after dinner. Goodness only knows what he thought.

At any other time, it would have been an elegant dinner, but I was so purely furious that I can scarcely remember anything about it, except that the beef was really tasty. There was one specially pleasant couple, lovely wealthy people who had a house on a hill overlooking the harbor. Since I was so upset, I had a couple of drinks beyond my customary quota, and though I'm not strong on wine, the wine was very good, I imagine. But my stomach was seething, and I sat there in my really nice dress with a dinky golden cat—solid gold, but still—where my heart should have been.

Finally—I thought it would never happen—I got Mr. Rufus alone. I beat about no bushes. "Hubert," I said (last week he had insisted on "Hubert"), "it pains me to say this, but Cecilene has now stolen my diamond heart, worth God knows what." (I never pressed Mr. Hadley for what it cost, but I had a good idea from the insurance.)

I explained the whole thing, the ring and the mirror, and Hubert was really sweet about it. He said it was basically his fault, though I had read right on my bedroom door that unless you took them to the safe, the Regency took no responsibility for your jewels or cash. He kept saying he really blamed himself, but when I said that was ridiculous and what a ninny I had been about the ring, he said, "No, no. Do you know why Cecilene lost her last job, before she came here?"

I said no, of course, and I had a feeling I knew what he was going to say, and he said it. "For stealing," he said.

Well, I was stunned—that he would have taken her on, I mean. "Food," he said. "She got caught stealing food. The Abernathys, the people she worked for, suspected it, and they finally caught her flat, as she was leaving the house. She had cristofine in one pocket and half a loaf of bread in the other. She had a fine job there, with good pay, as things go here. She carried on so to me that I fell for it—hard luck story, of course. I had already heard about it—the Abernathys were disgusted, and they spread it about pretty well. They're fair, but very very firm. I shouldn't have taken her on, of course. But she isn't exposed to food here, and she's a good worker—even more willing to work when I took her on after that. A name as a thief doesn't help a girl on a small island like this."

He really seemed so upset that I felt bad for him, though I was still fit to be tied. He kept repeating how she knew she'd be watched, and he'd had no trouble until this terrible thing . . . "Oh, Mrs. Hadley—Irma—why didn't you tell me about the ring? For heaven's sake!"

I tried to explain to him that good-hearted people make mistakes—look at him. He wanted to know, was it insured.

"Of course it was," I said, "but you talk like I'm not going to get it back?"

After a second he said, "How are you going to?"

Well! I hadn't thought about that, but I said couldn't we have her house searched?

He said, "Well, that wouldn't take very long, Irma. But you realize that's a tricky situation. There are people among the locals who can get very nasty about certain things, and I run this hotel, on this island. We could try to catch her wearing it, but I can tell you that by this time, it's in Charlotte Amalie or Trinidad. She'd never wear it in a million years. Your best bet is your insurance."

I was so furious I'd almost forgotten. We had a night cap on that, and I felt a little better, but not much. It's really upsetting to have your good disposition trampled on.

"Well, she won't find a job on this island," said Hubert, "if that's any comfort. Three times is out. With her looks, Trinidad should be the job." I felt the way Hubert said this was rather gross. "Before she's fired, do you want to tell her what you think of her?"

"I don't ever want to set eyes on her again," I said.

And I didn't. Lay eyes on her, I mean. I threw out those shells in the trash. I couldn't do anything about the arum lilies or, naturally, the flying fish.

The new girl was named Esmeralda, and though I've no complaint against her, she was, as far as I'm concerned, as ugly as sin. I couldn't help wanting to know what had become of Cecilene, who could certainly live off her money like a princess, if she wasn't scared to wave it around. I knew there was a big grapevine, like nothing on earth. Hubert had told me, but I could figure that out for myself in a place like this.

One morning when that ugly face was looking at me over a pile of fluffy towels, I couldn't stand it any more. "Esmeralda," I said, "did you ever know a girl named Cecilene, used to work here?"

"No ma'am," she said right away.

"Do you know anyone who knows her?" I said. "Is she working here on the island?"

She just went on hanging the towels on the racks. Then when she got ready to leave, she said through the open door, "I think she go away. Someone think she in Trinidad; I don't know she is where."

That was that. I never got any further.

This island is really funny. I mean, things are different. The Regency is the best place, and as I say, it's fixed up to be really nice. And yet, with just that little run to the beach, where the road goes round a curve, just off there to your right, there is what they call the Old People's Homes, though I'd say it's the Poor House for all intents and purposes. These really old women sit on the little porch, I guess all day, and there's one old man on the men's porch who waves when the station wagon goes by. Of course we wave back, except maybe a new person who's surprised. You wouldn't think it would be that close to the Regency, but that's just typical—a gorgeous garden, really elegant, and around the next curve under a palm tree, a bunch of trash. No hygienic conscience whatsoever.

But the really strange thing is, there's this small graveyard right opposite the porches—I wouldn't say fifty yards away; ten or twelve graves so far (though there was another yesterday—you could tell by the raw earth). There are little wooden crosses, but the weird thing is the flowers. With all the stuff growing around here, the ones on the graves are *cellophane.* All sorts of colors, mainly yellow and red. Maybe they just like to have it done once and for all, or don't like it fading, or maybe they just think it looks better. Big roses and lilies, cellophane, like they were floating on the dust. The beach itself is gorgeous, but the people on the porches might as well be a mile away, though they can certainly hear the sounds . . . The waves here are really small, but they make some sort of sound all the time.

I can rise above things; I've really had to. But I did watch to see if I could see Cecilene's grandmother on the beach with her candy. I really didn't want to meet her, though, that old woman in shame. I'd only seen her the one time, so it's a wonder I knew her when I saw her next. You have to drive really slow on the road down to the beach, at least you *should.* But Geoffry never heard of that, in spite of complaints. Like those calypsos, loud enough to break your ears. Some guests would say, really nicely, "Would you please turn that off?" and he'd do it, and the next morning it would ruin your ears again. Anyway, he had slowed down, and just as we passed the women on the Old People's porch, I thought the next minute, that was her grandmother! But the look was different, somehow. Frankly, I stared, and I was perfectly sure that it was the same old woman without the candy, and staring straight ahead at the cellophane lilies as if she'd never seen them.

When we pulled up at the beach, I fussed with my beach bag and was the last one out, and I said to Geoffry before he got back in, "Wasn't that Cecilene's Grand, right there on the porch?"

Geoffry said, "Yes, ma'am. She be there a week now."

I was getting a question together when Geoffry said, "She had a stroke and so she don't know where she is. They can't tell she that so she understand."

Well, I thought, as he got in the station wagon, she's not the first Grand to suffer from a granddaughter's doings.

The Regency's pool was really quite nice, but it was all people lying around greasing themselves. Not that you didn't have to do that, but at the beach there was at least some sort of action— the old women coming along with things on their heads to sell (and I will say, they didn't really bother you when you said no), and the conch man coming along with a big heavy bag of shells (he was really a sight, with red dredlocks, a Rastafarian, but he turned out to be harmless), and quite often, launches from the cruise ships that stood there outside the harbor, which was usually too small. Lots of Germans, and lots of Americans too, and sometimes actually Russians. The majority of the women had very large rears, really unpleasantly so, especially for bikinis. I don't know if the locals—the men (not many women seem to come), who seem to have waists like Scarlett O'Hara—thought these were sort of the flags of the countries. What you can't see on the beach!

Well, it really took me days to get over the whole enchilada. My insurance company was very nice about it, and I knew I could get another diamond heart, but I began to wonder if something else might not be a little more desirable. After all, it had been Mr. Hadley's idea, not mine.

Three of Hubert's dinner guests were really nice to me, and some bridge and dinners came out of it . . . But I don't know whether it was the upset to my nervous system, or the fact that I

had really been getting bored anyway. Hubert had finally come
a step further, and when he found there was really no future, he
stopped all the nice little attentions, and I finally made a reser-
vation at the Caracas Hilton. That should really have been the
end of the whole stupid story. But the important part is, look
before you leap, and reason things out really well. And that's
what I—knock wood—had the chance to do.

I was due to leave the Regency on a Tuesday morning, and I
wanted to pack before retiring Monday night, so I wouldn't be
rushed. I had gotten out all my bags—two big ones, and the
little green overnight bag—and laid them on the beds. It's so
easy to pack when you don't have to choose and are just going
to take everything. It was the Monday night crab-racing night
(which I'm good and sick of), and I could hear the screams, and
the drum crashes for the winner, through the open window. The
air smells really good at night here.

I filled the two big suitcases, after deciding on my traveling
costume, but the little green one held just overnight things, and
I left that empty. The quilted lining was a little rucked up at the
bottom, and I felt a little sharp lump in the zip-up side pocket. I
stuck my hand in, and . . . Well.

What it was, was my diamond heart. I really thought I must
be crazy. I just looked at it winking in my hand. It was more
like finding a snake in an Easter basket.

I just dropped down on the foot of the bed and stared at that
thing. How *could* it have been there, I said to myself. Someone
must have *put* it there. Then I remembered the whole thing—
how I'd decided not to take it, and then decided to take it after
every other earthly thing was packed away, and stuck it in that
little zip-up to put it in my jewelry box when I unpacked. And
it had been there the whole time, in the dark.

Well, I was really upset—all that fuss about my insurance
company, and Hubert—let alone Cecilene. Well, it just couldn't
have been more unpleasant. After I got my box out and put that
heart in the lower drawer, I went to bed. But I was just sick
about what I was going to have to go through the next morning.
I didn't even see how I was going to make my plane.

I tried to figure out how to put it to Hubert and the insurance company; but the worst part was having to back down before Cecilene. Then I started to wonder how on earth I'd get *hold* of Cecilene. I couldn't even talk to her grandmother, and I knew Hubert didn't even really know where she was. Trinidad is a really big place.

The whole thing depressed me, so it really went to my stomach. Finally, I took a Seconal, but I woke in spite of that. Maybe because the moon had gotten so bright. But *any*way, it was as though something good had occurred in my sleep. Like my good angel had visited me. Instead of being really upset, and also confused, my mind had settled to good sense, and that brought me calm. It was like my mind had sorted things out while I was asleep.

I realized that actually I had nothing to do with events. I wasn't responsible for Cecilene putting on my jewelry; I certainly wasn't responsible for her stealing food. I had leaned over backwards and never said one word to Hubert until my diamond heart vanished. Cecilene had borrowed my jewelry after she had lost her job for stealing. If there had never been any consequences, she might have gone on and on, turning into a full-time thief. Hubert was certainly better off without that possibility on his mind.

What I hadn't really solved in my sleep was my nice insurance company. I knew that required really careful thought later, but the funny thing was that before I *finally* got back to sleep, I remembered a movie I saw (I could not for the life of me remember the name). A man who worked in a bank, and was mad at it for some reason, kept putting tiny amounts of money *into* the bank, that they couldn't account for, and in some way this ruined the whole bank. I remember they had to keep people working at night to try to get things straight, and as I recall, the bank was actually ruined.

When I applied for my insurance, as far as I was concerned, my diamond heart had been stolen, and that was the Lord's truth. Now all those gears would have to be thrown in reverse, so to speak, and that would be very unpleasant for them. And also, if something of mine did subsequently get stolen, it would lead to a very unpleasant atmosphere. It was really very complicated, and I decided it needed later thought. You can't think matters like that out on a plane to Caracas.

I thought about sending a gift to the grandmother after I got to Caracas. At least I knew where *she* was. But I didn't even know her Christian name, let alone any other, and anyway, what type of gift can you give to anyone who spends her time looking at cellophane lilies?

I think the whole thing had thoroughly upset my nerves. I am very open to being upset, and harboring scruples. But I guess it's the physical things that make for problems.

I really must have gotten myself wrought up, fussing around in bed, trying to get back to sleep. Because the last time my poor tired eyes popped open, the moon was really very very bright on the pier glass, and for a second, it was like two girls were in the glass, jerking their hands back and forth and grinning at each other to beat the band. Just for a second.

What you can't see in mirrors!

Steven Schwartz

MADAGASCAR

This is a story I know so well.

My father, who is twenty-one, is on his way home from finding food for his family. He has traded a gold brooch for a bottle of milk, some vegetables, and a little meat. With his blue eyes and blond hair, my father is the only one in the family who has any chance to pass for gentile on the streets. He makes sure to sit on a public bench, to pick out a paper from the trash and look comfortable, then go on. Among the many edicts against Jews—no traveling in motor cars, no leaning out windows, no using balconies open to the street, no going outside after dark—is one that forbids them to sit on park benches.

On the way home he takes another chance, meeting his fiancée in South Amsterdam. Before the deportations started they were to be married; now they must wait until the war ends, each of them hidden in different areas of the city.

After dark when he returns to the apartment cellar where his father, mother, and sister hide, he sees the Gestapo drive up. It is May 26, 1943. Tomorrow he will learn that the Great Raid has taken away all the remaining Jews, those in rest homes, in mental institutions, in orphanages, those too sick to walk, those who have cooperated with the Germans thinking it would spare them. Even the entire Jewish Council will be shipped to the labor camps. Now he knows nothing, only that he must avoid the house, that if he is caught out after curfew he will be imprisoned or shot. He steps into a bakery where the baker—a gentile though trusted friend of the family—offers to hide my father. If someone has informed on the family and the Gestapo do not find all the members, the baker knows they will search the whole block; they have been through here before. They will check the back room, the bins of flour, the attic above. They will tap the floor and walls for any hollow spaces. But, ironically, they will not check the ovens.

The baker tells my father to climb into an oven no longer in use. At first my father resists. He is afraid. Afraid he will die in there. But there is no other way. The Gestapo will not think to look in such an obvious yet unlikely place.

My father crawls in. The sirens stop. His family is taken away to Majdanek, never to return. He lives in the oven until the end of the war, coming out every two hours when business has slowed sufficiently so that he may stretch. Some days the baker stays so busy that my father must be inside for three, four, and once even six hours. Without room to turn over or extend his legs, he remains curled up in a ball. On one occasion, much to his humiliation, he must go to the bathroom in his pants. The baker and his wife kindly provide him with a long apron while his trousers are washed in back. In the oven, he makes up waltzes in his head and has long, complex discussions with himself, marshaling arguments for each side, as to which of the two Strausses, father or son, is the true Waltz King, despite the son being known by the title. He re-creates each note of their compositions and discusses the works with a panel of experts, but always delays the final vote another day so he may weigh the evidence more carefully and reconsider the merits of "Joy and Greetings," "Lorelei-Rheinklange," "Shooting Stars," and a hundred others.

After the war my father will listen to music in a high-backed chair. The record player during my childhood, a hi-fi, will be near a whisper in volume, perhaps the loudness at which he originally heard the melodies in his head. When I come into the room, he does not mind being disturbed, but asks me to sit and listen with him. I am ten. "Ah, now," he says raising his hand when the French horns begin to play. "Our favorite part." I do not know if "our" includes me or someone else or if he just speaks of himself in the plural. Soon he closes his eyes, smiles, and extends his hand for mine. Although we are sitting down, me at his feet, our arms sway together, my father waltzing with me from this position. Softly he releases my hand, tells me I have good timing and to remember practice practice practice. Mastering the clarinet is no easy task—even for a bright ten-year-old. He rises from his chair, pulls down the sides of his coat—on Sunday afternoons he wears a jacket and tie at home—returns the record to its sleeve, closes the lid of the hi-fi, and stands with his hands behind his back for a few seconds as though making a silent prayer. Then he says, "Ephram, would you like to accompany me on a walk in the park?" I have my coat on within five seconds.

In ninth grade, I am caught shoplifting. I steal a silver pen from a drugstore. I am taken to the police station in Haverford, the small town where we live outside of Philadelphia and where my father teaches European history at Haverford College. My mother is in New York visiting her sisters, so I must call my father. The department secretary informs me that he should return from class within the hour.

"Are you at home, Ephram?"

"I'm at the police station," I say, shocked by my own admission. Perhaps I want to confess right away and get it over with, not hide the shame I feel, or perhaps I want to boast.

Without comment, she makes a note of my situation and promises she will get the message to my father immediately.

While I wait for my father in front of the sergeant's desk, on a plastic chair of a faded aqua color, I think how I've wanted to succeed at something, most recently sports. The basketball game I made sure my father attended, positive I would be put in since we were playing a much weaker team, we wound up only narrowly winning, coming from behind. I sat on the bench the whole time. "Very stirring match," my father said afterward, walking me to the car, his arm around me. He knew I felt bad, of course, but there was nothing he could do, nothing I could do.

I lack the speed and agility to be first string; and by this season I've lost interest in sports, don't even try out for the team, and instead have fallen in with a group of kids who hang out at the edge of the parking lot, wear pointed shoes with four-inch Cuban heels, pitch quarters during lunch, comb their hair in ducktails (a style that requires me to sleep with my hair parted the opposite way so that the curls will straighten out by morning), and who generally get in trouble for everything from smoking cigarettes to belching "The Star-Spangled Banner" in back of Spanish class. It is 1964. School has become intolerable.

My father soon comes to the police station. I am released into his custody and we leave the old armory building of massive, buff sandstone, me in a blue corduroy coat that says Haverford Panthers, my father with his walking stick and tweed overcoat, a cream-colored scarf tucked under his chin. He puts his hand lightly behind me and I involuntarily sink back against his open palm, no easy feat going down a flight of steps. I keep expecting him to ask me what happened. Though I know he won't raise his voice, he never does, let alone physically punish me, I anticipate a lecture, as is his custom when I've misbehaved, which to be honest has not happened all that often. An only child, I have learned how to fulfill my parents' wishes better than my own. They have little reason to find fault with me, so trained am I in the most subtle of ways—a raised eyebrow from my father, a frown from my mother—to find fault with myself first.

"Why don't we walk a little bit, Ephram." We stop at the post office. My father buys a roll of stamps and some airmail envelopes for letters to Holland. We have no relatives over there anymore but he keeps a regular correspondence with friends and some members of the Amsterdam Symphony. Before the war he, too, had studied the clarinet and planned to become a professional musician, a source of conflict with his father who wanted my father to have a career in business like himself. When I was younger I always eagerly awaited the letters from Holland so I could steam off the stamps for my collection.

We sit down on a bench in front of the post office. It is December but the sun is bright enough for us to rest a moment outdoors.

I am prepared to apologize, no longer able to stand my father's silence. At the same time I want to explain that school offers me nothing but hypocrisy, lies, false values, and mush-headed teachers who haven't read a book themselves in years, and that I know this frustration has something to do with what I've done. But before I have the chance, he says he wants to tell me something about the war, one subject in which I am intensely interested because I always hope he will speak, as he rarely does, of his own experience.

"You may not know," he says, "that Hitler had several plans for the Jews. The camps came much later, after he had ruled out other possibilities, such as selling Jews to different countries. He also considered sending the Jews to the island of Madagascar. He wanted to permanently exile them there. Not destroy them, just isolate them on a remote island. This was to be his answer to the Jewish question. I have imagined many times what this situation may have been. I see the beaches, I see the shops, I see the clothes my mother and father wear there—light fabrics, colorful, soft cotton, a little lace on holidays. The sea is blue, the houses white. My mother does not like the heat, but my father welcomes it every morning by doing calisthenics on the balcony. They have settled here, done well, as Jews will do most anywhere, even in Nazi Madagascar. But you see how childish this is of me, don't you? That I want there to be a refuge in the midst of such undeniable evil. Perhaps it is why I decided to study history after the war. I have the liberty to make sense of the many possible pasts historians can always imagine—but the duty to choose only one. Sometimes I fail to honor my task because it is too unbearable. I do not think you are in a very happy period of your life now, Ephram. We are perhaps letting you down, your mother and I. I hope, though, that you will see I am far from perfect and struggle to make meaning of things as much as you do. It is my wish only that you will not harm others in the process, nor assault your own dignity. Leave yourself a small measure of respect in reserve. Always. You see, even in my worst memories—and I know nothing that can be worse for a man than to remember his mother and father and sister while he walks free in the world—even here I have left myself an escape to Madagascar. So allow yourself the same opportunity and do not think so poorly of your own promise that you must succumb to the disgrace of crime. You are bright, imaginative, resourceful. Surely there is a way out of whatever hell it is you too experience. I do not doubt that you can do better than this."

Chastened, I sit in silence with my father while we drive home. After his intercession, charges will be dropped by the drugstore. My mother learns nothing of the incident, and I soon separate from the group of misfits I've joined earlier. I also give up the clarinet when I discover—as my teacher agrees—that I feel nothing for the instrument.

My college roommate freshman year is named Marshall X. Tiernan. I have chosen to go to a small liberal arts college in Ohio that is not too far from Haverford but far enough so I feel I'm leaving home. Every Tuesday afternoon he asks if I can vacate the room for three hours and fifteen minutes (exactly) so he can listen to music.

"I don't mind if you listen while I'm here," I tell him.

He shakes his head. He must have privacy. Marshall X. Tiernan, reedy and tall as elephant grass but not nearly so uncultivated, has an enormous collection of classical records that takes up one quarter of our room. He is studying to be an engineer. Unlike the rest of the men in my dorm, who in the fall of 1968 have grown their hair long and wear patched jeans and army surplus coats, Marshall dresses in Arrow shirts with button-down collars and keeps a well-inked pen protector in his pocket. He has an unfortunate stutter and does not socialize beyond a fellow engineering student he knows from home. We have a respectful relationship, but I can't say that Marshall is a friend.

I agree to leave him alone on Tuesday afternoons, but one time I come back early. I have forgotten some notes that I need to take with me to the library. Expecting to hear music outside the door, I hear nothing and decide to go in. On the bed, with large padded earphones, is Marshall, his thin body rigid as slate. He sees me but does not acknowledge that I am here. His clothes, the sheets, everything is drenched with sweat. His legs tremble, a kind of seizure starts. When the record ends, a composition by Satie, Marshall sits up, quickly strips the bed, throws the sheets in the closet (Tuesday the maids bring new linen), changes his clothes, and returns to his desk to study.

We do not discuss the incident.

Shortly afterward he drops out of school and moves home. I have the privacy of my own room, a lucky situation that enables me to spend time alone with Jessica, whom I've met at an antiwar meeting. One night while I am telling her, with some amusement I am sorry to say, about Marshall X. Tiernan, I suddenly stop. Jessica says later the look on my face is as if I've seen a ghost, for that is what happens. I suddenly see—no, *feel*— a twenty-one-year-old man curled painfully in a baker's oven, his body kept alive by music.

Thanksgiving vacation my sophomore year I bring Jessica home with me. Several years older than I and a senior in anthropology, she helps my mother with Thanksgiving dinner, talks at length with my father who retains a lifelong interest in Margaret Mead, and makes such a positive impression on them both that my mother whispers to me as we are about to leave for the airport, *"She's a jewel."*

But at school I sink into a profound depression. My grades plummet and although Jessica tries to stand by me, I manage to chase even her away. She finds her own apartment yet continues to call every day to check up on me. I become more withdrawn, however, and after a while I ask her to stop phoning. I watch television and eat chocolate donuts, drink milk from the carton and stare at the dark smudge marks my lips leave on the spout.

My father appears one afternoon, a surprise visit, he says. I know by the look on his face, though, that he has come because of Jessica. I burst into tears when I see him.

"What has happened, Ephram?" he says.

But I don't know what has happened, only that I can no longer study, I don't care about school and have no chance of passing finals; I don't care if I flunk out.

"Your mother is very worried. She wanted to come with me but I thought it best if I came alone. Is there anything I can do to help you? Is there something wrong in school, you don't like your courses, the pressure perhaps of too many hours . . ."

"I haven't been to class in weeks," I say. "I can't go. Even a trip to the store is overwhelming." I start to cry again. "I want to go home. I want to go back with you."

"But what will you do back there?" my father says. "There is nothing at home for you now. You have your studies here, your friends."

I look at my father. As always, he is dressed neatly, and warmly, a blue blazer and gray slacks, a wool vest under his coat. Meanwhile, my apartment remains a mess, dishes in the sink, clothes everywhere, my hair unwashed.

"I'll find a job, I'll work and make money."

"And live at home?"

"Yes, what's wrong with that?"

My father pauses. "I don't know. I would think that you'd enjoy the freedom of living on your own."

"I have freedom and privacy at home. You've never told me what to do or when to come in. I'm not happy here."

"But Ephram, changing the place you live will not solve your problems. You need to get to the bottom of this."

"I don't care, I just want to go home! Can't you understand that?" I am almost screaming. "I have to go back. I can't make it here!"

For the rest of the winter, I work in a bubble gum factory near Philadelphia. It is miserable, but the more miserable the better because I feel as if I deserve the punishment of tedious, demeaning work for failing in school. I am paid minimum wage, $1.85 an hour. So much sugar hangs in the air—we throw bags of it into a mixing contraption resembling the gigantic maw of a steam shovel—that the people who have worked for years at the factory have lost many of their teeth. The gum itself comes out on long (and unsanitary) splintered boards that I carry to racks, which are taken to another station where these long tubular strips of bubble gum—more like waxy pink sausages than gum at this stage—are cut into bite-size pieces with a tool akin to a large pizza wheel.

One day at the beginning of spring I receive a letter from the draft board. According to their records my student deferment has expired; I am now eligible to be considered for military service.

My father comes home early from his office hour at school. He himself hates the war, the senseless bombing and killing. He has marched with his college's students and protested the presence on campus of recruiters from a chemical company that makes napalm. He has, in fact, been more active than I, who have withdrawn into the routine and oblivion of factory labor, for which there are no deferments.

"What are your plans?" my father asks.

"I don't know. Canada, I suppose, if all else fails."

"And what is 'all else'?"

"A medical deferment."

"On what basis?"

"My mental condition."

"But you have never been to a psychiatrist. You have no history."

"I don't know then." I shrug. I feel numb, resigned. Why not basic training and then the jungles of Southeast Asia? Could it be much worse than the bubble gum factory?

"You will not go. That is all there is to it. We will make sure of that."

"And how will you do that?"

"We'll hide you, if necessary."

I look at my father and almost laugh. But I can see he is serious, alarmed.

"What are you talking about—hide me? Where?"

He picks up his newspaper and folds it back once, twice, three times until he has a long strip of news in front of him. It is the idiosyncratic way he likes to read the paper—folding it like a map until he is down to a small, tight square of information the size of a wallet or obituary. I think that it must make him feel some control over the world's chaotic events to read about them in such miniature, compressed spaces.

My mother brings in a stuck jar for one of us to loosen, and my father puts down his newspaper, which pops open on his lap like an accordion. I am still thinking about his wanting to hide me, aware that the draft has touched off buried fears for him, a flashback to the war, some instinctive response to the personal terror of his family being taken away from him. "I'll get out of it, Dad," I say. "Don't worry. I won't go."

"Don't worry, don't worry, is that what you think is the problem here? You have put yourself in this position, though I begged you not to. What is there to do now but worry!" He stands up. "I am *sick* with worry, if you must know. This is my fault. I should have demanded you stay in school, not let you come here!"

I have never heard him raise his voice like this. His body begins to tremble, and from the kitchen my mother hurries in with her hand over her heart. "What is going on here?" she says. "What are you arguing about?"

"Nothing," my father answers. "The argument is finished," and he goes into his study and closes the door—a sight I am used to from childhood. I hear him weep but rather than sadness I feel a great relief; finally, something I've done has touched him.

I do not get drafted but receive a high number in the first lottery. The long and tiresome depression, the deadness I have felt, is replaced with the exhilaration of a survivor, a life reclaimed. I make plans to visit Europe, use the money I've saved from the bubble gum factory to travel for three months. Guidebooks about England, France, Spain, and Italy cover my bed. I pore over them and come up with a tentative itinerary. But when I actually get to Europe, I find I make a detour from England to Holland. I locate the Jewish quarter where my father hid during the war, find his school—the Vossius Gymnasium—and then what I've come for: the bakery. It is still there, although the original owners who saved my father have long ago died. I explain to the current owners who I am; they tell me in broken

English that yes, they have heard what happened here during the war, they know about my father and the Koops, who saved him; the story is legend. "Does the oven still exist by any chance?" I ask.

They take me to the back, outside to a shed. It is here, covered with a tablecloth. I ask them if I can be by myself for a few moments and they say certainly, no one will disturb me.

A squat and solid object, the oven stands only chest high. I pull open the door and look inside. The opening is deeper than it is wide, the height a little less than two feet. I hoist myself up to sit on the edge. Then I swing my legs around and push my body in feet first. My neck is back against the left edge. I cannot go any farther. My shoulder sticks out too much even when I bend my knees into my chest. I do not understand how he did this, but I am determined to fit inside, so I slide out again and try to enter without my shoes and without my jacket. I tuck my legs under and pull my head inside, my back curved tight as an archer's bow. I hook my finger through the match hole and close the door. The stove smells of mildew and carbon; the scaled roughness of the iron ceiling grates against my cheek. It is pitch black except for the match hole through which I can see. I put my eye up to it and watch. Soon I hear footsteps and I feel frightened, but the footsteps recede into the distance and the bakery becomes silent.

Many years later my parents come out to celebrate the occasion of our son's fifth birthday. My father helps Philip build the space station they have brought him. I watch them play together, my father with no awareness of the world around him other than this mission to be his grandson's assistant.

While my mother and Judith, my wife, put Philip to bed, my father and I have coffee on the porch. It is a cool summer night and we are in Boulder, Colorado, where the shimmering night sky looks, to my parents, like a planetarium. Judith works in the university's office of communications, while I teach literature. Like my father, I have become a professor.

"What are you going to do now?" I ask him. He is on transitional retirement, half-time teaching, and is scheduled to leave the college next year. "Will you finally go to Europe?"

"Perhaps," he says, "but your mother's back may not permit it."

I nod. The trip out here has cost her a great deal of pain, which she has accepted stoically. If she walks for more than half an hour or sits for that long, the result is the same, inflammation.

"Have you thought of going yourself?" I ask.

"I could not leave your mother for that long. She would not be well enough."

My father sits with the hiking boots he has bought for this trip out west laced tight on his feet. They are spanking new and he has already cleaned them of mud from our climb this afternoon. I take pleasure in seeing him so fond of the mountains, so open to the world out here. "You and I could go," I say. "Together. A nurse could help mother if we went next summer."

"I will give it some thought," my father says, but I can see that the veil has already dropped—the complex configuration of blank terror that can still scare me with its suddenness, the yearning on his face vanished. He has gone to Madagascar. He empties the coffee he has spilled in the saucer back into his cup. "I have made a mess here," he says, replacing the dry saucer underneath. He stands up. Pulls down the sides of his jacket. Despite the hiking boots, he has dressed for dinner. "Would you like to go for a walk with me, Ephram?"

Yes, I say, and get my coat, eager as always.

Last summer Judith and I took Philip to Europe because I wanted to show him where his grandfather grew up. Though the bakery was no longer there—an insurance office now—I described everything about the original building, and the oven. I held him in my arms while he listened with intelligence and care, and I kissed his long lashes and felt his soft cheek against mine. I wondered what he knew that I would never know about him, what pleased him that could not be spoken. When would he grow past me, leave his fatherland, hack and chop and hew whole forests until he could find one piece of hallowed ground to plant the seed of his own self?

One night in our hotel I could not sleep and began to write: "Every son's story about his father is, in a sense, written to save himself from his father. It is told so that he may go free and in the telling the son wants to speak so well that he can give his father the power to save himself from his own father." I wrote this on a note card, put it in an airmail envelope, and planned to send it with its Amsterdam postmark to my father.

The following morning a call from my mother let us know that my father had suffered a stroke. We flew home immediately, and I rushed to see him in the hospital while Judith waited with Philip at the house. My mother was there by his bed. An IV bottle was connected to his wrist. His other arm I saw had purplish bruises from all the injections and from the blood samples taken. The effects of the stroke made him confuse the simplest of objects, or draw on archaic uses—a pen became a plume. A part of his brain had lost the necessary signals for referencing things and faces with words, and now dealt in wild compensatory searches to communicate. When he spoke of Judith he referred to her as my husband, called me "ram" trying to pronounce Ephram, and, saddest of all, could not understand why I had so much trouble understanding him. He had once spoken three languages fluently, and to see him in this state was more of a shock than I could bear. When he fell asleep, I left his room to speak with the doctor, a neurologist who explained to me that a ruptured blood vessel was causing the illogical and distorted speech. Bleeding in the brain. The image for me was vivid, his brain leaking, his skull swelling from the fluid's pressure inside, and all one could do was wait.

One day while I sat and read by his bed, he said my name clearly and asked if I could help him get dressed. He had a white shirt and tie in the closet. He spoke with difficulty from the stroke, although his condition had improved and we all believed he would be released soon. I dressed him and because he was cold I put my sweater over his shoulders and tied the arms in front so he looked like a college man again. While he sat up in bed I held onto his hand to steady him, reminded of how we used to waltz together when I was ten. I said something to him that I had carried around with me for a long while, something that had no basis in fact, only in the private burden of a son traversing the globe for a father's loss. "I'm sorry if I've disappointed you," I told him and he answered me in speech slowed by his stroke, "I forget everything, Ephram." I nodded, but then cried later at his funeral because I thought and hoped he had meant to say forgive.

BIOGRAPHIES
and Some Comments by the Authors

(Author's first appearance in *Prize Stories: The O. Henry Awards* is indicated in parentheses.)

Alice Adams (1971) is the author of four collections of stories and seven novels, including *Almost Perfect*, to be published by Knopf in May 1993.

"Quite devastated by the death of a long-loved cat, I began to think in a serious way about the nature of that love, our love for our animals, and those thoughts led to this story. There was also, I suppose, a desire to memorialize—as best I could—this particular and most individual cat."

Rilla Askew (1993) is a native Oklahoman. She's the author of *Strange Business*, a work of fiction published by Viking that chronicles twenty-five years of memory and experience in the fictional small town of Cedar, Oklahoma. Her short fiction has appeared in a variety of literary magazines. She received her M.F.A. in Creative Writing from Brooklyn College and is currently a visiting professor at Syracuse University, where she teaches in the Creative Writing Program.

"I had long known this story. It's a true story—or based on a true story, for much here is imagined. It took place not far from the small town in the mountains of southeastern Oklahoma where I come from. The tale has been handed down for generations like legend, has found its way into history books, been immortalized in paintings on the walls of local banks. I'd known for a long time I wanted to someday tell the story of Silan Lewis, but I'd thought I would tell it from the point of view of his white wife in the wagon on the way to the execution. She haunted me; that wagon ride to attend her husband's death haunted me.

"Yet, when I began to write, the voice in this story started talking to me; it was not the voice I'd wanted but it was the voice that insisted, so I wrote listening to it. It's an old voice, an old man's voice, and I don't know who he is. Later, I remembered an old photograph I'd seen once of the execution, and I think now it was an image in this photograph that was the source for the voice in the story. In the picture, the body of Silan Lewis lies sprawled on the ground in a white shirt, feet toward the camera, arms stretched out to the sides, surrounded by Choctaw men in dark cowboy hats. Silan Lewis's face is hidden from the viewer by the form of a man kneeling beside him. This man—lean-faced, dark, wearing a mustache and a white hat—is looking directly into the camera. His eyes are haunted. His hand is resting on Silan Lewis's chest."

Stephen Dixon (1977): "I was born and brought up in NYC, and was educated in the public schools there. After that, for around twenty years, I worked as a reporter, news editor, magazine editor, radio producer, salesman, artist model, public school teacher, bartender, waiter (I'm enumerating these chronologically), and lots of other jobs in between till I landed a job teaching in the Writing Seminars at Johns Hopkins University in 1980, and where I still am today.

"I've been writing for more than thirty years, turning out stories and novels without letup during this time. I am always writing because I'm always finding new things to write about and explore. I haven't tried not writing in thirty years, but I probably would find it a little like getting off a serious addiction. Writing keeps me alert and my mind lively and imagining; it's a very satisfying struggle where I'm always the loser but a willing combatant.

"As for 'The Rare Muscovite,' I don't like to write about myself, in autobiographical pieces like this, and I also don't like writing about a piece of fiction I've written. I've always felt the work stands for itself and anything I'd say about it would only detract from the reading of the piece. I will say this. I got the idea for the story after my wife and I returned from what was then the Soviet Union. We'd gone there so she could interview the widow of Isaac Babel for a book she's writing. I went along for the ride, so to speak, but I also hoped I'd find some material to write about. I did, the story herein, though the story's very much changed from what actually happened in Moscow and after."

Charles Eastman (1993): "For years I worked in motion pictures, writing original screenplays, a couple of which have been published in hardback at Farrar, Straus & Giroux, *Little Fauss and Big Halsy* and *The All-American Boy*. Before writing for films I worked at fiction, wrote some short stories and several plays. Two of my long short stories have appeared in *Santa Monica Review*, and at present I am working on two novels.

" 'Yellow Flags' was begun many years ago, an early effort, heavily overdone. Five years ago I returned to it, cleaned it up, shook it out, held it under the faucet for a while in the hopes of washing away all the clumsiness and crud, some twenty pages of it at least. What is amazing to me is that while my father did not come one day to take me to the beach, people now presume that he did; they speak to me as though 'Yellow Flags' is autobiographical, and I have come to feel that that must be the case. I can now remember sitting in the car with him under the streetlight trying to find something to say. Which maybe happened, but on another day and on some other street. I made it all up at the time, that is, or so I thought, borrowed from this impact or that in my life, because I wanted to write a story. But as a dream is composed of the psyche's essentials and is always true, so I think 'Yellow Flags' has now become an accurate representation of something that actually happened to me once. I remember it now as though it was in fact my experience after all."

Jennifer Egan's (1993) short stories have appeared in *The New Yorker*, *The New England Review*, *Mademoiselle* and other magazines. She lives in New York, where she is at work on a novel.

"I do remember renting horses in Puerto Vallarta as a child of eight or nine, being stunned by the world which opened itself to me in the back streets beyond the hotels and tourist restaurants. The experience left a strong impression, almost a taste.

"I often have written about Americans in foreign countries. For me, travel involves both a heightening of experience and a compression of time—the world is made strange, the boundaries provided by one's familiar, daily routines, are lifted.

"In 'Puerto Vallarta,' the irrevocable exposure of hidden tensions—in this case, secret knowledge and allegiances among a family—under pressure of foreign surroundings seems not just the vehicle for the story, but its actual subject. My thoughts while writing it were not nearly so abstract, though; I was pulled along by a sense of reckless, dangerous tension between a girl and her father, the choice it finally pushes her to make."

Josephine Jacobsen (1967) has won numerous awards, most recently the Lenore-Marshall Award, given for the best book of poetry published the previous year, for *The Sisters;* a fellowship from the Academy of American Poets for service to poetry; and the selection of *On the Island: Short Stories,* as one of the five nominees for the Pen-Faulkner fiction award.

Ms. Jacobsen served two terms as Poetry Consultant to the Library of Congress, and four terms on the Literature Panel of the NEA, and is a Literary Lion of the New York Public Library. She lives in Baltimore with her husband, Eric Jacobsen.

"I am always a bit diffident about discussing my own work, preferring that it should speak for itself. What can I say of my intentions and their expression in 'The Pier–Glass'? The story is quite different from any I have written. For me in this case the challenge was the struggle to be honest, never to have the protagonist say anything—however helpful to my point—that she would not naturally have said; but to have her report—quite sincerely in her own mind—her actions, while telling the reader another story.

"Primarily, two things appealed to me in this attempt: the contrast between the reality and the ego's perception; and below this, the elements of true sorrow and loss, of vulnerable lives radically injured. Having had favorable criticism of my 'style' (which after all is the mode of the author's viewpoint), I wanted to see how I would manage speech in a totally uncongenial voice.

"And mirrors—both mental and physical—have always fascinated me by their duplicity."

Charles Johnson (1993): "Between 1970 and 1972, I wrote six books I call 'apprentice novels' then the seventh, *Faith and the Good Thing* (1974), which was the first to be published. I next wrote *Oxherding Tale* (1982), a neo-slave narrative that explores freedom from the standpoint of Hinduism and Buddhism. I've studied Eastern thought and Chinese kung-fu for over twenty-five years, and I presently codirect a studio for the Choy-Li-fut system in Seattle. One story in my collection, *The Sorcerer's Apprentice* (1986), draws on material from Asian martial arts and philosophy, as does my novel *Middle Passage,* which won the 1990 National Book Award for fiction.

"As a lay Buddhist who meditates daily, I have always been passionate about the underlying values behind martial arts practice—personal discipline, service to others, the steady perfection of physical skills with a deepening understanding of the self's nature. 'Kwoon' is about a crisis faced by David Lewis, a teacher who believes in those values, and how he overcomes an opponent by eliminating in himself and Ed Morgan the egotism that gives rise to the illusory notion that there is even an 'opponent' at all. The only adversary to be beaten, he learns, is his own rigid sense of identity."

Thom Jones (1993) is a graduate of the University of Washington and the Iowa Writers' Workshop. His work has appeared in *The New Yorker, Esquire, Harper's, Story, Mirabella* and *Buzz.* A collection of his stories will be published by Little, Brown in June 1993.

"The Persian Gulf War was in progress when a casual remark that this was the birthday of a dear friend who died in Vietnam provided the impetus for 'The Pugilist.' Most of my stories come to me in this way. I hear a line and then perhaps a few weeks later I have my voice, and like a method actor, I fall into character and write instinctively without a plan or an idea as to what will happen. The day I wrote this particular story I remember that my wife and daughter and I had intended to go shopping. Whatever we were going to buy wasn't really essential however and it was raining very hard; each of us wanted some separate lunch and we weren't really getting it together to go out. It wasn't in the cards so to speak. Although I wasn't feeling very good I was eager to take a shot at this story. I loaded my stereo with *The Doors* and after I wrote the first few words I began to feel better and better until I fell into a kind of controlled ecstatic frenzy. I was writing about a buddy and it was coming straight from my heart and thus it seemed good and true. I didn't finish the first draft until about two in the morning and I remember being surprised at how late it was as I emerged from my strange trance, and I recall that I was very hungry. I made myself a fried egg sandwich as the story printed out and when I read it over, I was pretty sure I had something good.

"It strikes me that Vietnam is an indelible part of my generation and always will be. I would like to dedicate 'The Pugilist' to Lance Corporal Rolf W. Jorgensen of Seattle, Washington who was killed in Vietnam on July 20, 1966. I also wish to acknowledge Force Recon Marine Corporal R. Stan Joy who did not make it back from Vietnam alive, and Sergeant Tommy Evanoff, USMC, who did—heroes all. *Semper fidelis*."

Andrea Lee (1993) was born in Philadelphia, attended The Baldwin School, and received B.A. and M.A. degrees from Harvard University. She is the author of the nonfiction *Russian Journal*, which was nominated for the National Book Award, and the novel *Sarah Phillips*. She is a staff writer for *The New Yorker* and lives in Turin, Italy.

"I got the idea for 'Winter Barley' when I was rereading *King Lear* and came across the beautiful little speech made by Lear to Cordelia that begins, 'Come, let's away to prison:/ We two along will sing like birds i'the cage . . .' In the midst of the most extreme human misery and the breakdown of all civilized order—a king and his daughter have been made prisoners by members of their own family—these few lines suddenly sketch out the image of an idyll: a fragile perfect moment between two people that holds not only mutual love but humor, ironic complicity, defiance of the world outside, of the fatal workings of the tragedy that will inevitably crush them. I wanted to write a story about such an evanescent paradise. The image of caged birds singing together made me think of a duet, and so 'Winter Barley' became an interchange of the emotions and memories of two lovers. I was still thinking of *King Lear* when I created Edo and Elizabeth, who quite obviously on a certain level are father and daughter—in fact, it is this facet of their relationship that helps foredoom their brief pleasure in each other.''

Diane Levenberg (1991): ''I am deeply indebted to Joan Dash's excellent biography, *Summoned to Jerusalem: A Life of Henrietta Szold*. At the age of forty-three, while studying at the Jewish Theological Seminary, Szold fell madly in love with Louis Ginzberg, a blue-eyed professor of Talmud. His goal in life was to become the greatest Jewish scholar living. For a man with such aspirations, the aging Henrietta would not be suitable. He married someone else and Szold, after suffering a physical breakdown, left for Palestine where she spent the rest of her life devoting herself to Zionist causes. She became the first president of Hadassah, promoting its medical enterprises in Palestine. She worked tirelessly to create what is today the Hadassah Hospital and the Hadassah Nursing School. As the director of Youth Aliyah, the woman, who never married, saw one of her dreams fulfilled in mothering the thousands of children whose lives she saved. Deeply moved by her story, I wanted to see how it might play itself out had she lived in my generation.

''The result is 'A Modern Love Story.' While writing it I became fascinated by how the details of Szold's life and my own intersected. It made it that much easier to create this 'variegated fiction.'

''Like Szold, I was an editor at the Jewish Publication Society, I studied and worked at the Jewish Theological Seminary, and I was for years engrossed in scholarship (writing a dissertation). At an age very close to hers, I too, physically ill and feeling like one who had experienced a long history of unrequited love, felt myself summoned to Jerusalem, where I have continued to live.

Here, everyday, I thank God for the small and not such small ways I experience the miraculous gift which is this land and its people."

Lorrie Moore (1993) is the author of a novel, a children's book, and two collections of stories, the most recent of which is *Like Life*. She is also editor of the anthology *I Know Some Things: Stories About Childhood by Contemporary Writers*. She teaches at the University of Wisconsin in Madison.

"Aglow with the holiday spirit, the author sat down to write a nice little Christmas story."

Antonya Nelson's (1992) stories have appeared in *The New Yorker, Esquire, TriQuarterly, Story*, and elsewhere. Her first collection, *The Expendables*, won the 1989 Flannery O'Connor Award for Short Fiction; a second collection, *In the Land of Men*, was published this year by William Morrow. She teaches literature and creative writing at New Mexico State University in Las Cruces, where she lives with her husband, author Robert Boswell, and their two children.

" 'Dirty Words' is the only blatantly political story I've written. As I see it, the characters are representatives of the worlds they've come from, sunny California, U.S.A., and 1930's Poland. It is America's unique brazenness that fascinates me, its aggressive intoxication with itself, its audacious self-importance. Our confidence in our own significance—our robust fecundity— seems to me both seductive and destructive, the characteristics I meant to bestow on Bette."

Cornelia Nixon (1993) is the author of a novel in stories, *Now You See It*, which was published by Little, Brown in 1991, and also a book about D. H. Lawrence. She lives in Bloomington, Indiana.

" 'Risk' began as an attempt to deal with something that happened to me and my husband late one night while on vacation in San Francisco. We were conned by a hitchhiker named Rhonda, who said she was pregnant and disabled and sick and needed a ride to the hospital; she got us to give her twenty dollars and drive her to a gambling parlor in a scary part of Oakland, where she could have done much worse to us if she wanted to. I worked obsessively on that story every day for a whole summer, and by the end of it Margy and Webster had become so large in my mind, with so much history behind them, that I realized there was no longer room for Rhonda.

"Since 'Risk,' Margy and Webster have taken over my life, and I am now writing a novel about them. But it all started with Rhonda, and I'd like to say: Rhonda, baby, if you're out there reading this, thanks very much. I hope you won something with that twenty bucks."

Joyce Carol Oates's (1967) most recent novel is *Foxfire: Confessions of a Girl Gang,* to be published in August 1993. She has three times received the Special Award for Continuing Achievement in this series.

"A short story, even one so tightly crafted and small in scale as this, comprised of no more than two characters, with a shadowy third, and imagined in terms of an Aristotelian unity of time, place, and action, is the consequence of numerous elements that flow into one another like tributaries into a river. Like these tributaries, some are visible and definable, others are subterranean and mysterious.

"Rereading 'Goose-Girl,' one paragraph leaps out at me as a spark of a motive that prevailed from the first, in fact pre-existed any thought of this particular story:

> In families, courtships prevail. Someone is forever pursuing
> someone else; that person, another; and there are those who, so
> strangely, so perversely, prefer, yes unmistakably prefer, to be
> alone.

"In time, we inhabit all these roles. They are not necessarily linear, they surely overlap, and double back upon themselves and repeat themselves, whether tragically or comically, to the very hour of death.

"But 'Goose-Girl' in its specificity was inspired by the image of the 'goose-girl'—the female figure who is objectified, reduced in scale, purposefully and meanly derided by those who view her without sympathy. She is the outsider, she is the predator, or perceived as such. Of her ravenous hunger and need, a cruel comedy may be invented. Of her vulnerability, a community's rectitude. We all know a goose-girl and some of us have been a goose-girl, with or without knowing it. For the goose-girl will never know how she is perceived, only what, to herself, she *is*.

"The young woman in my story, Phoebe Stone, will not strike most readers as sympathetic. I might have sentimentalized her a bit, but I chose not to. Sympathy, felt for those who seemingly don't deserve it, is the rare thing, the gift.

"In art, as in life, I'm most powerfully drawn to people who simply *are*, in the face of others', sometimes an entire community's, disapprobation.

" 'Goose-Girl' is set in a fictitious 'Hazelton' that most closely renders the tone and quality and moral ambiguities of life in Princeton, New Jersey, where I've lived since 1978."

C. E. Poverman (1993): "In 1976, my collection *The Black Velvet Girl*, won The Iowa School of Letters Award for Short Fiction. Since then, I have published three novels, the most recent being *My Father in Dreams*. In 1992, Ontario Review Press published my second collection, *Skin*. 'The Man Who Died' is one of these stories.

"I'll write now what I said then. I don't feel that I'm in any school of writing or fighting any rearguard action with a style. Every time I sit down to write, I go to the same place in myself. There's some sense of imbalance, curiosity, playfulness, some question I can't answer, an image that keeps asking me to look at it, or a voice. That's all. I translate them however I can. I'll always follow the material as far as I can and take it on its own terms.

" 'The Man Who Died' came out of some talk I'd heard about a teacher. Later, I saw a picture of him in the paper. As in the end of the story, he was awaiting sentence. He looked completely composed, at peace: the end of a journey. I cut it out and looked at it for months. I have a number of friends who are lawyers and have worked on and off for a private investigator, so I had a feel for how a case like this might go. I was, of course, interested in what could have led a man to such a terrible moment."

John H. Richardson (1993) grew up mostly in Asia, the son of a CIA station chief. He started his writing career as a police reporter at the Albuquerque *Tribune*, working his way up to his current job as a senior writer at *Premiere* magazine. All along he wrote short stories. The first to see print appeared in *Black Warrior Review* in 1988. His first novel, *The Blue Screen*, will be published by William Morrow & Co. in 1994.

"I had been trying to write fiction for years without much success. My stories suffered from too much thinking, from graduate school and grandiosity. Then one morning I decided to try a story closer to the bone, about staying with my family in Mexico. My goal was to keep the story as simple and straightforward as possible. A year later I tried the Mexico theme again, writing 'The Pink House' in two or three effortless evenings. But for me the really interesting part came later: I worried about how my father would react to the story, since the father in it was rather blatantly modeled on what my sister calls 'Dad at his most pathetic.' But when my father read it he just shrugged and said, 'But you weren't *here* when we bought the house.' And he was right. I had *forgotten*. I made the whole thing up. Later I realized that was why I had written it, because I *wasn't* there—I felt excluded, part of a larger exclusion, so I wrote myself in. For a while that thought made me very happy."

Steven Schwartz (1983) is the author of two collections of stories, *To Leningrad in Winter* and *Lives of the Fathers*. This is his second appearance in the O. Henry Awards anthology. He teaches at Colorado State University and in the Warren Wilson M.F.A. program. "Madagascar" is also winner of a Nelson Algren Award.

" 'Madagascar' grew out of a family story. My uncle, a German Jew, crisscrossed fourteen borders escaping from the Nazis during the early part of World War II. He wound up in Holland and, as the story goes, hid in a baker's oven there. I first heard this story when I was five (my brother passed it on to me), and I suppose my imagination had worked on it ever since. One after-noon years afterward when I was stuck writing, wandering around the house looking for a distraction, I turned on the TV. Two historians were discussing an early plan of Hitler's to send the Jews to Madagascar and then ransom them. It was enough—the spark needed—to awaken the old family story of my uncle: an encoded tale of survivors and war, joined with my own concerns about fathers and sons."

Daniel Stern (1987) is the author of nine novels, two short story collections, a play, two screenplays, and numerous essays. He is Professor of English and Creative Writing at the University of Houston.

"At the end of the 1980s, after a life spent writing reasonably long novels, I seemed to want to write short stories. However, each story I wanted to write insisted on being called by the title of someone else's story or essay. After having been deeply moved by love, ambition, family, hope, and other such, I was finally in the grip of my lifelong love: literature.

"The first story I wrote in this mood was called: 'The Liberal Imagination by Lionel Trilling, A Story'—as it turned out, a story of youth and lost love. I then wrote 'The Interpretation of Dreams by Sigmund Freud: A Story' (about a man who marries widows), and a literary adventure had begun. My feelings for certain great writings of the past was impossible to separate from the stories I wanted to write—so I didn't try. I let them merge, and the engine that drove my writing became the themes, sometimes even the characters, in works by Heming-way and Henry James—though my own themes and characters were central—as well as essays by E. M. Forster and Freud. These were collected in 1989 in *Twice Told Tales*.

"I don't know if it was the encouragement I received from the response to that collection, or if I was just a man enthralled by a passion for a literary form that was taking me into emotional, comic, and literary areas I'd never explored before. In any case I closed my eyes and leaped. I took several of the most loved masterpieces by Kafka, Melville, and even by one of my favorite poets, Wallace Stevens, and wove some kind of personal fic-tional tapestry from their work and my own.

"These were published in the collection *Twice Upon a Time* in 1992. The story included here, 'A Hunger Artist by Franz Kafka: A Story' was the first in the book. If I continue this love affair with the dead writers of my imagination, what comes next: *Thrice Told Tales?*"

Linda Svendsen (1983): "I was born in Vancouver, Canada, received a B.A. in English from the University of British Columbia, and an M.F.A. from Columbia University in 1980. My first collection, *Marine Life*, was published by Farrar, Straus & Giroux in 1992; one of the stories, 'Heartbeat,' was included in *Prize Stories 1983: The O. Henry Awards*. I currently teach Creative Writing at the University of British Columbia.

"I started writing 'The Edger Man' in the summer of 1988. I knew I wanted to write a story about Adele, the first-person narrator who links the family stories in *Marine Life,* and her elderly father. I was about forty pages into the story and was having trouble keeping Humphrey on the page. I'm still not sure he is enough *there,* but since I was writing a collection, I found that he did shadow cameos in the final drafts of the others."

John Van Kirk (1993) was born and raised in northern New Jersey and attended college in St. Louis, Missouri where he remained for nine years. He held a variety of jobs, from caddying to carpentry, telemarketing to tending bar. He was in the U. S. Navy from 1980 to 1988. After the navy he earned an M.F.A. from the University of Maryland. He has been writing fiction since the mid 1970s. "Newark Job" is his first published story.

" 'Newark Job' evolved from a single descriptive paragraph written on a file card sometime in 1984 or 1985. That paragraph, a forerunner of the paragraph in which Henry first enters Ms. Williams's apartment with his father, came out of scenes remembered from accompanying my own father on jobs not terribly dissimilar to the one recounted in this story, as well as scenes remembered from my own work experience in the housing rehabilitation business. A story began to form itself around that passage.

"Equipped with a setting and characters, but no real plot, I fought with the story for two years. Then, by chance, I reread Hemingway's 'Indian Camp.' Shortly after that I got through to the end of my first complete draft. There were many more drafts over the next several years. The epigraph is meant as an acknowledgment of my debt to Hemingway, without whom this story may never have reached completion. I regard the work as it stands as part homage, part critique."

William F. Van Wert (1983) teaches film and creative writing at Temple University. He has written two film books, two short story collections, and a novella. Recent fiction has appeared in the *North American Review, Western Humanities Review, Tri-Quarterly, Boulevard, Four Quarters, Nimrod,* and elsewhere.

" 'Shaking' is part of an unpublished collection of stories I wrote entitled *Amen, the End of Grace.* I meant the title to go both ways, of course, proclaiming as it does both the renewal of grace and the loss of grace. 'Shaking' is a typical story in this collection in that the tone strives to be more humble than apocalyptic, while the effect on the reader should be that of a continued haunting. The Shaker woman is the fascination, of course, but the haunting for me is in the emotionally wounded doctor, who first gives her the story's focus, then takes it back, and who can neither accept her miracles nor prevent them."

Peter Weltner (1993): "A greek head similar to the one in my story once sat on a coffee table in the apartment on Telegraph Hill where my lover at the time and I lived. The poet Linda Gregg had loaned it to us after she had been loaned it by a friend when she was hospitalized with pericarditis. After we'd kept it for a couple of years, Linda's friend understandably asked for it back. I'm sure that black marble head had something to do with the years that Robert and I were together. And I think I know why I started to remember it so often almost a decade later after several friends had died of AIDS and the plague had become the essential fact of so many lives. But, however much a story may begin in personal emotion, for me it never stops there. The Greek head in my story is also very different from the one Robert and I used to hold and admire, knowing someday we'd have to give it back.

"I live in San Francisco with my lover, Atticus Carr, a medical social worker, and teach modern and contemporary English, Irish, and American poetry and fiction at San Francisco State. My articles and stories have appeared in *ELR*, *Ironwood*, *Parnassus*, *Five Fingers Review*, *The James White Review*, and *American Short Fiction*. Three of my books have been published: a collection of stories, *Beachside Entries/Specific Ghosts*; a novel, *Identity and Difference*; and a collection of three short novels, *In a Time of Combat for the Angel*."

Kate Wheeler (1982) has published half a dozen short stories and essays in literary journals. This is her second O. Henry Award; her work has also been chosen for *Best American Short Stories* and the Pushcart Prize. Her first collection of short stories, *Not Where I Started From*, will be published in 1993 by Houghton Mifflin. She grew up in South America, and still travels widely.

"My family lived in Cartagena when I was in seventh grade. After that, this story came together from many nameable and unnameable sources, not least of them the heat of the summer while I sat writing it. My middle sister, Margaret, who's in medical school, told me on the phone how painful it was to watch other people suffer. I looked at Alex Webb's photographs taken in the tropics, and laughed with Jeanne Anne Whittington about how each of us tried to get saved. My writing group explained Estrellita's romance.

"This story is dedicated to the men and women who served my family over the years, especially to Maria, who taught me to speak, and whom I haven't seen since I was five.

"I gave as much to it as I could."

MAGAZINES CONSULTED

Agni, Boston University, Creative Writing Program, 236 Bay State Road, Boston, Mass. 02215

American Short Fiction, University of Texas Press, P.O. Box 7819, Austin, Tex. 78713

Antaeus, 100 West Broad Street, Hopewell, N.J. 08525

Antietam Review, 82 West Washington Street, Hagerstown, Md. 21740

The Antioch Review, P.O. Box 148, Yellow Springs, Oh. 45387

The Apalachee Quarterly, P.O. Box 20106, Tallahassee, Fla. 32316

Arizona Quarterly, University of Arizona, Tucson, Ariz. 85721

Ascent, P.O. Box 967, Urbana, Ill. 61801

Asimov's Science Fiction Magazine, Davis Publications, 380 Lexington Avenue, New York, N.Y. 10017

The Atlantic Monthly, 745 Boylston Street, Boston, Mass. 02116

Blue Light Red Light, 496A Hudson Street, Suite F-42, New York, N.Y. 10014

Boulevard, P.O. Box 30386, Philadelphia, Pa. 19103

The Bridge, 14050 Vernon Street, Oak Park, Mich. 48237

Buffalo Spree, 4511 Harlem Rd., P.O. Box 38, Buffalo, N.Y. 14226

California Quarterly, 100 Sproul Hall, University of California, Davis, Calif. 95616

Calyx, P.O. Box B, Corvallis, Oreg. 97339

Canadian Fiction Magazine, P.O. Box 946, Station F, Toronto Ont., Canada M4Y 2N9

Capital Region Magazine, 4 Central Avenue, Albany, N.Y. 12210

The Chariton Review, The Division of Language and Literature, Northeast Missouri State University, Kirksville, Mo. 63501

The Chattahoochee Review, DeKalb Community College, North Campus, 2101 Womack Road, Dunwoody, Ga. 30338-4497

Chicago Review, 5801 S. Kenwood, Chicago, Ill. 60637

Chicago Tribune, Nelson Algren Award, 435 North Michigan Avenue, Chicago, Ill. 60611-4041

Christopher Street, 28 West 25th Street, New York, N.Y. 10010

Cimarron Review, 205 Morill Hall, Oklahoma State University, Stillwater, Okla. 74078-0135

Clockwatch Review, James Plath, Department of English, Illinois Westleyan University, Bloomington, Ill. 61702

Colorado Review, 360 Eddy Building, Colorado State University, Fort Collins, Colo. 80523

Columbia, 404 Dodge Hall, Columbia University, New York, N.Y. 10027

Commentary, 165 East 56th Street, New York, N.Y. 10022

Concho River Review, c/o English Department, Angelo State University, San Angelo, Tex. 76909

Confrontation, Department of English, C.W. Post College of Long Island University, Brookville, N.Y. 11548

Cosmopolitan, 224 West 57th Street, New York, N.Y. 10019

Crazyhorse, Department of English, University of Arkansas at Little Rock, 2801 S. University, Little Rock, Ark. 72204

The Cream City Review, University of Wisconsin-Milwaukee, P.O. Box 413, Milwaukee, Wis. 53201

Crescent Review, 1445 Old Town Road, Winston-Salem, N.C. 27106-3143

Crosscurrents, 2200 Glastonbury Rd., Westlake Village, Calif. 91361

Delos, The Center for World Literature, Inc., P.O. Box 2880, College Park, Md. 20741

Denver Quarterly, Department of English, University of Denver, Denver, Colo. 80210

Epoch, 251 Goldwin Smith Hall, Cornell University, Ithaca, N.Y. 14853-3201

Esquire, 1790 Broadway, New York, N.Y. 10019

Fiction, Department of English, The City College of New York, N.Y. 10031

Fiction International, Department of English, St. Lawrence University, Canton, N.Y. 13617

The Fiddlehead, UNB, P.O. Box 4400, Fredericton, New Brunswick, Canada, E3B 5A3

The Florida Review, Department of English, University of Central Florida, Orlando, Fla. 32816

Four Quarters, La Salle College, Philadelphia, Pa. 19141

Free Press, 306 Fifth Avenue, Brooklyn, N.Y. 11215

Frisko, Suite 414, The Flood Building, 870 Market Street, San Francisco, Calif. 94102

Gentleman's Quarterly, 350 Madison Avenue, New York, N.Y. 10017

The Georgia Review, University of Georgia, Athens, Ga. 30602

The Gettysburg Review, Gettysburg College, Gettysburg, Pa. 17325-1491

Glamour, 350 Madison Avenue, New York, N.Y. 10017

Glimmer Train, 812 SW Washington Street, Suite 1205, Portland, Oreg. 97205-3216

Grand Street, 113 Varick Street, #906, New York, N.Y. 10023

Granta, 13 White Street, New York, N.Y. 10013

The Greensboro Review, Department of English, University of North Carolina, Greensboro, N.C. 27412

Harper's Magazine, 666 Broadway, New York, N.Y. 10012

Hawaii Review, Department of English, University of Hawaii, 1733 Donaghho Road, Honolulu, Ha. 96822

High Plains Literary Review, 180 Adams Street, Suite 250, Denver, Colo. 80206

The Hudson Review, 684 Park Avenue, New York, N.Y. 10021

Indiana Review, 316 N. Jordan, Bloomington, Ind. 47405

Interim, Department of English, University of Nevada, Las Vegas, Nev. 89154

Iowa Review, 308 EPB, University of Iowa, Iowa City, Ia. 52242

Kalliope, a Journal of Women's Art, Florida Community College at Jacksonville, 3939 Roosevelt Boulevard, Jacksonville, Fla. 32205-8989

Kansas Quarterly, Department of English, Denison Hall, Kansas State University, Manhattan, Kan. 66506-0703

The Kenyon Review, Kenyon College, Gambier, Oh. 43022

Key West Review, 9 Avenue G, Key West, Fla. 33040

Ladies' Home Journal, 100 Park Avenue, New York, N.Y. 10017

The Literary Review, Fairleigh Dickinson University, Teaneck, N.J. 07940

Mademoiselle, 350 Madison Avenue, New York, N.Y. 10017

Magic Realism, PYX Press, P.O. Box 620, Oren, Ut. 84059-0620

Manoa, English Department, University of Hawaii, Honolulu, Ha. 96822

The Massachusetts Review, Memorial Hall, University of Massachusetts, Amherst, Mass. 01002

Matrix, c.p. 100 Ste-Anne-de-Bellevue, Quebec, Canada H9X 3L4

McCall's, 110 Fifth Avenue, New York, N.Y. 10011

Michigan Quarterly Review, 3032 Rackham Building, University of Michigan, Ann Arbor, Mich. 48109

Mid-American Review, 106 Hanna Hall, Bowling Green State University, Bowling Green, Oh. 43403

Midstream, 110 East 59th Street, 4th Floor, New York, N.Y. 10022

Mindscapes, 2252 Beverly Glen Place, Los Angeles, Calif. 90077

The Missouri Review, 1507 Hillcrest Hall, University of Missouri, Columbia, Mo. 65211

Mother Jones, 1663 Mission Street, San Francisco, Calif. 94103

MSS, Box 530, Department of English, SUNY-Binghamton, Binghamton, N.Y. 13901

Nassau Review, Department of English, Nassau Community College, Garden City, N.Y. 11530-6793

Nebraska Review, Writer's Workshop, ASH 210, University of Nebraska at Omaha, Omaha, Neb. 68182-0324

New Directions, 80 Eighth Avenue, New York, N.Y. 10011

New England Review, Middlebury College, Middlebury, Vt. 05753

New Letters, University of Missouri-Kansas City, 5100 Rockhill Road, Kansas City, Mo. 64110

New Mexico Humanities Review, The Editors, Box A, New Mexico Tech., Socorro, N.M. 57801

The New Renaissance, 9 Heath Road, Arlington, Mass. 02174

The New Yorker, 20 West 43rd Street, New York, N.Y. 10036

The North American Review, University of Northern Iowa, 1227 West 27th Street, Cedar Falls, Ia. 50614

North Dakota Quarterly, University of North Dakota, Box 8237, Grand Forks, N.D. 58202

Northern Lights, P.O. Box 8084, Missoula, Mont. 59807-8084

The Ohio Review, Ellis Hall, Ohio Unviersity, Athens, Oh. 45701

OMNI, 1965 Broadway, New York, N.Y. 10012

The Ontario Review, 9 Honey Brook Drive, Princeton, N.J. 08540

Other Voices, The University of Illinois at Chicago, Department of English (M/C 162), Box 4348, Chicago, Ill. 60680

The Paris Review, 541 East 72nd Street, New York, N.Y. 10021

Paris Transcontinental, Institut du Monde Anglophone, Sorbonne Nouvelle, 5, rue de l'Ecole de Medecine, 75006, Paris, France

The Partisan Review, 128 Bay State Road, Boston, Mass. 02215/ 552 Fifth Avenue, New York, N.Y. 10036

Phylon, 223 Chestnut Street, S.W., Atlanta, Ga. 30314

Playboy, 680 North Lake Shore Drive, Chicago, Ill. 60611

Ploughshares, Emerson College, 100 Beacon Street, Boston, Mass. 02116

Prairie Schooner, Andrews Hall, University of Nebraska, Lincoln, Neb. 68588

Puerto del Sol, College of Arts & Sciences, Box 3E, New Mexico State University, Las Cruces, N.M. 88003

The Quarterly, 201 East 50th Street, New York, N.Y. 10022

Raritan, 31 Mine Street, New Brunswick, N.J. 08903

Reconstructionist, P.O. Box 1336, Roslyn Heights, New York, N.Y. 11577

Redbook, 224 West 57th Street, New York, N.Y. 10019

Sailing, 125 E. Main Street, P.O. Box 248, Port Washington, Wis. 53074

Salamagundi, Skidmore College, Saratoga Springs, N.Y. 12866

Sandhills/St. Andrews Review, Sandhills Community College, 2200 Airport Road, Pinehurst, N.C. 28374

The San Francisco Bay Guardian, Fiction Contests, 2700 19th Street, San Francisco, Calif. 94110-2189

Santa Monica Review, Center for the Humanities at Santa Monica College, 1900 Pico Boulevard, Santa Monica, Calif. 90405

Self, 350 Madison Avenue, New York, N.Y. 10017

Sequoia, Storke Student Publications Building, Stanford, Calif. 94305

Seventeen, 850 Third Avenue, New York, N.Y. 10022

The Sewanee Review, University of the South, Sewanee, Tenn. 37375

Shenandoah, Box 722, Lexington, Va. 24405

Short Fiction by Women, Box 1276, Stuyvesant Station, New York, N.Y. 10009

The Short Story Review, P.O. Box 882108, San Francisco, Calif. 94188

Snake Nation Review, 110 #2 West Force Street, Valdosta, Ga. 31601

So To Speak, George Mason University, Fairfax, Va. 22030-4444

Sonora Review, Department of English, University of Arizona, Tucson, Ariz. 85721

South Carolina Review, Department of English, Clemson University, Clemson, S.C. 29634-1503

South Dakota Review, Box 111, University Exchange, Vermillion, S.D. 57069

Southern Humanities Review, 9088 Haley Center, Auburn University, Auburn, Ala. 36849

Southern Reader, P.O. Box 1827, Oxford, Miss. 38655

The Southern Review, Drawer D, University Station, Baton Rouge, La. 70803

Southwest Review, Southern Methodist University, Dallas, Tex. 75275

Sou'wester, Southern Illinois University at Edwardsville, Edwardsville, Ill. 62026-1438

The Spirit That Moves Us, P.O. Box 820, Jackson Heights, N.Y. 11372

Stories, Box Number 1467, East Arlington, Mass. 02174-0022

Story, 1507 Dana Avenue, Cincinnati, Oh. 45207

Story Quarterly, P.O. Box 1416, Northbrook, Ill. 60065

St. Anthony Messenger, 1615 Republic Street, Cincinnati, Oh. 45210-1298

The Sun, 107 North Robertson Street, Chapel Hill, N.C. 27516

Tampa Review, Box 135F, University of Tampa, Tampa, Fla. 33606

The Threepenny Review, P.O. Box 9131, Berkeley, Calif. 94709

Tikkun, Institute of Labor and Mental Health, 5100 Leona Street, Oakland, Calif. 94619

TriQuarterly 2020 Ridge Avenue, Evanston, Ill. 60208

The Village Voice Literary Supplement, 36 Cooper Square, New York, N.Y. 10003

The Vincent Brothers Review, 4566 Northern Circle, Mad River Township, Dayton, Oh. 45424

Virginia Country, The Country Publishers, Inc., 113 East Main Street, P.O. Box 798, Berryville, Va. 22611-0798

The Virginia Quarterly Review, University of Virginia, 1 West Range, Charlottesville, Va. 22903

Vogue, 350 Madison Avenue, New York, N.Y. 10017

Washington Review, Box 50132, Washington, D.C. 20091

Webster Review, Webster College, Webster Groves, Mo. 63119

West Coast Review, Simon Fraser University, Burnaby, British Columbia, Canada V5A 1S6

Western Humanities Review, University of Utah, Salt Lake City, Ut. 84112

Whetstone, P.O. Box 1266, Barrington, Ill. 60011

Wind, RFD Route 1, Box 809K, Pikeville, Ky. 41501

Witness, 27055 Orchard Lake Rd., Farmington Hills, Mi. 48018

Woman's Day, 1515 Broadway, New York, N.Y. 10036

Yankee, Main Street, Dublin, N.H. 03444

Yellow Silk, P.O. Box 6374, Albany, Calif. 94706

Zyzzyva, 41 Sutter Street, Suite 1400, San Francisco, Calif. 94104